ROYAL ESCAPE

ROYAL ESCAPE

SUSAN FROETSCHEL

FIVE STAR
A part of Gale, Cengage Learning

GALE
CENGAGE Learning™

Detroit • New York • San Francisco • New Haven, Conn • Waterville, Maine • London

GALE
CENGAGE Learning™

Set in 11 pt. Plantin.
Printed on permanent paper.

LIBRARY OF CONGRESS CATALOGING-IN-PUBLICATION DATA

Froetschel, Susan.
  Royal escape / Susan Froetschel. — 1st ed.
    p. cm.
  ISBN-13: 978-1-59414-717-3 (hardcover : alk. paper)
  ISBN-10: 1-59414-717-5 (hardcover : alk. paper)
    1. Princesses—Great Britain—Fiction. 2. Great Britain—Fiction. I. Title.
  PS3556.R59353F76 2008
  813'.54—dc22   2008037616

First Edition. First Printing: December 2008.
Published in 2008 in conjunction with Tekno Books and Ed Gorman.

Printed in the United States of America
1 2 3 4 5 6 7 12 11 10 09 08

For two caring aunts, both named Betty

ACKNOWLEDGMENTS

With warm thanks to editors and the team at Five Star—including Deborah Brod, John Helfers, Tiffany Schofield, and many others. Special thanks to Irene Vance, good friend who offered valuable advice as a librarian and researcher, and Amy Suntoke for reading the manuscript and offering suggestions.

Warm gratitude to the steady influences and invigorating ideas from colleagues and friends Holly Algood, Eila Algood, Rahima Chaudhury, Debbie Campoli, and Nayan Chanda for many hours discussing security, politics, the pressures of modern family life and other themes touched on in this book.

Finally, the book would not have been possible without my husband, Douglas, who inspired the idea and offers constant support and love, and my son, Nicholas, who encouraged me to resurrect the draft manuscript after I had shelved it more than eleven years ago.

Friendship is the best form of security.

CHARACTERS

Family:

Catherine II, Queen of England, a widow
Emma, Queen Mother

Edward, Prince of Wales
Elena, Princess of Wales
Prince Richard, age 13
Prince Lawrence, age 10

Princess Caroline, Edward's sister
Kenneth Livingston, Duke of Whitehall, her husband
Princess Waverly, age four

Staff:

Gregory Johnstone, Elena's great-uncle
Henry Pindlow, chauffeur
Walter Draker, security
Derry Sanders, Richard's valet
Michael Barringer, Queen's secretary
Hugh Fanley, Elena's secretary
Timothy Barnes, Edward's secretary

Larky Jones, Pepperell caretaker
Stephen Jenkins, head of security
William Cooke, senior security consultant
George Canton, chauffeur
Jonathan Giller, security

Acquaintances:

Derrick Wilson, divorce solicitor
Kay Danvers, mistress to the Prince of Wales
Kevin Tilton, friend of the Prince of Wales, anthropologist
Michael McLarrity, freelance reporter from the US
Paul Miggins, computer consultant
Roger Miggins, professor of law
Rita Whittaker, hospital nurse
Douglas Hill, friend of Michael McLarrity

Police:

Chief Inspector Timothy Maitlin
Inspector Cary Thornton

"Honi soit qui mal y pense."
("Shame on him who thinks evil of it.")
—Motto of the Most Noble Order of the Garter

PROLOGUE

The venerable stone office block was quiet, its hallways dark, with patches of light coming from city lights through the graceful arched windows. The only hint of movement came with shadows. First one, then another, both moved slowly toward the one office with the open door. The streets of the financial district were quiet at midnight and so too were the esteemed law offices of Wilson & Haggert. The clerical help had left sharply at six, and most of the legal professionals followed not long afterward. A group of custodians took over for about two hours to sweep, collect shredded trash, and polish exquisite wood and beveled glass. Derrick Wilson had asked the custodians to leave his massive corner office for another day and they happily obliged. After ten, the sound of vacuums and soft chatter had vanished.

The shadows merged, as two men padded, shoeless, on plush oriental rugs toward Wilson's office. There, with the lights turned low, the lone solicitor leaned back in his chair, his legs propped comfortably on the old mahogany desk. Holding a crystal goblet of red wine, his drink of choice for any celebration, he studied the scene beyond his window. A smile lingered on his lips. The call had come in late. He had worked hard for his most famous client—and together, they had won. Again.

Years ago, Wilson had met Elena, Princess of Wales, at a formal dinner party at the start of the Christmas season. The woman was gracious, tall, lovely—more of a listener than a speaker and yet the center of attraction in every room she entered. Most amazing was how her poise seemed so effortless. He had moved close enough to study her cobalt blue eyes— intense in their ability to convey kindness, enthusiasm, concern, curiosity, every feeling connected with virtue. She had sensed his interest and walked over to him after the dinner, while couples were dancing, and asked about his job. He was a solicitor. One who specialized in divorce, he added a tad sheepishly. He was among the best in Great Britain, but what did that matter in a roomful of artists, academics, politicians, and other celebrities? But Elena had been intrigued, and after glancing furtively at the small groups of people standing near, she leaned toward him.

"Do you help the women more or the men?" she inquired, with soft voice and direct gaze. She did not want to be overheard.

"I represent men more often than not," Wilson responded quietly. "I may have helped a few women along the way."

"Ah, so you're intimate with all the flaws made by the other side, the women," she teased, in a sly way that suggested the two were already confidantes. "And tell me, what's the most common mistake women make when pursuing a divorce?"

He thought a moment. "Thinking that a man might change. Thinking that he only cares about the money."

"And what should a woman do to protect her interests?"

He shrugged. "Monitor her behavior. Keep quiet about what she really wants. And as soon as she suspects trouble, keep a journal—selective, of course, about everything that's gone wrong with the marriage. You'd be surprised. One tends to forget the details—dates, witnesses to the little cruelties, both physical and verbal."

She dipped her chin, tilted her head and lifted her long lashes as she murmured her thanks and moved on to talk with others in the crowd. The pose, an odd combination of mischief and modesty, had been caught in thousands of photographs over the years, but remained enchantingly fresh and natural in person. Sixteen months later, Elena called and asked Wilson to initiate procedures for a separation. She also handed over a journal that began the night of the dinner party, with a vivid description of her husband dancing six times with his mistress, later following the cloying woman into a small room, with a posted guard ordered by the host. The two remained in there, away from other guests, for more than forty minutes. Other entries were more troubling. Reconciliation was impossible, and divorce negotiations began.

The family was not happy, but Elena got what she wanted, with credit largely due to her meticulous journal and her own public generosity. Rather than monthly payments of alimony, she negotiated a lump settlement of nearly seventy million pounds. She did not get custody—that would never happen for an outsider to the royal family—but she had veto power over the children's schools and was guaranteed a majority of their leisure time. To save the children embarrassment, the palace permitted Elena to retain her title. No other woman could be the Princess of Wales during Elena's lifetime. And after the death of her mother-in-law and husband, she would be known as the Queen Mother.

Wilson did not think much of royalty, but he could understand why Elena had earned the right to remain a woman of influence in the world.

Throughout the separation, Elena and her husband had few disagreements over custody—appropriate times for delivery of the children, adjustments due to vacations, palace visits coming out of the mother's time or the father's. Wilson admired Elena for how she had listened closely to the reasons and tried to base decisions solely on the best interests of the children. She did not resort to threats of releasing the contents of the journal—

not until the most recent disputes over Elena's financial status.

Strangely enough, the bitter arguments did not emerge with the separation or the divorce negotiations. Instead, controversy began after Elena had announced her intention to begin her own private trust fund for charities, separate from the trust funds established by the royal family and her husband, the Prince of Wales. She explained to Derrick her need to emphasize issues of importance for her and her children. The palace objected, accusing Elena of manipulation, corruption, and obsession with money. Lawyers for the queen retaliated, demanding more time with the two boys and expecting Elena to sacrifice additional weekends. Derrick had responded by forwarding a sample of entries from the journal and financial statements that showed her charitable work to be far more lucrative than that of all other members of the royal family combined. It wasn't Elena's idea, but Derrick insisted on his own that her work be separated from that of other family members.

He chuckled remembering the look of horror on the barrister's face after reading the selections. Elena had offered to start her charity trust with a portion of her own divorce settlement and not depend on money from the prince's trust. The palace had insisted on wording the announcement. After months of negotiations, documents clarifying the settlement, severing Elena's work and funding from the palace, would be filed in court the following day.

A sharp noise came from the hallway. Wilson left his desk and paused by the doorway. He waited a moment, but the sound was not repeated, and he was annoyed by his imagination. Nothing was waiting for him in the hallway, the same way nothing was waiting for him at his home. Still, it was long past time for Wilson to hop into his Jaguar and head for his lonely estate in Oxfordshire, about fifty miles west of London. Weary, Wilson wished he didn't have to drive. He should install a simple lavatory and single bed in some extra space near his office. The image, the simplicity of having no home, repeated itself in his mind hundreds of times since his own divorce. But thinking was easier than doing—and the call to the appropriate contractor was never made. Maybe next week. Because in truth, he didn't want to admit that his office was his one true home.

Wilson sighed, drained the remaining wine in his glass and switched on his small desk lamp, rubbed his eyes from the sudden burst of light, and gathered the papers and journal. He headed for his fireproof wall safe, located behind a set of law books and massive bookcases along the far wall and entered the combination that only he and his personal secretary knew.

As the door to the safe popped open, a shape emerged from the shadows and an arm slipped around his neck. Wilson gasped and twisted in alarm. The prowler was clothed completely in black, even his face covered with a black nylon stocking. The man tightened his grip, while another man crept silently from the hallway and headed for the desk. He shoved papers about and swore, before heading to the safe. Wilson noted that the man ignored an envelope of cash, a package of bonds and some jewelry. Finally, the man dropped to his knees and searched through the pile that Wilson had dropped in surprise.

"This is it," said a young male voice. He waved the journal. "I found it!"

"The original?" asked his fellow intruder, not loosening his grip on Wilson.

"You can't take that!" Wilson cried out. "Why, that's not worth anything!"

"That's what you think," said the man as he placed the small book covered in pastel silk into his small pack. Then he extracted a syringe and approached Wilson slowly. "You take it easy. This won't hurt if you stop thrashing about . . ."

The first intruder threw Wilson to the ground, knocking his

head sharply against the oak floor. Pressing a knee to Wilson's abdomen, he kept one arm clutched tight around the solicitor's neck and another about his arms. The second intruder loosened Wilson's pants and lowered his silk underwear.

"My God, what is this?" Wilson screamed and jerked in fear. But the younger man was stronger.

The second intruder cuffed Wilson on the head, enough to jolt him into silence.

"This isn't going to hurt. Not if you cooperate." He gripped Wilson's thigh—and stretched the leg out at an odd angle. Taking his time to find the proper spot, he aimed the needle for the creased skin where upper leg met the pelvis, piercing the skin and vein. Wilson tried to jerk away, but the older man held the needle in place. After removing the needle, the intruder checked the injection site, applied a small amount of some ointment and then wiped any remnants away. Moments later, Wilson felt sweaty and tingling pain. He could not easily move his fingers, neck or legs or fight as the man bent over and checked the leg again with a small torch. Wilson's muscles tightened, as though all pulled toward the center of his chest. Short of breath, he gave up struggling and could only watch the two men at work. They returned his clothing to order, and Wilson realized his legs had enough hair to make any needle prick hard to spot. One of the men grabbed the wine bottle and dribbled the remaining liquid about, before dropping the empty glass not far from Wilson's body. The other man gently placed Wilson's hand over his heart before closing the safe. Exiting the block as silently as they had entered, the men carried away the journal.

CHAPTER 1

Two servants huddled together before the odd collection of vases.

"The silver won't do. Too large, she said."

"Tsk. Here's this crystal one. But she'll butcher the stems."

"She plans to mix roses from the royal greenhouse with lilacs sent from some ordinary garden."

"A gaudy display—she worries about all the wrong things."

Elena stood before a crystal urn, toyed with some stems thick with lilacs, all in white, and waited for the telephone to ring. She despised waiting for the calls from the palace. Waiting was especially annoying today, a day that was supposed to bring her closer to freedom, the day when some more stray details from her divorce would be resolved.

The call was due shortly after ten-thirty a.m., according to the daily appointment sheet prepared by her staff and approved by the palace. Accordingly, her staff eliminated a visit to a nursing home celebrating an anniversary to make room for the call. The time slot had been no accident. The royal family proper did not devote much time in the way of charity to nursing homes and had first teased and then criticized Elena for insisting on such visits. They resisted publicity associated with nursing homes, a reminder of infirmity and death. For the royal family, aging offered no pleasure, only pain, lack of control, and the knowledge that one's children impatiently coveted wealth and title. But Elena's imagination played mean tricks with fears avoided. Better to confront her fears. So, she had penned a memo to her secretary to reschedule the visit to the nursing home, with more time at that.

As she trimmed the woody stems of the lilacs and mixed them with the roses, she tested potential conversations with the queen. All ended with petulance on her part. She sighed, and hoped that the call would focus less on the latest divorce conflict and more on official plans for her older son's birthday, a few weeks away. She knew her input on the official party would be minimal and less than welcome. But she needed to know the time and arrangements, so that she could make plans for a small and private celebration of her own.

The stems of the roses were stiff, and she added some wire to give the illusion of a graceful curve while she fretted about the upcoming birthday. What did a mother buy for her first son, Richard, who would turn thirteen? What should she give to a child who was far too serious? What could a boy want after having been the center of an acrimonious, public separation and divorce? She bit her lip and shook her head, knowing full well that her sons wanted their parents to reunite, to fall in love again. Like most children, hers were dreamers, readily capable of forgetting harsh memories of the past, not ready to calculate how disastrous any future relationship between the two mismatched people might be.

There was no perfect gift, only poor substitutes. Like time and the creation of memories. Elena would love the opportunity to escape on some wild vacation with Richard and Lawrence. How the two boys had reveled in wild snowmobile rides on a ranch in Colorado a few years ago. But the queen had complained and accused Elena of endangering the heir's life. Ever since, Elena had difficulty arranging vacations that were normal and fun. The queen required explanations, itineraries, and forms. Spontaneity was impossible. The bodyguards answered to the queen and not the princess.

Richard deserved something special. The past year had been difficult. His days of childhood were dwindling fast, yet surprises and birthdays were still precious. Her husband, Edward, always an impatient man, had already presented his gift, arranging the services of a personal valet. Boring and presumptuous, Derry Sanders lacked any real life of his own and accompanied Richard everywhere—school and home. "I received my valet when I was thirteen, and he was always there for me," Edward had said. "Richard will appreciate the continuity, the guidance, someday."

Elena held off from snapping that Edward was the one who instigated events leading to the divorce and disrupted the family's continuity. She bristled inside, annoyed but no longer amazed that her husband had felt the need to "purchase" a servant to fill empty spaces in her son's life. Friends and family should fill any empty spaces—or reading and introspection about one's own true interests. Even more troubling was the fact that Richard seemed to enjoy the company of the shallow man. She kept her disdain to herself. Really, a valet was merely an adult version of a nanny.

Derry had been in Richard's life for less than two weeks, but already Elena felt as if all her conversations were monitored, analyzed, and filtered by a servant! Of course, the children didn't recognize the inconvenience of the stranger in their midst. No, the attention of another adult was bliss. Derry was always there. He played games, helped with homework, and knew good jokes. He listened. For adolescents, parents became less important than friends—and Derry acted more like a friend.

The slow process of separation from one's parents was natural, Elena knew, as children spent more time away from home. She trusted that Derry would eventually become an annoyance. So, she didn't fight or cling. She would remain close to her sons, a confidante. The boys were about to become teens, but that didn't mean they wouldn't talk to her.

Her gift had to be special, different. Competing with the gift of one's very own human being was a particular challenge, she thought, pursing her lips and deciding to add more lilacs to the bouquet. Elena had spent most of the week shopping—wandering about a nature store, a bookstore, and then a store with expensive electronics in search of Richard's gift. A cellular telephone was out. Telephone calls, so ordinary. Passing an aisle with personal computers, she had noticed a young man tap diligently away on a keyboard. Nothing held any interest for his large brown eyes other than the computer screen before him. His hair was light brown and too long. Dark wire glasses drooped on his nose. Elena had found herself imagining her younger son looking somewhat haphazard and nerdish only a few short years away, especially if he didn't always have palace staff telling him what to wear.

She had smiled, and stood behind the man, watching as a series of darting medieval figures filled the screen. The store manager directed another associate to keep customers away from the area, before stepping forward to introduce Elena to Paul Miggins, computer consultant for the store. The young man invited her to try her hand at the game and guided her moves in directing the figures.

"I've never done anything like this before," she murmured.

"It's easy, really," Paul replied shyly.

"How old are you?"

"Nineteen." He showed her some of the most popular programs and games—and then showed her how a player could make moves over the Internet and E-mail. She asked a number of questions, and the boy answered as the manager watched from the background. Elena shook her head and expressed polite amazement, explaining that she couldn't possibly learn such technical maneuvers.

That had been three days ago, and she had studied the newspapers closely since. None contained articles or references to her visit to the store, no repeat of her silly questions or her assertion that she couldn't learn. Young Paul Miggins had passed her test for trust.

Elena smiled. Communication was an ideal gift. The boys had computers, which were linked to the palace system. Elena decided to call a trusted friend that afternoon and arrange for the purchase of two state-of-the-art laptop computers, decoys for two BlackBerry systems. She would also ask the friend to contact Paul Miggins in the store and request his services as a consultant to set up private and anonymous accounts that would allow her son to join the online games. The young man had mentioned security features and demonstrated a range of tricks; Elena would need all the protection that was available. Unfortunately, Paul could only help out after school. She had instructed her friend to propose that Paul leave the store out of the arrangement and that she pay a separate fee directly to him. Fewer people knowing about the consulting contract would increase the safety for her and everyone else involved.

In the meantime, Elena was confident that the Prince of Wales, who despised technology, would never bother figuring out the new toy. She felt a tad guilty. Richard would enjoy the computer, but in a way, the BlackBerry was as much for her as for her child—instant contact, as Paul had promised. Elena hoped Richard would understand why she had decided to buy two devices, one for him and one for herself. Not that she'd demand constant contact. Instead, she'd wait for Richard to take the initiative. At least she stopped at two. She wanted to buy another for Larry, but that would diminish the special quality of her eldest son's birthday. She and Richard would let Larry use their laptops. When it came to a BlackBerry, Larry would have to wait a few more years.

The phone rang, and Elena glanced at her watch in surprise. She had been told to expect the telephone call shortly after ten-thirty, and it was at least ten minutes before the time. Odd, Elena thought.

"Good morning," said Elena, nervously waiting for some assistant to ring the queen.

"Ma'am, it's me, Lisa," said the operator, hurriedly. "Her Majesty has not rung yet. But another call came through."

"But . . ."

"I think you'll want to take it, Ma'am. Your solicitor's secretary, Dolores Enfield. She said it's urgent."

"Put it through. And . . ."

"I explained to Miss Enfield already. If the queen rings, I'll cut the line immediately. Beauty of this old phone system."

Elena waited for Dolores's voice to break through.

"Excuse me for calling so unexpectedly, Your Royal Highness, but something horrible has happened."

"Please, Dolores, you can spare the formality with me."

"Yes, indeed. It took so long for me to get through and you never know who might be listening." Derrick Wilson had always insisted on speaking with Elena in person, in public areas. Wary of listening devices, he refused to discuss any details of her case over the telephone. He had promised that the trust settlement was final, only paperwork needed to be filed.

So the call caught Elena by surprise. "Yes?" she asked anxiously.

Dolores spoke quickly, her voice breaking. "Derrick died last night. The doctor said it was a heart attack. In his office—he must have stayed late. You know he's had a history."

"The poor man," Elena cried out.

Dolores started crying. "He had heart trouble, but he had

been taking such good care of himself. I never dreamed that this could happen."

Elena slumped against the wall. "My divorce killed him—all the arguing and pressure."

"I knew him better than anyone. He thrived on the challenges. Why would he be upset? You kept winning. That's what kept him going. No, it was his time."

"He was a good man," Elena said.

"I'll miss him," Dolores said forlornly.

"But what will I do without him?" Elena asked softly.

"But that brings me to another point. I'll pack your files first—before any of the others. I can forward them to another law office, the solicitor of your choosing. Just let me know."

"You know better than me. The process should be easy. The divorce is over with. Even our battle over the charitable trust funds is settled. Derrick was going to file those papers in court today!"

"Derrick's death makes that impossible, I'm afraid. A friend of Derrick's telephoned the courts this morning and obtained a continuation. You have time. I'll forward all the files as soon as I hear from you." Her voice was hurried, awkward. Elena sensed the hesitation.

"What about Derrick's partner?" Elena asked. "Or surely one of the younger people in the office could handle the case at this point."

Dolores took a long breath. "Haggert won't touch it, Elena. He always claimed that Derrick did not understand the repercussions of taking on your case."

"Poor Derrick," Elena said. "He never told me."

"He put up with a lot. This is an old and conservative firm that has worked with the aristocracy for a long time. Derrick didn't want to worry you or make you upset, but Haggert never forgave Derrick for taking on your case. He thinks the firm has lost enough business already."

"They must have picked some up, too!" Elena protested.

"And the firm lost the types of cases Haggert prefers—any friends to the queen. Elena, I'll be frank with you. The younger ones around here—they're simply not experienced enough. Not for a case of your magnitude. Making amendments to such a financial settlement is no simple matter. The entire matter could be open for review. Derrick would want you to plan a strategy. The continuation is in place. It's in your interest not to move quickly."

Elena struggled for words. She felt abandoned and waited for Dolores to continue.

"Choose a good solicitor. I can call friends of Derrick's. They could give you some names."

"But Derrick was the best."

"He was. But then, as you said, he did the groundwork. Someone simply has to carry on."

"Thank you, Dolores." Elena hung up, and checked her watch. The queen had not called yet—only a few minutes after the scheduled time, an unusual delay. Elena stared at her bouquet and felt sick inside. She touched a lilac. It was hard for her to believe Derrick was dead. The soft tone of the telephone made her jump.

She allowed two rings before answering.

"Hello, Elena." Queen Catherine's voice was calm.

Elena was taken by surprise that the queen herself would call. Normally, she'd be put on hold for five minutes. "Good morning, Your Majesty." Elena focused on keeping her voice soft and polite.

"I trust you're doing well these days," the queen asserted. "I haven't read otherwise in the morning papers."

Elena paused. She hadn't read the papers yet and didn't know if they had already reported Derrick's death. She wasn't ready to talk about her divorce and the new complication. She had not thought of the implications beyond the tragedy of Derrick's death. No. Focus on her sons and the party, Elena told herself. She forced her voice to be cheery, which wasn't hard. Elena had years of practice of feigning happiness with her husband's family. "Yes, I'm fine, thank you, Ma'am. And I trust all's well with you?"

Catherine's sigh was audible over the phone line. "My life would be perfect if my family could solve their problems without involving the press."

"I wish for the same." Elena tried to find agreement with the queen whenever possible. "But it's difficult when reporters bribe our staff and photographers stalk us everywhere we go! Why, they'd hide under our beds if they could!"

"We could all do a better job of living quiet lives and leading the way in modeling duty and responsibility," Catherine insisted. "In part, that's why I'm calling—about Richard's birthday. He's no longer a child. He's old enough for a substantial celebration. I plan on two hundred guests."

Elena rolled her eyes. A huge party that weekend would be a major annoyance. "He'll be honored," she conceded.

"The usual list—and I suppose we could invite a few schoolmates."

"He'd enjoy that."

"Staff will call for a list from the school. Security will check for safety and staff will check for suitability."

Elena shook her head in disgust, but remained silent. No mention of consulting with Richard on matters of camaraderie. No inquiries made of Elena or Edward, who might know something about the boy's friends. No, the queen would rely on servants and security and would not regard friendship as an essential qualifier. This was the first party since the divorce. Elena wasn't certain whether she would be invited or welcome, but was determined not to plead or bring the matter up.

Catherine continued: "His birthday falls on a Wednesday, I see—not very good for a party of this order. I scheduled the party for the Saturday following, a luncheon. Already had the invitations sent out."

Elena nervously ran her finger down her personal calendar. "That's my weekend with the boys. Can Richard and Lawrence visit me at Kirkington afterward?" Derrick's office had always monitored any changes in the children's scheduled visits. Damn, she hurt inside.

A long pause, and Elena refused to oblige her with nervous chatter. "I suppose, my dear, if you deem it necessary. But remember, it's unwise for children to spend too much time with their parents. The small creatures are not so different from prize roses. The parent plant creates the flower and seed. But then that seed needs distance to grow properly. The plant depends on the objective assessments of the gardener for proper water, nutrients, and soil."

The queen paused again. "But then, you were never one for gardening." Elena did not argue. Long ago, she had learned to argue only for priorities. "Well, plan on Sunday, and that's of course, if the boys don't have schoolwork. And you won't take off for any adventures that weekend? We mustn't wear the poor child out."

Elena crossed her fingers and forced her voice into sweet politeness. "No, Ma'am, and do you think the party will last into the night?"

"All right, take them Saturday evening, too. The weekend's hunt has been canceled. The party's quite enough! Oh, and Elena, there's no need for you to sound so distant. Of course, I expect you to attend Richard's party. This event will test your divorce diplomacy skills. And Edward's."

Elena's sigh of relief was almost audible. She had not spent much time with the entire royal family in recent years. They despised her—ever since a candid interview on American television as well as an argument over a movie she had watched with both boys. She made sure her voice was calm and steady. "Thank you, that's gracious of you. I'll look forward to the celebration."

"Elena, as you know, the papers on the amendment to your settlement require the signatures of not only the prime minister but myself. My staff assured me that there's no hurry, and I've not had the opportunity to read them as yet. I don't have to remind you how much it pains me to pick up the pen for such a deed." The woman's voice was more clipped and businesslike than usual.

"But my solicitor said . . . that agreement was to be filed in court today." Elena stopped herself. Derrick had always warned her to let him do the talking and refuse to enter negotiations with anyone in the family, especially the queen. But Derrick was gone.

"Barristers, solicitors, and courts—don't delude yourself into thinking they care about either you or the children. Your legal team may have led you to believe that agreement had been reached. I understand what you want from us. Fame and involvement. And I know what Edward wants. My crown. But the responsibility for these family decisions is mine. And mine alone. I have not signed the papers. I plan to read them and consider the issues carefully. What I decide depends on whether you and Edward prove that you can behave in public, whether you manage to keep personal problems out of the newspapers, whether you can put duty to your children and this family above selfish interests. Your behavior and loyalty, Elena, are vital for the future of your family and mine—not exactly two separate entities even though you decided to go ahead with this divorce and now this odd attempt at financial independence."

Elena held the phone in front of her face and stuck her tongue out to the receiver. She wanted to spit the words *duty* and *loyalty* out of her life. Duty worked well for people at the top of the royal chain—and those below who manipulated the system. It did not work well for independents who believed in fairness and the dignity of all human beings. But Elena had long ago learned that she could never convince her mother-in-law of the sense behind such a philosophy. She held the phone back to her ear and pinched herself. Don't talk too much, she warned herself. "I understand," Elena replied.

"I'm not sure you do. Heaven help the monarchy should I die before the two of you settle your differences—I refuse! I have to know that I can trust that Edward and you can appear in public in peace. The parents of that fine young man cannot constantly be causing a spectacle. And Richard's birthday celebration will be a test!"

Elena wanted to scream in frustration. The family had always blamed her for becoming the center of media attention. Massive, worldwide attention to her clothes, her hair, her activities, her smallest comments, her moods. As if she wanted to be the center of attention, like a tiger in a circus cage. Elena had tried to explain so many times. She closed her eyes and kept her voice pleasant, pretending to be an operator forced to deal with an angry customer. "The prince should have his day."

"Hmm. Keep your emotions in check. I want no photographs of you and Edward glaring at each other over Richard's head. In fact, it's best if you avoid appearing in any photos with Richard or Edward at all. Remember, it's Richard's day. You may attend the party, and that's enough. Also, be sure your staff has your outfit approved by my secretary. A subdued suit, my dear, why not pastel? No blacks or bright colors—and no hat!"

"I rarely plan that far in advance." The fools in the palace who made such suggestions wouldn't be content until they had

Elena wearing a castoff garment from the Queen Mother, three sizes too large.

"One can never plan too far in advance. You'll be expected at Wyndham Castle shortly before eleven that morning. Good day, Elena." A click instantly followed. The queen must have had her finger on the button, anxious to avoid an awkward farewell or additional comment from Elena.

Elena gently returned the receiver to its place, forgetting the queen's stiff and out-of-date maxims, as she returned to her flowers. The aroma of the lilacs overwhelmed the other blooms, filling the elegant sitting room, as large as it was. Lilacs were among her favorites, but these were extraordinary, each stem laden with at least a dozen clumps. The massive bouquet had been a gift from a plumber in Lancaster. He had included a handwritten note on plain paper, explaining that gardening was a hobby. He had planted the lilac shrub when his daughter had been born and never neglected to tend it all these years. In the early years, the little girl with brilliant white-gold curls had helped, applying lime in the fall and a special mix of bone and fish meal in the early spring. As time passed, the daughter and her father grew apart, and the attractive and curious young woman had left for London and eventually died of AIDS. But not before she had a son, who also had the disease. The plumber wrote how Elena's visit to the baby's hospital and her willingness to hold his grandchild had quelled prejudice in his village along with his own anger. He explained the source of his bitterness was not the flightiness of his daughter or the ignorance of those who shunned anyone with the disease. No, he only wished that he had sent some lilacs to his daughter and written a note to remind her of happier days for them both. He expressed support for Elena during a time of personal difficulty, gratitude for her constant ability to display unconditional love, regardless of irreversible mistakes of the past or potential ones of the future.

Elena had folded the note and asked her secretary to file it with her pile of correspondence that deserved an immediate reply.

She touched the petals of one bloom. Ordinary people adored her, and the royal family would never understand. They failed to realize that their criticism of her unconventional ways and her subsequent withdrawal from the public eye only increased the intense curiosity swirling about her.

Elena placed the arrangement on the sofa table covered in lace, admiring her work and promising herself to have her tea near the bouquet later that day. The queen had not mentioned the death of Derrick Wilson. Perhaps she had heard only about the continuation and not the reason why. That news would emerge soon enough, and the palace staff would develop a strategy. Derrick had been so sharp about points of British divorce law. The palace solicitors had quaked in the presence of the man and his letters. Would the palace balk at the settlement? She shrugged. But that was all right. She would find another solicitor, and as long as the members of the family were never sure about what she really wanted, then she had the advantage. And Derrick, more than anyone else, had taught her how vital it was to hide her goals and motivation, even after the divorce.

CHAPTER 2

"She has shown ample self-control lately."

"Remarkable—considering the delays in her legal matters."

"The papers haven't touched the anorexia issue in months. Be creative."

The Rolls entered the grounds of Wyndham Castle. A light shower had fallen earlier that morning, so the gardens shimmered with emerald green under a dazzling pure blue sky. A rush of nostalgia hit her. The place still resembled the storybook castle she had fallen in love with as a child. Henry, a favorite and loyal driver, kept the speed at less than twenty miles, knowing that the Princess of Wales gazed out the window at one of her favorite views. The constant queries of her friends—Why don't you just put up with him? Can't you have your own affair? Won't you miss it all?—they almost made sense.

She would miss the history, the mystique of being part of the royal family, but not the pressures of empty pomp and constant resentment. She would not miss the cruel but subtle hints of inclusion or exclusion, constantly practiced by family members. Perhaps that's what made the family despise Elena more than anything—her refusal to play. She could not manipulate her judgment of others, based on minor points of etiquette, on what a relationship could or would not do for her. Worse, Elena had done all she could to thwart palace efforts to teach the children the game. Often, she feared that she had not done enough. But then, the recent divorce was another step in instigating more change in the lives of her two sons.

Her Rolls went at a slow pace, following several service lorries onto the estate's grounds. Elena was amused at her driver's increasing embarrassment for her, ever since passing through the security gate. There, Walter Draker, her new security guard, had exited the vehicle and reported to the main security office—obviously nervous about his role and so much extra protocol since the divorce. Her driver, Henry, looked at Elena and rolled his eyes. Henry had insisted on holding off their typical banter while the new guard sat in the vehicle.

Walter, a young man with a sandy crewcut and freckles, had the appropriate rank and training to be her guard and had been assigned just that week. Yet he was too earnest, trying to overcome the fact that he had never before protected a member of the royal family. "I did join a contingent guarding the prime minister on a visit to Japan," he had offered by way of introduction. Elena had scowled. Even she knew that Japan was virtually free of crime. She had protested the change in her security staff, but the palace insisted and then went to scold the young man, citing her dissatisfaction. Elena tried to explain her feelings to him, her concerns that he had to be sophisticated enough not only to out-think terrorists, but newspaper reporters, freelance photographers, and ardent admirers. "I need someone who knows my every move, who learns to recognize the pitfalls." She offered her concerns as kind advice. "You're too young for that sort of drill. You shouldn't limit your personal life so drastically."

Walter gave a dogged response. "I want the job, Ma'am. I know I can handle it."

"All right," she said reluctantly. "But it's not always easy to keep up with me. So perhaps I can add a few tricks to your training." He looked puzzled, probably thinking to himself, what would a princess possibly know about high-tech safety precautions? But she knew that guards were trained in humoring their charges, within reason. She had no doubts that the security administrators also expected reports on her activities and comments, even the most mundane. All in the name of her safety, of course, palace authorities would assure him. In a few weeks' time, she would know the guard's standard for such reports—whether he was discriminating or liberal about reporting her every idle comment. She certainly would test him in the weeks ahead.

"Walter seems sweet," Elena offered, after they had dropped the guard off and pulled away.

"Not the best attribute for a man in security," Henry commented.

"Good for a chauffeur, though," Elena teased. "Perhaps he'll put in for a transfer."

Henry snorted. He didn't have to remind her how much security training he had undergone as a driver for the family.

"The palace despises me so much that they're using me as a training ground. With that man in charge, they must regard me as quite dispensable."

"They don't realize how much you can take care of yourself." Henry chuckled as he followed vans until they turned toward the service entrance. The Rolls moved smoothly, slowly toward the main entrance. Elena had been summoned to arrive almost two hours early, along with catering wait staff. She had never received a formal invitation to the event, only the one curt call from the queen. A mother of one of Richard's friends had called to ask about gift ideas, before proceeding to confide everything she knew about the guest list and actual time for lunch.

The family probably wanted to avoid an entrance by Elena. They still did not understand that she had never aimed for the

drama and attention. Elena merely focused on walking gracefully, head dipped, trying to avoid the attention. Yet, there was
always the wild crush of press and well-wishers whenever she
entered a room.

Henry held the door, while Elena stepped neatly from the
gray Rolls-Royce. The staff was still in the early stages of party
organization, and no footmen were in sight. Elena smiled her
appreciation at Henry and advised that she would be leaving
with the boys as early as possible, without being impolite. She
stepped lightly up the stairs to the massive entrance, and the
door was immediately opened by a butler who bowed and stared
at the floor, murmuring words of welcome to the Princess of
Wales. Unlike other family members who avoided eye contact,
she smiled and strolled briskly to the middle of the entrance
hall toward the main study. The servant did not smile back and,
head down, scurried to catch up with her. Obviously, the family
intended to treat her as a guest, distant and not especially
wanted. The escort meant that Elena no longer had free run of
the queen's palace.

"Your sons wait in the upstairs study, Lady Elena," the man
mentioned, beckoning her to follow.

"I remember," she responded quickly, with a little smile.
"Could you send some tea up, please? The car ride was long."
He hesitated, like so many of the queen's staff members who
despised taking any order from her. But they dared not refuse.
She was still the Princess of Wales. "Earl Grey would be fine,"
she insisted. And then she moved quickly up the stairs,
concentrating on striking each with the toe of her high-heeled
shoes.

The butler fell hopelessly behind, but still tried to follow,
coughing when she tugged on the massive door leading to her
sons' suites. Elena paused a moment in the doorway, and looking at him plodding along behind, thought about holding the

door open for him. That would cause some chatter downstairs.

"Really, no need to accompany me—I know the way," Elena chided. With that she let the door close, forcing the butler to give up. She hurried down the hallway, passing old portraits and wallpaper with an overdone pheasant design and looking forward to surprising the two boys.

Long ago, she would have caved in, allowed silly staff with absurd loyalties to tug her about like a puppet. But since reaching her thirties, she had developed a strong will. She came to the realization that she had to set an example for her sons on how to survive and achieve contentment within this troubled family. And that meant appropriating every chance for solitude, if only for a few moments.

She reached the final set of stairs and kept her hand just above the banister. She wished that she could see a photo of herself. She wore beige, as requested by the queen. But the new suit was silk, in small textured checks, designed especially for her athletic build. Simple, the short jacket emphasized her small waist and confident posture. A black shell of lacy folds peeked from underneath the jacket. The only jewelry she wore was striking onyx-and-gold earrings from a designer in Italy. Elena abided by the queen's wishes and wore no hat. Her blond curls were swept back by a thin black bow. If any photographers captured the new look, a stampede would descend on stores that sold the ribbons and they would be sold out the following day. Early in her marriage, she feared setting fashion trends. But now she reveled in it, selecting simple, inexpensive, yet dashing touches.

As she reached the top of the stairs, a door burst open, and a red head popped out. Larry, her younger son, greeted her with an impish smile. "In here!" he whispered, pulling her in excitedly. "Oh! We've been waiting for you all day!"

Elena ran to her child and knelt, taking him into her arms.

"Darling, how have you been? Having fun?"

He looked about. Even the little boy had learned that privacy was no privilege for members of the royal family. His blue eyes twinkled. "Not as much as we do with you," he whispered, then squirmed out of her grasp. Still clutching her hand, Larry pulled his mother into the room where the boys had an elaborate village designed with Legos. And there, sitting in the middle of the room was Derry. He was adjusting the drawbridge to an elaborate castle, surrounded by a moat brimming with water.

Elena paused. "I'd like to have the boys alone before the party," she said, smiling brilliantly, with only the slight hint of giving an order. The man didn't move or look up and so she said more firmly. "You're excused, Derry, until the party begins."

The valet looked at her and then Richard. "I'm just helping Prince Richard here," he said, keeping his voice jolly, but forcing the boy to make a choice.

Richard shot a nervous glance at his mother. "That's okay, Derry, we'll be doing more of this later."

"You'll be returning to London with me after the party, but I imagine you can keep this arrangement in place for a good long time." Elena tried to sound cheerful. When she had lived in the palace, she had insisted that servants leave a few toys about, that they didn't have to be immediately returned to shelves every time the boys left the room. "My, it's fabulous."

"Derry's idea for the moat," Larry added, with admiration.

"Clever." Elena was agreeable and sweet, but refused to sit or give more than one-word responses until the valet left the room. "Derry?"

He checked his watch and turned to Richard. "You should begin dressing in fifty minutes. I'll be in your dressing room, waiting to assist you, Sir." As he left, he looked disappointed, as though he had lost a contest. Elena was livid about the tension. The man should have the sense to excuse himself and not force the child to make a choice. She would speak to Edward about the valet's arrogance. After many years, she knew her husband's weak points, and one was his refusal to condone outright arrogance from staff.

She sat with her sons and began to play with the pieces herself. By the time Richard delegated a regiment of black knights to the moat around the castle, a woman knocked on the door bearing a silver platter with tea prepared for the princess, as well as milk for the boys and some small biscuits. While setting out the dishes and pouring, the maid glanced with curiosity at the Princess of Wales. Elena did not recognize her and made a point of giving the woman a warm smile. So many strangers worked in the palace. Elena had heard rumors—the queen was ordering changes in staff at least every three months. Too many books had been written about the family, and she must have decided that three months simply did not provide enough fodder for the tell-all books penned by staff that had become so popular.

Richard handed Elena a tiny white knight. "Sorry, Mum, we have no princesses."

"That's okay, this one's a princess in disguise," Elena retorted with a smile. She maneuvered her knight into some of the strange crevices, following Richard's man. Richard insisted on leading, and Larry cheerfully complied with his older brother. The three sat around and made up stories, loosely based on their ancestors and their enemies. Both boys were too young to know that the two were often one and the same, thought Elena ruefully.

After several rounds of strategy for the tiny men, Larry decided even more pieces were needed and left for his room.

Elena used the few moments to speak with Richard. "You received the boxes, my gift, at school?"

"Is it true?" he asked. "Just a secret for you and me?"

She nodded and reached for her bag, plucking a small print-cartridge box from her handbag. "The laptop is a decoy. You can still use it, of course. But here's another gift—a way to check E-mail securely. Keep it in this box so none of the staff comes across it," Elena murmured. "They won't find it in there."

"Or Larry . . ." Richard commented. His tone was cheerful, but he did want to set limits on his brother. Elena could only hope that the attitude was normal sibling rivalry and not the arrogance of rank.

Richard held the small device with buttons and tiny screen in his hand. "If they do, I'll tell them it's another video game," he whispered.

She nodded and handed over directions on how to use the new E-mail account, salamander@exchange.com.uk, and then she whispered his password in his ear. "Memorize it," she cautioned. "Change it every week. Never use names. Erase all the messages from me, mouser@exchange.com.uk, after you read them."

"And I'm the only one who can connect with you?" he asked.

"Only one," she promised. "Larry's a bit young, no?"

He smiled. "I might let him use it once in a while," he admitted. With that, he slipped the terse directions inside one of his schoolbooks, just before Larry returned to the room.

Elena changed the subject. "Richard, Larry, I want to warn you that I won't be with you much during your party. We won't be able to talk much until afterward."

Richard scowled. "But why not? That's not what I want."

"Is it because of the divorce?" Larry was pointed. "Divorce wouldn't be so bad if ours was normal and we could spend more time with you."

The comment hurt and Elena felt so helpless. She sighed. "Your father and I have less control than other parents. I know it's not fair, but as long as we live—here—we must follow the protocol. With luck, we'll sit at the same table. But we'll be on display."

"We're always on display," Larry complained.

Richard positioned his knight so that it was clinging bravely to a stiff little tree, an effort to keep from falling into the moat. "Grandmother already spoke to me. She explained that my primary duty is for my father and my country. I don't know. It's my party and I wish our family could sit together. I wish we could talk and have fun." His voice broke.

Elena bit her lip and looked away, even as she defended her mother-in-law. "Your grandmother loves your father as I love you. I understand her distress. She doesn't want difficulties or photographs of frowns and worried looks. She doesn't want any controversy."

Richard studied the man in the tree. "I wish we could be like other families, too."

The words pierced her heart, and she didn't have any answer for her sons. Living as a member of the royal family attracted enough attention. Walking away from the royal family attracted even more attention, as she had learned with her decision to divorce. She looked into her son's eyes—and agreed with him. But she wondered if he was really willing to walk away from all the comforts of the royal way of life.

"We have love—and as long as there is love between people, we can endure these events." She ran a finger through her hair and then pointed at the two boys and herself. "We have so much more than others—and we can't ask for more beyond that!" She shook her head as if to convince herself more so than them.

Richard looked away, while Larry stared at her with his large blue eyes. Even though Larry was younger than Richard, he understood how much his parents did not get along, that the royal family somehow resented his mother's behavior, and how much they resented any shift of attention from the queen and her most immediate heirs to the throne. Larry confronted the challenges, looking anyone in the eyes, straight on through the most uncomfortable of conversations. Elena continued: "All I can say is that you shouldn't argue with your grandmother or father. Neither should I. Alone, we can love one another and express that love in our own way."

Richard scowled. Elena loved her older son, and knew he could not help how he was raised with the expectations of special attention—and the façade of getting what he wanted.

"Look, Richard, this is your party. So if you have something urgent to tell me, why then, scratch your left ear and that forces me to smile. And if you scratch your right, then I must look all worried and important." She paused dramatically. "And if you touch your nose, then I must immediately sneeze at your command and rush away inside to meet with you." She gathered the giggling boys into a huddle about her, whispering about strange little codes that only the three of them would know.

But, sadly, Elena knew that escape from the party was impossible, especially for Richard. While Richard enjoyed devising the codes, he probably would never dare use them—unlike Larry. Elena returned to her chair and tried to straighten her skirt.

"The queen's only doing what she thinks is right," Elena said, more to comfort her son than excuse his grandmother's control. "Today is not a day for people looking for arguments or gossip. We can be separated. And civilized behavior on all our parts does not mean we deny what our hearts insist."

Richard nodded. Reaching for his knight and swooping it downward, he tapped the white knight in Elena's hand.

A knock on the door interrupted, and another stranger of a servant summoned the boys to get dressed. The boys reluctantly stood. "Larry, do you mind if I keep my princess?" Elena asked. "I want to remember today." Her son laughed and said yes.

She pocketed the little white knight, then bent over and wrapped one arm around each of the boys. "I can't wait until we ride back to London together," Elena whispered.

"But we . . ." Larry started to speak.

"Young Sir, I must insist," the nervous servant interrupted. "We'll be in trouble if we are late for your brother's party." The servant hurried the boys out of the room. As soon as the group left, Elena collapsed into the nearest chair and reached for some tea. Time to return to the royal world, where she and her sons had as much control as the little figures who were part of the Lego set.

About an hour later, guests began to arrive. Lovely packages of all sizes waited in elegant piles around the prince's table. Adults gathered about with cocktails.

Elena stood back and observed the interaction of the guests and particularly how they greeted the various members of the royal family. She decided against approaching any of the groups, instead waiting to see who would approach her, willing to speak to the woman who had dared to walk away from a royal marriage and make specific demands. Patience would provide a hint of who stood on Edward's side and who stood on hers.

Because of her early arrival and the tension with the servants, Elena felt a little worn. She had played with the boys rather than taking advantage of the offer to rest in a private room or fix her hair. She wore only light makeup. Her sister-in-law Caroline passed by without any hello, only a stern look at Elena's outfit. Playing on the floor with the boys, crouched over Legos, may have put some wrinkles across the front of her skirt, but she was in a good mood, her eyes and smile more serene than any others in the room.

Girls and boys in stiff party clothes played croquet on the lawn. Poor Richard was overdressed in a suit, undoubtedly chosen by the staff who served his grandmother. He looked utterly bored. He had long preferred American sports like baseball and basketball. But, of course, he could dabble with such games only when traveling with his mother, when she could guarantee privacy from the horrible "snappers." Elena nudged her son to try another team sport, a favorite game for most British and Europeans, except of course, the royal family. They regarded soccer as common and rough. As Richard grew older, he was forced to abandon sports that required large groups of other willing children.

All about, guests sipped champagne, while most of the children took careful sips of flavored sparkling water. Raised to resist eating much in public, Elena gently refused offers from any who brought her refreshments. One servant approached with a full tray of small squares of bread, decorated with cucumbers and rosettes of cream. She declined, but he continued to press close to her, insistent. Elena frowned about having to tell the servant no twice, that she didn't want to be bothered with food and drink.

He stood between her and the rest of the crowd, and extended the tray. "Please, Your Royal Highness," he whispered quickly, "I'm sorry. The queen's secretary asked me to deliver this note to you." His worried eyes pointed to the tray and she saw the folded paper. "Please, take it. Or he'll be most annoyed." With that, he covered the note with a napkin, topped with a tiny cucumber square—and transferred all to a plate for Elena. Elena accepted the stack.

"Thank you, Ma'am," he said with relief.

"Can you believe that I'd do anything to change places with you at this party?" she muttered. She turned and looked about for a quiet spot. How did the secretary expect her to read this note?

The servant's voice came over her shoulder, surprising her.

"Yes, Ma'am, I can imagine that. Is there anything else I can bring to you?" She shook her head and flashed an engaging smile. He smiled before bowing and moving away.

She wished she could tell which servants were her friends and which were not. The signals were rarely so obvious.

She wandered slowly to an empty bench and set the plate aside, unfolding the note and using the napkin as a shield. As more guests filed into the dining tent, she noticed that many, especially women, searched around a bit, before pausing to look at her. Then, many kept stealing glances her way. Peers were more difficult than servants. Royal pettiness made privacy and friendship impossible. Anyone who engaged in genuine conversation with the Princess of Wales could anticipate fewer invitations to royal events, as her dearest friends had already discovered.

Elena bent her head and pretended to be fascinated with the details of the sandwich as she flattened the note against the plate. The note with no signature was brief: "It would be helpful if you stay to the northwest corner of lawn." Elena crumpled the paper and held it inside her hand. Idiots, she thought. Elena wasn't even sure which part of the lawn was the northwest corner. They simply wanted to prove that they could control her.

She stood and returned to the edge of the tent, close to the sidelines along the lawn game—and reminded herself not to act surly and foolish like her husband's family. She refused to play any part in ruining her son's birthday party and would stand by quietly and watch the children have fun. To blinking hell with the queen, she thought. Let Edward be careful about space and stick to this corner of the lawn or that! Her son slammed a solid shot through his wicket, and she politely applauded along with the rest of the crowd. A thick finger tapped her shoulder. Elena turned, her face neutral, ready to counter friend or foe.

"I'm surprised to see you here today," said the gray man standing behind. Her great-uncle on her father's side, Lord Gregory Johnstone, had colorless hair, a gray suit, and a pallor that matched—except for the nose, of course, which was bright red from excessive gin. Johnstone was a member of her family, not her husband's, but he was also one of the queen's closest advisors.

"Are you more surprised about the queen's invitation or my acceptance?" Elena countered.

"Both, I suppose. You've been away for so long. You must miss . . ." He paused and gestured with one hand. "All of this."

She lifted her head high, flashing a brilliant smile. She used to hesitate and slouch around shorter men. Now she relished her height and the discomfort it could create. "You flatter my husband's family," she teased, keeping her voice low and gentle. Elena had promised to behave for the queen.

"You're angry about something," he said dryly, scanning the lawn and the players. "Why else would you demand a lump settlement of seventy million pounds? You'll dispose of the sum handily in a few years, and then come crawling back for more. Why couldn't you accept a monthly retainer like most sensible women? You know, Elena, all the money in the world won't allow you to buy what this family represents."

"Believe me, dear Uncle," she turned back to the field, raising her arms and clapping once more for a steady shot by Larry. "I know what money can and cannot buy. I know what money and status mean to Edward's family, and I also know how to negotiate."

"What's your bottom line, Elena? When will you be satisfied?"

"Let's play a guessing game, Uncle Gregory. Do you remember how we used to play that game during summers at Sandrings Hall when we were young? But oh, no, of course not.

You slipped away for hours, leaving dear Aunt Margaret and your staff to spend time with us. You were never one for watching children play. I recall how you once described it as a task for women. With much disdain, I might add."

"And still do!" he snapped.

"Unless, of course, an heir to the throne is playmate—and then you and all the rest of the court officials gathered around, always on watch to make sure that none of us behaved like children. All that fawning over one child—we pitied the poor Prince of Wales. I hope you know that it was more horrible for Edward than anyone else."

"You're jealous! You don't like the attention that he deserves as Prince of Wales."

"Not at all," Elena said, struggling to keep a simple smile turning into a smirk. "You turned Edward into a miserable and uncertain person, and you'd like to do the same for Richard. But this divorce forced all of you to deal with me—publicly. I refuse to treat my son like an entitled fool."

Johnstone's neck gleamed with sweat.

"Guess what I want," Elena challenged. "It begins with an R."

Her uncle scowled. "Riches. Royalty. Ruination for Edward." He paused. "Richard?"

"I already have Richard." She crossed her arms in a relaxed pose, such that her uncle could not avoid missing her trim waist, her confidence. "Three guesses and I'm already bored," she said, with a laugh. "No, Uncle, all I want is respect."

"Respect from whom?" he started to bellow. He looked around and lowered his voice to a whisper. "If you want respect from the queen, I wouldn't recommend your ongoing plan of extortion."

"If you don't think fighting back as hard as I can wins the queen's respect, then you don't know her well."

"So money and title equal respect for you," he said, his tone snide.

"You've read your history. I'm on the defensive, and the reason for a fight sometimes matters less than how the fight is actually conducted."

"Elena, you're my niece and I don't understand you." He truly looked puzzled. "Why don't you just take the monthly retainer. They would treat you well."

"That would mean the family would still control me."

He shook his head and sighed. "The queen gives you more respect than you deserve. Why do you think Edward annoys her so?" He shook his head. "Yes, you're a scrapper, but what are your principles?"

"All that matters is that I know what they are."

"At least your boy's different—than both you and Edward. He does his duty and enjoys himself. He's comfortable. Staff did well by him. His spirit is more suited for leadership despite all Edward's efforts to compete with him and yours to baby him."

"You fool!" Elena responded quickly, keeping a pleasant look on her face as she faced the crowd. "Don't you understand where his spirit and self-confidence come from? Since he was an infant, he knew that he could ask me anything! He could try some activity and not worry about failure. That's what increases a child's confidence. Not discussions with adults, pushing a child into activities that he's not ready for, dressing and parading him about the country with shallow praise. That's why Edward doesn't know the difference between genuine feeling and posing. If you and Edward and Derry and others had their way, the boy would be afraid of the real world and all the decisions that must be made."

"I can't win. You argue and talk in circles. Edward always complained about it. Damn, Elena, this is no time to be cryptic about what you want. Stop arguing like a woman. For your sake, be straight with the family on what you really want!"

She gave a sparkling laugh. "I am a woman, and so is the one person who matters when it comes to winning my argument. The queen knows what I want. I want respect and enough money to survive. I want to love my children and provide care. Like it or not, Uncle Gregory, divorce or not, I will not fade away and live my life as merely the mother of our future King, like some potted plant in the background."

"You silly thing. You could do yourself a favor by remarrying and disappearing. No more problems with the press. You could enjoy a normal life and not be a pariah."

She stared into his old, watery eyes. "I agree. That sort of life sounds heavenly. But I'd never leave without Richard and Lawrence." Some music started and staff scurried near the palace, signaling the entrance of the queen. "Better run along, Uncle Gregory," she said, waving her hand as if swatting a gnat. "Edward's coming soon. He won't like it that you've joined my long line of admirers. You don't want to appear in tomorrow's *Daily Post,* counted up in the wrong camp!"

Visibly startled, Gregory scanned the large crowd gathering near the tents and started to walk away. He paused. "You yearned to marry the Prince of Wales. I implore you, think twice before you hurt this family and your son's future. If I didn't know better, I'd think you were deliberately out to destroy the monarchy—and yourself." Shaking his head, he walked away from the field and toward the party tent.

"Only if the monarchy tries to cut my ties with my children," Elena murmured to herself. She turned and walked along the edge of the playing field, moving closer to the action. She noticed one of Richard's friends strike the mallet against the red wooden ball. The wicket was close, but John's shot missed by a foot, a mistake that could only be deliberate. John dramatically slapped the side of his head with his hand and pointed out his foolish shot to Richard. Her son patted the boy's back before taking his shot. John preened—so young, and already the subtle fawning had begun.

Derry Sanders called Richard to the sideline opposite from where Elena stood. He straightened the prince's silver and black tie and offered a towel to wipe the boy's brow. He pulled the older prince away from his younger brother and leaned over to whisper in his ear. Richard's face did not change, but he nodded while listening intently to Derry's instructions.

Watching, she thought how strange it was that the royal family relied on servants to tell them constantly what to do. What was it this time? Not to get overheated? Not to let one's friends or younger brother get too close or forward? Not to ignore one's dull father who just entered the party late, so as to gain maximum attention, and followed at a barely dignified distance by his frumpy, controlling mistress, Kay Danvers. Elena observed as the valet led the boy to the small group, where Edward was clearly the center of attention. Kay stood back, in deference to Edward, her face aglow with pride. Elena moved close enough to see the expressions on their faces and hear Edward's hearty question, "How goes it with the boy's training, Derry?"

Elena could not hear her son's reply, but Richard's face remained hopeful, solemn, as he waited for his father to turn his way. Her husband had always treated the child before him as an object—valuable or priceless perhaps, but an object nonetheless and a replacement part at that.

Derry's expression was hearty, confident. "Coming along, Sir. We're most proud of his progress."

Edward absently patted his son's shoulder. "Spending time with his schoolmates?"

"Yes, Sir, they seem a good lot."

"Enough time for that. Time for Richard to greet some of the more distinguished guests."

"Certainly," Derry said, happily, pointing toward the tents where guests gathered for a light meal of watercress salad, chilled shrimp with lemon sauce, salmon soufflé, and delicate tea sandwiches. The menu had not been chosen by a child, let alone a boy.

Edward's small and exclusive entourage moved away, but not before Elena saw the pain in Richard's eyes, after being so obviously dismissed by his father. Her husband's chief concern was that Richard keep good company, not for fun but for social development. He only cared that the boy never reflected poorly on his father.

Elena could tell from the gestures and expressions that the father had not extended his child a simple birthday greeting. The boy blinked and the pain vanished. Richard was like his mother and had learned to mask his emotions well.

A servant interrupted her thoughts. "The northwest corner is this way, Lady Elena."

CHAPTER 3

"She does not know about the arrangements for the weekend."
"She could make a scene."
"The chaps will not leave with her. That's final."

Elena endured sitting through the meal. The table arrangements were satisfactory. She sat at the main table, along with twenty others, although at a far end, where she could barely see the center where her son and husband sat. One gesture was made to Elena's status, however, by seating her across from the ever-smiling Queen Mother, a demure woman, in her nineties and hard of hearing. And Elena noted that Kay was in a far corner of the room—a small consolation that the queen was more dissatisfied with Kay than with Elena.

At Elena's right was an anthropologist in from Thailand, introduced as Doctor Kevin Tilton. The man was weathered and more than six feet tall, a feature always appreciated by Elena who stood at five feet, ten inches, herself. Tilton had none of the awkward ways that tall men often develop upon reaching their forties. His thick golden hair strayed about his dark green eyes and tanned neck. He was attentive and apparently fascinated about sitting next to a princess, albeit one who had been recently divorced.

"So you're only in London for a week," Elena said. "My, you'll have to hurry if you want to visit all the best places."

His cheeks flushed slightly. "I feel like I've had the best today."

"Not really, you're too polite," she said, with a smile. She caught herself wondering what it would be like to camp out under the night stars in the jungle or desert or wherever it was that an anthropologist worked.

"No, merely enchanted," he replied, before turning to his food.

Elena picked up her fork, asked about his research, and glanced down at her plate. Six sublime shrimp were arranged on the plate, the lemon sauce sprinkled in an abstract design. On the inside curve of the largest shrimp was a gray smudge, twitching ever so slightly. Elena turned her plate slightly, and poked the gray with her fork. Gray legs extended from the smudge, the legs of a half-crushed silverfish, struggling against inevitable death. Elena gasped in horror, but then as quickly turned it into a deep if awkward breath, simultaneously slamming her fork down to put the creature out of its misery. Dr. Tilton paused and touched her shoulder.

"Is something wrong?" he inquired. "You look dreadfully pale."

At all costs, she wanted to avoid explaining her reaction or ruin the meals of nearby guests. She took another deep breath, knowing the insect was deliberate and her meal was the only one with a problem. What she didn't know was who did it.

She gently pushed her plate aside, so that she could no longer see the small creature—and tried to compose herself. Answering his question was no simple matter and would take hours. He pressed her again, asking what was wrong.

"No." Elena held her head high, trying to stay calm. Good manners demanded that she keep her discomfort to herself, and instead she reached for her crystal water glass. She twirled the glass in her hands and studied it carefully before taking a sip.

Any tablemates looking on could not tell if she was fascinated or disgusted with the meal. But she could not hide her lack of attention to the nearby conversations. And so, the eager chatter around her subsequently drifted. Elena felt ill, and didn't care that the Queen Mother gave a small disapproving look. It was only after the server came to Elena's place and removed her plate that she could speak again. Those sitting nearby nervously resumed eating. Later, she realized that she had forgotten to make little faces at her sons during the most pompous speeches.

After the luncheon, Edward presided over the large birthday cake decorated with cut Wyndham roses. Father and son stood side by side. For the sake of photographers, Edward placed his hand lightly, protectively, on the boy's shoulder, as Richard cut his birthday cake. He walked away when the photographers finished.

"Don't act so damn stoic, Edward," Elena thought to herself. She no longer felt ill and maintained a polite smile on her face. God knew who among the guests carried miniature digital cameras to record the events, including her refusal to eat. The British economy, with its uncertainty in the job market, along with high taxes and immense debt, made life hard even for the upper class. A good shot of the royal family could be worth a month's income. Any unusually embarrassing pose, an exclusive, was worth a small fortune.

After the gifts were open, the youngest children ran about wildly on the lawn, and Elena sat in a chair under an umbrella, admiring how Richard stepped forward to organize a game.

"Do you mind?" Tilton asked, surprising her by coming up from behind and pointing to the nearest chair.

"Not at all, please." She didn't mind the company, but kept watching the interactions underway on the lawn. She could not take her eyes off Richard, explaining rules to the other children. Was he being bossy, or was he a natural leader? Did the other children admire him in earnest or only because of his position? Most important, did the boy recognize the difference? She should have so many conversations on such matters with both her sons. But time with them was scarce. Elena had always tried to emphasize laughter and fun.

"I would have thought all the single people would have vanished from this party by now," she murmured.

He smiled like a conspirator. "Why do you assume that I'm single?"

She glanced at his hands, rough and without rings. "Most women I know would prefer coming to this function more than their husbands. Unless you're lucky and married an extraordinary woman."

His eyes stayed with her. "No. I only met her today."

Elena shook her head, deliberately turning away with a sharp look to the children on the lawn. He was nice and she didn't want to sit alone, but she had no intentions of flirting. So she changed the subject. "When you were little, which one would you have been?" She pointed to the different groups of boys—a few running about madly, others cooperating with Richard in his attempt to organize the giddy group, others drifting off and finding distraction among the adults along the sidelines. Larry was nowhere in sight, but that was not unusual.

A small girl with long blond curls and an elaborate Laura Ashley print skipped to Elena and gave her a hug. Elena happily took her niece into her lap and welcomed an interruption that forced the uncomfortable conversation with Tilton to take a lighter note.

"Waverly, you've been such a big girl at this party today," Elena exclaimed. "Why, most of the guests would never dream how much younger you are than Richard and Lawrence!"

"Thank you, Auntie Elena," the four-year-old replied with a happy smile. "Mummy was so unhappy with me before. She said I didn't spend enough time with Richard. But it's hard when he's playing with his friends. The older boys don't want me about." With that, she leaned her party-weary head against Elena's chest.

"Of course," Elena murmured. As she stroked her niece's hair, the little girl closed her eyes. Elena had not lost her allure with the children. "I thought you were the perfect little girl here today," she whispered. A royal photographer snapped the scene. Elena wondered if he would lose his job. Or more likely, the photo would never see the light of day.

Then Elena turned to Dr. Tilton. "When you were little, did you recognize differences in other children? Did you ever feel caught in some role that never seemed to end?"

"You sound more like an anthropologist than I do," he said with mild envy. "You're a perceptive woman. But you must hear that all the time."

She laughed and closed her eyes so that he could not see her true reaction. "When I was a little girl, I stood alone and watched the others play. While others talked and joked, I pondered all the comments in my head, wondering how others managed to find a way to fit them in so quickly into the conversation. Somehow, I always felt behind. Looking back, I realize I thought about each and every statement far too long. The only way this party would have been any fun for me would have been if I had explored the upstairs rooms until I found one with a television and an immense sofa with lots of plump cushions. I'd find a silly or sad show—and escape!"

"We could do that now," he said in a conspiratorial whisper.

Elena frowned. She was disappointed that he misunderstood her, especially as she held her niece. Suddenly, her sister-in-law, Princess Caroline, emerged from the crowd, obviously annoyed. She stormed to Elena, snatching Waverly away and setting her promptly into a standing position. Waverly looked alarmed as her mother used a firm hand to smooth the dress.

"I've been looking for you all over," Caroline scolded. "Crawling into laps is not how one behaves at a formal party, my dear." She cast a scathing glance in Elena's direction and directed her reprimand that way, not that Waverly knew. "Apologize to your aunt, please!"

"There's no need for that." Elena tried to be serene and pleasant with her sister-in-law. "I welcomed your company immensely, Waverly."

The little girl looked frightened. Elena felt sad, knowing that the royal family was probably warning its youngest members to stay far away from the foolish woman who dared to divorce the Prince of Wales. She watched as Caroline quickly led Waverly away.

"They tell me to follow Caroline's example as a mother," Elena said flatly. "I care too much for my children, they claim. Should I act stern, like Caroline?"

Tilton spoke softly. "To judge by Richard, you've done a marvelous job as a mother. But he's older now. You could start letting go."

Elena did not respond. She should not be so particular, but she could not help but think, What about Larry? People constantly overlooked her second child, but he was special, too, despite the fact that he would never be king.

Tilton touched her arm. "Look, you know London better than anyone. We could return to the city tonight—together. I'd be honored to have the best tour guide in all of Great Britain. Or we could relax . . ."

She smiled warmly. It was frightening how easily her smiles could come, even when she was annoyed. "That sounds grand—if you want to be followed by a mob of photographers," she said. "But the answer is no. My children are returning with me tonight."

He pleaded: "Are you sure? Don't they have a nanny? Couldn't you this once?"

She shook her head firmly, turned to the lawn, and waved her hand gently in Richard's direction. She was pleased that her son spotted the gesture in less than ten seconds. Time to think about leaving, she thought wearily. Guests were preparing to say farewell—and Elena and the children had stayed long enough. She couldn't wait to have the children that night and the following day—on her territory with her rules. Not that she had many rules.

And she had enough of Doctor Tilton, despite his good looks and intriguing career. "Thank you for putting up with me today." She stood, flustered, as if late for an important appointment. "I must have said some silly things, and you may have the wrong impression of me. Despite what you read about me in the papers, I'm simply the mother of two boys, frightfully boring for most men, I'm afraid. And I'm an empty shell when I'm not with them. Please enjoy your stay in London, Doctor Tilton." She already had too many admirers who didn't know her at all and she knew deliberate abruptness would chase most away.

Guests waited for the drivers, and court photographers drifted away. The queen had left the party long ago, after posing for an official portrait with her son and two grandsons. Edward and his mistress had not been around since the cake had been distributed. At last, Elena could gather her children, collect their suitcases and take off for London.

She headed for the palace, in search of Larry, when her Uncle Gregory stopped her. His face was flushed with too much gin. "The queen's secretary asked me to inform you that your driver has been called. For your convenience. He also offered his compliments. The queen was most pleased with the outcome of the party and your behavior."

"Wonderful," she said. "The party was grand. All I have to do is locate Lawrence. I assume the boys' belongings have been loaded?"

Gregory frowned. "But the boys are staying here."

"No," Elena said coolly. "I arranged it with the queen. Why, it was posted on my schedule this morning!"

"Oh, dear," he said, in mock distress. "That's most annoying—there must have been some mix-up."

"Fine, that's no problem—I have plenty of clothes for them back at Kirkington. They're boys, and other than school, they have no obligations."

"Everyone in the royal family has obligations—especially those two children. They're part of a hunting party that was arranged by their Aunt Caroline for tomorrow. She went to a lot of trouble gathering the right sort of people. The guests would be terribly disappointed if the boys were not present."

"A group of people who care more about titles than children," Elena said. "But I made plans, and I'm their mother. My schedule does not belong on the back burner. I planned a small celebration for them tomorrow with friends."

"Don't you think that's a bit much?" Gregory said with a patronizing smile. "I mean, the boys are worn enough after today."

"Caroline's hunt is more relaxing than a small party with friends?"

"To be honest, dear girl, you did not look well during the luncheon today!"

"And I'm sure you know the reason why," she snapped. He showed no sign of understanding what she meant or didn't care. "Look, I haven't seen my children in a week. This party hardly counts. I played by the queen's rules today. We had an understanding. The boys were here all day yesterday for hunting parties or whatever nonsense Caroline had planned. They're coming to London with me."

"I'll relay the message, Elena. But don't count on having the boys. Perhaps you can arrange a dinner with them some night here at the palace, before they head back for classes at Van-Crendon. Don't you think that would be more convenient?"

Getting nowhere with her uncle, she walked away, searching for Richard. Maybe Gregory was confused. The boys had not mentioned any interruptions for their scheduled weekend visit when she had visited them privately before the party. She found Richard under a tree with a small group of cousins. Derry stood close at hand, always ready to do Richard's bidding. Elena found it grating and odd how her interests always clashed with the plans of the valet. Didn't her son notice? Had her husband deliberately planned it that way? Did Richard realize that the man was a ball and chain? Derry was around only to push the boy in a certain direction, shape him into a royal mold without feelings or goals. Or did the boy blame his mother for the tension and discomfort?

She had to be careful. "Richard, darling," she called out in a friendly way. "Can I see you a moment?" Derry started to accompany the boy. "No need to leave the fun, Derry," she ordered.

"Yes, Mother?" Richard hurried to her side.

"Darling, I thought you were coming back to London with me tonight."

The boy looked uncomfortable as he stared at his feet. Damn, Elena thought, they should not put her child in the middle, making him feel guilty for their treachery. She had to be careful, refusing to fall into their game of retaliation. She bent low and looked into his eyes, keeping her own open and friendly, her smile comforting.

"But I was told that the plans had changed. That you had other plans and that we could not be included." Richard sounded genuinely confused.

"Who said that?" Elena asked.

"Derry."

Elena's throat was tight and her chest hurt. But it would do her no good to stand on the lawn and argue with a servant. "Not true at all! A mistake of some sort, but don't you worry, sweetheart. I've been looking forward to seeing you all week! I'm more than ready for you. Maybe we can clear it up. Why, I had planned a small party tomorrow, with some of your friends in London. Laser shooting! It was supposed to be a surprise."

"I would have liked that, Mum . . ." The boy was glum.

"I will go talk to the queen myself. We had this weekend arranged all along. The staff must have mixed it all up."

"I hope you can get it changed, but Aunt Caroline's party sounds important. Are you sure you didn't make a mistake?"

"Not at all!" Elena was irritated. "It was on my schedule this morning." She lowered her voice and reminded herself not to take her frustration out on the boy. That's what Derry and the servants wanted. "I'm going to find your grandmother. Do you want to come with me?"

Richard shook his head. "No, I believe you. I thought it was funny, because Derry said not to talk about it before the party."

Good, Elena thought to herself. Her son was already learning not to trust the valet. "The queen will decide. If she can't change the plans, then we'll reschedule. I promise. I want you to have a wonderful day tomorrow either way and not to worry about any of this. Promise?" She placed her smooth hand under his chin. He nodded.

"Where's Larry?"

"He got restless during the party and Nanny Ryan took him away." He pointed to the higher points of the castle. "He's probably in playing some game or taking a nap."

"Oh, shoot naps! Who needs a nap at that age!"

"I'm made of stronger stuff than he!"

She couldn't tell if the boy teased or not. Servants and members of the family had expressed similar sentiments often enough, even when they were not true. She had constantly urged her boys not to engage in comparisons, but she decided to ignore his claim and press on with her curiosity. "When were you told about the change in plans for this weekend? Did you talk about it with your grandmother?"

"No," Richard said, looking behind him. "Derry told me this morning and Larry didn't find out until later. He was very upset. Derry suggested that we not talk about it, that our disappointment might hurt your feelings."

"How considerate," Elena said sarcastically. The bastard, she thought to herself. She wanted to warn Richard about Derry, but that would take careful thought. It wasn't wise to rush into such a task at the end of a long and stressful day. "I hope you believe me," Elena insisted. "It's some kind of a mix-up."

"I do, mother, and I'll miss you. Please try to talk to Grandmum."

She appreciated her son's understanding, but over the years he had become used to such disruptions. "I'll try. Now, return to your guests—and do your best to look happy."

The boy dashed off to his group, and Elena was sure she saw the hint of a smile on Derry's lips. He knew. He probably knew more than anyone in her family. One could never tell who made the decisions around the palace—the queen or the odd and rigid staff vying to serve her interests.

Elena stormed off toward the offices inside the palace in search of the queen's secretary, Michael Barringer. She ignored the receptionist and opened the door to Barringer's grand office—larger and with finer artwork than her own office at Kirkington Palace.

"I want to know what's going on," Elena demanded. "The boys were supposed to leave with me. I spoke with the queen about it weeks ago."

Barringer gave her a quick bow, but his tone was insolent. "Ah, Lady Elena, we were so glad you could make it today. Please have a seat. Would you like a glass of claret? I opened the most delightful bottle."

"I won't be staying. According to my schedule for the day, I was supposed to leave with the boys directly following the party. And we're obliged to meet these schedules, as I've been constantly reminded over the years." She remained standing and leaned over his desk.

"The party was a success for the young man, don't you think?"

"Like a shot of Novocain. What could be more fun for a child than prancing about in a silly suit before hundreds of adults he couldn't care less about! He was supposed to spend the rest of the weekend with me. I discovered a few moments ago that his valet told him that I changed the plans."

"Oh, dear, there's some misunderstanding. The queen may have mentioned something about your request a few weeks ago. But then Caroline invited some important guests who will spend the weekend here—a philosopher from Latin America and a watercolor artist from Spain. She thought it would be an enriching experience for the boys. Don't you agree?"

"But what about my plans?" Elena, about ready to go hysterical, tried to keep her voice steady.

Barringer shrugged. "If only you had called and spoken with me. Someone, I'm not sure who, mentioned that you had changed your mind."

"The least you could have done is call and check. Or ask Richard and Larry for their opinion. I'd like to talk to the queen about this matter. Now. This is most annoying."

"She's unavailable for the rest of the day."

"What!" Elena was horrified. She was not going to have the

boys for the rest of the weekend. Derrick was gone, and they were testing her mettle. Only the queen could overturn Barringer's schedule and she was unavailable. "What do I do?"

"My advice? Have a quiet weekend and enjoy yourself. Believe me, Caroline has high regard for your children. They adore her. If you truly love them, you'll allow them to enjoy the benefits of the royal family."

"Caroline resents my children. She's jealous that they're first in line for the crown."

He chuckled. "I know Caroline as you never will. She grew up in this family. She's utterly loyal to her mother, her brother, and to his sons. Your sons mean more to her than you can imagine."

"Only if she can influence them and use them. And for what? What does it all mean to be queen or king? A few extra party invitations and more groveling from the servants?"

"I suppose it's difficult for you to understand, not having lived with such duty your entire life. You came upon your role suddenly. You were and continue to be obviously unprepared."

"Ordinary citizens overlook my failings. If only the family could be so forgiving."

He shuffled papers idly about his desk. "I have the boys' calendars here. If you want time, you had best let me know."

"The court has established the schedule!" Elena shouted, in a panic.

"Elena, be realistic. Your solicitor is dead. You chose to reopen the settlement. We consider any agreements under discussion with him, including the schedule, as null and void. You must start over—and I would suggest that you not be tardy about choosing another solicitor. And for once the queen agrees with you. Perhaps for everyone's sake, more negotiations are necessary."

"What are you talking about?" Elena asked.

"The trust settlement does not stand alone." His tone was patronizing. "Time with the children is another issue on the table."

Elena swallowed and tried to control her agitation. "When is the next time I can be with them?" she questioned, keeping her voice soft.

Barringer smiled as he looked down in his book, assuming that she had given up. "Hmm, next Sunday, after attending church with their father. I suggest that you save everyone time and drive here to meet them."

"Most of their belongings, Larry's toys, are at my home. How can you deprive them of time with their mother, something they want?" Elena asked, her voice broken.

"They're growing older." The man was haughty. "They're uncertain about what they really want. But they no longer need toys, and in fact, Derry told me he was packing some of their more inappropriate belongings for storage. Those boys no longer need coddling. That's always hard for a mother to take, but the queen understands."

"What would happen if I suddenly changed plans?" Elena questioned. "The next time they're with me!"

"Your plans are secondary," he said coldly. "Your behavior and these irrational comments confirm my fears. The boys won't accompany you to London—and in fact, I believe they have already been whisked off for some activity with Caroline's husband. Once you heard of Caroline's plans, you could have simply complied. By coming to my office and trying to argue your case, you missed your opportunity to say farewell."

"You bastard!" Elena asked. "How dare you?"

He gave her a smug smile.

She shook her head and spoke low. "Don't you realize that those two children know what you're doing? That they believe my explanations and not those of some silly servant? You can do little things to annoy me in the short term. But over the long term, you and the entire royal family lose credibility. It happens over and over, and you never learn from your mistakes. The boys don't trust you."

"I'll pass your concerns along."

"Do." Elena's reply was cool. "Richard knows me. I tell the truth. He asked me to plead our case to his grandmother—and I wonder how you can possibly explain this nonsense to him?" Barringer cocked his head, and turned his attention to paperwork on his desk. He did not have to explain. She was a blond pretender. She had no more royal blood than he did. Her royalty came by virtue of marriage, and that was over.

Elena stormed out of the office, desperate to find her children and explain. As she turned a corner, she ran into Edward. "Oh!" she said, startled.

"You're still here!"

"Don't worry, I'm on my way out!" She crossed her arms and stood to her full height, with the help of three-inch heels. That annoyed him. Before they were separated, she wore flat shoes, never challenging his height. "Without the children, I might add."

"They're staying here?" he asked, puzzled. "But why aren't they going with you?"

The staff enjoyed punishing Edward as much as Elena for the divorce: Their arrangements typically meant she had less time with the children, and Edward had less time with his mistress. "Ask your sister, Caroline. She has plans for them and your intellectual lackeys."

"Damn," he said, staring out the window. "I had other plans."

"Didn't we all?" she snapped. "Give my regrets to Kay." She leaned back against the wall. His confusion was genuine. She couldn't decide whether to be pleased that he was not part of the plot to keep the children away from her or angry about his eagerness to be away from the boys. She loathed her husband's family and pitied him, but the boys needed and admired their father. In truth, she had to admit that Edward was decent in many ways, except for his inability to stand up for himself and his sons to his family.

"Do you know what really bothers me? I doubt your mother had anything to do with these plans. Or even Caroline. I think the servants did it. They hate being servants, and they hate us. And in some underhanded way, they do whatever they possibly can to make our lives absolutely miserable."

He laughed at her. "Really, Elena, you imagine more power than the servants could possibly handle. And my dear, that's been one of your problems. You've always had difficulties with the servants. You can't say I didn't warn you. The secret—relax, and let them handle matters."

"And lose all control in my life?" Elena said with a laugh. "I refuse to follow their whims blindly! I won't have them telling me how to conduct my affairs and live my life."

"That's unfortunate. If only you had tried more, our life together could have been so much easier. Royal duty isn't merely playing to crowds, smiling and shaking hands, and giving little speeches. That's the easy part. Royal duty is also about tradition, order, a family setting a good example."

"Royal duty!" she scoffed. "The details on royal duty have changed every day since I met you!"

"Duty comes minute by minute. We have protocol and responsibility. You never understood."

"Save that pompous crap for the papers. Or pillow talk with Kay."

His back stiffened and he looked about to make sure no one had heard. "Don't forget that I'm the Prince of Wales. I expect appropriate language."

She threw her hands up in surrender. "All right, Edward, I'm grateful you had nothing to do with this mix-up this afternoon. I get on well with the boys, you know that. We both do. Perhaps you could talk to your mother. Explain . . ."

"Those boys do well going back and forth," Edward agreed. "But Mother will get annoyed. She's always after me to spend more time with Richard. If I speak up for you, she'll only accuse me of trying to avoid him. Besides, her secretary told me that she'd be busy for the rest of the afternoon."

"She's avoiding us," Elena said. "Can you say something about next weekend? At least try. Surely you don't need the boys every weekend."

"Certainly not. I'll say something to Barringer."

"Thank you," Elena said sincerely. "That's fair of you."

He nodded his agreement. "Kay said today's party was delightful. She thought Richard remained the center of attention and had plenty of fun."

"But then her idea of fun is a dead pheasant!" Elena quipped. She appreciated him working to give her more time with the children, but she didn't want to hear about his homely, self-centered, smug mistress. What kind of woman would cling to a man for more than twenty years after being told that she was not good enough for marriage? "I still don't understand why Kay cares so much about the protocol of these events. It works against her. And good lord, Edward, you could have greeted Richard with a birthday wish. A little hug wouldn't embarrass you. He's still a child!"

"Richard understands. He's more than a child and must behave accordingly in public. And he's doing a fine job getting accustomed to protocol. Derry is a good influence on the child. Have you noticed Richard's ordering the servants about?" Edward chuckled and didn't notice her grimace.

"I want him to be spontaneous. I worry that ordering servants about will spill over to bossing friends about."

"Derry will take care of that," Edward said dismissively. "The boys needed us when they were young. It's a childish fancy to think that must continue. Believe me, this is something I know." He sighed and looked out on the grounds. Servants were lugging away the debris. Cars were driving away. Edward's tone was flat, but the look in his eyes was wistful.

Elena never met Edward's childhood guide and always wondered if the valet had been like Derry. Edward was sentimental whenever he reminisced about those days. "But why's it better for the boys to rely on servants more than us?" she asked. "We're their parents. We can give good advice and care. And we do have the time!"

"The boys need independence. They need to control themselves and others."

"Edward, you were close to others besides servants," she said softly. "My Uncle Gregory was a good man, but he essentially worked for your parents. Later, you had your valet. The servants cared for you, but you can't imagine how different it might have been if you'd been close to your parents."

"You don't understand," he said, more distant than harsh. He had never learned how much his tone of dismissal, his entire manner, infuriated her and motivated her to assert herself as an individual, separate from the family.

"For whatever reason, they were incapable of showing love," she insisted. "Your mother did her best by finding nice people, but . . ."

He gave her a look of fury, and she felt chilled. The sun was going down. The party was over. She steeled herself against any reaction. It was no longer in her interest to educate her former husband about human relations. In the early years of her marriage, she had tried. He and the rest of the royal family refused to listen, refused to consider any other approaches.

They all regarded her as an uneducated twit. True, she had

barely completed her education after failing all her O levels, but the fiasco had not been because she was dim. No, the girls at the exclusive boarding school had been given an array of incentives to do poorly at school, convinced that their priority in life was preparing for good marriages. Instructors repeatedly advised the young ladies that the wealthiest, most powerful men did not appreciate the most intelligent women. Elena wanted a happy marriage and complied.

The school had never tested its students for their observations of the web of relationships among teachers, friends, family—but Elena learned how to listen, analyze, and express her opinion when it mattered, with a smile. Her school experiences did not diminish her social instincts, which would have been coveted by the world's finest advertising and marketing executives. Her survival instincts were even better.

"Thank you, Edward, for your part in inviting me today," she concluded with remote politeness.

"And thank you for your discretion. It's for the best, you know. For you and me and the boys."

Shaking her head, she left the hallway, intent on being graceful. Hot tears burned her eyes, but she would not allow anyone to see. The butler joined her in the lobby and bowed.

"Your driver has been waiting," the butler noted solemnly.

"And he can wait a few more minutes," she replied. "That's his job. Where are my children? I expected to say farewell to them."

"I believe they left with Princess Caroline's husband," he said hesitantly. "The nanny upstairs would know."

"Call and check," Elena demanded.

He rang—and shrugged. "No answer," he apologized. "After the party . . . Everyone has taken off."

She could stay and make a scene. But Wyndham Palace was immense, and it was unlikely the boys would hear and come running. She wondered if she could count on the children feeling as frustrated as she felt. The two boys could make a point to the queen and their father far better than she ever could. She rang Barringer's office. He refused to take the call. "Leave him this message," she advised the assistant. "I'm worried about staff's inability to locate the boys. As far as I'm concerned, it's a serious lapse in security."

"They're on palace grounds," the assistant said soothingly. "The boys are always safe as long as they're running about on palace grounds. Especially with Derry around."

Elena asked for stationery and wrote an apologetic farewell note to Richard and Larry, hastily explaining her efforts. She sealed the envelope tightly and handed it to the butler and then ran for her car, eager to leave the stifling palace, still bustling with post-party activity.

Henry slowly guided the vehicle away from the imposing building. "Off to Kirkington, Your Royal Highness?" Henry queried, his voice soft with sympathy. He knew how much she enjoyed spending time with her children and her keen disappointment about leaving the boys behind.

"Yes, yes, yes," she murmured, staring out the window. The car slowly eased its way through gardens where she had played with the boys as toddlers and then a patch of forest. The boys had nicknamed the patch Sherwood. Back then she had complained about a lack of time with the children. If she had only known that the situation would not improve as the children grew older. She had always calmed herself by expecting, searching out more choices. She stared out the front window, the main palace gate just ahead.

"My God!" Henry swore and stopped the car. Elena sat up and followed his eyes. A small figure stood by the edge of the road and waved frantically at the Rolls and then darted back toward the woods.

"It's Larry!" Elena exclaimed.

"The master of the carriage house kept reminding me to get this car off the grounds by six," Henry fretted. "Explained that they would be working on the gate and . . ."

Elena didn't wait for him to finish, and flung the car door open even before he came to a complete stop. He didn't quit the engine and looked worried. Ignoring Henry, she ran off the road, through the high grasses, toward the edge of the wood, where Larry waited next to a twisted oak.

"You didn't say good-bye!" The boy was distraught.

"I couldn't find you, sweetheart. Richard said you got restless during his party."

"Nanny Ryan was furious!" The boy beamed, always expressing pleasure about irritating the nanny. "I refused to sit still and she said I would detract from Richard. I played with my napkin even more, so that I could leave the stupid party!"

"Oh, you're clever." She gave him a hug. "I wish that I had thought to play with my napkin."

A frown crossed his face. "Aunt Caroline said I was naughty and wouldn't allow me to go with Richard and Uncle Kenneth. That's all right. If I can't go with you, I'd rather be alone!"

Clutching him close, she wanted to whisk the boy away with her. All the family really cared about was Richard, the future king, so why couldn't they allow her time with Larry? But they knew enough to care about appearances. Photos of Lawrence alone with his mother, without his brother, would start the gossip stampede.

Larry must have shared her thoughts, because he started pleading to join Elena. "Please, Mother. I counted on going to London with you tonight. Derry packed my science set with your bags. You're the only one who allows me to do the kind of experiments I like."

"I counted on your visit, too," she admitted. "Someone

changed the plans on us. I tried to talk to your grandmother after the party. But it didn't work."

"I don't believe anything she says!" Larry said, with a child's petulance. "Derry told Richard at some point during the party that he 'thought your mother' had changed the plans. After I had left the party, I was looking for some paper and went down to the offices. I heard Derry speak with old Spot." That was the nickname the boys had for Barringer, because of a prominent mole on the back of his balding head. The boy pinched his nose and spoke in his snootiest imitation. "The queen thinks that two parties in one weekend are entirely too much for the young princes. Besides, laser shooting in a public place is most inappropriate. Better the boys practice at a real hunt."

He reached out and wrapped his arms around her shoulders. "Mum, as long as we're around here, we have to do what everyone else wants us to do. We never get time to ourselves!"

Elena frowned. She looked toward the car, where Henry looked worried. What had he said about the gate closing? But Larry was insistent. The boy tugged on her hand. "Please, Mother, let me come with you. Let me climb into the boot. No one will notice if I'm not around."

The boy's protest was loud and long. If she took him away in the car, the queen would label her a security risk. If she took him back to the palace, then Larry would face punishment. She took his hand and sat with him on the grass. The servants, even Henry, wouldn't like a change in the schedule, but she couldn't simply dismiss her son's concerns and drive away. Just around the corner, a mob of photographers waited, ready to document another painful moment in her life.

"Darling, if I took you without permission, we'd both be in trouble," she confided. "It could mean us not getting together for weeks."

"They don't care about me. They only care about Richard.

I'm old enough to see it, and I know why!"

She longed to comfort him, but also wondered what he meant. "Oh, honey, that's . . ."

A deafening roar from behind interrupted her. Feeling a burst of hot air on her back, Elena pushed Larry to the ground, before turning around to look.

A ball of orange flames engulfed the back of her waiting car, which quickly turned to billows of thick black smoke. Choking from the horrible smell, she wasn't sure if bits of glass and metal stung her skin or just the heated air from the blast. Using her body, she shielded her son from the explosion and urged him to crawl deeper into the woods. But the boy was confused, his eyes wide with fear. So she linked her hands under his arms and dragged him back. "Hurry," she cried.

The boy squirmed once, struggling to look back at the car through the trees. She examined his face and head. "Are you all right?" she asked, touching her son's face. The back of her neck and arms stung, but she ignored the pain. The boy's eyes were dazed, locked onto the roadway.

"Are you all right?" she pressed.

He stared at her. "Mother, you look frightful!"

"Stay here," she ordered. "Don't move from this tree." She turned and saw for the first time the Rolls, its back ripped open, puffs of black smoke drifting toward the sky. "Oh dear God, poor Henry." Security had always trained her to remove herself and her family from any scene of trouble. But Henry, of course, she had to help him. She ran back to the Rolls. The heat and smell of burning metal hurt her nostrils as she approached. Some flames still leapt from the back seat, where she had sat only moments earlier. Smoke filled the vehicle. Inside, a panicked and bleeding Henry coughed and fumbled with the door. She grabbed his door handle. It was locked.

"Unlock it," she screamed. "I can't get it open!"

He shook his head, his eyes full of tears.

"Open the window," she screamed.

He pounded the buttons, but the car's complex electronic system did not respond. She tried the door handle again, while Henry struck feebly at the glass. The smoke was getting to him, making him weak. Removing her heel, she slammed it against the window. Damn bulletproof glass. She ran back to the edge of the road, searching for the odd sharp stick or rock that might have been overlooked by groundskeepers, anything she could use to pry at the door or break the window.

Glancing up, she saw the palms of Henry's hand fall away, his face slumped against the window. That was when the final explosion hit. The car turned into a huge ball of flames as the full gas tank exploded. The blast knocked Elena backward more than several feet and she landed on the ground, her head striking one of the ancient rocks lining the palace drive. She went dizzy—and fought to retain consciousness. The crackling sounds of a ruined car, the smells of burning gasoline and singed silk helped her to keep focus. Henry was gone, but she had to reach Larry. Clawing the dirt and long grass, Elena hoped to return to Larry, making sure that he had waited by the tree and had not tried to follow her. She tried with all her might to move, but only managed to clutch a tiny pebble. Her eyes closed, and an image of Henry beaming at his wife and new baby filled her mind before she passed out.

CHAPTER 4

"My God, look at all those flowers. The florists must be in their glory."

"Yes. Strangers love her more than her own family does."

When Elena regained consciousness in an all-white, crisp hospital bed, two sights greeted her eyes that suggested she was in for a rough week.

The first was an attractive, beaming young nurse, her wispy hair pulled back with a thin black ribbon.

The second was some newspapers on the chair next to her bed—the top one showing an out-of-focus full-page telephoto shot of a determined Elena, running from the burning Rolls, young Larry in tow. Larry had claimed she looked frightful, but Elena could not help but think that he was wrong. She looked rumpled but daring, and the effect was quite fetching.

The headline screamed: "ELENA, HERO OF WALES"

Another: "TRUE GRIT—BRIT GRIT!"

The full shock from the car bomb returned and Elena suddenly had so many questions. "Oh, no!" she cried out and tried to sit up. "What about Larry and Richard? Are they safe?"

"You're awake!" the nurse said efficiently, quickly moving the newspapers aside to the other side of the room. "How wonderful! Both sons are perfectly safe. The younger was checked at the hospital last night and released almost immediately. I'm thrilled to be the one to see you awake and tell you."

Elena closed her eyes in relief. Larry was fine. "Thank God," she murmured.

"Are you ready to sit up?" The nurse arranged two more plump pillows behind Elena's back, helping her to sit up. And the young woman stood over the bed, studying Elena with a direct, assessing gaze. "In the meantime, what can I do for you? How about a nice drink of ginger ale?"

The nurse's voice carried hint of an Irish accent. Soft and lyrical, the voice was soothing, almost hypnotic. "That sounds delicious," Elena said, suddenly feeling her dry mouth, sores along her back and a lump on her head.

"And my name's Rita," the nurse explained, as she opened a small refrigerator. She placed plenty of ice into a plastic cup and poured from a small bottle, placing the cup in Elena's hands. "Sip slowly," she advised, before pulling it away after a few sips. "Let me know when you're ready for more. Ask if you need anything at all. But, first, I should call the doctor in, tell them that you're up. He can let your family know that you're awake."

"No! Not yet!" Elena protested, jerking forward. Nausea and a headache overwhelmed her. She desperately needed to be alone. Her voice was weak, "Please, give me a moment. Just you . . ."

"Of course, Your Royal Highness." The nurse looked alarmed, and hovered near the bed, helping ease Elena back to her pillow. "It's best if you take it easy. No sudden movements, please. Not after a head injury."

"I need time to think," Elena repeated. "How long ago?"

"The accident happened yesterday."

"Henry?"

"He's dead," Rita replied, compassionate but firm.

Elena took a deep breath. That's probably fortunate, Elena thought to herself. No one would understand that sentiment unless they had witnessed the horrible scene, a man trying to escape an explosion, suffering, knowing he was about to die in a burning vehicle. The pain must have been dreadful—she had been outside the car, not very close at all, and yet her arms and neck were bandaged, the skin felt tight and burned. She hesitated to ask how she looked or about the extent of her own injuries. It was enough that Larry had escaped injury, and she tried to be thankful.

Her mouth still felt dry, and she suddenly felt the urge to try moving about on her own, to stand. She turned her head toward the bed stand, wondering if she could reach the ginger ale on her own. A small vase featured a single bough of plump lilacs in rich purple. Next to the vase, as if on guard duty, was the tiny Lego knight that had been in her pocket. His Lego smile was big and happy, and she could not help but smile herself.

"Your clothes were completely ruined, I'm sorry to say," Rita murmured. "The investigators took them away. Before we took them off, I hope you don't mind that I went through the pockets. Thought that someone might want the little man." She placed the plastic toy into Elena's hand.

"It's a princess," Elena corrected her, realizing even as she spoke that her comment did not make much sense.

"Yes, of course," Rita said in her affable way, but nodded as if something else had been confirmed. "I thought it might be special."

"The pieces are my younger son's favorite." Elena stared at the toy. "We played with them before the party, and he let me take this one with me. When we have time together, we build and tell stories. But there isn't much time, even when we all lived together."

Rita sat on the edge of the bed. "The investigators from your palace were demanding, but I couldn't imagine how a toy would be of much use for them."

"It's not my palace," Elena corrected again, almost speaking to herself. She didn't want to be bossy, but she wanted the woman to understand that being a princess was nothing special.

Rita paused and then changed the subject. "And the lilacs, they're from my neighbor's garden. I heard they're your favorite—I hope that's true."

Elena nodded. "Thank you. Yesterday seems so long ago, almost like it never really happened."

"Your mind will be foggy for a while. But you remember the accident?"

"Yes, after we left Richard's birthday party." Elena pointed to the stack of newspapers across the hospital room. "May I look at some of the newspapers?"

Rita hesitated, tucking a stray lock of hair underneath the ribbon. "Maybe it's better you rest."

"But there was news about the party, wasn't there?" Elena asked.

"After the accident and all the commotion, the party was largely forgotten." Rita stood and sorted through the stack, at last plucking out one tabloid that favored the royal family. "It's too soon for you to start reading much, but there's a small photo of the young prince in here. Plenty more of you." Elena shook her head and groaned. Her headache immediately worsened. The family would never forgive her.

Rita was puzzled. "I understand how you must hate the photographers, but you were sensational! The one man described how you moved your son out of harm's way and then went back to help the driver."

"He couldn't open the door," Elena murmured. She stared in disbelief at the newspaper—at the photograph of her and Larry, wishing that she could have saved Henry the same way.

The nurse stayed close, smoothing the covers on the bed, asking questions and glancing at Elena constantly. Elena realized that the woman's busy movements had a purpose.

"What are you checking me for?"

Rita looked up with an appreciative smile. "Just checking for any symptoms of shock or bleeding on your brain. You took a nasty blow to the head. But so far you're coming along nicely—alert, good memory. Though the bruise on your head must hurt?"

Elena nodded. "And these burns?" she asked.

"Mostly minor and will heal quickly. The arms and neck took the worst of it. But head injuries are fickle. So while you're at it let me check your eyes." Rita held a small torch and asked Elena to stare straight ahead. "No sign of blood. Your pupils react normally to light. How's the vision?"

Elena looked around the room and then glanced out the window. "Excellent." Elena appreciated Rita's style, how she focused on care, while giving information. Once Rita called for the physician, the palace would send security details and press assistants who would take over, all telling her what to do or say. "I hope you will stay with me for a while. I really can't handle the whole crowd right now."

"I can talk to the doctor in charge. He's very nice and will understand. Really, little can be done for a concussion beyond keeping the patient quiet and relaxed. I'll talk to him and he'll insist that your room be kept quiet. Only one visitor at a time. Would that help?"

Elena nodded, and closed her eyes, leaning her head against the pillows. The room was quiet, white. She enjoyed talking with a new person. It was best if she came to terms with the accident privately, without all the interpretations of palace staff. Then she opened her eyes again. "Can you let me read one of the newspapers? Best to know what I'm in for. Do they know who put the bomb in the car?"

"No, they haven't caught anyone yet." Rita examined the

newspapers, and finally handed over the most distinguished of the bunch. The account would be short and formal, and signal what was being said in the international press. "Just one for now. Try not to worry, Ma'am. They all call you courageous."

"Please call me Elena." Her eyes swept back and forth, trying to absorb the subtle messages beyond the words:

In the spirit of Great Britain's finest heroes, Elena, Princess of Wales, saved her younger son from a car bomb late yesterday—and then returned to the flaming wreckage in an attempt to rescue her driver.

"Mama pulled me away from the car and made me sit by a tree, and then she ran back," explained ten-year-old Prince Lawrence. "She tugged and tugged. Then she hit the window with her shoe. There was a great big explosion, and she got hurt. It was the most horrible thing I've ever seen. But she was wonderful and never looked scared."

Investigators with the Metropolitan Police refused to comment on the explosion. But palace security hinted that a bomb had been placed behind the back seat of the Rolls-Royce owned by the palace and frequently used by Elena, as well as other members of the royal family. The anony-mous source added that the bomb was unsophisticated and similar to those relied upon by insurgents in the Middle East. As of press time, no organizations claimed responsibility for the bombing.

Elena was injured and struck unconscious when the gas tank of the Rolls exploded. Hospital administrators reported her condition was stable. Young Prince Larry suf-fered minor injuries and Henry Pindlow, driver for the royal family, died of burns at the scene.

Prince Larry took up where his mother left off, rushing

to her side and working to pull her away. A photographer with this newspaper came to the child's aid and obtained exclusive photographs and comments.

Palace staff immediately issued a release, criticizing photographers and journalists for taking photographs of the tragedy, and then collecting comments from the young prince before palace representatives arrived on the scene. That release was followed shortly afterward by another expressing outrage at the incident and sympathy for Pindlow's family.

Despite much talk to the contrary, the finest of Britain's chivalrous traditions still survive among members of the royal family, if only a few . . .

Elena crumpled the newspaper and started to weep. "Poor Henry," she said softly. She looked up at the nurse, her eyes wide. "I tried. Really I did. I can see his wife holding his beautiful little baby." The nurse wrapped her arms around Elena and tried to comfort her. "And Larry, you're sure his injuries are minor?"

"He's fine, a wonderful and brave little boy." Turning abruptly, she snatched a note from the nightstand and handed it over. "And that reminds me, he left something with his nurse, just before he was released last night. The dear child asked that it be handed to you as soon as you regained consciousness."

Elena accepted the grubby little patch of paper. "You're the best mum in the whole world. I love you." The note was signed by Larry. She held the note to her chest, leaned back against her pillow and realized how much her head ached and her arms stung from the burns. She could feel ointment along her arms, neck and face. She reached for her hair, felt frayed locks and closed her eyes. She needed to think.

"Terrorists," she murmured. "I never dreamed that I was in

danger, especially since the divorce."

"You're still part of the royal family." Rita rubbed her right hand and studied it closely. "And the most popular one, at that."

Elena frowned and shook her head lightly as if annoyed by a buzzing insect. "It's wrong to ask, why me. I stopped asking that question ever since the prince chose me to be his wife." But why now, she thought. The militant groups had never targeted her before. The Rolls had been assigned to her driver for at least six months. No one could have mistaken the owner. Most worrying was that the boys were supposed to sit in the back seat, one on either side of her. Of course, the palace firmly believed that a few people hated the royal family enough to kill two innocent children. But Elena always had doubts. She reached for the nurse's hand.

"Don't let anyone else come near who doesn't need to," the princess whispered. "Make the security stay outside, the family, everyone. Except the children. And you. If you don't mind, of course. You must have a family?"

"Only an ornery brother," Rita confided. "But he's a handful and it's good to get away from him." She looked toward the door and dropped her voice to a whisper. "Are you afraid that someone's out to hurt you? Like terrorists? Or could they have been after someone else?"

"I really don't know." Elena gave her a wry smile. "No, I fear the family even more. I just need time alone, without others telling me how to think about all this."

"That's not a problem." Rita nodded with efficient approval. "It's been a traumatic time for you. A concussion requires quiet. I have my orders. The hospital wants to make you happy, whatever it takes."

"And my children—if you contact my secretary, she'll tell you how to reach them." Elena was embarrassed about having to ask.

"I'll try again." Rita looked guilty. "The nurse upstairs told me that Larry tried to visit before he left. But his security officer refused his request. I thought then that it would be helpful for you to hear the children's voices and made some inquiries. But your staff filed a complaint against me with my supervisor. They claimed that hospital staff has no place questioning the whereabouts of the princes. They're short on nurses, or I might not be here." She shook her head. "But you're lucky, the hospital cares more about you than the palace staff. So I'll keep trying—and let you know what I hear."

"The boys have probably been whisked off to Scotland," Elena said. "Thank you for telling me the truth and not pretending that the boys can't make it for this reason or that." She leaned back and closed her eyes. "This room is plain, but it has a certain peace. And what's your name again?"

"Rita Whittaker."

"Thank you so much, Rita." Elena drifted into an uneasy sleep. "If I can't be with my children, then I just want to be alone."

CHAPTER 5

"All she cares about are clothes, shopping, her children."
"She's an ordinary woman."
"Then how does she manage to grate on our nerves so much?"

"So?" Elena held up two comfortable outfits to show Rita. The first was a black Walker with distinctive silver buttons and long sleeves. The other was a pale coral Verani, with a full skirt, scoop neck, and short sleeves.

Rita felt the texture of the material. "You want to be careful about the burns. I vote for the pink. It's softer, lighter. And the sleeves will be more comfortable, of course."

"I don't want anyone to think that I'm showing off my wounds on purpose!" Elena said.

Rita tossed the black suit aside and held out the coral dress, instructing Elena to lift her arms. Just then, a small phone buzzed. "Excuse me," Rita said, turning toward the corner. "It's my phone."

"Hello . . . I'm at work. Why are you calling me here? . . . No, I won't do that . . . You're wrong, that's not me . . . We'll talk later, when I get home." Rita looked distressed as she pressed a button and shoved the cell phone in her pocket. Quiet, she proceeded to help Elena with the dress.

"A boyfriend?" Elena inquired.

"No, just one very bossy brother," Rita said. "He thinks that I'm his baby sister who must drop everything to do his bidding.

Somehow I grew up faster than he did. He's controlling, maybe because he loves me."

"I'm not sure about that. Control does not mix well with love." Rita pulled the dress over her head. "Ow," Elena said quietly.

"Sorry about that. Lower your arms. Slowly."

"Oh, I'm not blaming you. My skin feels stiff." Elena stretched her arms a bit.

"No, you're right about control. But it's so hard saying no to one's family, isn't it?"

"It's tiresome," Elena agreed.

"But I don't want to think about him now. You're lucky, if you take proper care, the burns won't leave scars. Try to put on that ointment at least twice a day. And when you get home, change into a light shift. Cotton is best."

"I should walk out in the hospital gown," Elena said. "I wish we had a full-length mirror. People care so much about what I wear. Do I look all right?"

"Stunning." Rita smiled.

"And you're sure you can't tell I don't have on a bra?"

"Not at all."

"Good. The British undergarment industry would never forgive me. Did you call downstairs about how it looks outside?"

"A crowd. At least a hundred. Growing by the minute."

"Photographers?"

"Plenty, and of course the well-wishers."

Elena sat on the bed to slip on soft leather pumps that matched the dress perfectly. "Rita, what are people saying about what happened?"

Rita shrugged. "They're puzzled. Everyone adores you, and no one can understand why anyone would attack you and two children with a bomb. Why the princess and not the prince or queen? There have been some mumblings that you were a target because of the divorce. Others counter that you're the perfect mother!"

"That's not me."

"That's what people say. That and wondering why the lout of a husband . . ."

Elena held her hand up and dropped her head to break eye contact. "Former husband and father of my children, let alone the future king."

"I'm sorry, Elena. I shouldn't have said that."

Elena cocked her head and smiled, as if to suggest she didn't care. "He hasn't said a word, has he?"

Rita shook her head. "He can talk tough about security when he's behind his palace walls—how he'll protect his children and not allow them to be targets of extremists! But could he have done what you did? I'm sorry, Ma'am, but the man's a fool. And then, for none of the family to stop by and visit or send flowers until . . . why, the nerve!"

That tidbit of gossip made for big headlines. The day following the accident, hundreds of bouquets lined the lobby of Quincy Medical Center, some handpicked from country gardens and tied with a ribbon, others elaborate displays ordered from florists. The hospital administrator called in extra volunteers, who organized the gifts and bouquets, and selected their favorites. The volunteers then brought the sample of gifts to the princess's room for her approval before delivering them to wards of the elderly, the terminally ill, and others who had fewer visitors and well wishes. Another volunteer packed all notes and cards into a box for delivery to the palace, so Elena could write individual thank-you notes to every well-wisher in the weeks ahead. Elena hardly needed another bouquet, but the volunteers were shocked about the slight from the royal family.

A day after the newspaper criticized the royal family for its lack of acknowledgement, an unwieldy bouquet of burgundy roses arrived, accompanied by an unsigned, printed card from the palace—an impulsive gesture by anxious staff, who agonized over any hint of bad publicity.

Elena insisted on giving the flowers away. The family resented any show of attention on her. They despised her and could not understand reporters' untiring fascination with her. Elena wasn't sure either. She was hardly the most beautiful woman. She suspected that the journalists detected the constant conflict with the family. Every snub by the royal family intrigued the public, who identified with the princess, a one-time commoner.

But Elena didn't want gestures or flowers. She wanted to see her children. "I'm not even sure where they're staying," she said to Rita.

"Try not to worry. As soon as you get home, the excitement will fade. They'll visit and you'll have a wonderful time."

Elena shook her sadly. "You don't know how it is, Rita. My life's nothing like that at all. I'm lucky to have a few minutes alone with my children anymore." She looked about the room nervously. "Are you sure no one has entered this room?"

Rita shook her head firmly. "Only when you were awake—and once last night, and then my good friend Lydia covered for me. This room cannot be bugged. Not that they didn't try! That foolish young man kept trying to relieve your guard and convince me to leave. And the older man kept asking me to go get him tea and cigs. Like I was a maid or something! Fools. The bunch of them! But don't you worry. Your privacy is secure."

Walter Draker had diligently remained posted outside her door throughout her stay. At one point, he knocked on the door and asked to speak to Elena alone. Elena nodded, and Rita returned to the nursing station for a break. As Walter spoke, Elena kept close watch on his hands, wary of any sleight-of-hand tricks.

First, he apologized for waiting in the gatehouse on the day of the accident. "I'll never leave the vehicle and you again."

Elena stopped him. "Don't blame yourself. We shouldn't have to be so careful on palace grounds. And you've done a remarkable job of protecting me. To be truthful, I highly doubt that any real terrorist wants to get at me."

"They want every member of the royal family." Walter repeated palace convention. "There are plenty of groups who want to destroy the monarchy, as a symbol of Western civilization."

She shrugged. "I'll be returning to Kirkington tomorrow, and you'll have a well-deserved break. And again, you have my complete appreciation for standing by."

"Along with that nurse," Walter grumbled. "She refuses to leave."

"But I like her." Elena picked up a nail file. "She's nice."

"I don't trust her." The guard stood to his full height.

"She's an intensive-care nurse who loves her work. How dangerous can she be? Why, if she were to pass out the wrong medicine or commit some other awful deed, she would have done it the first night!"

"She's pandering to you," he argued. "Don't you see? A normal woman would have a life, a boyfriend. She wouldn't stay at a job round the clock!"

Elena let out a crystal laugh that always signaled her most teasing nature. "Why, Walter, you're describing yourself! Perhaps you two should get together . . ."

Walter did not appreciate her observation on his lifestyle. "I don't know what's going on in here. The palace demanded a bedside watch. I want to respect your privacy, but I also don't want to make another mistake."

The man was sincere, even if it was only about doing his job properly. "The palace is more worried about photos than gunshots or poison." Elena dismissed his concern. "Rita's not interested in selling photos or stories to the press. Believe me, nothing of great interest happens in this hospital room!"

Walter shook his head glumly. "The press is a minor problem after what happened on Saturday. Somebody wants to kill you—and that nurse is in here giggling with you all day. I don't like it!"

Normally, Elena would have felt that this was another attempt from the palace to stifle her feelings, her fun, her life. But Walter appeared genuinely concerned. Elena could not forget the exact timing of the bomb. Staff had urged Henry to leave the palace grounds. She was sure that if Larry had not stopped the car, the bomb would have gone off outside the palace boundary, killing not only the driver but Elena and Walter, too. As her personal bodyguard, Walter had good reason to worry.

She tried to reassure the man: "You're outside the door and in charge. You search everyone coming in. I'm in your hands, Walter, and I feel safe."

He scowled. "Give her no information about your home—nothing about your schedule or the children's. Absolutely no personal information."

"She's expressed no interest in such matters," Elena protested. "Only my health."

"I'm being up-front with you on this," Walter confided. "She's gained your trust, and if she's going to try anything, it will be during the hours just before you're released. Please, may I leave this bug here, under the edge of your nightstand?"

Elena tossed her nail file to the side and accepted the small electronic listening device. She twisted it about in her hand to examine it.

"It's a safety precaution. For my ears only—please."

She stared up at him in amazement, and the man who was normally nervous and polite held his stare. "No one ever asked my permission before." She dropped the small piece of plastic back into his hand. "Walter, I have new respect for you, but the answer's no."

He swore under his breath. "My supervisors think that you are stupid. I tell them that's not true, but when you do things like this, refuse the bugs and dart off on your own, it makes me wonder." He shook his head. "No, if you had a deficient intellect, you'd be much easier to guard."

"This is not a casual decision on my part," she said. "And believe me, I won't forget your kindness."

A soft tap came on the door, and Rita poked her head inside with a bright smile. "Would either of you like something to drink? Some tea, perhaps?"

"Sounds lovely," Elena said with a smile.

"Not for me," Walter growled. "As you like, Your Royal Highness. It's up to you. I'll be outside if you need me." He nodded curtly, before storming out the door and returning to his post outside.

Elena smiled as she remembered the exchange and Rita poured two cups of tea. "Our last cup together," the nurse said.

Walter's warning from that day still haunted her, and Elena wondered if the comment invited protest, perhaps even insistence from the princess that the nurse would be welcome at Kirkington Palace for future cups of tea. Damn, Elena thought to herself. Walter's worry made her suspicious and unkind.

"I'm ready to leave the hospital—but I'll miss seeing you." Elena deliberately kept the comment innocuous. Rita did not look disappointed.

A firm rap on the door interrupted them once more. The two women looked at each other. In less than one hour, security and selected hospital staff were going to escort Elena to a waiting limousine. Photographers had been invited to show the world that Elena was in good health. The women had hoped to have a quiet moment together, but the time was dwindling fast. Rita went to the door, opening it a crack.

"Yes?" she demanded. Despite Walter's obvious irritation, Rita blocked entry to another distinguished gentleman following closely. "And who may this be?"

"May I introduce Sir Timothy Barnes, secretary to His Royal Highness, the Prince of Wales?" Walter intoned, while standing at attention.

Rita offered a slight shrug and glanced in Elena's direction. Walter bristled at the arrogance, while Elena nodded unhappily and stood. Barnes bowed and offered a formal greeting, but was visibly startled by her hair. Rita stayed in the open doorway, to keep the others out.

Elena stuck out her bottom lip, letting out enough breath to fluff the straggly hair on her forehead. The uneven tufts, what was left from the flames, gave her the rakish look of a wild adolescent. On her own, Elena would have never dared make such a request of her stylists. But, with the fire and the hospital stay, well, she wasn't in a hurry to change the unusual look. Let the tongues wag!

"Speak up, Barnes." Elena's order was pert. "I'm preparing to leave the hospital. Are my boys all right?"

"Please excuse us, young lady," Barnes barked, as Walter held the door open, ready to escort Rita away. "I'm here in the service of the Prince of Wales."

"That's not necessary, Rita," Elena said and turned to Barnes. "She'll stay. She's cared for me nonstop. She knows practically all there is to know about me, and you're not about to chase her out!"

Barnes pursed his lips. "You put too much trust in strangers." He emphasized the last word with a haughty lift of his chin. She knew he meant commoners.

"I prefer people who like me for what I am—and not out of

deference to title, position, or some sense of duty," she countered.

"As you wish." Barnes's response was curt. He glanced quickly at Rita and Walter and then the hallway beyond, suddenly recognizing the need to take care with his words. Word leaked so quickly to the newspapers and blogs these days.

"Where are my sons?" Elena repeated.

"The young princes are enjoying time with His Royal Highness."

"And Larry? He's recuperated?"

"The injuries were minor," Barnes admitted. "You protected him well."

"Thank God. But then why didn't the boys visit me here?"

"*Both* princes are fine and the palace wants to keep them that way," Barnes continued, with a hint of a smile. Elena recognized his subtle criticism that her concern for Larry was off-balance, inappropriate. She fumed inside. Caroline and the others would never be chided for excluding Larry.

"Of course, the palace wants to keep them safe." Elena tipped her head slightly and narrowed her eyes into a blue glare. "I do, too! What do you mean?"

"The palace deeply regrets that you were a target of an attack. The family wants to do everything in its power to protect the entire family, including you and, of course, the two boys. Security advisors to the queen have suggested that it's best if the boys are separated from any known target. Specifically, you."

"I'm not some target," she said in a low voice, gritting her teeth. "I'm their mother."

Barnes glanced at Rita who had paused while selecting and packing ointments and other prescriptions. "We understand the pain and difficulty of such an arrangement. It's only temporary. It's for your protection and that of the boys. That's the bottom line for us all, isn't it?"

Elena thought a moment and then gave her famous serene smile, the one that the Prince of Wales had gradually learned to dread. Without comment, she moved closer to the bed and helped Rita transfer some clothes and jewelry into the plain suitcase.

"Yes, yes," she said, with a hint of impatience. "So, it's all right for the boys to spend time with Edward? I thought he was *supposed to be* the ultimate target. But what I'm hearing you say is that I've become the ultimate target?" She kept her voice airy, as if to sing a happy melody. She gracefully leaned over the suitcase to hide the triumph in her eyes. "I do believe the entire ward just heard what you said."

Barnes looked confused, because of Elena's knack for voicing the real fears of staff or the royal family. Her conversations took a different track than those typical of palace insiders. "That's not it at all," he said, floundering and backing away. His only recourse was to end the conversation and retreat for more discussion of strategy.

Elena smiled and remained unflustered. If anything, the damn divorce had made her stronger.

"I'm not qualified to interpret the wishes of security staff or the palace—both of whom value the lives of the young princes above all else," Barnes said with irritation. "The palace will be in touch. If the Lady Elena will excuse me . . ." He clawed at the door handle, in a hurry to leave. Walter paused, shrugged his shoulders, and quickly followed the man outside.

Elena stopped packing, and looked at Rita, waiting for a reaction from an objective person.

"A tough old nut," said Rita.

"You called that right," said Elena. "My poor boys. I miss them."

"Surely they could protect all of you together."

"Of course!" Elena scoffed. "But they don't want it that way. They want my life to be hell."

Rita shook her head in sympathy.

Elena continued: "Rita, how much do you make here monthly?"

"Oh, about 2,000 pounds per month. Excluding the taxes."

"I imagine you could stand for some extra."

"Couldn't we all? My mum does not get along with my dad. She works awfully hard, but he takes her check each week. Spends it at the pub. Whenever I can, I try to send a little along to her . . . She enjoys going to the store to buy something extra for herself."

"Why does she stay?" Elena murmured. "But you're a sweet girl to think of your mother." The princess sat on the bed and folded her hands. "You know, you could make a bit extra if you called some of the papers and offered to tell about the conversation you just heard."

"I'm not a gossip," Rita protested.

"I noticed, after reading the papers." Elena gestured to the pile beside the bed. "And I'm grateful. But surely a measure of gossip is natural, almost healthy for humans. Don't you agree?"

"Maybe . . ." Rita nodded.

"Call the *Post* and the *Union*. Talk to the editors, not the reporters. Get them to make offers, and don't take the first."

"But why would they believe me?"

"Here now, I can help with that!" Elena had a mischievous plan. She went to her bag, removed a small digital camera, marched to the bed, and threw back the sheets. "All right, I'll close my eyes, and you take a couple of shots."

"But . . ."

"Oh, do it. It's an easy way to make money, I tell you! You deserve it as much as those vultures waiting downstairs. You can offer an exclusive—the only photo of Princess Elena in her hospital bed. Wait now, let me close my eyes and relax." She arranged herself and then pulled the white sheets up snug about her neck. "Must clean the smile from my face, so that I appear to be sleeping. Move in a bit closer? That camera can handle it. And take the shot at the right. That's my best side. Go on, now. Hurry!"

Rita snapped the camera twice.

"More!" Elena urged. "We want to give them a choice! They always appreciate that!"

Rita took four more photos from different parts of the room. Sunlight poured like silver rays into the stark room and made the princess's hair and skin glow.

Rita checked the image, then showed Elena. "With the light, you look like a sleeping angel!"

"Thanks to you!" Elena shoved the covers aside and stood, straightening her jacket about her shoulders and smoothing her skirt. "All right, I guess I'm ready to leave. You packed plenty of that ointment?" She handed the camera back to Rita.

"Yes, the ointment's in the side pocket." Uncertain, the nurse held the camera. "You know, I don't want to lose my job over this. I love nursing more than anything."

"When you call the papers, don't give your name. Arrange for a post-office box. Once you come to agreement, send a print. Tell them you were in the hallway and overheard a riveting conversation between the princess and the secretary to the Prince of Wales. Use that word. 'Riveting.' "

Rita nodded.

"You remember the conversation, now, don't you?"

"Yes . . . I think so."

"Here's my private phone at Kirkington. Call me if you have any problem. Be subtle, but hint that the palace seems worried more about me than either the queen or the prince."

Walter would be so annoyed and blame Rita. He might even

guess that Elena was the instigator. Still, he couldn't prove anything. Other hospital staff had drifted through the hallway the entire time.

Rita nodded again and looked nervous. "Are you sure it's all right, Ma'am?"

Elena smiled. "Of course. It was my conversation. It's my life they're talking about. I have no problem at all with this. In fact, you might save my life by making the problem public. At the very least, the release may win me some public sympathy, and that will hasten my reunion with the boys."

"I understand," Rita said, reluctantly.

Elena stepped over and gave the woman an impulsive and gentle hug. "Thank you for your care, but also for being a friend. My life will be hectic in the next few weeks. I have to see to my children . . ."

"Of course," Rita replied quickly, cutting Elena off.

"But I hope I can see you again someday. I want to talk more about nursing and politics and us. I sincerely mean it. I hope we can get together."

Rita wore a little frown, as though she suspected that a visit would never happen.

"What's the matter?" Elena questioned.

"My supervisor criticizes me for becoming too attached, too close, with my patients," Rita explained. "They expect professional distance, particularly in a National Health Service hospital."

Elena knew that hospital directors carefully considered Rita's bedside manner before choosing her to assist the Princess of Wales. The royal family often relied on national hospitals for publicity purposes, but then administrators defeated the equality factor by automatically arranging for private rooms, the best nurses, and exclusive treatment. "I can write to you, care of the hospital?" Elena questioned.

"I love all my patients and try to make each feel special." Rita looked about the room and was matter-of-fact. "Once they don the street clothes, though, I can disconnect."

Elena knew that Rita was comfortable with any decision about future contact. The nurse, quiet ever since Elena shed the hospital gown, went to a drawer for paper and a pen. She scrawled for a minute and then handed the paper to Elena.

"I don't expect an invitation to your next royal function," Rita joked. "But this is if you ever have a question or need me . . ."

The paper listed a telephone number and address in Brent. Elena carefully pocketed the paper, and then took the pen and another slip of paper to write her own personal phone number. "Thank you. You've done so much for me. I hope we meet again someday."

"It's my job." Rita smiled and gave Elena a quick hug. "Now, no tears."

The two women parted, and Elena insisted on walking out alone. "It's best the photographers don't take any shots of us together, especially before you hand over my photograph."

Walter carried her bag and was followed by palace security, hospital administrators, and a few local politicians who accompanied her into the lobby where a mob of photographers snapped thousands of flash photos.

Elena smiled graciously and thought about how much she hated the palace staff, the courtiers, the lifelong servants, people like Barnes with all their empty pomp, meaningless etiquette and stuffy ways. The best etiquette should connect people and not separate them. The staff thought that they could control her like a puppet. And when they couldn't, they lashed out at her looks, her lack of royal lineage, and poor education. Years ago, a group of people who made a very good living off the royal family had decided that Edward must marry a young, simple, empty-headed virgin so that the monarchy could survive. The courtiers had chosen her as the brood mare when she was a mere nineteen, a young girl who was tall and gawky, insecure because of her own upbringing, and too intimidated to try her best at school. How she had scorned attention back then. The court had chosen her for all the wrong reasons, and Elena would never forgive them for that. Barnes was part of the crowd. So was her uncle. They refused to accept blame for the outcome—her outstanding popularity. She was their mistake, and that meant they were her fiercest enemies.

CHAPTER 6

"The children keep complaining they're bored."

"Our job is to keep them away from her, and make them enjoy their father."

"She spoiled them, especially the younger one."

Larry leaned back on a large smooth rock along the bank, and tossed a pebble hard into the silver ripples of the brook.

"Will you please?" Richard said heatedly, looking up from the knotted mess at the end of his fly rod. "It's most difficult to fish when someone's tossing rocks and scaring all the trout."

"You're not fishing this exact moment! Besides, for all you know, tossing rocks over there could scare the trout over to this side. You're just mad because I caught two!"

Richard scowled. "That's because you use worms like a little child. I fish with flies that I have made, like a grownup."

"Whatever it takes," Larry said, nonplussed. He tossed another rock out into the middle of the stream. "Richard, why do we have to wear these skirts when we come up here?"

"You know what they're called. I get tired of talking about this every time we visit Pepperell Hall."

"But these clothes take all the fun out of it," Larry lamented. "This could be a great place for hiking and swimming and exploring. If only I could wear jeans."

"This is Scotland, and we're the only ones who can wear the Pepperell tartan."

"If the guy who invented these was around today, he wouldn't be caught dead wearing one," Larry complained. But he lowered his voice as he watched his father approach.

"It's what Father wants," Richard chided. "Shhh, you'll hurt his feelings."

"He doesn't have any feelings to hurt," grumbled Larry, repeating a sentiment attributed to his mother by one of the tabloids.

Edward strolled along a winding path, edged and shaped by human intervention. Larry studied his father as he walked slowly, never looking ahead or smiling at his sons. Instead, the man looked out over the fast ripples of water with a nod. He bent over and examined an ordinary weed with a frown. He followed the flight of a mallard with intent concentration. The man never spoke much about what these inspections revealed. Often, Larry felt like another object along the path.

Edward spoke as he neared the two children: "Not many ducks this fall. I hope Benson's men are keeping watch over the nesting sites."

"You can check, Sir! Take us along!" Richard exclaimed.

"Surely you're not suggesting that we take on Benson's duties?" his father asked.

"But it might be fun!" Larry shouted, agreeing with his brother.

"Not part of the day's plan. Today we fish. Three men together and we'll deliver what we catch to the chef."

"Fishing's not going all that well, Sir," Richard said.

"Let me check what's wrong."

Edward seized another rod and let the silver strand whirl about the air. The fly landed neatly in the middle of the stream as the boys stood and watched. Rushing water swept the end of the line downstream, and Edward slowly pulled the line toward him.

"Not biting today. You two boys stand too close together. Impossible to have quiet that way. The skilled fisherman, like the hunter, doesn't start flinging his rod about or start shooting as soon he arrives. No. He approaches the habitat, listening and learning, gradually becoming an accepted part of the scene. Only then he becomes predator, top of the food chain."

"I didn't do any of that, and I caught two!" Larry piped up.

"You're too young to understand these matters," Richard scolded. "And you didn't use a fly rod."

"And I never intend to," Larry replied stubbornly.

Edward didn't show that he heard, and placed his arm around Richard's shoulder. "Let's walk down to Andell Clearing. That's a pleasant spot. I've always had luck there!" The two walked away.

Suddenly, a groundskeeper emerged from the shrubbery to retrieve the rods and antique baskets used for tackle. Larry reluctantly handed over his own rod, a favorite because it had been a gift from his mother when he had returned the summer after his first year of boarding school.

"Nice work, young man!" Larky exclaimed softly.

"Thanks for saying so," Larry responded. "They are good-looking trout, aren't they?"

"Your brother is a tad green, I'd say," Larky said with a chuckle.

"He wishes he could use a rod like mine."

"Never pays to stand out much at your age," Larky said, dipping his head. "Not much point to it anyway. Believe me, there's more fun to be had blending in and having no one notice you. Count yourself lucky, Larry."

"You'll bring my fish along for tonight, won't you, Larky?"

"I'm going to deliver them to the man with the big white hat myself! You better run along and catch up."

"Thanks, Larky." Larry smiled, and looked forward to eating

trout with Larky and other groundskeepers. Palace staff would never serve fish caught by Larry, not unless Edward or Richard caught some as well.

He ran along the path, not wanting his father to get irritated and guess that he was making dinner plans with Larky.

His father would never turn around and call out for one of his sons. No, he expected the two boys to follow meekly about and regard even the oddest of his comments as wisdom. Deviations from the pattern annoyed the Prince of Wales, who would respond with testy comments or snubs that only ruined a good day in the forest.

Larry hurried to catch up.

". . . glad to have this time with you. I must return to London at the end of the week." Edward paused under a willow tree and examined the leaves along one branch that arched over the pathway. Then he sat and the boys followed suit.

"Can we go along or must we stay here?" Larry questioned.

Edward gave him a hard stare.

"It's never as much fun without you around," Richard interjected. Larry admired his older brother's ability to soften the younger brother's questions. Indeed, Larry could be as blunt as his father was. "When will you return?"

"I'll be there for the weekend and perhaps for another day or two. I have a speech before the board of directors of some corporation. Then . . ."

"You'll check on Mother, too, won't you?"

"Yes, yes. She's out of the hospital and recovering nicely. I understand she was horribly frightened by the bomb. And like all of us, she's relieved that the two of you are far, far away from . . . the madness." The man spoke carefully. Larry knew that his grandmother had more than once chastised her son for making negative comments about his wife. The queen had even urged him to read a book she had bought, *Sensitive Divorce for*

Sensible Men. Not long afterward, Larry had heard servants laughing about his father tossing the book into the trash. But his father didn't dare cross his mother.

"Father, who hates her so much? Or us? We were supposed to be in the car that afternoon."

"I told you," he said curtly. "Extremists, from Ireland or the Middle East, with some cause that resists everything Great Britain stands for. They do not appreciate what we have done for them all these years—introducing progress, welcoming them as immigrants. They're selfish and will do anything to get attention."

He paused. "I suppose you're old enough to know the details. The police investigators looked the device over and said it was one of those homemade bombs used to blow up buses and subway cars. These characters are bullies who think senseless threats will frighten an entire country into giving in to their wishes. It's the policy of the British government to go about its business and ignore the rabble rousers. Prove to them that they have no influence. And believe me, they have none here at Pepperell. It's been glorious not looking at a newspaper or a television all this time!"

Larry sighed. He hated vacations at Pepperell, and one reason was because staff enforced instructions to bar newspapers from the Scottish castle. Whenever Elena made headlines, his father sought the boring peace of Pepperell. Larry had been fascinated by the newspapers, ever since he had heard about the story of his birth, when his father had been quoted as preferring a girl, so as to eliminate any immediate competition for Richard. His father expressed equal shock that the child had been born with what he called a "carrot-top." Articles about Larry often went on to report that the queen had scolded her son and that Edward had long denied making such comments.

A testy tone, some comment about terrorists from his father, jerked Larry from his private thoughts. For once, the tone was directed at his brother.

"But the terrorists do have influence." Richard was indignant. "The IRA is a political party now. And these terrorists keep us away from our work and studies and friends. Everyone is afraid and it's annoying. This would be a nice holiday, but not when we remember why we're here."

Larry had long observed that his father resisted arguing facts with his sons. The boys performed, and the man appraised. "You're sensitive. That's a good quality in a leader. Keep it in balance, though. Don't let it overtake the other essential qualities: deliberation, discretion, dignity. Your safety is paramount. You can return to the daily routine once the investigation is through."

"How did someone manage to slip into the palace garage and get that bomb into Mother's Rolls?" Richard had asked the question dozens of times, to Larry and others.

Edward shook his head, but Larry could see that he was already distracted and not going to answer the question. A small spider tiptoed its way down a nearby branch—part of a triangle of anchors for a web. Edward took a long stick, and teased the spider, by taking small jabs at the center of the web. Not enough to destroy the web completely, but enough to goad the spider into thinking that it had trapped some prey.

Thinking about the newspapers again, Larry suddenly felt sorry for his father who was a bit like the little spider who built a web to control its world. But something bigger could always come along. The newspapers had tremendous power over the family, so much so that Larry enjoyed comparing the newspaper accounts to test his own observations about family routines and reactions. For the most part, the articles were accurate—and without question, Larry believed the story about his father criticizing his gender and hair. The staff at Pepperell

sneaked a few of the London papers into the country estate occasionally, but refused to lend them to the child, fearing
Edward's wrath should they get caught. So Larry was forced to
rely on gossip about his mother from the nanny or the upstairs
maid, while Larky shared news about politics and the outside
world.

Normal families had privacy, Larry thought perhaps for the
thousandth time in his life. Privacy meant power over one's self.
Anyone important enough for the newspapers had to behave according to others' rules. Larry felt genuine relief about his place
in the family. He really wasn't jealous of his brother—and he
hoped that he made his attitude apparent enough to the world.

Richard didn't notice his father's or brother's distraction and
pressed on with questions about terrorists and their motiva-
tions.

Edward sighed. "The investigators aren't certain. The bomb
could have been inserted during the party. Or, security suspects
that the bomb could have been there all along, before Henry
entered the grounds. They're checking the history of the car.
Anyone who came near it. But then, the day of the birthday
party was quite the spectacle. All the guests, caterers, servants—
they're all being checked out, of course." Edward held his
tongue to the inside of his cheek for a moment, thought a moment and then rushed ahead. "And they must check your
mother, too."

"What do you mean?" Larry burst out. Richard gave the boy
a furious glare, a warning to keep quiet until the man got
finished talking. Larry glared back, but knew Richard was right.
The older boy was always reminding the younger brother that
children learned more from adults with silence than with questions.

"Your mother's unhappy. Our divorce. She wants it and she
doesn't. Maybe inviting her to the party was too much. The

queen meant well by the invitation, but maybe the thought of walking away from the family is overwhelming. Maybe she wanted to hurt herself."

"With a bomb?" Even Richard forgot his own rules on self-control. "That's ridiculous because Mother would never hurt Henry or us!"

"A bomb has never gone off on palace grounds before," Edward said tersely. "It's strange that your mother was the target. She's popular, yet . . ."

"And she was brave," Larry interjected. "She tried to save Henry! And I tried to help, too."

"That was foolish!" Edward exclaimed harshly. "And you should not have been anywhere near there. You have a duty to the country to keep yourself safe and not make it any harder than necessary for security. Especially with the taxpayers complaining constantly, nitpicking at every expense."

Larry held his annoyance in check. The newspapers and public had lavished praise on the exploit. All his father did was issue criticism.

The Prince of Wales continued: "You're not to wander off again. The next time I won't leave it to the staff to punish you! What did they decide on, anyway?"

"Oh, don't worry, he was punished. A favorite toy was taken away." Richard didn't go into detail.

Larry was glum, thinking about the nanny hired to accompany the boys for this brief stay at Pepperell. Undoubtedly under the influence of Derry, the woman had announced that it might make good practice if the older boy applied the punishment. Richard had balked and hesitated a few days, hoping the matter would be overlooked. But Derry took charge, and removed all the Legos, a favorite of Larry's when it came to toys. Still, his older brother managed to salvage a small medieval gate and a few knights and a skeleton and urged his brother to keep them hidden. Larry vowed that he would get even with the servants, especially Derry, even though Richard begged him not to try. His older brother deplored conflict of any nature, yet somehow always found himself in the middle of his parents' troubles and his brother's disagreements with staff.

"Don't you worry about Mum being alone?" Richard asked. "Did you call for extra protection?"

"That herd of photographers following her provides plenty of protection."

"She hates them, Sir," Richard said. "She tries to get away and sometimes we manage. Actually, Mum taught us quite a few tricks."

"Hmm," Edward grunted.

"When do you think we'll see her again?" Larry pressed.

"Soon enough," Edward replied, with irritation. "First, we must assess security. And we must allow the inspectors to do their work. Finally, we must make sure that your mother is calm and contains the publicity. This family does not need to attract more attention. I'm not sure how to handle your mother . . . She has set out on her own path, but then, that's not the problem of two boys. Everyone at that party will be checked, I guarantee it."

Knowing the palace ways, neither boy commented. Pleading too much about visits with their mother would only prolong the separation. Edward stood and spoke in a jovial way, urging the two boys to try tossing a few more lines before heading off to their rooms and dressing for dinner.

They rounded a curve in the path and could see the clearing, with its ancient trees and clipped grass, and the dancing stream beyond. The rods leaned against a willow hanging out over the water and the antique basket with tackle was nestled in the long grass underneath.

"Larky won again!" Larry cried out in delight.

Edward scolded in a stern voice, low enough to be heard by only the boys. "And a good thing for him. Lawrence, please refrain from constant comments on the servants' movements. Surely you have better things to observe. Your brother, for example."

Larry wrinkled his nose, and Richard blushed. Edward stepped close to the bank, searching for the best place to launch the first casts.

"The servants are almost always more interesting than you," Larry whispered to Richard.

"Than you, too!" Richard countered. "Off with your head, you twit!"

Larry giggled and rushed toward the water. Opening the basket quickly, he found his container of wiggling worms, which he had caught himself earlier that morning. He wrapped the smallest worm around the hook, piercing its body twice.

"Boys," Edward spoke solemnly. "We're out to enjoy a day in the forest. But we can't forget protocol."

Both boys stopped and waited for their father to take the lead in picking up his rod and flinging the line into the water. Edward took his time, standing on the edge of the bank, hands on his hips, as he surveyed the gurgling water, the towering firs, and low mountains beyond. Larry slouched against the nearest tree and Richard straightened his back and waited. The sun was low in the sky.

Soon after his father threw out the line, Larry was ready. Standing on a rock downstream, so as not to disturb the others, the boy snapped his wrist hard, and the hook soared and landed into a deeper pool midstream. Moments later, the line jerked.

"Another one! I caught another one! It's big, too!" Forgetting the rod had a reel, Larry backed up, jumping from the rock to shore, yanking his line hard. The fish leaped from the water and Larry shrieked with delight. Despite excitement and poor form, the boy managed to move the flopping fish to the bank. A color-ful trout, sixteen inches. The boy knelt to unhook his catch.

Triumphantly, he carried his catch to show his father. Edward looked at Richard with a smile and shook his head. "He's young," Edward murmured, with a hint of disdain. He leaned against the large oak tree and patted the shoulder of his eldest son. "Fishing—indeed, life itself!—is not measured by how many fish one catches. It's the process, the anticipation, the intel-lectual appreciation. But Lawrence is too young to realize this."

Larry looked down at the gleaming trout, opening its mouth uselessly for air. Instead of placing the fish in the bucket for Larky to retrieve, Larry turned and bent over a deep section of the stream, moving the trout back and forth, allowing oxygen to filter through its gills.

The fish dove deep and disappeared. No point in going after any more trout. His father didn't care. Larry did not like the royal system, the protocol, but he was stuck with it. Only a few more years, his mother had promised him. He looked over at Richard and saw his brother's cheeks burned. At least Richard sensed the lack of fairness, and that's why Larry loved his brother. Richard was less insecure than their father and that's how the system would gradually change. At least that is what his mother had promised.

Larry put his rod to the side. Somehow, he'd talk to his brother later, and try to make amends. The other fish would be cooked and eaten by servants later that night—and Richard would probably accompany Larry in stealing to the kitchen to try a bite. If Richard or Edward had caught fish, the entire set would have been served and celebrated at the royal dining table. So much for process and intellectual appreciation. And later, the two boys would avoid talking about their father, because they didn't agree.

Larry might be young, but he knew that he did not want to

be anything like his father, a man who didn't understand what he really wanted.

CHAPTER 7

"She spends too much time in her room."

"That computer is another toy. She doesn't know what she's doing."

A small, lovely bouquet of exotic white flowers arrived from Doctor Tilton. She read the note before tossing it aside: "The city was not nearly as much fun without a princess. Horrified about your accident and tried to call. Grateful you're out of the hospital and well, wishing you and your sons the best." The card listed two telephone numbers—one in Australia and the other in London.

Elena had been out of the hospital for a week and still had not seen her sons. One of the servants whispered that the children had left Pepperell for another of the family homes in Wales. Another insisted the boys were still at Pepperell. She had tried calling all the possible places, but servants at every location apologized that the boys were unavailable for security reasons.

And her unexpected stint at the hospital delayed her accessing any BlackBerry messages. She desperately wanted to contact the boys. While in the hospital, she couldn't check or use her own BlackBerry, still hidden away in her bedroom. She wasn't sure how to use the device and did not trust anyone to retrieve it for her, wanting to keep the secret.

With any luck, Richard had managed to carry along the

BlackBerry that she had sent for his birthday. She only hoped that he still kept the secret and found the skill to set it up on his own, away from Derry's prying eyes.

She patiently waited three days after returning home from the hospital to invite Paul Miggins, who arrived in an ordinary delivery truck from a local office-supply company. "I'm arranging my office and don't want to be bothered for the rest of the afternoon," she informed staff before he arrived. Paul was so young, Elena really didn't worry about what they thought of him. And if there were any prying eyes among the staff, they would focus on the new laptop.

She looked over Paul's shoulder as he downloaded software and typed away on the tiny keyboard. "Do you think Richard could follow your directions?"

"We'll soon find out. You sure he'd send a note? Most boys aren't great on correspondence, especially with their mums."

She nodded. "I'm sure he sent one. And then he probably worried when I didn't answer. He likes gadgets and he likes that this is our secret."

"Okay, if that's true, then he's on. This stuff is made for kids. Trust me . . ."

"I never could connect on my own," Elena said, shaking her head, staring at the glowing pearl-gray screen.

"You could if you had to," Paul had said, tapping some buttons. "Just try hitting buttons and searching about. I called down the office, and your account's in order. The BlackBerry automatically collects, encrypts and pushes messages to your account. And no worry about phone lines."

"That's a relief. A few years ago, I asked for my own phone line that I could answer and use as I please, and the servants were horrified. They want no extra wires in these rooms, where as they put it—'history took place.' And they don't even like me answering my own phone, let alone adding a phone line for the computer." She frowned. "They still don't like that I carry my own cell phone."

"I don't get it. It's your space. A staff person's life would be easier if you answered your own phone."

She shrugged. "I suppose that if I do more, then they eventually lose their jobs," she said. "That's one concern. . . . I can only imagine the staff's so bored that they want to check on everything we do. It gets on my nerves. So, I can retrieve my messages from both the computer and BlackBerry?"

"Yes—but with the laptop, you'll have to leave palace grounds for wireless, I'm afraid."

"And the system's secure?"

"Yes and no," he cautioned. "CEOs and top security officials all over the world use these. But you should change the password frequently. Never leave the handheld on. If you leave it somewhere, anyone can read your inbox. If you lose the device, contact me immediately and I can put a hold on the account. And remember the best protection is using no identifiable words—no names, phone numbers, addresses . . ."

She broke in. "I know. Don't sign notes. Only make comments that I would say to a person's face. I gave all those instructions to Richard along with his gift."

"But it's easy to get excited, jot a note, and forget. For now, these accounts are anonymous—not attached to your name or financial records. They're part of my research project at the university."

Elena looked at him, waiting for him to explain.

He shrugged and smiled. "My research focuses on security—and so you're part of my study. It should be one of the more secure systems on the continent. My brother teaches at the university and he's after me to get the work patented." He punched in a series of codes on the keyboard and handed over the BlackBerry. "Here, I downloaded your messages before coming over. You have three new messages from Salamander. And we'll change your password so I can't do that anymore." He showed her what keys to hit to read them and then moved to her office computer. "While you read, I might as well check this over—make sure it's compatible for files from the laptop."

He continued typing for a while, but did not like what he saw on the screen. "I know this computer is ancient, but even so, it's acting odd." He typed again and pointed to the screen, which kept repeating a cryptic message about the system lacking security support from central authority. "That's strange," he muttered.

"Richard is at Pepperell!" she exclaimed. "He's bored out of his mind and has not heard any news!" Elena leaned against her desk, typing a note to Richard to assure him that she was out of the hospital. She looked up to see the young man typing a baffling sequence of numbers and letters. "I'm amazed you know what you're doing. I'm used to electronics that plug in and then work—phones, televisions and the like."

Paul laughed, going back and forth between the office computer and the laptop, not missing a beat with his typing. "Any computer can do a lot more than any phone or a TV."

"So your brother, the professor, does he teach about computers?" Elena asked with a smile. The boy's hair curled about his collar. His clothes were oversized and wrinkled. Two thin gold hoops that had not been visible in the computer store were added to his left ear. Everything about him was smart and confident and free.

Paul laughed. "I taught him how to use the computers, even though he's twelve years older." He didn't take his eyes off the screen as he continued to type furiously. "No, he's a professor at the law school. Pretty traditional, but at least he understands why I do what I do. Maybe that's why the rest of our family doesn't understand either of us!"

"I know that feeling," Elena said. "Sometimes I don't know what I'm more nervous about—family reading my E-mails or the general public."

"You don't have to be nervous yet, just avoid too many specifics." He pushed his chair back and stared long and hard at the computer. "This desktop computer will have nothing to do with the laptop. The laptop keeps suggesting a security problem. I'd like to find out about that. Do you have some time?"

She nodded and studied her screen. "Richard's complaining about Larry catching more fish. If the two boys quarrel enough, perhaps staff will get weary and send them back to school where they belong." She typed a long note.

Paul typed in more code. "Damn, everything looks right."

She looked over his shoulder at the message on the screen and saw the gray box with the warning, as he continued to check plugs. "You really should have wireless and not dial-up. It would go much faster. Do you mind getting a phone to plug in here? Let's see if we get a signal that way?"

She ran down the hall and unplugged a staff phone and ran back. "Hurry with this. I don't want them to know that I moved it."

"Who's the boss around here, anyway?" He plugged the phone in the jack and picked up the receiver. "Dial tone." He dialed a number.

"Who are you calling?" Elena asked.

"First number that came to mind," Paul said with a shrug. "My brother." He held out the receiver. Elena could hear an answering machine kick into gear. A droll voice gave office hours for students and promised to return all calls. Elena reached over and hung up before the message finished. "Don't make personal calls on these phones," she whispered.

Paul looked at her and then examined the telephone, unscrewing the receiver and shaking it. Nothing. Then he pulled out his pocketknife and quickly removed the plate to the phone jack. A small circuit board dangled, attached to thin wires. Paul gently disentangled the wiring and transmitter from the jack. His mouth was set tight. He stared at the disk for a long minute, flipping it about in his palm. "Damn it all," he muttered. "Here's our problem. I should have looked before making that call."

"You didn't leave a message," she tried to assure him.

"If this is what I think it is, this bug doesn't just follow your phone conversations. It tracks phone numbers dialed out."

"Then it didn't pick up much. I only use this jack for the computer."

"So you're only contacting the server. It's the same phone number over and over for how many years?"

"At least five, and I'm sure they stopped monitoring this jack years ago. Or they'll think it's a wrong number." She felt some relief. "What kind of law does your brother teach?"

"Divorce law." Paul paused. Then he laughed. "No, he teaches international law, and focuses on human rights and security issues. Nothing to do with divorce. And you're right. I didn't leave a message. If anyone asks, you called a wrong number. Let's get rid of the bug and get your E-mail going."

"They might know I removed the bug," Elena cautioned him. "Another one will take its place."

"I can put it back in, if you want. The BlackBerry will have nothing to do with the system in place here anyway." He lowered his voice, less confident than before. "I take it having your phone bugged is not too unusual?"

"It happens all the time," she said with a sigh. "They install a phone line and automatically add a bug. It's standard security around here. I'm sure every phone in the palace is stuffed with these devices."

"Your own security gives you no privacy?"

"My God, no. That's gone on for years. For our protection.

They probably have thousands of tapes on file of my husband and me arguing back and forth. After a while, one tends to forget security and other staff. In this world, after a while you get used to living life in front of other people."

"Sounds perfectly dreadful."

"Take my advice. You're young. Keep your life simple . . . despite those exorbitant prices you charge. What do you do with your money anyhow—besides splurging on clothes?" She gestured toward his worn jeans and faded button-down shirt.

"Not much. Mostly new computer gadgets. The rest goes into various savings and stock accounts. It takes some research. Most computer companies are trash. But there are still a few out there that could revolutionize their part of the world."

"Impressive. This is a land where the children want to be rock stars, soccer players or fashion models. How did Britain create a boy like you?"

"I despise sports. Prefer to read and muck around with electronics. My brother bought me a computer a few years ago—and arranged for an Internet account. That got me going." He glanced at the small device. "This is a sophisticated bugger."

"If you trash it, would they know about the call to your brother's office?"

"Too late for that, I'm afraid. Why don't we put it back inside this phone jack. Use the BlackBerry for any private chats between you and me, between you and your sons. Let the snoop think it's working. That way, they might not come in and tinker with the computer."

"Not a bad idea. Could that device possibly pick up my E-mail?"

"I don't think so. But something was interfering with the laptop. I wouldn't trust any of this older equipment, and I'd keep the laptop and BlackBerry under lock and key." He knelt on the floor and restored the listening device, connecting wires and returning the cover plate to the jack. "Remember, accidents are easy with E-mail. You hit the send button too quickly, and the wrong message goes out. Don't say anything about anyone that you wouldn't say to their face. Change codes and passwords regularly. And remind your son." He showed her how to change her password. "This all sounds a bit less fun now, doesn't it?"

"Richard will like the subterfuge."

"Close out and try your password again." Paul stood and watched her. "I want to make sure you're completely comfortable with the BlackBerry." Elena's typing was slow on the small keypad. A few minutes later, she was back online.

"And another message!" she whispered with glee.

But the note was signed by Larry: "Hi, Mum. I miss you. Richard probably didn't mention it, but I figured this out before he did. Boy, he's annoyed. When he cools down, I'll show him how to do more. But he knows more about the Internet. We're trying to figure out how to do some games, like Halo. Any ideas? Love, Larry."

"Write him back and tell him not to use names," Paul warned. "And tell his brother to be more careful not to leave his Berry out and about."

"Yes, I'll do that, we'll get used to being careful." Elena could not hide her pleasure. "But this is great! Do you realize how long it's been since I've talked with them?"

Paul insisted that she write immediately, reminding the boys of the ground rules and Elena followed his instructions. When finished, she read Larry's note again and smiled. "I can't believe Larry's asking me to tell him how to work the contraption. Maybe you can help. What's Halo, anyway?"

Paul chuckled. "Popular game—kids can play online with people all over the world."

She typed: "My dearest, what a clever boy! I miss you, too, darling. Don't forget that this belongs to your brother. I have no idea about how to call up the game. But I know someone who might have some ideas . . ." She handed the device to Paul, who explained that Halo was too complicated for BlackBerry and typed in some tips for other games. She looked over his shoulder as he ended the note: "Erase this note so your brother doesn't get angry. And no more names." He clicked send and the note vanished.

"That's wonderful, better than the post or phone."

"But just as insecure if you're not careful. I installed a software version of a shredder. Don't forget to use it. And log out of your BlackBerry after every use. Richard must have forgotten—or do you think he gave Larry the password?"

"The boys are close," she admitted. She wondered if he would keep the secret from Derry.

"Keep yours hidden, especially from the prying eyes around here," he advised. He showed her some other features and then logged out and watched as she returned to the E-mail program. "And erase your notes as you go along, especially any sensitive ones. You shouldn't have much trouble. Have fun playing around with it, and call if you have questions." He stood, ready to leave.

"This has been wonderful," Elena commented after thanking him. She tucked the BlackBerry into a biscuit box and walked with him downstairs. In the hallway, he paused by another telephone on the antique table. He looked both ways.

"I wonder whether this phone line is clean," he whispered.

"It's a staff phone." She shrugged.

He knelt and had the jack apart and back together in less than three minutes. "Not a bug in sight. But then, they could be using something tricky."

They started to walk away and the phone rang. Impulsively, he picked up the receiver before the second ring with a pleasant hello and handed it to Elena. "They want you," he said.

She made a face and accepted the phone. Staff was not

around and she didn't want to miss a call from the boys. She offered a tentative hello.

"I have a message for the princess." The voice was rough.

"Go on," Elena replied with impatience. "I'll see that she gets it."

"I've heard that before . . . This is important. She deserves to know who her real enemies are. Last week's bomb. It had nothing to do with the IRA."

"Who is this? How would you know?"

"Ah, so you're more interested than the stuffy goat who answered last week. Who set the bomb? I wish I knew. Most radicals are content to take credit for every problem, right down to a late bus at rush hour. But others of us are choosy about our targets . . ."

"So who are you? A terrorist?" she snapped. She immediately pressed a button to start recording the call for security staff. "Why should I believe you?"

"I was active once with the Irish Republican Army. We have as many factions as the royal family does and agreement's rare. But we hear quickly about any action from our more radical counterparts. Catch my drift?"

Suddenly she realized that the caller didn't recognize her voice and thought she was a servant. Her public comments had been rare since the death of her divorce solicitor and the hospital stay. "How do I know this is not a crank call?"

"You only have my word." The phone clicked.

"Damn," Elena said.

"A threat?" Paul asked.

"No. Stranger than that, I'm afraid. A man calling with a cryptic warning about who set the bomb off."

"You can't believe an anonymous caller. They're a nasty lot."

"I don't know what to believe. I only know that I can't trust anyone." She sighed and leaned against the wall. "And as a result, how can I expect anyone to trust me. God, my life's a muddle. I'm going to have to report that call. They'll insert more bugs everywhere!"

She reached for his arm as he headed for the exit. "You better call your brother. Tell him what happened here."

"Tell me the truth." Paul's voice was low. "Do you think he's in trouble?"

"I doubt it." She remembered Derrick; he had never told her how much his partner resented the divorce case. "But he could be harassed . . . He should deny knowing me. He can claim that he refused to take the call. That he has no idea what it's about. And that's the truth. I don't want to involve you or your family with my problems."

"Knowing him, he'll be curious. But I'll give him a call and warn him."

She nodded. "Thanks again."

"Call anytime you have questions or need help. My E-mail address is in your BlackBerry."

"I'm sure that I'll need plenty of help."

CHAPTER 8

Two sets of hands ironed and folded bed linens. The meticulous folds and stacks would never be seen by the Royals. That had been the way for hundreds of years. "She looks worn these days." "The glamour takes more time."

"This is most irregular," sputtered Lord Stephen Jenkins, to no one in particular. A group of eight men sat in a circle with Elena in a meeting room of Kirkington Palace. She had demanded a meeting of her security personnel. The palace sent along her Uncle Gregory and Stephen Jenkins, the director of security for the entire royal family. Walter Draker, her personal guard, sat to the side and remained silent.

"But these are most irregular times, aren't they?" she replied. "When a mother and two children must worry about car bombs on palace property! When the only recourse that security can come up with is separating boys from their mother!" There was no denying that she was at least half the age of every man in the room, except for her guard, Walter. Elena was pale and somber in a simple black linen dress. The low neck, tight waist and a flowing skirt emphasized her femininity and youth. A single large red polka dot sat off-centered near the hem of the skirt, a fashion detail she had found useful for testing others' distract-ibility.

Johnstone coughed and replied: "I beg to differ, Lady Elena. I assure you that safety is our sole concern. Everything we do is for the safety of you and your children!"

"And we have affairs under control!" snapped Jenkins. "There's more going on than *you* could possibly understand." He wore a dark gray suit. A dark tie gripped his neck and Elena thought she could see his pulse struggle against the collar of his shirt. She wondered if the disdain was due to her gender or her title.

"Hah!" she said with a haughty lift of her head. "I have legitimate concerns about my sons' safety, let alone my own."

Jenkins placed his pocket watch on a nearby table. "I can spare exactly twenty minutes for this nonsense."

Elena looked about the room. "Why haven't detectives with the police interviewed me about the car bomb? Is anyone really checking the source? Do I need to remind you that I'm the only surviving adult witness?"

"We wanted to spare you discomfort, embarrassment. Besides, the car is with the police. They want real evidence. Physical evidence. Not theories from a hysterical victim. We handled their inquiries."

"Did they speak with Larry?"

"No."

"Did they want to?"

The men looked at one another. They had anticipated fear from the princess and were not prepared for her direct confrontation. "The detectives filed a request with the palace," Jenkins responded shortly. "A spokesman for the queen requested that a list of questions be submitted for both of you."

Elena shook her head in disbelief. "Don't you fellows watch television? Read books? As time slips away, evidence disappears, memories fade."

"You watch too much American television," Jenkins snapped. "We don't need you to tell us how to do our job. We held off on interviews out of consideration for you."

Elena addressed her own secretary. "Put it in the record that I offer no objection to an interview with detectives." She looked down at her hands and waited until the scratching of the pen stopped. "I received a telephone call yesterday from a person who claimed to be with the IRA."

The room of men fell silent. The group that had once been a major threat for any British institution. Forming not long after the Easter Rebellion in 1916, the Irish Republican Army alternated political action with bombings, assassinations, and kidnappings to convince the British to relinquish control over Northern Ireland. After years of threats and terrorism, the IRA declared a ceasefire in 1997.

Jenkins shuffled his papers about rapidly. "I didn't see that listed here on my morning report." He glared at Walter.

Elena spoke up: "That's because I answered the phone and not a member of staff."

"And that's why you have problems," Johnstone scolded. "What do you expect when you deviate from routines established by palace security?" He held out his hands and smiled at the circle of men. No one smiled back.

"Which phone?" Jenkins asked. "We may have the conversation on tape."

"The upstairs hall."

Jenkins studied a printout. "Are you supposed to answer that one?"

"It's a long story," Elena replied.

"It always is," Jenkins snapped, slapping his list. "So, tell us, what did the bloody bastard say?"

She didn't answer, instead lifting her head and giving Jenkins a hard look, encouraging him to change his tone. Jenkins didn't flinch. "If you don't like the way we talk at these meetings, don't call one. This is like the chickens telling the farmer how to keep the fox away!" The man snapped his papers inside his briefcase, ready to leave. "Besides, that rabble has not been active for years."

"Now, now," Johnstone said, as he frowned at Jenkins. "We cannot overlook any detail. It's true that we haven't had many problems with the IRA in recent years." He quickly reviewed the history for the group, reminding them that after the IRA declared ceasefires in 1994 and 1997, the group secretly disarmed, intent on pursuing Irish unification through the political activities of Sinn Féin.

But a few members scorned the peace process and formed small radical groups, including the Continuity IRA and the Real IRA. Such groups continued selling drugs, counterfeiting, and plotting robberies, all the while siphoning money to sympathetic Sinn Féin candidates.

"The spin-off groups are extremely small and do not get much publicity," he noted. "No one wants to give them attention by labeling them terrorists. They're small-time criminals. So let's get back to the telephone call . . ."

She might be divorced, but her uncle never forgot that Elena was still Princess of Wales and would always be the mother of the most important man in the country. She paused, going around the circle to look at every man. "The caller claimed that the IRA did not plant the bomb. He said I had other enemies."

"Rubbish!" Jenkins scoffed. "Of course, it's CIRA or RIRA, trying to throw us off track."

"They're notorious for playing these mind games." Johnstone, more conciliatory, was still patronizing. "Did you recognize the voice?"

She shook her head.

"Well, Lady Elena, you should not answer the phones!" With that, Johnstone turned to the rest of the men and held out his arms, as if he had discovered a solution and was presenting evidence obvious to all. "Palace organization and routines—

that's the key to proper security."

"We have a record of a voice, but we can't trace the call." Jenkins was annoyed and followed Johnstone's lead in blaming the problem on Elena. "All we have is your word."

"Now, now, let's stay calm," said Sir William Cooke, a former commissioner for Scotland Yard and the man with the most law-enforcement experience in the room. He only consulted with palace security staff when emergencies arose. "The call was undoubtedly from a crank. It's regrettable that you even had to hear it. Members of the royal family should never experience such intrusions."

"But that raises another point," Elena said softly. "The man said he had called before to warn me. I can only assume he spoke with some member of my staff. Why did I not hear about that call?"

"We refuse to be alarmists. The butler took the call and followed *proper* procedures," Johnstone said.

"Then I'll fire Humphrey this afternoon," Elena retorted.

Jenkins rolled his eyes. "The constant rotation in staff is expensive, Lady Elena," he exclaimed. "Before every staff person comes on line, they're trained in security measures and protocol. It costs the taxpayers almost eight thousand pounds for training every new man!"

Elena leaned back and crossed her arms. "I prefer frequent changes. That's the best security measure as far as I'm concerned—especially when it comes to my privacy."

"Security requires sacrificing privacy," Johnstone wheedled.

Jenkins went through his notes. "Humphrey made a brief report," Jenkins read. "He said the phone call was short, that the man demanded to speak to the princess himself, that the threat fell into a category D range. Hardly a huge threat." He put the papers down and stared at Elena. "What more can you want from the man? He did what he was told!"

"He should keep me informed," she insisted.

"Category D—that means we strongly suspect the caller's lying," Cooke said. "It's a crank, I tell you. Or one of your many admirers who wanted to have a talk with you."

"What proof do you have that CIRA planted the bomb?" Elena demanded. "Have any police detectives been to Wyndham Palace to check? Could it possibly have been a disgruntled employee?"

"Staff is thoroughly screened." Jenkins turned to the former Scotland Yard commissioner, who was so highly regarded for his law-enforcement skills. "Cooke, I tell you, this demonstrates why we can't have amateurs messing around with security!" There had been some public grumbling about allowing members of the royal family to take on more responsibility for their personal safety. But security and staff resisted.

"It's my life, my family!" Elena insisted. "It's not unreasonable for me to receive warnings about any dodgy act!"

Johnstone sighed and spoke in the gentle, wise tone he used when other people were near. "Elena, I suggest you leave the security detail to us. Jenkins has years of experience, frustrating groups like the IRA by protecting you and the rest of the family. He never lets up. Why do you think they detest him so much?"

Jenkins held his bald head high and sat straight in his chair, holding in an oversized stomach. Elena studied the pompous, close-minded man. How did he manage to carry so much credibility? Why did they automatically assume her theories were wrong? No member of the royal family had come so close to death from a bomb. She struggled to keep her voice from getting querulous: "Regardless of how you feel, I trust you'll report the latest call to authorities. Perhaps they can lead the investigation." She looked at Cooke, but Jenkins answered.

"Their time is valuable. The public expects the royal family to shoulder the burden of sorting through the hundreds of calls, threats, complaints, and irregularities that the royals undergo everyday. We work very hard to screen you from such annoyances. And I might add, this is the first time in my thirty-four years of service that my work has been met with such ingratitude."

"Jenkins, Lady Elena has not expressed displeasure with security," Cooke interjected. "And Ma'am, please understand that Humphrey was acting under orders. We can change the procedures."

She thought a moment before acquiescing.

"We have noted the content of the call. That's all we have right now. Correct, Elena?"

She nodded.

"So, that settles it." Cooke concluded the meeting with efficiency. "The call's on the official record. The princess will refrain from picking up her telephone. Staff will notify security and the princess on any threatening calls. Security probably should apply some extra surveillance on lines going into that home . . ."

"Yes, it's settled," Elena interrupted. "In the meantime, I'll make the call to the detectives myself."

Jenkins's mouth dropped open. Elena wished that she knew what apoplexy was because he seemed a likely candidate.

"But why? You have us."

She closed her own notebook. She looked at the face of every man to make sure she had their full attention. Then she spoke softly, "You said it yourself—a major bomb that went off on palace grounds. A life was lost. And the bomb could have taken the lives of my two sons as well. This meeting has done little to reassure me. I may be paranoid or naive, but I will do whatever it takes to feel safe—and to be reunited with my sons." She paused before continuing. "Besides, I believed the man on the phone. It was not the splinter group of the IRA or Islamic extremists. He suggested an inside job . . ."

"This is a slap in the face to the royal family and its loyal staff!" Jenkins said stiffly.

Cooke cut him off: "Your call won't be necessary, Ma'am. I'd be honored to file the complaint for you."

Lord Stephen Jenkins stormed away from the conference room and angrily called for his driver. Cooke pulled out a cell phone and started dialing. Elena sat with her hands folded while the commissioner rang the Metropolitan Police and asked for Chief Inspector Detective Timothy Maitlin.

"Elena, the Princess of Wales, has graciously volunteered to answer questions from the authorities. . . . No, that won't be necessary. . . . That's right. She deems the interview a priority, no objections at all. . . . She offered to allow you to set the time." Cooke looked up at Elena for approval and she nodded. "She'll be at her home in Kirkington Park." He returned the receiver slowly to its place, almost as if he regretted making the call.

Cooke turned toward Elena but avoided eye contact. "Four o'clock, today."

"The palace will assist you by sending a legal representative," Johnstone added.

"That won't be necessary," she snapped. "I'm a witness, not a suspect."

"I hope you know what you're getting into." Her uncle spoke with sympathy.

She smiled serenely and stood. All the men's eyes went to the polka dot. "The truth," she announced.

CHAPTER 9

"She has another five years before her beauty vanishes, before the people stop caring."

"At this rate, the monarchy won't last that long."

Elena ordered tea served directly at ten minutes after four, and decided to hold the meeting with Chief Inspector Timothy Maitlin in her most formal receiving room—with its elegant ivory walls, floral fabrics and royal blue accents.

She requested the staff to leave her alone and arranged the furniture herself. She angled two chairs close to the floral sofa. She moved a table near the sofa for the tea service. She moved a smaller table between the sofa and chairs—convenient to hold individual cups and saucers. Studying the room, she admired the intimate seating arrangement.

She would preside from the blue armchair—large and comfortable, it made a nice frame for her tall athletic figure. She had changed into casual, yet neat jeans and a white cotton sweater. Her hair was brushed and held back with another thin ribbon. She checked a mirror in the hallway. With no makeup, she looked vulnerable, cooperative, and ready to help.

The door rang promptly at four, and Humphrey passed in the hallway.

"Show them directly into this room, Humphrey," Elena called out. "And have Martha bring in tea soon. Before we get too settled in our conversation." The man nodded and closed the door. She went into the room, moved a few pillows from the sofa to the remaining armchair and then claimed her seat by sitting and holding a magazine in her lap. She pretended to read an essay until she heard footsteps approaching in the hallway.

"Lady Elena, Princess of Wales," intoned the butler, as he had been instructed by some palace training program, much like the long line of servants who came before him. Elena stood, dropped the magazine to her chair and shook hands with Chief Inspector Maitlin and Inspector Cary Thornton. At the same time, Martha brought in a large tray with tea and small chocolate-covered biscuits from Belgium. Elena nodded at the butler, who returned the gesture and left the room. Martha poured three cups of tea and then also left the room, closing the door without a sound.

"Please, call me Elena," she directed. "And make yourselves comfortable." Without moving away from her chair, she forced the two inspectors to sit side by side on the sofa. She offered sugar and cream, with a smile. Maitlin was tall with brown eyes and dark hair that could use a decent trim, and the younger partner, Thornton, was young, serious, obviously awed with the setting. Both men wore traditional dark suits. Maitlin extracted a notebook from an inside jacket of his pocket. Thornton awkwardly held the delicate teacup, but Maitlin left the tea untouched, impatient to conduct the interview.

"Thank you for coming by," Elena said.

"It's our duty, Ma'am," Thornton said. Maitlin merely lifted his eyebrows.

"I wanted to speak with you about a telephone call."

"We'll get to that," Maitlin interrupted. "The investigation will move along more efficiently if we ask the questions."

Elena nodded.

"You're welcome to continue with your tea, but we want to go through this systematically and take careful notes." He shot a sharp glance at Thornton, who immediately moved his teacup to the table. "Start by telling us about the day your car was bombed on Wyndham grounds. Tell us everything you know about who handled the car that day."

Elena was anxious to tell them about the telephone call. But instead, she sorted through her memories of the gruesome day, repeating how Henry had pulled the Rolls from her Kirkington garage, and drove directly to Wyndham without stopping. Henry had left her at the front door and that was the last she saw of him and the car until the end of the party. She explained how she understood that the servants who were not working the party, including Henry, stayed out of sight and enjoyed their own celebration. She saw him once again when he returned with the car later that afternoon, ready to drive to Kirkington. They asked about the car, but she could only offer speculation: She suspected, but could not be sure, that the car had been parked with dozens of other vehicles, out of sight of her and other guests. Henry probably had not stayed with the Rolls the entire time, but again, she couldn't be sure.

Thornton interrupted her a few times to inquire on minor details. Maitlin tapped his pencil, with an impatient and disjointed rhythm, throughout the monologue. Elena emphasized that the boys had been scheduled to leave with her for the weekend, but last-minute plans had changed.

"How was Henry?" Maitlin asked. "Disagreeable?"

"Not at all," Elena insisted. "He was a gentle man."

"A man with strong political opinions?"

Elena did not like the questions and felt increasingly nervous. "Not really. He preferred the Labor agenda, with the health care and education benefits. But we didn't discuss politics all that much."

"Did you discuss much of anything at all with him?" Maitlin questioned. "He was a member of the staff, after all."

"He's been my driver for more than eight years." Elena's reply was defensive. "We spoke a great deal, about our families, our dreams and disappointments."

"And what were his disappointments, Ma'am?"

She responded without hesitation, to prove that she was not ignorant about the cares of others who happened to work for her. "Not pursuing more education when he was young, before he had children. Not having the opportunity to start his own business. He liked to tinker. He often wondered what would have happened if he had studied mechanical engineering and gone into manufacturing. But he settled into his work as a mechanic and later became a driver, because it paid well."

"Was he bitter?" Maitlin asked, his tone softer, as though he was more ready to believe her.

"Not at all," Elena said firmly.

"But those discussions were only in the car? Never in here?" He waved his arm at the furnishings and the tray with tea.

Elena shook her head slowly. No point in trying to explain that was not her choice, how such a meeting would infuriate her ex-husband and the family. She could tell him how she had secretly visited Henry's wife in the hospital and their small home. But that wouldn't help solve their case, and she didn't know how tight the detectives were with palace security. They would blame her and Henry for security risks and take steps to tighten her protection.

"How long did you know Henry?"

"He was a driver for the family for almost ten years. Not long afterward, he transferred to my staff. He worked with me longer than most."

"Is that because you are a hard woman to please, eh?" Maitlin said.

"Only when gossiped about," she said, with a cold stare. Thornton offered a quick smile and looked down, as though embarrassed to be with his partner.

Maitlin looked at his notebook. "Did Henry have marital problems?"

"Not at all! His wife had a baby not so long ago."

"Any problems between Henry and your security guard?" He checked his notebook. "Walter Draker?" She shook her head, and he pressed on. "Was it typical for Henry to retrieve the guard at the gate?"

"Yes."

Maitlin put his pencil down as if to point out her words were worthless for the investigation. "But they're servants," Maitlin said. "You don't really know much about Henry or the others."

She tightened her lip and waited for the next question. She refused to argue with him.

"Your husband, did you talk with him much that afternoon?"

"A bit, but after the party. We were inside the palace."

"How long did you talk?"

"About ten minutes."

"How would you describe the tone of that conversation?"

Elena laughed. "Measured against our track record, the conversation was civil, even pleasant—like two strangers meeting on the Underground."

"What did you talk about?"

"The party. The boys not going home with me. He knew that I was disappointed."

"You were annoyed?"

"Yes. But I also knew that it wasn't his fault. He understood my disappointment, because the change disrupted my husband's plans, too. The decision was made by the queen or someone on her staff."

"How did he react to your disappointment?"

She shrugged. "Somewhere between mildly sympathetic and unconcerned. But he was not mean about it."

"Was that attitude typical?"

She lowered her head and smiled. "Don't police detectives read the papers? Yes. That's typical Edward. He refuses to interfere with protocol and family tradition."

Thornton smiled and then coughed. Maitlin scowled.

"Any reason for the staff at Wyndham to have a grudge against you?"

"No reason except for the divorce. I haven't stepped foot in Wyndham for months."

Maitlin coughed. "But you were at this party. Could you check this list of staff and guests for unfamiliar names?"

The staff list included more than one hundred names. "May I borrow your pencil?" She studied it and checked the names she did not recognize. Many of the names were Irish, she noticed. Then she shook her head, refusing to get caught up with Jenkins's old prejudices. "Most are new to me. But I really doubt that my problem is with either the staff or guests." She paused. "Please, can't I tell you about the telephone call I received yesterday?"

"Go on," Maitlin said curtly.

Nervous, Elena hurried. "I answered the telephone yesterday afternoon. A man said that factions of the IRA did not plant the bomb."

"That's most helpful," Maitlin said with sarcasm. "We have plenty to keep us busy, without having to focus on every person and group who didn't have anything to do with the bomb." Maitlin leaned forward. "Your Royal Highness, surely I don't have to remind you how these cases attract crank calls."

She nodded slowly. "But this call was different. The man was earnest, almost as if he knew something more."

"Did you tape the call?" Maitlin probed.

"It's with my security staff—not long at all. The man spoke and then hung up on me. The call took less than a minute."

The two men looked at each other.

"Well?" she pressed. "I'm not comfortable with palace security. They want me to be quiet and I refuse."

Maitlin leaned forward and whispered in a snappish way. "And that is why we're showing you the list of staff and guests."

Even the younger man looked annoyed. "Tell us exactly what the bloke said?"

"That the IRA did not try to kill me. That there were IRA extremists who would take credit for anything. He spoke in a rushed way, as if he did not want to be overheard. But he also sounded pleasant . . ."

"A polite radical." Maitlin rolled his eyes. "And how do you know it wasn't a prank, from a friend who handed out your telephone number? Another idiot wanting a scrap of attention from the princess?"

"It sounded real," Elena insisted. "Almost as if he was trying to be helpful. I know that sounds odd."

"We'll check on it." Maitlin gave a dutiful nod. "If it's not IRA, then it could be Islamic extremists."

Elena frowned. "It must be comforting to have so many stereotypes for suspects. Do you really think that makes your job easier?"

Thornton smiled, then ducked his head. Maitlin ignored her question. "How did you feel about going to the party?"

"I looked forward to celebrating the birthday," she said. "I couldn't wait to spend time with my sons after the party."

Maitlin took notes. "What was your frame of mind that day? And the few weeks before the party?"

The question was odd and she thought a moment. "Nothing unusual. I'm tired of the horrible gossip about me in the papers. I miss my boys when they are at school or with my husband. But I have plenty to keep me busy."

"How much have you talked about the divorce around your

staff or with the family?"

"I only spoke with my solicitor," she said firmly. "I didn't trust anyone else."

"Could someone have been angry—about your request for divorce?"

Elena worried about how many questions focused on her. "The divorce proceedings have been going on for months. Besides, with the death of my solicitor, Mr. Wilson, I'm the only one with cause for anger."

"Interesting—that you suggest you're the only one with cause for anger." Maitlin's eyes locked onto hers.

She refused to let him bait her. "I want to control my life and be with my boys," she said. "That's all I want. I'm not suicidal. I'm not making extraordinary demands. You might understand if you had to live with this family for one week." She paused, glanced out the window and then turned to him again. "I have cause for anger, but no reason to hurt anyone or myself. All I can say, Inspector Maitlin, is that, like the caller, I'm another negative for your notebook—the bomb had nothing to do with me."

"I didn't think so, but we must clear rumors."

"Hints from my in-laws?" she asked.

"Not directly, instead vague suggestions from staff," he responded. "I'll be frank, Ma'am. Some question your mental stability."

Elena scoffed. "Anyone who questions the status quo around here—senseless palace protocol—is considered unstable. Fortunately, most intelligent psychologists do not regard 'questioning authority' an official diagnosis. Not yet, anyway." Her head dipped as she tried sincerity. "Ever since Henry died in the awful explosion, I've been frightened about getting into a car. It's under constant guard now. I must worry about what I eat and where I visit. Most of all, I miss my boys. It's not right that we're separated. It highlights just how inept our security force is, whether they're starting or chasing down such foolish rumors."

He cocked his head. "Not all foolish. More than one person said you were visibly upset during the party, particularly during the meal. We spoke with palace officials while you were in the hospital . . ."

She sat up in her chair and waited.

"They mentioned you were distant that day," Maitlin explained.

"The queen specifically requested that I remain in the background during the party."

Thornton jumped in. "Another said you looked pale and ill."

"A minor problem. I found an insect on my meal. It disgusted me, but I didn't want to complain or make a fuss. And another man, one of the guests, was a bit forward. But that's to be expected since the divorce. I manage to fend off these annoyances. Most of the time, I watched my son having fun. I attend these horrible functions to see my children."

"Did you have an invitation? The staff mentioned that your arrival was unexpected."

"Of course I was expected! It was my son's party. And I spoke to the queen herself!"

"Some confusion, I suppose. Barringer mentioned that all arrangements, invitations for the party went through him."

"She called me at my home and we had a pleasant conversation."

"I have notes from Barringer here. He states that, 'All invitations come through his office.'"

"That's rubbish!" Elena retorted. "Why would I suddenly barge in at Wyndham after six months? Ask Richard. Why, ask the queen. We talked about the party weeks before."

"Is it true that after the party, you stormed into the queen's office with some complaint?" Maitlin asked.

"I had expected the children to come home with me."

"So you didn't leave the party directly. Who did you speak with after the party?"

"I only had the conversation with Barringer, the queen's secretary, and my husband. That was in the hallway."

"No one else?"

She shook her head.

He turned a few pages back in the notebook and then looked up. "The palace didn't mention the talk with your husband . . ."

"It was quick and unplanned. I wasn't marked in his schedule book for the day. And he can tell you he was disappointed in the change of schedule. It ruined his plans, too. Both our schedules were disrupted and we commiserated. We have little control over our own lives, inspectors."

Thornton tightened his lips. Elena could understand why he didn't have much sympathy for wealthy people who claimed to lack control over their lives.

"Why did you wait until now to talk with us?" Maitlin's puzzlement was genuine.

"I was waiting for you! Palace security discouraged me from calling you."

"You didn't get our messages?"

"Why, no! I called a meeting of the security team yesterday and insisted on seeing you. I'm the one who wants a complete investigation!" She stood and headed for the phone. "Let's call in Jenkins and the others now. He can't deny that I called yesterday's meeting and insisted on involving proper investigators."

"No," Maitlin said. He dropped his voice to a whisper. "Let's not. I suspect the staff is being . . . difficult. They keep making contradictions, suggesting at one point that you cling to the children too much and then later that you want nothing to do with them."

"Why do you think the palace staff withholds so much information from you?" Thornton murmured.

"They want to be the buffer between us and every part of the public. I think they want to protect us but . . ."

Thornton held a finger to his lips, pointed about the room. "The government condones it by setting odd standards for your family."

"That's not my style, I can assure you," Elena replied.

"Then if we have more questions, we can drop by?"

Elena nodded. "Anytime. I want you to catch the person who tried to kill both me and my children." She handed over a card. "This is my direct line."

"Again, the palace staff said you were the only one with the impression that the children were supposed to leave with you."

"That's simply not true," she insisted. "They're lying to make themselves look less foolish. Both the children and the prince know the truth about this."

"No need to bother them at this point." Maitlin stood. "We've done enough for one day. Not much in the way of substance, I'm afraid."

"And you'll check the phone call? The man sounded reasonable."

"Reasonable? Not if he has anything to do with the IRA, Ma'am. Once a group resorts to terrorism, the idea never vanishes. Extreme members embrace the strategy."

Suddenly he reached for his pocket. "Excuse me while I take this." Then, answering his cell phone, "Maitlin here." As he listened, the frown on his face deepened. "What time?" A pause. "Any witnesses?" Another pause. "We'll be right there."

Thornton looked up, alert to the shift in tone and pace. Maitlin pocketed the phone and hurried to the doorway.

"We must leave now—another bombing," Maitlin announced

to Thornton. "A car job—similar design as the one at Wyndham."

"Tell me, it wasn't anywhere near Pepperell!" Elena exclaimed.

Both men exchanged a glance. Undoubtedly her security people had told the inspectors that the princess didn't know the whereabouts of her children. The staff relished having more information than the family members themselves. They spied on the family, limiting excursions and allowing wiretaps—playing games as the detectives called it. "Nothing to do with your family," Maitlin said. "A professor."

"Where?" Elena asked tentatively.

"Cambridge," said Maitlin. "Please excuse us, Ma'am. And call if you have anything to add."

A chill went through her. She stopped, too flustered to speak, worried that the bomb was connected with her.

But the two detectives hurried away, not waiting for her response.

CHAPTER 10

"The visit from the inspectors was not what she expected."
"Good. Perhaps she won't call them again any time soon."

Elena ran upstairs, avoiding eye contact with the few servants she passed along the way. She was tense, after hearing about another bomb. She didn't like the boys being kept away, and violence anywhere would give the staff an excuse to prolong the separation.

She had kept calm with the detectives. Any display of temper or panic would have validated the rumors spread by staff. The palace had control over her in their own way, causing her to worry, then hinting that her unpredictability and anxiety were good reasons for keeping her sons away. She knew how most of the public made judgments: Flighty royals were unstable, thoughtless, thoroughly undeserving of public protection, inviting trouble. So far, Elena had always managed to prove in a public way that she was quick-witted and well-adjusted. But now she could not attend any public events—shopping, mixing with crowds at the ballet, enjoying dinner parties, would be poor form. The reporters would take note of a mother enjoying herself without her children.

But if she didn't get out, she'd look like a recluse, timid and fearful. She could try going to Pepperell uninvited. But that would raise the ire of staff and family to unbearable levels.

Removing her BlackBerry from its hiding place, she typed in

a short note to Richard: "Hope you're enjoying time away with the trees and streams. Catch any big ones? Wish I could be there for some smoked trout! Any idea on when you'll be back? Or any word on engagements? I could arrange a surprise. Say hi to Larry . . . Love, M."

She sent the note, slouched back and stared at the tiny empty screen. No notes had arrived from the boys that morning. But then, the sun was shining brilliantly up and down the coast, with a teasing breeze, a wonderful day for stomping around the woods. She couldn't expect the boys to stay in and think about typing notes to their mum. She started to return the BlackBerry to its hiding place when the screen flashed to announce a new message.

She clicked the key for her inbox. The message was from an address she did not recognize. Nervous that some stalker discovered her E-mail address, she hit enter and the message popped to the screen: "Turn on telly." The note listed no sender, but she knew that it had to come from Paul.

She ran to the nearest room with a television, the playroom between Larry and Richard's rooms. Wiping away dust from the television screen, she felt morose. She had to get in touch with the two boys. Two weeks was far too long. Everyone, especially the boys, would wonder if she really cared about them.

Frustrated, she pressed the remote. Emergency news was on. A tall reporter, with dark hair pinned high, stood in front of a parking garage. Cars had been torn to shreds, and a column to the garage looked as if it had been hacked away. The woman reported that a car bomb had killed three people, including Cambridge law professor Roger Miggins. The bombing in Cambridge. Paul's brother was the professor at Cambridge.

"The bomb went off shortly after 4:45 p.m. today," the young reporter droned on in a somber tone. "That's shortly after Professor Roger Miggins left his office here on the Cambridge campus. He started his car, when the bomb exploded. Two other drivers, in different vehicles, were also killed. A passenger in yet another vehicle was seriously injured. Inspectors report a telephone call came in about twenty minutes after the blast, with the caller claiming to be with the IRA and taking credit for the explosion. Police ask the public to call with any information at all. Identification of the other victims is pending notification of family."

A reporter gestured toward the scene, as the camera moved in for a close-up of devastating damage. "The bomb is the second to rock the country this month . . ."

Elena turned the sound to mute. She closed her eyes, remembering how Henry had clawed at the window, trying to escape the Rolls. She had watched as an awful explosion had turned a frightened man into a lifeless form in seconds. The same cruel death had been slated for her. Now Paul's brother was dead—one day after Paul had made the mistake of dialing the man's office from the telephone in her private bedroom.

That call had caused Roger's death. Maybe she was paranoid, but she could reach no other conclusion. Paul had good reason for blaming Elena.

She ran back upstairs to her office and noticed her computer was on. Geometric patterns—her screensaver—darted off the screen into space. Damn, she had left the machine on. Anyone could have come in, tapped away at the index and read her documents. She stood at her doorway and listened for quiet patter noises of staff. The hallway was silent. How long had she been with the inspectors? Less than an hour surely. She was safe this time, but she had to be more careful.

Plopping back in her chair, she reached for the biscuit box and checked her BlackBerry once again. Nothing from Richard. She found Paul's note and hit R for reply: "I'm stunned. This was no coincidence. Can we meet? You name place. My thoughts are with you."

She sent the note. He had been waiting. In less than a minute, another new message flashed on her index: "Change password before replying. Scoozie's, tomorrow at ten. Sit toward the back. Order a cappuccino with nutmeg. Don't try to talk to anyone. No one who works there knows anything. Go alone."

She pulled out the small slip of paper that detailed how to change a password. She went from Mouser to Un1c0rN, following the advice to use nonsense mixtures. Then she typed her reply: "It's difficult for me to do anything alone. I must ditch security. Please, be very careful."

She checked her mail again. Nothing. Had Edward or Derry discovered the BlackBerry and learned its true purpose? Did some member of staff simply find the BlackBerry and toss it? Or, had the boys grown weary of a gadget that was a poor substitute for a real mother? She could carry her own device and wait.

CHAPTER 11

"The press hasn't noticed that the children spend no time with her."

"She's stayed at home more than we expected.

"Let's entice her away."

Upon exiting the palace, Elena lingered on the stairs, under the shadows of wisteria vines, and adjusted a long chiffon scarf attached to her black hat. She wore her tallest black heels, hidden underneath the long legs of a black pants suit, her largest and darkest sunglasses. Just beyond the stone wall, reporters waited with telephoto lenses, some on stepladders. She climbed into the limo, which drove slowly through the gate. Rather than wait for Walter, she ordered the new chauffer to drive to the end of the driveway and the gatehouse. Photographers crowded around, forcing the vehicle to crawl by. Security officers at the gate managed to hold the reporters back physically, but verbal restraint was impossible.

"Elena, any comment on the latest attack? Who do you blame?"

"Your Highness, please look this way! If I don't get a decent shot, they'll fire me!"

"Have you seen your children lately? When's your turn with the boys coming?"

She whispered to her new chauffeur, George Canton. "Tell them I'm off to meet an ailing friend. I'll answer a few questions and allow some photos if they promise to give it up for the rest of the day."

"Are you sure, Your Highness? You can't expect this group to keep their word." She nodded. He raised his eyebrows, lowered the window. Elena thought about what she planned for the next few hours. How often did George think of his predecessor's demise? Did he blame Elena? Was this just a job, or did he fear her or resent her? She couldn't tell, and that bothered her. As he repeated the reason for her destination, she lowered the window a few inches, and cameras snapped furiously. With the oversized hat and sunglasses, the photos would be useless.

The photographers did not press forward and she opened the window a bit more. She kept her face somber as she spoke: "I want to thank you for the concern that you have all displayed in recent weeks following the attack. My injuries were slight, and I've fully recovered. Let it be noted, however, that I cannot forget how Henry Pindlow died. I spoke with the investigators and hope that those responsible will be apprehended soon. . . ."

"Have you talked with police?" one woman shouted.

She nodded.

"Do they have a suspect?"

"I don't know." She shook her head.

"The latest bombing? Did you know Professor Miggins?"

She shook her head firmly.

"Do you sense any pattern at all? He practiced law . . ."

"No idea at all," she insisted firmly, locking eyes with the man from the *Daily Union*. "My divorce is final and history. If— and I emphasize if—someone killed Professor Miggins because they thought he was working for me, a horrible mistake was made. My deepest sympathies are with his family."

"This is your first venture out since the accident? Are you confident about your safety?"

"No." But she smiled, and the cameras clicked furiously.

"Do you plan to curtail your activities in the future?"

Elena thought for a moment and spoke low, to force them to listen closely. "Bombs and threats are such a cowardly way of confronting one's problems," she said, tilting her head up slightly. "I refuse to alter my life for such a person. I alter my opinions and lifestyle based on rational thought and discussion. I'm not about to change now."

Walter hurried to the car and angrily ordered the photographers away from the door.

"Your children? When will you see them again?" Disappointment swept through her and she studied the questioner, a tall man who stepped forward, to determine if he was deliberately being cruel. His black hair was too long. His gray eyes, behind serious wire-framed glasses, were intense. He didn't look like a journalist.

Elena glanced at her hands, bare of rings, before glancing up at the group of reporters again. "Of course I want to be with my children. More than anything else on this earth. Palace security thinks it's best they're removed from public life for the time being. What's most important to all of us is that the children are kept safe. I don't agree with these arrangements, but I have no other recourse than to trust all safety measures recommended by the professionals for my children, regardless how painful they may be for me." Tears welled in her eyes and her voice broke. "Now, if you will excuse us," she said. A few scribbled furiously and others frantically shouted more questions, an unintelligible barrage.

Walter slipped into the back seat next to Elena. Calm but firm, he spoke to the driver. "From now on, you call me before you leave. You don't leave the house until I'm with the car." George eased onto the driveway, careful not to strike reporters who pressed against the car.

Most photographers did not pursue Elena so relentlessly

once they had a photo or comment for the day—though a few always remained alert for the embarrassing slip. But Elena had been wary for the past two years. She released announcements, any news or opinions and posed for photographs in public forums, so that exclusives had virtually become non-existent. She had learned the lessons of public relations well. Living her public life in a transparent way gave her freedom and privacy when alone.

At Elena's directions, George began a meandering drive toward a good friend's home, making a few stops for flowers and wine. She hoped the long, slow drive would eventually bore the journalistic stalkers.

An hour later, one small car, a new blue BMW, continued pursuit.

"What do I do?" George called out.

"It's all right." But Elena was impatient and didn't dare be late. Walter and the driver could fight it out with the pesky reporter at the restaurant—keeping both men busy and possibly giving her more privacy. "Let's head south to Willoughby Street. A small restaurant called Scoozie's."

"You didn't mention this earlier," Walter exclaimed. "Is this stop, a restaurant, really necessary, Ma'am?"

"The last attempt on my life was at a palace," Elena said. "Please, on to Scoozie's, George."

The driver accelerated and he reached the restaurant twenty minutes later. He took a few quick turns through lights, but the BMW did not fall behind.

"I'm nervous about him," Elena said, biting her lip. "Please, don't let him come inside."

Walter glared, and Elena sensed that he was angrier with her than with the reporter. But she didn't argue. Walter spoke to the driver about keeping the car nearby, and then they both ran inside. She turned to glance back out at the window, wondering if Paul was someplace near, and saw the BMW block Elena's car. Elena did not have much time and hurried toward the back of the restaurant, even though the place was dark and she wore the glasses. Walter was not far behind and managed to make the gesture of touching her chair as she sat at the table.

"Why do you run ahead of me?" Walter murmured. "You don't seem to remember that your vehicle was bombed not so long ago!"

She leaned forward. "Walter, security works so much better when there's less planning." She dropped her voice to an earnest whisper. "If you don't mind, I need some space. It makes me nervous to have you so close."

"That's not advisable after . . ." Walter began.

"Please," she pleaded. "It's best if you stand by the door. Look, this place is empty."

He gave her a stern look. "No tricks?"

"If anything happens, the palace will blame me. Believe me, they'll never blame you."

"That's not what I care about." He shook his head with misgiving. Without another word, he moved slowly for a table by the door and sat, his back straight, ready to move, not taking his eyes off her when a young and beautiful waitress with long dark hair handed him a menu with a smile. Her hair was long and dark, woven into two thick braids. He waved her away, his eyes locked onto Elena, even as the waitress hurried by and dropped a menu on Elena's table. The young woman then returned to the bar area, slowly stacking glasses while sneaking small glances at the overdressed customer in the back of the restaurant and the angry man near the door.

"Don't worry so," Elena mouthed the words at Walter. But her guard had good reason to be cautious. Frequented by graduate students and a young computer crowd, Scoozie's was in a district with dark, narrow streets and not on any typical list of royal haunts.

She scanned the menu quickly, hoping for a message from Paul, grateful for an excuse to avoid Walter's stare.

Elena couldn't get rid of Walter, but maybe Paul would still deliver the message.

The back door of the restaurant slammed open with sudden energy, distracting Elena and Walter both. Disheveled after some altercation with George, the dark-haired reporter looked more like a professor than a reporter. His shirt was blue denim, worn open at the neck. Walking quickly inside, he straightened the well-worn, once-expensive tweed jacket. Carrying a notebook and pen like props in his one hand, the man pushed his hair back with the other—and headed straight for Elena.

She checked him over. At least he didn't carry a camera.

Walter stood, took a few running steps and grabbed the reporter's arm. The reporter looked at the guard as if he were an annoyance and then looked at Elena with a smile, as though he expected her to decide. Though tall, the odd reporter was more charmer than bully. Don't be silly, she chided herself.

"Walter, it's all right," Elena called out. "Give us a few minutes." She detested how any request sounded as if she were calling a dog, how even the best members of staff put themselves in that position. She checked her watch. She was in the restaurant a few minutes early, and perhaps she could chase the man away quickly.

The reporter flashed a brief smile of relief as he sat, but his eyes were uncertain. Elena folded her hands and tightened the muscles about her eyes. The man had to be new and didn't know what he was doing, she decided. She was accustomed to reporters who thought they had something on her, a silly tape of a phone call or an embarrassing photo. They didn't realize that Elena had nothing to lose.

Walter glared at both women and Elena felt guilty as he

returned to his lonely seat—yes, he was a nice young man, but she could never forget that he was paid by the palace. Sadly, some distance kept them both safe.

Elena was stern. "I spoke to the lot of you this morning with the promise that you'd lay off for the rest of the day. You're not being fair to your colleagues, the ones who abide by their word. Do you think I'll favor the one reporter who chooses to harass me?"

"The rest of them are dim."

She raised her eyebrows. "For showing some integrity?"

"No, for the questions they ask. For accepting the word of any royal, including yourself."

She took a breath, let it out slowly. "Then I see no point in us talking."

Another waitress approached, waiting without a word and staring at the small pad in her hand. Barely an adult, she was tiny, no more than five feet tall, with dark red hair and exquisite pale skin. She was stunning, even with the distracting gold hoop attached to her lower lip. The young woman looked back and forth between the two, and then her gaze lingered with Elena.

"A cappuccino with nutmeg," Elena said. "Decaf, please. And tea for the man over at the other table, lots of sugar. And nothing for this gentleman—he's not staying."

The waitress locked eyes briefly with Elena and showed just the hint of a frown. Her message was clear: Elena was supposed to be alone.

The girl dipped her head and scrawled on the pad. Then she swung around and headed for the coffee machine, her long black skirt twirling about and showing her knees. Despite the casual attire, the woman was delicate, exotic. Elena remembered her childhood secret longings to be small enough to disappear. She turned away, but found herself wondering if the woman was Paul's girlfriend.

Elena turned full attention to the reporter. She had hoped to appeal to his sense of fairness and get rid of him. That had been a mistake. The jackals had no character. Grabbing photos and comments was their game. She vowed to keep her comments short. "What's your name?" Elena asked, not bothering to cover her irritation.

"Do you want to read some of my work?"

"No, I intend to file a complaint."

"And that won't be a first," he replied.

She remained stiff and didn't answer.

"Just hear me out. I'm Michael McLarrity—a freelance writer. Currently on assignment for *Intense*—it's a new magazine in the States."

She shrugged. "All the more reason not to talk with you."

He leaned over the table and whispered. "I know where your children will be this coming weekend. And unlike those other fools you call journalists, I know that you don't know." With that, he retrieved his notebook and stood.

"All right, wait!" she whispered, panicked, torn between learning more about the boys and hoping the woman would bring a message from Paul with the coffee. "This weekend where? And how do you know this? The palace has been keeping the schedule a secret. For their protection."

"Protection from what?" McLarrity asked harshly. "From you? Does your husband's status automatically make him more trustworthy than you?"

"Of course not," she snapped. Then she shook her head. "I don't know."

McLarrity sat again. "Have you tried to find them? Contact them?"

Elena held her tongue. She didn't want to get trapped into answering questions—not without finding out what he knew. The best tactic was delay. "I can't talk to you here. My guard is watching us. All I can say is that security will have fewer questions all-around if you leave here quickly."

"Do you want to know more about your children?"

"You can come to the palace tomorrow. Early, all right—nine?"

"I can be there at eight . . ."

"Yes, that's better." Elena felt a rush of conflicting emotions: She'd have to calm the secretary about tinkering with the schedule.

Elena was desperate to hear the journalist's report, but she had to maintain a fierce hold of her self-control, never letting anyone know how much she needed him. So, she didn't even ask for a way to contact him. Trust was impossible for her, Elena thought. Fewer words and emotions shielded her from public scrutiny. "Tomorrow," the journalist said with a nod and left the restaurant.

Elena pointedly ignored Walter and pulled a novel from her bag, staring without reading. Less than a minute later, the coffee arrived. Elena stared, a bit expectantly. But the woman's eyes darted away, keeping a blank face while placing some extra napkins close to Elena's hand. The petite woman pointedly did not ask if the princess wanted to order anything else, probably didn't care, and instead haughtily twirled away out the back door.

Worried, Elena studied her coffee, with its puffy white foam tumbling over the sides of the cup onto the saucer. She slowly sprinkled some sugar on top, watching it dissolve, then harden against the hot foam.

Walter suddenly stood and approached the kitchen, where the coffee had been made. Damn, what was the man up to, Elena wondered. Hoping that her hesitation did not trigger his suspicion, she lifted the cup and saucer, gulping some coffee. Or, did he sense something else? No obvious message on that napkin or inside. She looked at the little pile nearby and, with Walter's attention diverted, swept them all into her handbag.

The dark-haired waitress blocked Walter from entering the kitchen, and he shouted: "Where's the waitress who brought that coffee in here?"

"You have to speak with the owner," the woman said stiffly. "We don't have to answer your questions."

"Elena, don't drink that," Walter ordered.

"Please, this is not necessary," Elena murmured. But she put the cup down.

The waitress was skeptical. "You're pretenders," she countered. "There are too many pretenders in this country."

"Where's that waitress who brought the coffee?" Walter was insistent. "I'd like to speak with her just a moment."

"Clara deserves her break now, doesn't she? If you have questions or complaints, it's best if you speak to the owner. It's his niece, trying her hand at the job. Just an ordinary college student, trying to make money for books. But you must talk to her uncle, and he won't be back until four."

"She's not a waitress, is she?" Walter asked. "She never worked here before."

The dark-haired woman shrugged, but was less hostile, almost as though she agreed with him about something odd going on.

Walter pressed. "What is Clara's last name and where does she live?"

"Walter, I'm fine," Elena pleaded. She could not allow him to pry into the background of any of Paul's friends. Paul would never forgive her. "Let's not terrorize anyone over a simple cup of coffee."

Walter ignored the princess. "Surely, you have a number for getting in touch with the owner immediately!"

The woman leaned against the wall and smiled. "Not for you, mister," the woman snapped. "Next time bring in the real thing. We both know that the real Princess of Wales would never step inside here."

"Walter," Elena stood and pulled him aside, speaking under her breath. "I heard about this place and wanted to try it. I didn't mean to cause any trouble. It's my mistake. Let's just get out of here fast."

"Phonies," the woman said scornfully.

Perhaps the woman's disbelief convinced Walter. He scowled and turned toward his charge's table, pushing the coffee to the side. "Yes, it's time for us to leave."

Elena did not want him to file a detailed incident report, and she hoped that he would not remember the extra napkins left at her table. Walter tossed some pound coins on the table and did not look at any of the staff as they left the cafe. Elena could only hope that Paul's friends would understand. Palace staff always watched Elena.

The car sped away from the neighborhood. Walter urged that she return immediately to the palace, but Elena insisted on visiting her friend who was feeling poorly.

As the two men talked about the best route, Elena opened her purse, pretending to search for her mirror. The men didn't pay attention, and so she straightened the napkins, noticing a note written on the inside fold of one. Tucked in with the bunch was a white plastic card, with a red stripe. It looked like a credit card, but without any labels. She took a glance out the car window, not wanting to get caught staring at the napkins.

She searched through the Hermès handbag again, looking for a lipstick and a photo of her boys caught her eye. She stared at the happy faces, wondering why they didn't contact her. She laid the photo on top of her purse, ready to respond to George and Walter if they took their eyes off the heavy traffic. Walter continued to argue with George, questioning how the reporter got inside the restaurant, while scanning the roadway ahead.

George countered he could not park and keep watch on a restaurant door at once.

She unfolded the napkin inside the purse to study the note: "Get to main library at Cambridge. Alone. Key for gates. Enter library, turn left. Wait for computer along back wall, so no one can slip behind you. Open your account." Elena slumped back in her seat. Go alone, the note said. Didn't Paul realize that he asked the impossible of her?

She spoke up. "I changed my mind. I want to go to Lady Sarah's house."

"But that's so far away and will disrupt the schedule," Walter protested.

"I remembered something important," she said.

George made a turn and headed northward. "Ma'am," George interrupted her thoughts. "That car's still behind us, Ma'am."

"The BMW?" Elena asked, without looking. George nodded. "He'll get bored," Elena said.

"Central security's worried, Ma'am. They asked that we head back to the palace."

"Damn security!" she insisted. "They want to lock me in a cage. Makes their job easier, you know."

"At least Lady Sarah Pintner's better than Scoozie's," Walter muttered.

Less than an hour later, George stopped the car, and Walter accompanied her to the front door of the elegant home. The Pintners were not the most royal family, but they came from a long line of public servants and they were also extraordinarily wealthy. Elena slipped inside as the butler opened the door, and Walter made the routine call to the Pintners' security chief.

Sarah had an old and elegant home in north London. Her grandfather and uncles all had joined the Royal Forces during

World War II, leaving Sarah's grandmother home alone with three children under the age of five. The man flew planes that dropped bombs and understood too well the resulting destruction, fear and panic. So, as a precautionary measure before he left, Grandfather Pintner consulted with neighbors, and together they constructed and supplied a spacious, yet secret, underground bombing raid shelter, connected to two homes and one garage by tunnel.

About twenty minutes after Elena arrived, a woman hurried away from a nearby carriage house, not far from the Pintners'—her head down and intent on exercise. Bulky in size, she wore a gray sweat suit, running shoes and all hair tucked inside a baseball cap—and hurried to a parked car. Behind the wheel was a friend of Sarah's daughter, who drove quickly to the Cambridge campus.

The house with the tunnel, the exercise suits with quilted padding along her torso, thighs and upper arms, gave her a few hours of freedom every few months. Elena had to be careful about these visits with Lady Pintner. If some photographer blew her cover, if security realized that she had left the premises, then the few precious hours of freedom would vanish forever.

So Elena kept her head low and shoulders slumped, avoiding eye contact, as she followed the directions on the note and used the plastic card to enter secure areas. She entered the library easily and found an empty chair in front of a library computer. Most students were concentrating on books and one another, and none gave her more than a passing glance.

She sat close to the screen, to discourage any sidelong glances from students who sat at either side. Elena clicked about a few news sites and glanced around to see if anyone watched. But no one was curious about an oversized woman in gray.

She called up her own E-mail. A message from "anonymous" waited, nothing from either of her boys. She opened the message. "Wait for the computer under the red poster to get free. Once there, click on the program labeled 'visitor' with password aaaa1111. We'll have an open line and can chat anonymously. No names."

She glanced at the other computer. A young woman was frowning and typing away. As Elena waited for the computer, she called up generic news sites and read brief updates. The Miggins bombing topped the list.

The young woman stood and reached for her backpack. Trying not to hurry, Elena sat in the empty seat and followed Paul's directions. Nervous, she wondered whether Paul was really on the other end of the chat line. She wrote: "Never worked like this before." She hit send. A message bounced back seconds later: "It's ok if you type fast. You're mum of the former salamander, no?"

"What's his name now?"

"Red Scorpion."

"Where are you?"

"In the library. Saw you come in. But DO NOT look for me. Keep your eyes on screen. Did you get questions about my brother?"

"Only briefly."

"Damn brief with my family as well. They have no suspects."

"Did they talk with you?"

"They don't want to hear from a kid brother. Expect more questions, though. Give them a week to figure out the connection."

Elena couldn't type her questions fast enough. "What happens then? No one knows that you set up BlackBerry for me."

"Let's keep that way. But they'll trace that one call."

"Reporters asked if I had consulted your brother on my case."

"He's not that kind of lawyer," Paul wrote back. "But I don't think his death is a coincidence."

"Neither do I."

"One stupid call. That's not enough to change the status of any case. We don't even know if the call was the problem. But if it was, the call made someone afraid. And the police don't have a clue."

"Do we tell the police?"

There was a long pause. She typed again: "We can't afford another mistake. I won't mention you. But dare I wait until they come to me and ask? I could say a wrong number. I could say someone else made the call. I don't know. Help me."

"We have to decide. The police will automatically believe you, won't they?"

Elena sat with her hands poised lightly on the keyboard. He didn't realize that she lacked any real power. She remembered the antagonism when the two detectives interviewed her. Finally, she typed: "You'd be surprised. They'd probably believe you more than me. I don't want to take the chance of anyone finding out how you've helped me. I don't want you to get hurt. For now, I'll say the call was a mistake."

Pause. "Hope you understand if I can't come by your place again."

"Definitely."

"Let's think about this. I'll contact you. Always as unverified sender. Damn, can't exactly use you as a reference now. Can I?"

"I owe you," Elena concluded.

"You're ok. For a princess." The message flashed on the screen and then vanished as fast as a spark.

CHAPTER 12

"She has yet to hire a solicitor!"

"She's arrogant for a woman with less than a secondary-level education."

Elena woke early the next day and immediately checked her BlackBerry and again twenty minutes later. No messages. She'd check again after the meeting with McLarrity. She wondered if he truly had information about Richard and Larry or if he wanted to trap her into divulging secret fears. She vowed to be patient and give him no information of value until he demonstrated the source of his knowledge.

Of course, she'd proceed as if she had nothing to hide. Ever since she agreed to join the royal family, she could never be sure what she was supposed to reveal or hide. Early in her marriage, she discovered her minor missteps too late, only when staff working for the queen approached her with solemn disapproval. The queen never mentioned problems, smiling and chatting through dozens of luncheons, teas, receptions and balls. As a young woman, Elena was convinced that the staff could not possibly make decisions to reprimand her on their own; eventually she came to realize the family's insecurity, hiding their emotions and following rules reinforced by years of tradition. Indeed, the palace staff was autonomous when it came to anticipating, judging, discouraging feelings held by members of the royal family, and the royal family reinforced that control with complicit silence. At first Elena had thought that she lacked some form of self-control. Later she realized the control came from a pack rather than any sense of self.

Her husband's family had been raised to serve in the narrow roles of modern-day royalty. They were supposed to act regal and serve as public examples. They performed for the public and they practiced on one another constantly, accompanied by piles of paperwork. Royal life was a charade, Elena knew. Each member of the family must have reached the same conclusion at some point during the long and dreary parade of publicity. Not one of the Wyndhams could say what they truly meant or act as they pleased. So much acting led to lies, and no one in the family could ever trust another family member.

Poor, blinkered Edward. He refused to talk about the issue, but he had to know. He wasn't that stupid. But the truth was that only his royal status made him special, a message relayed to him repeatedly since birth by his parents and the palace staff. The line to the throne had diminished the worth of education, career, friendships, passions. Edward would be nothing without his royal lineage—his upbringing had discouraged him from exploring, creating, working, or thinking for himself. Oh, he did community service and served as an example to the citizenry, but he lacked the imagination, the curiosity, the hope, to trust that his sons could live a different life.

She could hide her feelings, but she didn't act. Elena wanted her sons to experience the real world. To learn that pain and failure and despair could not be easily thwarted, that such feelings could lead to relief and perseverance and motivation.

But she couldn't tell the reporter these thoughts. Elena dressed casually for the meeting. Loose eggplant silk slacks and a lilac sweater, with only slight makeup. And, for a woman who experienced divorce and separation from her children, she looked like a woman with few cares. People thought she was shallow and frivolous, but that suited her. Her greatest advantage against any potential enemy was their underestimating her skill.

He was announced, and she nervously fluffed her hair back before he entered the informal sitting room. The maid arranged petite pastries on a tray and poured two cups of dark tea. "But you're American," Elena said. "Perhaps, you'd prefer coffee."

He reached for his cup. "Breakfast tea is fine. I've developed a taste by now."

She nodded, all business, and reached for her tea. "So, you came to talk about my children. But let's be clear—this is not an interview. Privacy becomes more precious for them with age."

"Agreed, not an interview." He nodded and waited for the maid to leave the room. "Privacy is not usually a term applied to one's mother, however. You did that on purpose—led the maid to believe I'm here to ask about the children. Will she gossip?"

"We'll find out soon enough," Elena said shortly, and she sipped to gain a few moments to think. She had expected him to be more difficult than intelligent. But McLarrity was patient and wanted her to plead for his information. That would make a fine story: Princess in distress. But she refused. She crossed her ankles and sat up straight. "After the bombing my husband and I both had legitimate fears about the children's safety. The family decided to take security measures."

"If you accept that, then you've given up," he said, leaning back. "You'll take their money in exchange for your children's time."

"That's not true!" she shouted. The few tablespoons left in the cup sloshed out and stained the linen napkin. "If I could have my children, then I'd walk away with nothing. But money is power in this family. They agreed to the trust settlement and now they're backing off."

He had his turn to smile. "And I believe you," he replied. "So you do care. I told you I'm over here on assignment for *Intense*. It's part of the GC group."

"A men's magazine?" she finished. "Edward's staff must be thrilled."

He nodded. "Staff for your husband contacted me and suggested they could arrange a special interview with the prince on a sporting vacation with his sons. Once I arrived in the country, the negotiations switched. Suddenly, the staff tried to get me begging for the interview."

"They know how to play games," Elena said. She poured more tea. "Don't call them back."

"I did better than that. I called and told them I was no longer interested. Too much hassle for a puff piece. Takes me away from my main objective—finishing research for my dissertation."

"That must have upset them," Elena said.

He smiled. "It did, and I have more time than what was scheduled before."

She sipped her tea. "And what's your Ph.D. in?" Elena asked, curious about the man's persistence. "Journalism?"

"No. Political philosophy and constitutional crises."

She leaned back and stared at him. "And that's why you're interested in us. Our divorce is a constitutional crisis. Edward's staff doesn't know about your research."

"You took the words out of my mouth," he said. "Let's get back to your concerns. After years of accusing you of meddling in international politics, the people who work for your husband refuse to speak your name. It's as if you don't exist. I'm not sure separating the children from you is motivated by a concern for safety."

"But whining to you, a journalist, will not help my predicament, I'm afraid," Elena said.

He put his tea down and leaned forward. "Is it safe to talk?" he murmured.

She shook her head and then pointed to his notebook. He opened it to the first page and scribbled before handing the book over. The book was new, with no other notes, and she wondered again if he really was a reporter. She read: "Your husband's secretary called yesterday and suggested that I observe the prince and the boys during the botanical garden exhibit in Staffordshire next weekend, followed by an interview."

She wrote back: "At Biddulph Grange? The benefit for domestic violence shelters?"

Michael nodded.

"A charity that I sponsor. Not Edward . . ."

He wrote his response: "They're keeping you trapped at home and moving in on your territory."

Elena bit her lip. "But after the accident, I explained that I was sending a representative." He pointed to the notepad. She wrote: "Did they invite Edward, too?"

"Perhaps the palace decided to send Edward as your representative," he scrawled back.

"He'd never agree to that!" Elena spoke aloud.

He shook his head and wrote. "Perhaps you should find out who's substituting for you?" Then he handed the pad to her.

"I was ready to go, but a palace secretary called about another commitment and suggested that I not try to tackle both events."

"If you went, could they find some way to embarrass you? Such as keeping the children away?"

She shook her head firmly and inside wondered how much she could trust this man, a journalist. Would Edward and the children really attend her event?

He continued to write: "You could show up. The press can

capture a happy reunion between a mother and her two children."

She took the pad and replied: "Edward might cancel his interview with you."

Michael shrugged. "He thinks he can manipulate me, but he's also desperate for publicity."

"Why are you doing this?" Elena narrowed her eyes, and then reached for the notebook again. "Do you want to watch Edward and me behave like fools?"

"No," he said.

"Why would you help me?" Elena wrote. She handed the note over and stared at him as he read.

"I was working with Roger Miggins on some case studies." He handed her the pen. She held it frozen, not knowing what to write.

"But I didn't know him," she whispered.

Michael took the notebook again. "But he knew about you. His caller ID listed your number, and he knew that you had tried to call him. He had asked some questions about why and was getting ready to contact you directly. Please, you can't mention that I'm writing about Roger's work. That's a secret."

Elena bit her lip as she wrote. "I want no one else hurt because of me." She showed him the notebook, and then removed the pages with the exchange. Michael offered to take care of it, but she thanked him and shook her head no. It was a warm day, but she would start a small fire in the fireplace, making sure to destroy the paper completely.

At last, she knew the whereabouts of her children. She could only hope that they still wanted to be with her.

CHAPTER 13

"The children seem to be behaving."

"We promised to return the computer in a week if they kept it up."

Edward ducked his head slightly to speak into the microphone. The hostess had offered to adjust the instrument, but he liked tipping his head. He looked taller, friendlier, as his wife had suggested when they were first married.

A large crowd of people stood respectfully in a semicircle about twenty feet away, all somber, attentive. Edward was proud of Richard's stiff posture, his expressionless face. Lawrence squirmed and squinted, but then he was the younger of the two, always more enthralled by immediate blooms and insects crawling about a garden than the history of cultivation. A child who lived for the present, he was impulsive and prone to distractions—too much like his mother. Edward always had trouble approaching the child, let alone conversing with him. The boy got bored so quickly. Edward shook his head. He had to remain focused on his speech, his bearing, his destiny.

A few sentences later, Lawrence let loose with a loud yawn. Edward frowned at the two boys, furious with Lawrence and upset with Richard for not taking better control of his brother. As the Prince of Wales, Edward had to worry constantly about speaking with poise and sense, impossible with the irritations and distractions of two children.

Richard lowered his head and remained quiet. Edward wondered why the older son didn't have a word with the younger boy. He would have them both sit at desks later in the evening and write essays about failure to carry out duty. Perhaps Lawrence should have dinner in his room.

Suddenly Richard jabbed his brother hard, but Lawrence ignored the warnings, reaching out and picking thorns from a rose bush with large pink blossoms. He was tugging at the rosebush as his father concluded the talk and the audience politely applauded.

Edward accepted congratulations as he moved away from the podium. An assistant secretary to the Prince of Wales stepped forward and bowed his head. "One of the footmen just advised that a nanny's available in Cheshire Cottage, Sir." Edward looked at him blankly.

"For the children. Lawrence can't seem to keep his hands off the best varieties."

"Of course, by all means. Excuse them and let's enjoy some peace this afternoon." He then turned his back on the boys without a glance.

Elena could not bear a public display of any reunion with her sons. She watched from behind some hedges nearby as Larry fidgeted, then as Richard lingered, obviously hoping his father would call him back and praise him for rigid and regal behavior.

But no, as always, the boys were lumped together as children, ignored as individuals who had minds of their own.

As Edward concluded his speech, Elena retreated to the cottage, watching the assistant secretary hurry the boys along the path. He impatiently pointed toward the small cottage, surrounded by tall hedges and mounds of rhododendrons and azaleas. Larry skipped eagerly ahead, and Richard strolled. The man turned around, hurrying back to the crowd full of self-important nods and arched eyebrows. Elena leaned from the window a bit and let out a terse call of the chickadee, a high note followed by a low one: *Fee-bee.*

Larry paused and looked about. But he was the only one to notice that something unusual might be in store.

So much for security, Elena thought. Enraged, standing by the window alone, she studied the approach of her boys. She had given the destination to her driver at the last minute. Walter followed quietly, without alerting his superiors. His only comment: "They're keeping your husband's whereabouts a secret from us, and this is only a garden show, right?" He was enough of a dear to wait outside the cottage and give her some privacy.

She bit skin away from the edge of her forefinger, ignoring the pain. Damn Edward and his crowd, she thought to herself. They carped on about the boys' safety and didn't care to check on the qualifications of the supposed caregiver or even meet her! Elena had learned to take advantage of the loopholes created in the massive hierarchy of the palace, where a mysterious someone else always took care of details. In some ways, the system was a godsend, allowing her to slip into the gardens, enter the cottage as a nanny and have this unguarded moment with her sons. She stepped back from the window and waited for the knock, a child's hesitant thump. Elena lowered her voice and called out: "Come in!"

Larry burst through the door with his typical hard energy and Richard followed more slowly as Elena opened her arms and smiled. The boys looked amazed, and Larry was the first to reach her for a hug. "Mum, I can't believe it's you," he cried out. "Finally, it's like a dream come true!"

"Mother," Richard whispered. "Why did it take so long?"

The question stabbed Elena. She should not have allowed the separation to last so long. Maybe she should have fought the palace from the first day. If only Derrick were alive, but she wouldn't give the boys any excuses. Instead, she put her arms around them both and tumbled to her knees, all three of them squeezing and crying and kissing at once.

After a few moments, Elena put a hand to each boy's shoulder and looked at them both. "No one from the palace knows that I'm here," she whispered. "Where's your security?"

Larry shrugged. Richard hung his head. "This is the first that we've been out in ages," Richard said. "Dad's men have been watching over us."

"But no one checked? Did they just allow you two boys to walk in here?" Alarm spread over the face of her older son. Elena was furious, but not with the boys. All the pompous puffing about security was a guise to keep her and only her from the boys. "Have the guards been this lax all along?"

Richard and Larry looked at each other. "They were on top of us constantly after the accident," Richard admitted.

"But not much lately," Larry added.

Elena stood. Her first conversation should not be about safety, but after all, she was their mother. "It shows how each of us is ultimately responsible for our own safety. We must be vigilant on our own and can't depend on security. You can't rely on your father or me for that matter."

Larry looked frightened and Richard looked puzzled. Enough about security, she thought. "I love you both," she said, giving each a warm hug. "What were you told about me?" she asked softly.

"We were told that you needed some rest, some time away from us," Larry said sadly. "We missed you!" He wrapped his arms around her waist and refused to look at her face, with its mixture of sternness and fear. Elena put her arm lightly about him, and tried to soothe the anger inside with love, both for herself and the boys. She had not seen them for weeks and her first emotions were fear, anger, annoyance—all because of the palace. But she had to overlook that for the next hour or so.

"What matters is that we're here together now!" She forced her voice to take on a cheerful note. "Do you have ideas for what we can do?"

"Do you have your BlackBerry?" Larry piped up.

"Why, no, not with me. What happened to yours, Richard?"

"Father had our belongings packed and sent on to school. We were supposed to be back next week, but then the palace delayed that another week. The delays are irritating all of us, including father."

Elena vowed to keep the conversation positive. "But you're returning Monday," she said pleasantly. "That's good. You're good students and will catch up."

"Can't catch up on the sports and fun." Larry was gloomy about his parents' lack of control.

"Surely, you had some fun with your father." Elena put a finger to his chin.

"At first," Richard said. "But then, he got busy."

"Let's not waste time now then . . ." She led the way to a small table set outside on the old stone courtyard. A tray of large chocolate biscuits, fresh fruit and lemonade waited on the nearby table. "I brought along a book. I can't tell you how much I've missed us all reading together."

"What's the name?" Larry asked eagerly.

"*The Island of Blue Dolphins,*" Elena showed them the cover. "I heard that it's quite good. Although it is about a little girl."

"Yuck," Larry said.

"Hey, I'm a girl," she said, merrily. "Wouldn't hurt for you two to know a bit more about how girls think!"

Richard gave her a wary look. "That's a long book. If you start, you must promise that you'll stick around to finish it."

Elena understood. "I want the same. You must help me convince your father."

Larry looked at Richard and shook his head. "He doesn't listen to us about anything."

"Maybe if we work at it together," Elena said sadly.

"I'll refuse to behave if they don't let us be with you," said Larry, snuggling close to her and lifting her arm to drape it behind his neck. "Let's read and then can we go for a walk? I'd like to see if any bugs live in these flowers . . ."

Sitting on a blanket in a clearing, the threesome took turns reading two chapters each, before putting the book down and wandering off to examine a tunnel that led to another garden—and then beyond to a nearby field of wildflowers. Elena loved the little cottage. It was private, with no telephones, television or other annoying devices. She appreciated having her children all to herself for an hour, with no interference from the palace. She owed the director of the National Domestic Violence Organization a huge favor.

Elena wore a large, but simple straw hat and a sleeveless dress, in pale yellow cotton that flowed around her long legs. The boys had each picked a tiny bouquet before dashing off to search for insects. She lay stretched out in the long silky grass, content to pretend if only for a moment or two that she was on the island of blue dolphins. Only for a moment, because inside, Elena doubted that she could ever be like the self-sufficient little girl who learned to survive on her own happily without family or friends. Self-sufficiency. Elena had never known what that meant, but it's all she wanted for her children—the ability to go through life and make independent choices without relying on dreary, calculating palace staff.

She heard joyful shouts and leaned on her elbows to watch the boys as they darted about, competing to see who found the most unusual insects. Larry had aphids and an odd caterpillar to his account. Away from his father and staff, Richard joined the search and carried a tree-hopper and a large black beetle.

Suddenly, Elena heard voices. She glanced toward the vine-covered stone wall and path beyond.

A group of men approached slowly along the path to the cottage. Conniving staff surrounded Edward, Michael McLarrity and some other conservative reporters. McLarrity carried a small tape recorder and Edward answered questions. Elena wondered briefly if she should hide—and wait. But no, better to get it over with. If she had to confront Edward about the children, it might as well be in front of reporters. More often than not, they took her side.

Her boys paused when they heard the group and stood at attention. As always, the boys had to wait for their father to nod, the signal that meant they could continue playing. Elena scowled. When still living with Edward, she had insisted the boys did not have to follow protocol, that it interfered with normal childhood. But that obviously changed since the divorce and more so in recent weeks. The group passed the boys without comment and did not recognize the woman in the field.

Just as well if Elena didn't wait, so she stood and called out: "Game's over, boys. Let me see your lists. Who found the most insects?"

At the sound of her voice, Edward looked up, surprised. McLarrity grinned. Members of Edward's staff looked incredulous. McLarrity turned to Edward, as if to congratulate him, and then immediately headed in her direction. The rest of the group had no choice but to follow. Timothy Barnes, secretary to the Prince of Wales, formally introduced Mr. Michael McLarrity, the journalist from the United States, to the Princess of Wales.

McLarrity refrained from bowing, but nodded his head politely. "Your Royal Highness," he said. "I just complimented your husband on your family's progressive stance. Divorced and yet cooperative. Working together to protect the children's privacy. Living life and ignoring all the ugly rumors. It's refreshing, and our readers will want to know the secrets."

Edward nervously swallowed, almost as if he expected a tirade from his ex-wife. But she merely nodded. "So true," she agreed, then excused herself with a polite smile. "My children and I have little time together," she explained. "And I'm sure you'd rather discuss issues of importance with the Prince of Wales. Good day, gentlemen." With that, she turned and walked toward the children, ready to examine their insects.

Edward's secretary followed her closely. "What were you thinking?" he demanded. "Your presence here violates the children's security."

"I beg to differ, but the children are far more secure now that I'm here," Elena snapped. "If I'm so dangerous, how did I get on this property? Who decided to send the children off into some unknown cottage with a stranger of a nanny without any precautions? The lot of you don't care about my children. Your sole priority is keeping them away from me! Should I discuss my complaints with the reporter over there? He certainly seems interested in our family life."

Timothy Barnes growled at her. "You wouldn't dare."

"Try me," Elena said, lifting her eyebrows.

"He won't believe you!" Barnes exclaimed.

"Oh, but the children will help," she replied coolly. "Larry! Richard!" Both boys looked up immediately, and waved. Elena started to wave them over, but Timothy reached out and stopped her. "This interview is important for the prince. Please, tell me what you want. I'll see what can be arranged."

"A simple matter of resuming the children's normal schedule." Elena stood tall, watching Larry examine the inside of a bluebell. With any luck, a bee did not lurk inside.

"That requires palace approval," Barnes said helplessly.

"You have a cell phone," she said, keeping her voice low but friendly. "Call the palace. Talk to Jenkins." She glanced at her watch. "You have five minutes to get that request approved and set a meeting for me with queen, so that I can guarantee that the terms of the divorce settlement will be met. I'm tired of playing your games. I don't want to bother going back to court."

She put her long and ringless fingers to her neck to ease the weeks of tension away as she strolled toward the tangle of flowers being studied by her younger son. Richard stood to the side, no longer playing. Conscious of his father and the reporter, he focused on acting mature, another observer. She wished she could engage him in conversation, but that would only add to his discomfort. So, she huddled with Larry. "What's so amazing about that flower?" she whispered.

"Look." The child gently touched the stem and pointed inside petals. A minute spider had spun a delicate web underneath and busily repaired one ragged side. Struggling in the center of the web was a tiny white wrap. Larry pointed: "That gnat almost got away. At first, only one leg was stuck. But she moved in close, circling him and covering him in thread. Why does she keep returning and poking him with one leg?"

Elena grimaced. "I'm not sure we want to know." She knelt beside her son and whispered. "Darling, it's arranged—you and Richard can return to school. And I think our visits will begin again."

"Great!" Larry exclaimed. "You and I—we can take care of any terrorists!"

Elena gave him a hug, but remembered the bomb inside her car and hoped that she could keep her sons safe. Someone had managed to infiltrate the palace grounds. She didn't want her younger son to feel either too safe or too terrified.

But she would caution the boys later, now that she could count on more time with them. Elena looked off in the direction of Secretary Barnes who frowned and held the phone a bit away from his ear. His face was ashen as he undoubtedly heard a harsh reprimand about his inept handling of security. Or his failure to keep the Princess of Wales at bay. The palace thought of her as a spoiled brat who grew into an unpredictable manipulator. They failed to view her as a mother with fierce instincts to protect her children. Possibly they had never met such a person.

Barnes clicked his phone and returned it to his briefcase before looking Elena's way, extending a curt nod. An oblivious Edward and Michael slowly entered the garden. Edward gestured magnificently as he spoke, and Michael held the recorder high, listening intently with regular nods. The two slowly approached Elena and the children. "Your husband has offered many insights into the difficulties of raising the children, Ma'am. I was hoping that you could contribute some comment as well?"

She smiled shyly, but shook her head firmly. "I'm sure my husband provided more than enough. All I can say is, despite our problems, I truly believe that both my husband and I put the interests of our children first. That's the priority for both of us. Wouldn't you agree, Sir?"

Edward managed a nod and Michael scribbled. Elena walked away, not bothering to comment on the rarity of agreement between a woman and man about how to best raise a child, let alone a woman and man who had difficult childhoods. Both Edward and Elena had lacked reasonable models. Edward followed his mother's formula, based on a belief that distance fostered respect. Elena deliberately designed her own path. Unfortunately, raising children was a strange art. A parent could never be certain of the outcomes.

Chapter 14

"The queen insisted on keeping the appointment with her."
"We can't lose control."

Elena liked the sound of her heels clicking against the marble floor as she approached the queen's private study. Not her usual flats, the shoes were soft, comfortable, trimmed with a diagonal ruffle. She enjoyed looking at the world from a full six feet of height.

Her appointment had been for eleven in the morning, and Elena was kept waiting in an adjoining room for seventeen minutes. "A meeting with the assistant to the prime minister," the nameless clerk confided and mumbled an apology. Elena smiled with radiant patience. More time to think would only benefit Elena.

A phone rang, and she was directed to the queen's study. Elena wore a simple beige linen dress and deliberately carried no purse. No papers. No letters from barristers. Derrick had worked hard on details of the settlement and Elena refused to start all over again.

A footman held the massive door open for her. Elena entered the room with its tired, old maroon and dark blue furnishings—expensive, ornate, but not elegant. In Elena's mind, such dreariness turned any glamorous or important work into drudgery. Elena sat in the chair where she had sat maybe a hundred times: From the very first time when she was seventeen and awed by the queen to the last time when the gray-haired woman granted grudging approval for the royal divorce.

A meeting in this room signaled work and not pleasure.

Elena herself had toyed with the divorce idea for months before approaching the queen. Her motivation had been hard to explain, but Elena still remembered the exact moment when she knew the divorce was necessary, after a formal dinner at the children's school and one of Edward's reprimands.

"You pay too much attention to Lawrence," he had murmured.

"I love both children," Elena protested. "I treat him no differently than I did Richard at that age."

Edward kept his voice even, logical: "We can never forget that Richard has special standing. He needs to expect deference from others, get comfortable with it. He won't learn if his mother treats him as an equal with other children."

She stared at her husband with horror. He was serious. "I love both my children and treat them equally. I will not be told how to dole out my love to them. You credit me with more self-control than is humanly possible, Edward."

He lowered his tone to a steady monotone. "If I don't see serious effort on your part to set an example and show more deference to Richard in public, you don't need to come on the trip to Japan with us next month. Japan is important to me. People expect royalty to behave like royalty."

She had not answered and didn't change her ways with the children. Needless to say, she didn't go to Japan. Instead, Elena agreed to a candid interview on American television, finally convincing the queen herself that divorce was the only way to end the public bickering.

The queen interrupted the bitter memory, entering the room and sitting at a desk, ridiculously small for her girth and for the amount of responsibility she claimed. The tiny desk, with delicate carving, was the sort for occasionally writing invitations and thank-you notes, not for negotiations or diplomacy of national import. Elena dipped low in a polite curtsy and returned to her seat only when so directed by the queen. A lady-in-waiting, an assistant secretary, and a clerk hovered about the far corners, failing to look busy or essential.

"Your Majesty, thank you for taking time out of a busy schedule to see me," Elena said.

Queen Catherine nodded abruptly and impatiently looked about the room and waved the staff away. She wore a suit in a busy pink pattern, too busy for her ample frame. Her silk blouse was without a wrinkle and neatly buttoned to her chin. The outfit was intended for a harmless grandmother, invited to a distant relative's wedding. The queen preferred that image of kindliness, wisdom, and stability, although her stern eyes and mouth, steely with self-discipline, did not mesh well with the image. "That was a foolish risk you took yesterday, Elena," the queen began. "Sneaking away with the children, not taking proper security precautions, and then disrupting the interview of the Prince of Wales."

"I hardly disrupted that interview!"

"Edward did not expect your company. You threatened to disrupt. Or we would not be meeting today."

"Your Majesty." Elena struggled to keep her voice more courteous than argumentative. "I hadn't seen my sons in weeks. A mother who doesn't care to spend time with her children reflects poorly on the entire family."

The queen frowned.

"And security is dreadful. Staff heard about a nanny on the premises and sent the boys off to the cottage—without checking! I'm as alarmed as you are. Most of the staff care very little for those boys. They are more intent on keeping the boys away from me. I merely exposed the charade that staff calls protection."

Queen Catherine paused for a long time and tapped her pen. "I share some of these concerns," she conceded at last. "Staff has no explanation about why they didn't detect your presence. And the boys both have sent word that they miss you and feel very safe around you. Any specific lapses on the part of staff should be put in writing and filed with my security chief."

"Yes, Ma'am." Elena was surprised about the agreeable tone.

"You are in an awkward spot, dear," Catherine said. The voice was sympathetic, but her gray eyes were not. "Each member of staff is selected and trained for loyalty—unquestionable loyalty to the crown. Most perform remarkably well at putting personal feelings aside. However, resentment and difficulties emerge when they sense disloyalty among those whom they're expected to serve."

"I have worked hard for the crown and I love my children. I may question some traditions, but only to protect the happiness of two little boys. Does that make me disloyal?"

Catherine stood and went to the window, examining gardens surrounded by hedges that were trimmed to perfection. Elena was relieved to have a break from staring into the woman's intense eyes. "What else do you call divorce from the Prince of Wales?"

Elena let out air, forced her voice to stay low and calm. "He wanted it more than I. He loves Kay. You knew she was his mistress, even before our marriage."

Catherine turned and waved her hand at the troublesome detail. "A divorce won't necessarily lead to marriage for them." She returned to her seat. "You have your ways with the press. You could have worked on eliminating his foolish attraction for her somehow. Or, you could have been content. Designed a quiet and suitable role for yourself—and out-waited Kay. But you didn't even try."

"You expected me to stay quiet during his blatant affair, while he treated me as a . . . possession. So I did carve out a new role—trying to focus on charity work. And some became annoyed and jealous when the media expressed appreciation. You suggest that I could have made him happy by staying completely quiet, showing no feelings, fading into oblivion like the palace staff!"

Catherine lifted her hand to her throat. "Staff works to maintain a protocol for us all. Observing and accepting their advice would not have been the worst tack. A dedicated servant who maintains objectivity often knows what's best for our children and families."

"I don't agree," Elena said. "I feel like I can't do anything right—whether I'm quiet or outspoken, whether I stay at home or I'm active with charities. In the beginning, I listened to every bit of advice. Did you ever consider that someone fostered Edward's discontent for me? I could not go on trying to capitulate to whims and failing to please over and over. Living a lie and ignoring the children's emotional needs would only make matters worse." Elena tilted her chin with pride. "At least the children began their lives with some normality. My God, the staff would have never allowed those two children to play or get dirty."

"Those two need to prepare for responsibility."

"If they don't play now, they'll play later," Elena retorted. "Look at your own children."

Catherine's face went pale, her eyes like jagged points of dark glass. "How dare you judge my children—and connect their problems to my ability as a mother. Edward is a good man, twisted by an ungrateful society that refuses to respect convention, history, and yes, loyalty. Don't you dare pass comment about my children."

"Forgive me," Elena said quickly. "Of course, Edward's a good man. But he's unhappy and he's still hungry for a purpose."

"Bah, happiness, purpose. You two would not recognize happiness if you fell into a pool of it. But then, you're products of your world. The Americans started all this nonsense with their pursuit of happiness. A pointless pursuit at that! The citizens of this country once settled for comfort, satisfying questions of curiosity—in the world and in their homes. Once, I thought I could do my part to influence the world. Now, I can't even influence my own family." Catherine sighed, looking tired and old. "You know, I'd give anything to have kept you two together—anything."

"I appreciate that, Ma'am," Elena said with sincerity. But inside, she knew the divorce was for the best. Edward had ignored her and the children throughout the marriage, and now the targets of his attention no longer mattered. "The boys know that they're loved and valued. They don't have to go through life wondering why their parents live together, but share no love."

"You both could have done a better job of pretending." Catherine shook her head sadly. "What an odd world. Emotional attachments and needs—if not subdued and forgotten, they ruin a leader."

Elena studied her mother-in-law. The two women were amateur philosophers who would never agree, who had neither the time nor ability to collect the massive amount of evidence needed to convince the other. "I could better harness my own emotions," Elena admitted. "But denying feelings denies the truth."

The queen shrugged and unlocked a desk drawer. "Here are the papers that your barrister's team presented. They're in order. It's still hard to believe you did not struggle more to remain a part of this family."

"I love the family as people. Edward preferred another woman, wanting what the family said he could not have. I put up with that for years. How much better it might have been if you had permitted him to marry as he pleased."

"I urged him to be responsible, discreet."

"But even you couldn't force him to stop!" Elena said, with disappointment.

"We could have worked together," Catherine said. "We could still try."

Elena shuddered inside; how could she possibly explain to a man's mother that the love had vanished. "It's too late. We argue too much about activities, about public behavior, about how to handle the children." She didn't mention to Edward's mother that she shuddered at the thought of his touch.

"But you haven't been with any other men. At parties, you insist on carrying out protocol from the old days—dancing with men who are happily married, refusing to be alone with men who are single."

"Perhaps I dread the gossip."

"Or you still love your husband."

Elena pursed her lips and shook her head.

"I have not signed these papers yet. My solicitors tell me that they want to make changes."

"But we reached an agreement," Elena said.

"I'm on your side, dear," Catherine agreed. "I don't believe Edward deserves more power over the children than you. He needs your help."

"Go on . . ." Elena sat up straight.

"One minor change suggested by my solicitors would clarify the crown's control. You and Edward could share visitation. I don't fool myself that Edward will take advantage of many visits. But I have the final word on important decisions for the boys.

That prevents the bickering between the two of you."

"You don't trust either of us!"

"I trust you, dear, more than you think. Women are better with children. But the boys deserve stability in their lives. You and Edward have input, but no final say on the boys' schools or activities."

"I can't accept that," Elena said, her hands shaking. "If you suddenly died, God forbid, Edward would have complete control. And he doesn't know how to recognize or stand up to people who want to use him! You know that. That's why you and I were once close."

"I have no intention of dying, my dear."

"Neither do I," Elena exclaimed. "But someone put a bomb in my car. We can't stop tragic events. I can't sign this. We went through weeks of negotiations, and my solicitor drafted a fair agreement. Please, Queen Catherine, try to understand. I don't want to make all the decisions, and I don't plan to argue with you and Edward. But I think the boys should have freedom to make some choices on their own."

Catherine gazed out the window at her garden. "You insist that I went wrong with Edward and Caroline, but I did my best under the circumstances. If anything, I did not discipline and restrain them enough."

"I'll fight this in court." Elena found it hard to control her anger.

"There's another way," Catherine kept her voice soft.

Elena waited, too agitated to speak. She had to find another solicitor. The palace would never stop playing games with her unless forced to do so by a public court of law.

"You and I want what's best for those two boys, no? More than anyone else."

Tears burned her eyes. Elena could only nod.

The queen's mouth tightened. "And there was no other

reason for divorce other than Edward's inappropriate behavior, no?"

Elena paused and nodded slowly again.

"You're not in a relationship. No career. I know those children are the center of your life, and I admire that. Do you remember the excitement that went through this country when you two got married? The only event that came close during my lifetime was the end of World War II. For the sake of the children and the crown, you two could try to work your problems out— quietly, without interference from the palace staff and family or from the press."

Elena leaned her head into her hand, covered her eyes. The queen was right. She had nothing in her life other than her children. Her charitable work took a distant second.

"Long ago, marriages were arranged. Did you know that those marriages work out better than matches based on love? Edward doesn't realize it, but you and I do. A person can make a marriage work with just about anyone—especially with the father of her children. For the sake of her children."

Elena took a deep breath.

"What do you say?" the queen pressed. "Will you try?"

Elena spoke haltingly. "If I do what you ask, and Edward refuses, then would you please sign Derrick's version of the agreement?"

"Of course," the queen said. "You have my promise."

This was insanity, Elena thought to herself. But cooperating with the queen would allow the settlement to proceed far more smoothly than any court action. Derrick had always told her that.

"Good, it's settled," the queen concluded, with her brisk imitation of happiness. "I will speak to Edward and impose conditions. Let's give him time to get used to the alliance between you and me. Then the two of you can meet for a quiet and private dinner. I'll make the arrangements. It will be neutral territory, a quiet inn in Dover that's always been a favorite of mine."

CHAPTER 15

"Disaster has struck."
"We need incriminating photos."

"Look outside, will you?" Larry said, pressing his cheek against the old window. "Perfect day for the park, and we're missing it."

"You're not missing the day. Only the park." Richard spoke up from the book he was reading.

"Same thing," Larry retorted.

"Boys," Elena cautioned as she stepped into the center of the room. "We have only today and tomorrow together. I don't want to spend the time settling arguments between the two of you."

"Mum, please, I want to go to the park today. I was reading one of the papers last week . . ."

"You?" Elena asked. "Why do you read the papers?"

Larry shrugged. "I enjoy them. The staff selects articles for Richard, but I read more than he does."

"Newspapers are trash." Richard dipped his head lower into the book. Elena pretended to adjust a figurine on the tea table to catch a glimpse of the title—*The Escape and Adventures of Charles II.*

"He reads a chapter or two in the beginning and some more at the end and then pretends to know what's in the middle. Admit it, Richard, those old history books are boring."

"Not so," said Richard, remaining aloof.

"It's wonderful that he reads any history," Elena defended her older son. "Did your father give you the book?" Her children were growing in so many ways without her. Inside the palace, she felt like a trapped moth, fluttering against walls in a useless attempt to escape.

"No," he said, pulling the leather-bound volume closer to his face. "I borrowed it from his library."

"That library has some ancient books that are not meant for borrowing," she said. "You should have asked."

"Books are meant for reading, not collections. Don't worry, I'll return it next weekend. He'll never notice."

"If we go next weekend!" Larry interrupted.

"Why, of course you'll see him," Elena said. "What do you mean?"

Richard furrowed his brow, a warning signal meant to hush his younger brother.

Elena faced both boys. "Did your father cancel next weekend?"

"Big mouth," Richard muttered under his breath.

"Who knows?" Larry said, with a shrug. "He promised to take us to Pepperell last weekend. But then he canceled. A diplomatic matter, he said. So, I wasn't sure if he'd take us this week or not."

"You should have called me," Elena protested. "Where did you go?" Richard explained that he spent the weekend with a friend and Larry stayed at school. Elena took a breath and thought a moment, making effort at a reasonable tone of voice. "I was home. Why didn't you come here?"

Larry waited pointedly for his older brother to answer. But Richard kept reading and after a few moments, the small boy's voice chirped: "Don't blame us! Derry said Dad asked us not to call. Said it was good for us to spend time alone, without you or him!"

"Derry is not your parent," Elena chided. "You should have called me." The two looked at each other with guilt.

"Derry claims that Richard should tell you what to do and not the other way around," Larry explained. Richard poked his brother with his elbow. "Stop causing trouble," he muttered.

"Really?" Elena couldn't say more or it would turn into a tirade.

"Derry teases, Mum," Richard insisted. "We try to follow directions from you, Father and Derry, but it's hard when everyone wants us to do something different."

"When we make mistakes, they end up in the newspaper," Larry said glumly. "Like when I left the palace and the car exploded."

"The explosion had nothing to do with your behavior, Larry," Elena said, with impatience. "Whoever gave you such an idea?"

"Grandmum," he replied. "She was furious with me and still scolds me about it in her notes."

"She was worried, Larry," Richard inserted. "She told us that our behavior is watched by children around the world."

"Every—what was that word she used?" Larry continued.

"Antic," Richard replied, pointing to his brother.

"Yes, every antic of our family."

Elena wanted to smash a vase or shake her sons. But she couldn't touch the real target of her anger, the queen, for misleading the children so. She took a deep breath. "None of us are as important as Grandmum makes us out to be," Elena said. "Every child is responsible for his or her own actions, nothing more. And that includes you two." She knelt before them and gathered them into her arms. "Don't be afraid to talk to me. You could have E-mailed."

"We did!" Larry protested.

"But I thought you were with your father, and you could have told me more about what was going on. It's not as if I make scenes and drag you away from places where you want to be, now do I?" She cocked her head.

The boys giggled. "I suppose not," Richard said.

"We were afraid you'd get mad at Dad—and it would hit the newspapers," Larry added. "That gets Grandmum very upset."

"No," Elena said firmly. "We won't let that happen. And about another matter—our behavior: Grandmum is correct that good behavior is essential from you two. That includes courtesy, consideration, dignity and honesty. But she's wrong about the reason. Your behavior is not for anybody else. It's for . . ." She touched each boy on the nose. "You and you."

"Enough!" she said, standing. "Off to the park! Richard, bring your book if you like and you can read under a great old tree. Larry, bring something you can play with on your own, so you don't pester your brother." Larry returned with his largest and bounciest ball and a book on insects.

Not long afterward, the threesome entered the park gates, followed by three guards who argued among themselves.

"We're here!" Elena announced breezily. But Richard's guard stepped forward, asking the group to pause a moment. Elena rolled her eyes at her own guard, Walter, but knew that Jonathan Giller, Richard's man, was technically in charge.

Giller scanned the area. "The boys should stick to this clearing," he ordered. Giller explained how he would monitor the clearing, Larry's man could stay at the entrance gate and Walter could take the opposite side, with the men dividing the area to keep watch for any suspicious passersby.

"All right, we're set," Giller announced. The two boys took off running in separate directions. Richard found a large tree, and spread out with his book. Larry kicked his ball wildly across the field.

Walter was annoyed, and Elena reached for his arm and shook

her head. "Let it go," she whispered. "The boys need to play, and if you three start fighting, we'll have to leave the park . . ."

"Call me if there's any problem, Ma'am," Walter urged, before walking away.

Giller lingered a moment to answer some questions from Larry's guard, and as Elena passed she heard the man swear. "Bloody ridiculous, coming to the park," Giller murmured to his colleague. "For selfish reasons at that."

Royalty was expected to ignore guards and leave them to their duties, but Elena whipped about and faced the man. "Ridiculous? Boys in the park? I think not!"

"Excuse me, Lady Elena. But this area is too open and unsecured. Typically, we need a week to . . ."

"Oh, spare me. Nobody has plans to hurt the boys here."

"The palace has plenty of beautiful grounds. We have orders . . ."

"Why must you make our lives so complicated? Look, will you? Larry is bouncing a ball. He'll settle in a few moments. And Richard's under a tree. These children need a normal life more than anything else."

"Thank you, Ma'am. But I insist that if anything odd happens, we'll leave the park immediately." Giller turned his back to Elena, lifted his radio and began whispering orders.

Elena shook her head and headed for the line of manicured trees. Richard leaned against the largest of the trees, already absorbed in his tale. A child with a book was always a picture of contentment. She wanted to go near him, hug him, but that would be selfish. More often than not, it was best to enjoy children from afar, especially as they grew older and became teenagers, and wait for their approach. She found a grassy place for herself under a tree, arranged a blanket, and sat down. Only Giller was in sight and he focused on Larry, who darted back and forth, kicking his ball in what looked like an imaginary game of soccer.

She leaned back and stared up at the canopy overhead, the green leaves like sparkling emeralds against the sun-drenched sky. She tried to remember the last time she lazed about in a park. Too long ago . . .

A hand touched her shoulder, and she jumped as she twisted her head around in quick surprise.

Doctor Kevin Tilton leaned against the tree and smiled dreamily at her.

"Oh, it's only you," Elena said. "You startled me!"

"Only?" he asked, as if disappointed.

"The security men talk as if IRA terrorists lurk behind every tree," she said, leaning back again. "I thought you were supposed to leave the country weeks ago!"

"I left and came back. London intrigues me."

"Hmm, so historic and modern, a constant clash between the two," Elena said.

He stretched out beside her, close as he could without touching. "Perhaps I lie. It's not a city I love, but a woman . . ."

"Hmm, does she love you?" She watched Larry bounce his ball close to Richard, trying to get his older brother to play. She wanted to call out, but decided to let Richard handle the matter. Richard frowned, but he put his book to the side and gave the ball a tap. Larry smiled happily and returned the ball with a wild fling. Richard made a point of returning full attention to the book.

She gave the anthropologist a quick glance and turned to watch the boys. "I don't think she knows or cares," he pressed. Propping himself with his left elbow, he leaned over her, forcing her to stare into his eyes.

Elena caught her breath and backed away from him. "Why, I hope you don't mean me?"

He didn't say anything but moved his right hand across her

stomach. She moved to back off, but the tree was in her way. "We don't know each other at all," she reminded him.

"You are sensible, graceful, kind. What more is there to know?"

She noticed he did not mention beautiful. "And I'm a mother of two boys. Please!" Where were the guards when she needed them? She didn't want to make a big fuss though, giving Giller reason to make the group leave.

"And you're divorced . . ." He moved slowly as he leaned over to kiss her.

"That doesn't mean . . ." she gasped and angrily pushed him.

"Shh," Tilton covered her mouth with his hand. "Not another word. Your marriage is over and nothing else matters. You should go on with your life."

The large green ball bounced wildly into the stand of trees, surprising Tilton. Elena stood and scrambled away, taking a defensive stance, ready to run or strike. Tilton shook his head and sighed. "Children . . . remember that I love you and don't want to wait long." He jumped to his feet and walked toward the trees and out of sight. Elena brushed off her blouse and combed her fingers quickly through her short curls. Bits of grass and twigs flew off. Larry came out from behind a tree.

"I didn't like that man," the boy said, giving his mother a hug. "Are you angry that I chased him away?"

"Not at all," Elena said. "You came to my rescue." She reached for the ball, tossed it to him and told him to play some more while she went to find Giller. The guard leaned against a tree, not far from Richard, and had just lit a cigarette.

"Where have you been?" Elena snapped. "Why aren't you doing your job?"

"What do you mean?" Giller looked amazed. He stood upright but did not discard the cigarette. "We're doing our job! Properly, I might add!"

"Then why didn't you stop that man from bothering me? Dr. Tilton!"

"But he's on the clearance list for the palace." Giller looked sheepish, then challenging. "You have spoken with him before, haven't you?"

"Yes, but . . ."

"We were advised that you had arranged to meet him." The guard's tone bordered on snideness.

"I certainly did not arrange to meet him!" Elena said hotly.

"So, Lady Elena, do you want us to chase him down? Call authorities?"

"And make a scene in a public park?" she retorted. "Attract the news reporters? Certainly not. I just wish that you'd been closer." She crossed her arms and looked around. "He startled me, that's all."

Giller nodded, but looked puzzled. "Our apologies, Ma'am. We misunderstood and tried not to interfere." He dipped his head low, but not before she saw the smile on his face, as if they shared some naughty secret. She felt a shiver go through her, fearful of people making assumptions about what she really wanted. So often they were wrong! She shook with fury and ran to find the children. Walter and the other guard had reconvened on a nearby hillside that overlooked the grounds and were laughing. Did they laugh about her? Did they assume she was having an affair with Tilton?

The children were not far away, sitting quietly together.

"Boys, we should leave the park now." She kept her voice calm.

"No, Mummy, no," Larry pleaded. "We only just got here, and Richard just agreed to play ball with me. You can play too!"

"This ball is ridiculous but fun," Richard added.

Elena wanted to run away from the park, and go to the one place where she could shut the door and not see security. Her bedroom. But that would make them laugh more. Make them think they were right and she was wrong about bringing her children to play in the park. Damn them. Damn them all! If she left suddenly, that would confirm their suspicions that she had only come to the park to meet the mysterious Tilton—and they were wrong!

She started to run down the hill and stretched out her hands. "All right," she called out. "Toss that ball my way." Larry gave it a toss and she punched it back hard in return. Both boys merrily gave chase, and she studiously avoided the stares from the security guards.

CHAPTER 16

"How did the photos turn out?"
"We didn't have enough time. She looked annoyed."
"Is she clever or lucky?"

Elena smoothed out the sleek black jersey of her simple dress, sleeveless with a scalloped neckline and a full skirt, as the maitre d' seated her at a table in the small private room overlooking the harbor and channel lights. The table was set with pastel linens and gold-rimmed crystal that sparkled in the candlelight. The room was dark enough that she could see the shapes of fishing boats lined along the docks in twilight, dark enough that she could not see the expression in her husband's eyes.

"Such a lovely inn," she said, looking out over the dark water. Unlike her mother-in-law, Elena had no agenda for the night and preferred that her husband set the course on conversation. She was too weary to do more than listen and react. She no longer wanted much from the family, other than time with her children.

"It is," he agreed. "My mother has good taste and knows this country better than anyone. Too many people make the mistake of thinking that the family does not know how to enjoy life." Fishing vessels rocking back and forth with the waves were hypnotic. "My parents celebrated their anniversary here for years. I never knew."

"She manages to protect her privacy," Elena said, with envy.

"And she wishes we'd do the same," Edward countered.

"You act as if I enjoy the press." Elena tried not to argue. "What would you have me do?"

He spoke without hesitation. "Dress differently. Look more like a mother and a wife than a supermodel."

"Oh, Edward," Elena said, shaking her head. "Look at me. I'm wearing a simple dress. My hair is short and easy to take care of. When I do wear makeup, it's very little. No one ever thought of me as pretty when I was a little girl. I like the clothes, and the designers want me to like their clothes. What's the harm? Do you want me to look frumpy? Would that have really made the difference?" She stopped short as a waiter entered the room with several bottles of wine. Edward chose a merlot, a favorite of hers, and waited silently while the waiter opened the bottle and provided a taste. Edward nodded without looking at the man.

"I don't know," Edward said, with mild irritation, after the waiter left. "My mother specifically asked that we not complain or argue. That's not the reason why we came together tonight. But I must admit that it's difficult being your husband."

Elena was hurt. "Not the private me. Maybe the woman in the press. But that's not me. I can't control the attention."

"My mother manages."

"Tell me how I've been unreasonable," Elena insisted, but Edward didn't reply. "Don't you remember how much fun we had in the beginning? But I was supposed to act like a pet or a little sister. You tired of me and then you got jealous."

"I'm not jealous," he hissed. "But the people no longer take the family seriously."

"Because we're human? Because we make mistakes or want to make our own choices now and then? That's what most of our bickering is about—do you think we could possibly ever stop?"

"It's what Mother wants," Edward said despondently.

"Everyone can't get what they want all the time. Do you know what you want, Edward? If you want to be free, I understand."

"To marry Kay? I'm not sure I love her, but she understands me more than anyone. I loved her once, but . . ." He paused. "We're older now."

"If I had only known," Elena said. "I'd have stayed away."

"Do you honestly think that you could have said no?" His voice was kind, genuinely curious.

"Maybe not." Elena smiled at her own honest answer. "The prospect of being princess dazzled me as a teenager. And I always thought I could change you."

The waiter entered, carrying bread and a platter with an array of cheeses from around the country. Then he left the room again and closed the door.

"Mother wants us to reconcile and consider remarriage." Edward refused to look at Elena and stared intently out the window. "She's prepared to relinquish the crown immediately if we remarry."

"So, she had to dangle a prize," Elena said, almost to herself. "Do you really think being king will make your life better?"

"I'd have more control."

"Edward, Edward," Elena was gentle. "It won't work if that's all that you want. I want a real marriage with love. You could have real control now, if . . ."

"Don't tell me what to do," he said with contempt. "Our marriage was a farce. You're not the woman I married. I thought you could be quiet, deferential, someone who could raise our children in the royal tradition. I was misled."

"Never by me," Elena insisted. "Maybe I've changed some. I've grown older. I want to help others, but I also want my privacy. I want our children to be happy. And I worry if we get back together, then we will argue and cause them more pain."

Edward stared at her. "Are you playing a game? My mother assumes that you want to be queen more than anything else."

Elena shook her head, but kept a smile. "Sorry, Edward. You have known me for such a long time, and you still assume that I want what you want. And that's not how it is . . . I can't be queen the way your mother is queen. If anything, I'd step back from the role, try to live a more normal life."

"How do you expect me to believe that?" Edward exclaimed. "The way the press tracks you about!"

"I could try."

"Yes, you could," he said. "You don't have to worry yet. You can't be queen unless we agree to restore the marriage. She told me that she refused to step down unless I'm married to you! She promised that if we complied with her wishes—reconciling, making public appearances together as a family, behaving with absolute decorum, the whole blooming mess—that she would give up the throne and allow us to take over."

Elena shrugged. "It's what you always wanted."

Edward leaned forward. "No, you and my mother have always been wrong about me. I don't want to be king. I want respect. As a man and for my ideas. And I'm not sure that's possible if I agree to a reconciliation."

"Why?" Elena questioned.

"With you at my side, I'm always the second wheel. Maybe in some small way I do envy you. You captivated the world. Ordinary girl becomes princess. Your beauty and virtues should be a matter of course. Instead, they were regarded as extraordinary by today's shallow rules. I used to think the same might have happened for Kay . . ."

Elena tried to hide her smile by looking out the window.

"I often wonder," Edward pondered, "what would have become of you if you had not married me."

"I've often wondered myself," Elena said. "I probably would have married some businessman and been obscure and happy. No. The mad rush of the public remains a mystery to me. It makes me uncertain about what I really want. All that attention complicates our life."

He nodded.

"I wish your mother had allowed us to work this out without the bribe. At least you're up-front. She didn't mention anything about the throne to me—only that she'd agree to the terms of the divorce if I tried."

"Everyone is surprised that you didn't just walk away from the children." Edward poured more wine, and Elena carved some thin slices from the Scottish cheddar, the Stilton and the Yorkshire blue.

"Who is everyone? The staff?" she asked. "They want to raise them the way the royal family has always been raised—parents and friends kept at a distance. I can't agree with that. The upbringing, leaving it up to the staff, is why everyone in your family is so dissatisfied. But why are these strangers so intent on raising our children? Don't you every wonder about that?"

"I suppose they assume they can do it better," Edward replied. "Believe me, I'm much kinder to my children than my father ever was to me."

"I realize that. But there's so much to life, Edward. We're so shielded, and I simply want the boys to have real choices. They'll be stronger and happier if they make their own choices and mistakes. It would be so much more fulfilling for them. People learn more by mistakes than they do by constant success." She dropped her voice to a whisper as the waiter opened the door, escorting two other men bearing platters.

"But some mistakes can't be tolerated," Edward snapped in irritation. "The boys do not have time for silly behavior, for jokes, for associating with the wrong people. They don't have choices." Pretending not to hear, the servers briskly arranged the plates, as if the positions could not be too exact. One man asked Edward about more wine. Edward shook his head, without consulting Elena, and the man served a cauliflower soup, topped with toasted almonds.

Elena blushed. She could never get over his habit of speaking so personally in front of strangers, especially about the children. Edward refused to believe that other people were equal to himself, that they might not accept different standards for royalty. Too often the people who worked around royalty found some way to profit from the idle comments.

But that was an old and endless argument for the couple. So, she picked up her fork. The dinner was superb—filet mignon, large scallops with just a touch of cream and white port, and grilled exotic vegetables. Edward ate rapidly, as if to put the conversation behind him. Elena stubbornly waited for her husband to choose a subject and resume. But he did not speak. So they ate dinner silently, and the waiters cleared the plates and brought tea. Elena ordered a pear tart with almond crust, and Edward asked for a vintage port. When they were alone again, Elena spoke with impatience: "Neither of us has any idea what we want. From the queen or from each other."

Edward stared off toward the water. "I suppose that I want both the throne and the freedom to enjoy Kay's company. I'm comfortable with her like no one else."

"I'm happy for you, Edward. I hope that I can meet someone and feel that way again someday. In the meantime, it's hard for me to fit in with this family."

He shrugged. "Then continue doing what you do best—travel around the world. High-profile charity and good deeds. Glamour and publicity. While it lasts."

"What's that supposed to mean?" she snapped.

"Common sense, my dear," he said. "Mother believes that as

you grow older and your beauty fades, your influence will diminish. Perhaps that's why she waits to walk away from the responsibility. Less distractions for all of us."

Elena clenched her teeth and controlled the volume, if not the tone, of her voice. "And what about our children? I refuse to abandon them. They're my priority."

"The boys need consistency. We can't pass them back and forth. Staff keep pointing out the problems. While you travel as an ambassador of good deeds throughout the world, they can attend school and spend holidays with us. They can benefit from my good example. And Kay provides feminine encouragement in all suitable areas. We can all go on with our lives and get along. Perhaps you'll fall in love again, start another family, forget about us . . ."

"No!" Elena cried out. At the same time she pushed her chair back away from the table, more powerfully than she intended, and a crystal glass shattered to the floor. "No." She was firm, as she stepped way from the table. "Forgetting is not that easy for me."

Walter came to the doorway, followed by Edward's guard. Elena pushed past them. "I need some air now!"

Walter stepped aside as she headed for the nearest doorway into the hallway. Elena got confused about which direction to take, then saw stairs and raced down to an unfinished cellar of ancient stone. Finding a door to the outside, she pushed hard into the cool night air. Her flat shoes, made of leather as thin as satin, did not take well to the uneven path along the shore.

Elena breathed the salty air and walked away from the inn, down a grassy hill and toward rickety wood stairs that led to the dock. She sat on the bottom step and leaned her head against the post.

There was no choice, no winning, when it came to being part of the royal family. The family was skilled in using their children as a weapon, and Elena was not. She could not decide how she wielded the most power—married to Edward or not. A curse suddenly broke through the quiet noises of the night: "Damn the woman, where is she?"

"She's not out here!" another man shouted.

"Could she have left in a car?" the first shouted.

"We would have heard!" Walter retorted. "Give her a minute alone, for God's sake."

"Damn it all, find her!" came another harsh whisper. "Without getting a bunch of reporters down our backs."

Elena remained quiet, put her hand to her mouth and giggled softly about security. She evaded them without even trying, simply by not following formula. Surely, she deserved a few moments of peace now and then. How much did the security detail overhear and report of the dinner conversation? For all she knew, the room had been wired, and the queen already knew about Edward and Elena's inability to agree. Who would the queen blame for the impasse?

No moon was out and the night air was soft, velvety with light fog. Elena heard footsteps in the gravel not far away. She dipped her head and wrapped her arms around her knees, hoping to escape the inevitable scolding from security for a few more minutes.

"Elena, is that you?" Edward's voice was concerned. "Are you all right?"

She kept her voice friendly. "It's a wonder what a few moments alone can do. Yes, I'm fine. There's so much for us to think about."

"It's something you don't have to do. It makes you worry too much."

She didn't answer. How could he stand the agony of not thinking through his own matters, big or small?

"You dart about and elude security, making the whole job

more tedious."

She wished that he understood. "Security, the snappers, they make us out to be much more important than we really are, Edward. Out here, in the night, we're two people. No different from anyone else and I love how that feels . . ." Tiny cool raindrops touched her arm. She lifted her face, and wished for more.

"Elena, you're tired. It's starting to rain. Let's just tell Mother that we're considering her request. That we need more time."

"Lord, don't you realize she already knows? These security men—they all work for her. She cares more about the monarchy than about any of us—and that includes her own self. Your family has sacrificed too much."

Edward gave a short laugh. "I accused her of that once long ago, when I was in college. She agreed and said that sacrifice made her a less selfish person. We must sacrifice our individual goals."

"The logic is twisted," Elena said. "Children have more potential with choices. I can't do to my children what she did to you."

Edward sighed. "It's too late, Elena, to talk about this."

She stood. "Yes, indeed, a long night for us both. I'm sorry, Edward, that I didn't know what I was getting into with our marriage." She reached out for his hand and he pulled her up. "You tried to explain, but I don't think that's possible." She could not be annoyed with Edward. At least they spoke about feelings, and that's why the divorce had been amicable for the two of them, if not the family and the palace staff. Edward put his hand on her shoulder, and they slowly climbed the stairs away from the dock and black water.

A security man in a dark coat waited near the royal limousine. Another waited at the end of the circular drive that led to the inn. Elena yearned for a few more moments of freedom to talk without prying ears. She was not ready to return to the world of hectic self-importance. Even Edward paused.

Elena pointed to a path that wound behind the inn. "Let's just glance at the gardens," she whispered.

"But you won't see anything at this time of night," he protested. "And this rain is cold."

"I can't resist flowers, day or night." She tossed her head and headed that way. Elena guessed that her husband wanted to return home, crawl into his bed and read. But he had little choice but to follow her. The couple had arrived at the inn in one car, which waited near the front. The queen had left instructions—the car was not to leave without both of them. Elena wanted to linger. Alone, unwatched in the garden, they were two people who could talk and plan.

She didn't know the names of the flowers, but some white ones glowed like petite ghosts and beckoned her. She bent to touch the petals.

Edward slowly followed her through the garden that wrapped around the inn. Large drops fell, but he didn't talk or hurry her. Elena wondered if the silence was due to patience or inability to think of something to say.

Suddenly, the front door to the inn opened, jarring the silence of the night. One of the palace security men hurried out, talking over his radio. The owner of the inn followed, and then came a couple, huddled together underneath an umbrella. Both were tall, and both bent their heads against the rain.

Elena could hear the woman complaining, mixed with the sound of a moving car on the wet drive. "Of all the nights to come here," the woman fretted. "It was most inconvenient . . ."

Suddenly, shots rang out from a small patch of trees not far from the parking area. Elena wanted to run, but Edward grabbed her with both arms and pulled her low. "Don't move," he whispered. "Damn, we have no cover."

Men started shouting and running—all toward the front of the inn. The umbrella rolled down the stairs, and the woman who had been complaining looked puzzled—holding her hand up to shield her face from the cool rain. Meanwhile, her companion fell to his knees, looking about in horror. Then, another shot fired. The woman toppled down the stairs.

"Get off the path," Edward ordered with a whisper, as he rolled her into the flower bed. Wet, muddy, the two took refuge between a short stone wall and some of the taller plants. "Snipers."

Elena pressed close to him, staring at the steps of the inn. "Shouldn't we . . ."

Edward shook his head and put a finger to her mouth.

Shouts came from all directions of the parking area and alarms sounded. With guns drawn, one palace guard gave first-aid to the couple down and also radioed for an ambulance. Another man stood guard near the limousine sent by the queen. The owner of the inn, clearly distraught, tried to help the two fallen guests. Other men, including Walter, ran for the patch of woods, from where the shots had come.

Elena rose on one elbow to get a glimpse and Edward pushed her down again. "Who were those people on the stairs?" Elena asked.

"Ordinary people," Edward said dryly. "I fear they had the misfortune of being mistaken for you and me."

"But why?" she gasped.

"We'll stay quiet and wait here until more police come and the area's secured." He lifted his head and looked about. No one had spotted the prince and princess. Then he looked down at his ex-wife in exasperation. "Damn, Elena, why did you storm out of the restaurant like that? Did you know something was going to happen? Is this commotion because of you?"

"You're blaming me?" she snapped. "Had we walked out in

the typical parade, either of us could be dead right now." She pushed his arm away and stood on feet that ached with cold. Her dress stuck to her legs and she tried to smooth it back into place before heading directly for the commotion on the inn's front steps. Workers from the inn and palace security scurried about. The woman was motionless, sprawled at the bottom of the stairs, blood dripping down her neck. Her dark eyes were wide open and her face was gray under the torches. Her velvet hood had tumbled back, showing a brown bob, newly cut and styled. Nearby, her companion groaned.

Elena shivered, helpless, as a short woman wearing a violet suit pushed through the crowd. "I'm a doctor. Has anyone called an ambulance?" The men nodded and stepped aside, and the woman knelt on the ground to examine the shooting victims. She quickly turned her attention to the man. "You'll be all right," she said soothingly to the man. "Two bullets, one to the shoulder and one to the arm." She directed a waiter to find some clean towels, lots of towels, to slow the bleeding. The doctor didn't comment on the condition of the woman, who had taken one shot to the neck and another to the upper chest. "Why isn't an ambulance here?" the woman snapped. "Someone call again!"

Elena stood there shaking. "Why these two people?" she whispered. But no one was close enough to hear or answer her. Inside, she kept hoping that the shots had not been intended for her and Edward. She felt guilty standing around useless, looking on at wounded people who probably had been mistaken for them. Or maybe these people had problems, she thought. Maybe someone hated them over some grudge, an affair or debt. Elena stepped forward. "Can I help in any way?" she asked.

"Lady Elena!" One of Edward's security men angrily grabbed her shoulders. "Why are you standing out here?" he hissed. "Waiting for more shots? Or the cameras?" Infuriated at being treated like a fool, Elena shoved the man's arm away.

"Stop arguing," the doctor in violet ordered. "Where's that man with the towels? I do need help. Go gather some towels and hot water and get it here quickly!"

Elena ran into the inn and headed for the door that waiters had passed through. After two turns, she found the kitchen. The cooks quickly agreed to let her carry away a pot of hot water, kept on the stove for cooking pasta. She asked about some cloths, and they handed over a pile of dish towels and napkins, assuring her they were freshly laundered. As she hurried back to the inn's front entrance, some water sloshed down the front of her dress, but she ignored the stinging pain.

A waiter had started giving mouth-to-mouth resuscitation to the woman, while the doctor pressed on the woman's chest.

"Too late for her, I'm afraid," the doctor murmured to Elena, running her hands nervously through her tousled gray hair. "But the man might have a chance. If we can get him to a hospital."

"Who are they?" Elena asked again softly.

The doctor shook her head. "No idea. They sat a few tables away from me. It's my thirtieth wedding anniversary. They looked like they might have been here for the same reason. Not as many years." The doctor grimaced. She dampened some towels and asked another bystander to loosen the man's shirt. She gently cleaned around the wounds and then asked Elena to hold a towel in place.

"Press harder," the doctor directed.

"I found a cot!" one man shouted from the inn.

"We've done everything we can do here," the woman said. "All we can do now is make him as comfortable as possible." Her voice was weary, and she stood, asking the men from the inn to position the cot and lift the patient gently from the wet ground.

Some man's dress coat had been tossed to the side. Still holding the towel in place, Elena reached for the coat and tucked it under the man's head, for a pillow. Suddenly, a hand clutched her arm and pulled. "The car's waiting—we must leave at once!" Walter tugged at her, and Elena tried to jerk away.

"I have my orders," Walter insisted.

"Wait! She's helping me." The doctor glanced up and looked at Elena. "My God, it's you. I didn't realize. Are you hurt, too?"

Elena looked down. Her dress was splotched with mud, her stockings torn. She could only imagine what her face and hair looked like. But she shook her head and realized she had not felt so alive in months. "I'm fine," she promised, giving another tuck to the temporary pillow.

"Good," the woman said, glancing to the drive. "Thank you for getting the water. He might be okay—if the ambulance arrives soon. Perhaps it's best if your party leaves and clears the driveway."

"Now, Ma'am," Walter said. "The prince is waiting." Speechless, Elena allowed herself to be led away.

"Two civilians dead—God, everyone in security is in trouble now," Walter muttered, holding her arm tight and looking about the parking area. "Why did you run off like that? Did you see or hear something?"

"No!" Elena snapped with irritation. She should be grateful that he did not blame her for the shooting. He respected her intelligence more than most palace staff. She was upset that, because of her title, she could not help more at the scene. But she couldn't blame Walter for that. "Nothing happened. I wanted to get away from the table. Edward was talking about Kay and . . ." She waved her hand in disgust.

"Your sudden exit saved your life and your husband's life and perhaps mine as well, although I'm not sure the others agree."

"Who did this?" Elena asked, glancing back at the inn.

"Intelligence is looking into IRA splinter groups, says they've been making trouble lately."

She wondered if security wasn't just grasping at straws. She regretted ever reporting the one telephone warning. "What do you think?"

"No one cares what you or I think. I don't know who did this. But with the rain and confusion, I do believe that the couple was mistaken for you and Edward." Walter wiped his brow and continued. "I'll be lucky if I have this job tomorrow. My charge runs off and then some innocent couple gets shot! And if they know that I helped you by pointing out the exits before dinner . . ."

"That probably saved my life," she murmured. "But I won't say anything."

Walter was stiff. "Thank you."

"Let me ask you about something," Elena asked. "What happened last week in the park, when I was with the boys? Why did you go off and leave me with Giller?"

Walter looked surprised. "You yourself said you wanted some space with the boys."

"But how did Tilton get near me?" she pressed.

"Richard's guard said he was on an approved list for you and the boys."

"Walter, I only met him once. I'm worried about these lapses. It's as if strangers can come and go and loved ones are kept away. Don't you realize something's wrong?"

He hesitated and then nodded. "You're right, I've had the same feeling lately. But let's talk about this tomorrow—away from the others."

As they hurried down the drive, the limousine pulled up, the door opening before the vehicle even came to a complete stop. One of the security men lunged out and pulled her inside. Walter hopped in the front. "To the motorway," the guard shouted to the driver.

Elena turned and glanced back at the parking lot. An ambulance passed, its siren screaming. "But where's Edward? He was with me in the garden . . ."

"His men found another car and left immediately. You know it's against protocol to join a crowd after any sign of trouble. Your duty is to leave the scene."

"Those people were hurt. The woman's dead. I only wanted to help. They were mistaken for us."

"We're checking on it," the senior security man said smugly. "It's probably coincidence."

"Edward didn't think so. Neither do I. It's rare when the two of us agree about something."

"No more talking, please, Ma'am," he said shortly. "We have to concentrate on getting you back to Kirkington. Where it's secure." Walter started to make a comment, but the head guard coughed and stared pointedly out the window. The scolding was unofficial but real.

That night, Elena woke with a start and looked about her bedroom. All was quiet. She wanted to reach for the button by her night table. But her arms and chest felt heavy from fear. She was afraid to even breathe. Without turning her head, she studied the shadows along the walls and wished she could remember them like familiar knickknacks. The room looked and felt strange. Elena waited, wishing she had good reason to get up and walk out of the bedroom. Not long ago, she went to the nursery and checked the boys as babies. She had fought so hard to get the nursery located near her bedroom, and then had to argue with servants because she wandered in during the night.

Yet her fight was worth it. Otherwise, she would never have had the chance to see Larry smile in his sleep and Richard tighten his tiny fists to his chin. The memories were good. Now, the bedrooms were near but the boys were far. She took several deep breaths, and after what had to be at least ten minutes, she could relax. Still, she was certain that someone had been in the room. Turning her head ever so slightly toward the windows, she waited sleeplessly for the first pale hint of dawn.

Chapter 17

"So close, and yet, failure."

"She's unpredictable. That's why she must be stopped."

Soft morning light touched the room and revealed familiar patterns and shapes. Only then did Elena fall into a troubled sleep, not waking until after nine-thirty. She dressed quickly and headed for her computer.

She read her inbox. Richard spoke about using the computer for a research report on bats and echolocation. Larry added a quick note, with the permission of his brother, complaining that the other boys at school did not believe that he could someday bring dinosaurs back to life. Elena typed in a message to Richard, asking questions about his studies and suggesting that he try to E-mail some scientist via the internet and added a postscript for Larry—"The best scientists keep their important ideas a secret, particularly before they've done any experimenting. Try not to brag, and do start practicing now!"

She turned the computer off, called for her breakfast and sat in an armchair and waited for the palace to summon her to discuss security, ask questions, and determine blame. Without doubt, Elena would be a target.

The bagel with cream cheese, surrounded by six perfect blackberries, on translucent coral porcelain arrived on an ancient tray of etched silver and glass. She ate slowly and still the palace did not call. Elena went to pour tea when she found the small envelope, sealed but unaddressed. Elena tore the note open and read: "Sorry to hear about last night's horrible accident. It is up to every member of the family to take more precautions. MI5 will consult. You relax and take care. And thank you for trying. Sincerely, Catherine."

The note seemed simple enough, polite and innocent. But Elena sensed its real message. No one cared what she thought about the previous night. They would utterly ignore her opinions about the attack. And, what did Catherine mean by trying? Did she expect a decision, a change of heart, after only one night? Elena picked up her telephone and asked for Walter. A strange voice replied at the security station: "He's been reassigned."

"Last night was not his fault," Elena protested.

"A routine shakeup," the man at the security desk explained.

"Both my husband and I could have been killed if not for him . . ."

"I understand, Ma'am." The man was trained to be polite but follow his orders as neatly as a circus poodle.

"How can I get a message to him?" Elena changed tack. "I left some of my belongings in his safekeeping."

"I apologize, Your Royal Highness. I'm not authorized to say. Security reasons." His voice sounded bland, young, and honest. He probably did not know Walter's whereabouts. "Can someone else be of assistance?"

"No. Do you know who's assigned for my detail?"

He hesitated with a small cough. "No one will be leaving the grounds today. Until the investigation is complete."

"You mean I'll be kept a prisoner? Does this apply to the entire family?"

"I cannot say, Ma'am."

"I'd like to speak to Lord Jenkins," Elena demanded.

"He's in a meeting, Ma'am. They're all in a meeting."

"I expect a call when he returns. I want my car as soon as

possible." She thanked the man curtly and hung up the phone. Elena wondered what would happen if she tried to take a walk. Would security guards physically prevent her from leaving the palace? Could she leave unnoticed? While she stared out the window toward the gate, the staff telephone rang down the hallway. The security guard had relayed the message that the princess was restless. Probably someone calling to find out more about her plans for the day. Elena stood by the door, and counted ten rings. Why did the staff ignore the phone? Elena quickly changed into a sea-green top, short-sleeved, short-waisted, and snug.

She glanced at the queen's note again. Others would think Elena paranoid, but she knew every word had been crafted with disappointment. The queen must have heard how Elena had stormed away, but didn't realize that those few moments alone had offered the most possibility of the entire night. Surely, Catherine could understand—Elena wanted to restrict Kay's influence over the children's lives. Why, Catherine disliked Kay, too . . . Elena shook her head. But Edward was Catherine's son. Elena picked up the phone and dialed her own secretary.

"All your appointments have been canceled, Lady Elena, so you can rest."

"Fine. But meetings have been set with security and palace staff, no?"

"Um, no. There's nothing at all on your schedule."

"But surely they have questions about last night. We must meet with the police?"

"There's nothing, Ma'am." The secretary sounded nervous.

"Then call and find out what's going on," Elena ordered. "We'll arrange the appointments!" She hung up the phone and punched the number that McLarrity, the reporter, had given her. A palace operator intercepted the call.

"Yes, Lady Elena, may I be of assistance?"

"No. I was returning a telephone call from a few days ago."

"Who, Ma'am?"

"An acquaintance," she said shortly. McLarrity was a reporter, and no reporter was her friend.

"We have orders against internal direct dialing today. Security precautions."

"Oh, bother!" Elena slammed the telephone back. She crossed her arms and paced back and forth. A moment later, she was back at the telephone. The operator answered with the same helpful voice.

"Put me through to my husband," Elena ordered.

"Where, what . . ." the operator stuttered.

"Let me dial direct," Elena snapped. There was a pause and ringing began. After three rings, one of the assistants to Edward's secretary answered.

"I'd like to speak to Edward," Elena ordered.

"May I inquire as to the nature of the call?"

"I am his wife. We have two children together. Put him on the line immediately."

"Prince Edward is out walking. I would be happy to take a detailed message."

Elena shut her eyes, and remained calm. "When do you expect him in?"

Another pause. He probably was with Kay already, and Elena swore to herself. "He took a lunch and asked not to be disturbed."

"Walking, camping," Elena fumed. "He's never far from someone with a cell phone, and this is urgent."

"Hold on please, it may take a few minutes."

She waited standing. She refused to hang up, and getting Edward to a phone took ten minutes. "Just awful about last night," he said, adding how he had not slept well the night before.

"I'm glad you're all right. Really." Elena kept her voice sincere. "Did you talk with your mother?"

"Briefly. She was furious that the incident disrupted our talk. I told her these matters take time."

Elena bit her tongue. "I'm surprised you returned to Pepperell so quickly. Won't we have to answer questions from the police?"

"Staff will handle the details. Our security detail was there and can answer questions far better than we can. Besides, I work best here. No calls. No visitors. It's the last civilized place in the world."

She didn't ask about the nature of the work. "But what about the children, Edward?"

"Extra security has been posted at school. Jenkins is very upset about you breaking protocol, my dear. Puts us all in danger."

"Their idea of protection is locking us up! Treating us like criminals! Separating us and cutting off communication. Children should be near their parents when there are problems."

"If that's what you want, I can arrange for tutors at Pepperell." He sounded disappointed. Elena heard a woman's voice in the background. Did Kay advise him on what to say? Or was she just hurrying him? Edward's mistress was so complacent about allowing security to rule her life, always meek and never pushing boundaries. She adored Edward's status more than the man himself, and so the royal family condoned a woman whose lineage did not qualify her for marrying a prince and who agreed to be a mistress.

"That's too far. I can't tolerate another separation. The boys would miss school." And staff would blame their mother, she thought.

"I'm sorry, Elena, but you must admit that you're a dangerous woman to be around."

"What happened last night wasn't my fault. We must help the investigators. We can't simply hide!" He didn't answer. "Edward, our family should fight this together. You and I, with the children." Still, no answer—Elena was ready to plead, anything to win time with her two boys. "It's what your mother wants . . ."

The sound of Kay's voice came distinctly over the line. She was standing close. How could Elena compete with a woman who could whisper and touch him, who always complied with the family? "I yield to my mother's wishes when they're reasonable," Edward said, distantly. "I must go, Elena."

"Your mistress is nothing more than your ego," Elena snapped.

The phone clicked.

Elena hung up gently and decided to complain to the press. That always put the palace into a panic. She punched in McLarrity's number once more, trying to think how she would explain the shooting and the botched meeting. The operator again intercepted the call.

"Never mind," Elena said sweetly. She went to the computer, but the server was down. She reached for the BlackBerry, placed in a slot under her nightstand, out of sight from prying eyes. She typed an E-mail to Paul: "Did you see the news? The attack last night? They claim it's the IRA. Again. I'm not so sure."

She checked the "in box." Two notes from her sons.

"Hi, Mum! Saw you in the news again. Be careful. Then Derry snatched the paper away from R, and he was furious. He told D that we were no longer children. Told D he wouldn't have his job. Derry went all somber and concerned. The man is a fake. He gave the paper back to Richard, but told him to keep it away from me. Hah!

"I don't like the man. He manipulates us. He resents it when R and I get along. He laughs at us and thinks we don't notice. R pretended to keep the paper away from me when D was around. Then as soon he left, he tossed it my way. Richard's great about things like that. Please take care of yourself. Can't wait to see you again."

Names in the message. Alarmed, she quickly wrote a note reminding the boy to use no names, especially with all the security problems.

She read the note again. Larry had always been astute, chafing under any control that did not make sense to him. Years ago, when he first began school, he had been disappointed that he had not been firstborn. Elena had tried to reassure him that being born second in a royal family could have its benefits. Waiting for the crown, all the responsibility, only limited Richard's freedom and choices. With time, Larry had stopped complaining. Elena was certain that her younger son had come to agree with her and pity Richard, but of course, the two could never talk about such feelings.

She hit "Next" to read the note from Richard: "Mum, sorry to hear about the dinner last night. I'm relieved that the two of you are safe. I probably shouldn't ask, but did you and Dad make up? L and I would do anything . . .

"I'm annoyed. D tried to keep the news away from us! It's pretty embarrassing when we go to school and our classmates know more about our parents than we do! I promised D I would keep 'harsh realities' away from my little brother. That boy can handle reality more than anyone I know. For me, my little brother's the epitome of harsh reality!

"Don't worry, though. L and I get along well. Yesterday, D mentioned that we might have to head for P over the weekend. For an announcement. Then today, he said the event was canceled. Weekend with Dad was canceled, too. Our schedules are chaos. We hope to see you soon. Love you."

Elena read the note again. What announcement was Derry talking about? Paranoia seeped through her. No one had mentioned any announcement to her. Had the queen anticipated a reunion so quickly? Not with Edward already at Pepperell!

Elena typed brief replies: "Take care of yourselves. Stay alert. Thanks for not using names and tell your brother to do likewise. Use precautions even around the staff. Your father and I love you two very much. Let's take it a day at a time. I'm trying to arrange a meeting for us."

As she finished adding lines specific for each boy, the screen flashed that another message arrived in her in-box. She didn't recognize the E-mail address. Elena grimaced as she hit the button and read: "Rumor's out that some of the more interesting members of the royal family are into E-mail. Check the new game on the Internet—a race to find the young prince's password. I alerted the boys. In the meantime, change your password daily."

The message had to be from Paul. Bless him for looking after her. She started to change her password when there was a knock and the door opened to her reading room. Elena had forbidden staff from entering her private room without permission and she whipped around, ready to scold—until she saw Walter. "Thank God," she exclaimed. "I wanted to get out, and the desk refused to ring you."

Walter held his hand up, and listened at the doorway, checking to make sure he had not been followed. He moved close to her ear and his whisper was barely discernible. "Shh," he cautioned. "I came to say good-bye. I'm not with security anymore. I was fired this morning." He guided her close to the window, far from her desk, phone and bed, and then opened the window wide, leaning to avoid the listening devices. Even he wasn't sure where they were all hidden.

"No!" Elena gasped. "No one told me. They said you'd been transferred. But . . . this is so unfair."

He put his hand to her mouth and shook his head, moving

his lips close to her ear.

"They didn't fire me for a screw-up last night," he breathed into her ear. "I'm afraid that they fired me because they think that I saved your life last night."

Elena gasped. He put a finger to her mouth. "You heading out the cellar, and the prince following, didn't go over big with my superiors. They accused me of insubordination."

She paused before answering and glanced around the room, feeling anxious.

"Don't worry, they can't hear us, not if we really whisper. I know . . ." His mouth literally touched her hair and breathed the words.

"You've listened in my bedroom?" she murmured.

He nodded. "In the interest of safety—I used to believe that."

Elena shook her head. "They hate me that much."

"Someone obviously wants you dead," Walter said. "And security worries less about protection and more about avoiding blame. You must get out of here."

"But where?" Elena asked. "I have no other home. My parents are dead. My brother and uncle work for the palace."

"Abroad. Out of the country."

"Out of the question." Elena stepped away and put her hands to her head, trying to think. Then she moved closer once again. "They won't allow me to leave on an official vacation. There's so much with schedules and security."

"After what I've seen and heard during the past twenty-four hours, I would not step on any of their planes," Walter said. "You must find some other way."

"I can't leave the children."

He cocked his head. "You're not with the boys anyway," he pointed out.

She looked at him and wondered if the young man wasn't part of the snare trying to keep her away from the boys. Was this just another ruse to provoke Elena and make her look unstable? But he kept talking and didn't notice her suspicion.

"Trying to bring them along only makes escape more difficult. You needn't worry about the boys. No one seems to be after them. Yet."

"No one's talking to me about last night. And they won't let me make any calls at all."

"If it makes you feel any better, Edward's schedule has been canceled as well."

"But he's with Kay and not complaining," Elena retorted. "I can't live like this . . ."

"Your only recourse is to leave the country."

Elena had trusted Walter in a world where she trusted so few. "That seems so drastic. Surely, someone in my own country can stop this. The courts . . ."

"You need a solicitor, though frankly, I'm worried what would happen to another qualified solicitor hired by you. Jenkins found out that you called Roger Miggins. Initially, I thought he was alarmed out of interest in your safety. Now, I'm not so sure."

Elena took a deep breath. She trusted Walter, but decided against explaining that she had not made that call. She didn't dare let on that she knew the younger Miggins brother.

"I reported that call after reviewing the device on your phone. You can imagine my alarm about his untimely death, with a car bomb that was so similar to your experience. But then Jenkins reprimanded me for suggesting that it was anything more than a coincidence."

"When did you report the call, before or after his death?" Elena whispered.

"I reported it the day you made that call, later that evening." He shook his head, as if disgusted, when she didn't say anything. But she also sensed fury. He wouldn't be standing in her bedroom otherwise. "Believe me, I wish that I'd never reported the call. And I've edited my reports since." He looked at her and sighed. "I should have warned you how much we were monitoring your calls, particularly after the attack at the palace. I'm sorry."

She put a hand to his shoulder. "I'm sorry about you losing your job. I'll miss you because I trusted you, and you were very good. What can I do for you? Tell me."

"They plan to keep you away from the press. Any publicity of these goings-on will infuriate them. Perhaps you can find a solicitor secretly."

"I have an idea. The reporter from the United States—he could demand to see me. Perhaps he could put me in touch with a solicitor."

Walter looked doubtful. "Do you trust him?"

"As much as anyone else," she admitted.

"Don't call from here," Walter urged. "I'll go and speak to him in person. No one will follow me now."

"Are you sure?"

He nodded. "In the meantime, be careful of everyone," he urged. The words sounded so ominous. "I feel obligated to remind you that I now fall into the category of 'disgruntled former employee,' the most dangerous category, according to Jenkins."

"I trust you." She mouthed the words.

He looked out the window at the peaceful gardens. "I feel guilty about walking away from you at such a time. I want to make sure that you're in good hands."

She wrote down the telephone number for him, along with Michael McLarrity's name. She also wrote: "Thank you with all my heart—I feel so trapped here."

"I'll contact you as soon as I hear something. Otherwise, take a walk tomorrow evening on the grounds here. Alone. Try to be difficult all day—and then insist that you need a walk outdoors.

Wander about the gardens and then head for the bench by the pond, the one near the birches. I'll be there at eight and let you know how my meeting goes."

CHAPTER 18

"One never serves royalty by consulting with royalty."
"A terrible mistake."
"One that will be rectified. She can't be touched on palace grounds. But nobody cares about Walter."

By the following afternoon, Elena had received no word from Walter. Restless, she rang and requested her driver for what had to be the twentieth time. "Leaving the palace grounds is unwise, Lady Elena. We have yet to find the appropriate security man for you."

Elena asked to speak to a superior and received the same response. "What happens if I take my vehicle and drive away, alone?"

"That would be foolhardy!" the officer in charge snapped. "You would be stopped for your own safety."

"And how long does this order stand?"

"It's indefinite, Lady Elena."

Elena dined early, declined dessert, and then waited until when she knew most of the servants would be relaxing over dinner. The grounds surrounding the palace would be quiet. She changed into comfortable walking shoes, gray khakis, a bright white shirt. At the last minute, she snatched a paperback novel and a thick heather cotton sweater, and slipped downstairs and headed for the large garden. Along the way, she paused to pick off a few dead blooms and look about.

Oddly enough no one protested or followed her about the grounds. So, she was free to wander about outside. Gradually, she headed to the pond and its nearby stone bench, where she sat, with her long legs curled underneath. She donned her sweater to blend with the twilight. Elena tried to read the words on the page of the thriller, but the light was fading and she could not concentrate. Still, she dipped her head and put her hand to her chin, and regularly turned pages.

At least thirty minutes had passed. Elena was nervous and put the book down beside her on the bench. Twilight crept into the garden, long before it overwhelmed the open lawns. It was foolish to pretend to read in such light. Songbirds had fled the flowerbeds and nestled among the branches of trees and shrubs. The muffled sounds of London traffic could be heard in the distance. The night air was cool, and thin strands of fog emerged in the gardens of roses and lavender. Free from the distraction of other senses, Elena could detect the scents of some early blooms drifting through the night air.

She looked toward the palace and could barely make out the lights of the upper floor of Kirkington. Elena had claimed a headache with crankiness, hoping that would discourage staff from scurrying about and bothering her. Inside, she felt a twitch of fear, urging her to return to her private suite inside the palace. She worried that staff members, if they discovered her missing, might put even tighter controls on her. Yet she also wanted to talk with Walter.

She checked her watch. The meeting was minutes away.

But Walter was a dismissed employee, and maybe he had been overconfident about entering the palace grounds? Maybe the meeting didn't matter to him anymore? But then the young security guard had suggested the meeting, not Elena. He had told her to be careful, and seemed convinced that someone was out to kill her and maybe Edward.

Now, alone in the night, she feared every noise, every shadow, everyone including Walter. He had urged her to come alone to the garden at this time. Any number of accidents could happen, and all she carried was a silly book, a paperback no less.

He had told her to come to this bench, the one by the pond and birches. Maybe he had made a mistake and didn't know a birch from a willow. Elena hesitated, afraid that if she walked away from the bench that she might miss Walter altogether. A tiny voice in her mind chanted a warning, *You don't know Walter at all. He worked for the palace, not you. Get away from that bench.*

Slowly, she stood and moved away from the bench, all the while looking about. Maybe he had discovered important information and was delayed. If he didn't show, she didn't know how to possibly reach him. She could call the security office, invent some excuse, a lost trinket or a question about a recent event, and leave a message for him to call. Maybe he had nothing to report and decided entering palace grounds was too risky. Or, maybe he had lied. Just because he claimed to have been fired was no reason to think that she could trust him. Maybe he still worked for the palace. Or maybe he had simply given up on royalty and planned on avoiding all of them for the rest of his life. She couldn't blame him.

Or maybe he had come by earlier and left some note. She decided to search the area around the pond before returning to her space in the palace.

Darkness had already cast its veil over the lush garden, and Elena hoped that she blended in with the scene's intricate details. She pulled the hood of the sweater over her head and tucked the collar of her shirt away, hoping to blend in with the night even more. The birds had long stopped their chatter.

The garden was too silent. Instinctively, she paused and leaned against a large tree trunk, straining to listen for any sound at all. Low-hanging branches caught her hair and tickled her face, as she stood watching the garden bench slowly blend in with the night. A small ball of panic started in her stomach, as she thought about the next and following days, remaining trapped in Kirkington, away from the children. She hoped that Walter had not deceived her.

Palace staff had not deceived her in years, tricking her into a public or foolish mistake, because Elena had quickly learned that she couldn't trust even the friendliest. She had kept her thoughts and goals to herself, adding to her mysterious allure. But never before had she been literally trapped on palace grounds.

She sank to the ground and leaned against the shaggy gray bark, remembering when she had been young and new to the palace. She didn't know it at the time, but the family had agreed to assign the newcomer as a project for senior staff who served the Queen Mother. The women had helped her choose clothes, went over palace etiquette, explained history, and provided hours of gentle advice. They had fussed over her and given her attention, acting much like older sisters. And Elena had made a mistake by regarding them more as friends than staff.

Then one day, she was supposed to be walking with Edward. Her fiancé had canceled at the last minute, claiming a fierce headache. Elena had offered to bring him some tea, but he declined. Less than an hour later, she had watched as servants loaded a wicker picnic basket in his favorite coupe and he drove away. It was the first of many lies from Edward about not wanting to spend time with her, and Elena had fled to the darkest corner of her closet, underneath some of her finest new gowns. She bit her nails, but didn't cry. She just wanted to be alone in the dark to think. She even contemplated putting a stop to the wedding, then less than two weeks away. What would everyone do?

Two ladies-in-waiting had walked into her bedroom and

dumped an array of boxes onto the bed, either more items joining the parade of hats and outfits that had to be tried on or wedding gifts that had to be acknowledged by notes in her personal handwriting.

Amy, the friendliest and Elena's favorite of the assistants, flopped onto the bed. "I'm sick of dealing with a child. She knows nothing and has no style. The queen expects us to work miracles!"

"And she's so tall." Rebecca replied, straightening Amy's pile of boxes. "As much as she claims to hate horses, she looks like one!"

"That's what they get for wanting a virgin," Amy added snidely.

The two women giggled.

Amy continued her rant of gossip. "And how she looks in that wedding dress. For a wedding on the telly. Did you hear, it's to be broadcast all over the world! Why would you go out in public looking like her?"

Rebecca had laughed in scorn. "She's huge! A monstrosity in white."

"Like her awful Laura Ashley dresses. She might as well look for her clothes in maternity shops!"

"Do say, you're right!"

"Can you imagine what it would be like if we let her have her own way on clothes and style?"

"My God, and now they expect us to do something about her hair."

The conversation drifted down the hallway but remained etched in Elena's memory. Hugging her knees, she did not move for another hour, instead thinking about what she should do next. Damn them, she thought. Damn them all. Elena had not chosen the dress. Family members had forced the wedding dress on her, along with dozens of other dreadful decisions that left her feeling uncomfortable. Elena never felt quite right about what to say, how to stand, exactly when to enter or leave a room. No wonder she looked awkward.

In the wardrobe closet, Elena had resolved to make her own decisions and learn to live with them. She'd continue to be polite to the staff, but she could never trust them again. All decisions had to be her own. Edward had chosen her and she was sure that she had detected admiration, love, in his eyes early on. It was then that Elena had thought back and realized that her fiancé had grown increasingly distant ever since she had left her job, her comfortable flat with her friends, and moved into the palace, allowing herself to be molded by palace helpers who did not know her.

Elena had vowed to go back to being herself. Besides, she thought, men did not care about silly matters such as clothes and etiquette. Edward was an intelligent and older man and would never make the stupid mistake of marrying a woman he did not respect.

That afternoon, the princess-to-be left Wyndham Palace, climbed into one of the extra vehicles kept for palace errands and traveled alone to the studio of the man who was designing her wedding dress. A determined Elena presented her plea for simplicity and sophistication. The designer shouted with delight, then hugged her and eagerly invited her to his workroom.

On the spot, he himself had removed the frilly collar of lace and tulle. He had tightened the waist, and showed her how he would expose both her back, shoulders and more of her chest. "They had asked me not to emphasize your height," he had noted, an Irish lilt emerging with his happiness. "That's a silly mistake, but I thought it's what you wanted. You're a tall and beautiful woman. Statuesque. Anything else makes you look dumpy!" Then he had removed all the pearl clips that had gathered up sections of the skirt to the waist.

The result was a sleek, elegant dress that emphasized her long legs and skin that had the luminescence of a pearl. "Stand tall and be proud," the designer had said, standing back and admiring his creation. "I realize you're a shy woman, and I agree that you should never want to appear arrogant. But don't bend your shoulders so! Keep them straight and back. If you must detract from height, then dip your head like so." Then with both hands, he had clutched her head, and cocked it ever so slightly into what would soon become a world-famous pose. "At last," he had exclaimed, with awe. "A work of art."

"Can we manage to keep this a secret?" Elena had whispered. "The dress?" The designer, understanding her fears of the palace, smiled and nodded.

"And what should I do about my hair?" she pressed.

"Be yourself," he had advised. "If you try to please others, you'll be a sham." He wrote a number on a slip of paper of a young hair stylist who specialized in natural looks. Then he hugged her again. "Thank you for coming to me and speaking up. I should have said something and I apologize. But I was afraid to approach you. They told me I'd hurt your feelings. But I should have known better. A woman can only be beautiful if she's comfortable, and I was only aiming for your comfort. Now that we both know what you want, I can promise—you'll be beautiful."

And that's what papers and television commentators around the world had proclaimed ever since. Elena still remembered the delight on her husband's face as she strolled down the aisle in the wedding dress. In a stern voice, Elena insisted that Amy and Rebecca not be allowed near while she dressed, which began a long line of rumors about her rudeness with staff and a failure to appreciate their hard work.

Sighing, Elena touched the bark of a nearby tree. If only she had not been so wrong about Edward . . .

She could no longer see the bench. She held up her wrist, but it was too dark to see the time on her watch. Walter wasn't coming. Maybe he had no other news or maybe he had somehow left a message for her at the palace. She was nervous and wanted to run away, return to the safety of her bedroom in the palace.

Elena moved quickly through sections of the garden, hurrying back to the clearing where she could see the lights of the palace, when she stumbled over something in the dark.

She caught herself before falling to the ground, but her book flew out of her hand. Rattled, Elena paused to catch her breath and look about. But the book cover was dark, and in the shadows of the shade garden she couldn't see much. She thought about finding a servant, but Walter could be running late, and she didn't want to get him or anyone else in trouble. Every small bit of freedom was precious.

She chided herself for not carrying a torch. But such basic items for survival were standard equipment for staff and not royalty. Members of the royal family were trained to depend on others, she thought ruefully.

She took a few slow steps in a circle, hoping that she'd tap about and find the book with her shoe. She kept moving systematically about in larger circles, reaching out with her hands to avoid trees. The new tips of blue hostas, growing around the birches, tickled her legs.

Suddenly, her foot kicked into some bundle in the path, a bag of clippings or supplies left behind by some gardener. Not wanting to trip, she gently kicked again.

A chill went through her. Gardeners did the bulk of their work when the royal family was occupied with affairs away from the palace. The queen was fastidious about the gardens and expected impeccable work. Any tools or cuttings left about would be cause for immediate dismissal. All the palace gardens were among the finest in the world, and the master gardeners prized their positions and the status.

Elena held her breath and refused to run away or seek help. If anyone, including Walter, had been out to hurt her, she would have been long dead. So she forced herself to crouch down and touch the object that had caused her fall.

Her hand gently patted and she felt a metal button and then the smooth silk of a tie. Gasping, she shook gently and then harder. She couldn't see a face, but she knew it was a man. She grasped at his arm and tugged hard, but there was no response. Then she moved her hand to his face. The skin of Walter's forehead was smooth, cold as a leaf in the wet rain. Her hand moved down his chest, and she felt something wet and sticky.

Elena gave a soft cry and murmured, "My God." As her heart pounded, she stood and backed away in terror. Then she stopped and glanced at the dark pile that could only be Walter. "I'm so sorry," she whispered.

Then she turned and ran full speed for the palace. Once inside the hallway, she could see that her fingertips were streaked with blood. Frantically, Elena called out. No one came. She ran into the nearest bathroom, one reserved for guests arriving to check their hair and makeup before functions. She turned on the hot water, washed her hands, and stared at her flushed face in the mirror. Furious, she called out again.

But no staff came. None ever came when she really needed them. Elena sank to the floor, took a deep breath, and screamed.

CHAPTER 19

"She's distraught."

"The prescription is open. Use as much Xanax as necessary until Walter is cremated."

Elena woke up and felt something was wrong. A nurse, someone she didn't know, rushed forward with some pills and water. Elena shook her head and thrashed restlessly back and forth in her bed. "I want my sons here, now!" she insisted.

"Surely you don't want to see them like this." Hugh Fanley, her secretary, stepped forward close to the bed. He laid a sympathetic hand on her forehead. "You're distraught. Give yourself time to rest."

Elena shook her head, trying to emerge from the fog of sleep. "If Walter's not safe, then none of us are safe," she murmured.

"It was a traumatic experience. You need rest . . ."

"Poor Walter," Elena said. "What time is it? What did the police say?"

The secretary looked puzzled. "No police have been here. What are you talking about?"

"Walter. My guard. He was killed. I found his body in the garden."

The secretary put his hands together. "There, there, he was hardly killed. He died of a heart attack."

"A heart attack!" Elena sat up. "Impossible. I saw the blood." She looked at her hands, expecting to see some blood still left on her hands. But they were clean, impeccably manicured, and polished. There was also a bandage covering the base of her thumb on the left hand. Underneath was some wound that stung. Elena frowned. "The newspapers, what do they have to say?"

The secretary looked at her with sympathy. "Elena, don't concern yourself with gossip in the news or worries about Walter. He was hardly important enough to make the papers. It's not healthy for you. Yes, the poor man's dead. I suppose he could have fallen and struck his head, cut himself. Perhaps there was some blood. But he had a heart attack. You can't . . ."

"You must believe me!" Elena tried to move out of the bed. "Where's Walter now? I touched him, and you can't pretend that I didn't!"

The secretary made a soft noise of distress and glanced at the nurse, before stepping aside and arranging the flowers in one of more than a dozen arrangements. As usual none of the arrangements included cards. Staff, striving for efficiency, had already arranged the cards in piles—the large one for impersonal printed thank-you notes and the smaller pile for her own desk.

"Your Royal Highness, you must not worry so," Fanley said. "The man is already cremated and in his family plot. Palace took care of all arrangements, and his mother was most appreciative. She was less upset than you, dear. She knew her son was too fond of smoked meats." Fanley grimaced. "So bad for one's cholesterol."

"My God, what day is this?"

"This is Wednesday and you collapsed after finding Walter's body three days ago. We found you in the downstairs bathroom. You were distraught, in a panic. Please, don't let it happen again. You scared the staff out of their minds, and the stress can't be good for you."

Elena sank against her pillow. "But police inspectors, were they here?"

"There's no need for inspectors, Ma'am, except in your imagination. Really! The death of a servant is not worth your health. These tragedies happen." He lowered his glasses and gave her a pompous look, as if to ask if Walter had been something more to her than a member of the staff.

"The man was too young to die," Elena snapped. "And it's strange that he died so soon after being fired from here."

Fanley again shook his head in a puzzled way. "But he wasn't fired." He turned to the expressionless nurse, reaching for the ornate container. He extracted a white pill. "You're too confused to think about these matters now. Here, take this. You'll feel better."

"I don't need that." She stubbornly clamped her mouth tight.

"It's for the best," he said, holding the pill close to her lips.

Elena pushed his hand away, pressed her mouth tight, stared out her window. The day was well underway, yet she felt stiff and groggy. "How many of those have you given me in the last few days?"

"You were hysterical," Fanley counseled. "The queen's own physician recommends that you stay in bed for another day. I won't insist you take another pill, if you manage to stay calm. If you only recalled how upset you were that night. You had us very worried."

He handed the pill box to the nurse, who nodded and turned away.

Elena didn't remember much except running away from Walter's body. "A man who worked for me died," she said softly. "In the line of duty, I might add. I should have attended his funeral."

"You're in no shape for that," he said firmly.

"I've had way too much rest," Elena groaned, struggling to

sit up, and swing her legs out of the bed. She groaned. Pain shot up her leg from the bottom of her foot, and she felt heavy, as if an extra twenty-pound weight had been added to her frame.

The telephone interrupted with a shrill ring. Fanley answered and turned to the window. "I was told she was not well enough to take phone calls." He listened a moment and frowned, before pressing the hold button. "The palace would like you to take this call, but to speak only briefly." He held the phone receiver as if she were a child and had to promise to behave.

"Who is it?"

"A journalist." The secretary's voice was full of disdain. "A Michael McLarrity."

Elena pretended weariness. "What does he want?"

"He's working on a profile of the Prince of Wales, and the palace asked us to cooperate. Seems that he has a few loose ends to tie up and has some questions for you."

"You know I despise reporters!" Elena was stubborn. "It doesn't seem right to take a call from a reporter before I hear from my sons or friends—and I'll let him know that."

"The palace would like you to take this call," he insisted. "He knows that you don't feel well and promised to keep it short."

Elena took the phone with some reluctance and waved Fanley away. But he refused to leave the room. Elena ignored him and spoke sharply: "Hello, Mr. McLarrity, I'm surprised you telephoned here."

"Please," Fanley hissed, as he fussed about the bed. "Don't argue with the man. You should be resting."

"I need to see you." Michael was blunt.

Elena waved her hand to silence Fanley. "You could have arranged that with my staff."

"I tried, and they said you've been ill lately. They were vague and I got worried."

"But your story focuses on my husband."

He paused. "I understand. All right, the profile is incomplete without more about the children."

"The children are too young for that sort of coverage," Elena said, arching her eyebrows at Fanley.

"Mere details. Your husband offered some wonderful anecdotes, but couldn't remember the exact dates. Please, the article can't be written without that information. It must be accurate. I'm reminding both you and your employees that the Prince of Wales approved of this article."

Elena sighed. "What do you need to know?"

"It would be best to meet in person. Tomorrow morning, if possible."

"All right, if you insist that the story won't run without these details," she said, making a point of rolling her eyes at Fanley. "But lunch would be better."

"All right, we'll have lunch together. The Graycott before noon? And can you contact your staff to arrange release of some of your personal photos of the children when they were younger?"

"I'll try." Elena kept her voice cool, before hanging up. Surely palace staff was screening her calls, and she hoped the journalist understood her reticence. If she was less than eager for a meeting, then staff might allow her to leave the palace. She and Michael would learn whether the staff really wanted that article on the Prince of Wales. She leaned back and closed her eyes.

Fanley patted her shoulder lightly. "You handled that well," he said.

She sat up in bed. "I may cancel."

"But you look better already," Fanley said with his inane smile. "Back to your old self."

Which old self, Elena wondered. The secretary was not the most bothersome of her staff, but she never forgot that he had been hired for the position because he couldn't keep a secret.

He treated her like she was a dim little girl who did not know what was best for herself.

She stretched and yawned. "I feel so stiff and tired. It will be good for me to get out and about."

"As long as you're up to it." Fanley was stern. "I'm not sure you're ready for a meeting with a reporter, of all sorts."

"This one's safe." Elena was dismissive. "It's for Edward, so the world can see that he's good to his children, and that the children love us both. I want to get it over with."

Fanley nodded his approval. "No photos involved?"

She shook her head. "Not of me, but he wants to borrow some older ones of the children. In the meantime, I'm ravenous. Do you think I could have some biscuits and fruit sent up?"

"Certainly, right away." Fanley paused by the foot of her bed. "And about Walter, you're sure that you've come to terms with his death?"

Elena dipped her head and avoided staring at Fanley's eyes. "Really, I'm fine. He was so young. It's strange to think of a man alive and with me one moment, and in another to know that I'll never see him again." A real tear fell, but that only helped her lie. Lies were necessary to separate herself from the palace and its staff. "I overreacted. Please forget that I said anything."

Fanley's smile grew larger. "That's my princess. Remember, it was all a bad dream. I spoke with security myself, and you have nothing to fear. If you need anything, just ring. Meanwhile, I'll send someone to help you bathe and dress. The doctor said that you should expect to be unsteady on your feet." And with that he slipped away.

Elena didn't wait for help, but headed for the shower. As soon as the hot water hit, she felt coherence after being in a daze for several days. Someone had deliberately kept her quiet until after Walter's body was buried. She had no choice but to pretend apathy. Or that same person would prevent her from leaving the palace. Elena quickly changed into a tea-length black skirt and a close-fitting short-sleeved thin black sweater, embroidered with minute black beads.

Standing at the mirror, she knew she wasn't crazy, so why did she have to convince others that Walter's death was no accident? Maybe she would try to get McLarrity to ask some questions. She applied dark makeup around her eyes and studied the effect—she looked thin, fragile and trustworthy.

Dressed in less than twenty minutes, she left her room and headed for the library, where staff arranged recent newspapers at a reading table. She avoided glancing toward the corner that hid a surveillance camera, discovered by Larry long ago, and she selected a few fashion magazines, including the latest *Vogue*. She wandered about the room, turning pages, pretending to search for an article. As she wandered by the newspapers, she glanced at the headlines and didn't have to study them close to realize that articles questioned her health and stability: "The Princess of Wales has been despondent recently, despite rumors of a reconciliation," ". . . a long history of depression and eating disorders in her family," ". . . distant and moody . . ."

Elena felt sick and walked away, holding the *Vogue* close to her chest. The rumors could have only one source—the palace staff. She returned to her room, tossed the magazine to her bedside, and went to the BlackBerry to check her E-mail. One short, polite note from Richard, several days old, explaining activities at school and asking about her health. Elena dashed off a fast and cheery note, urging him not to believe what he read in the newspapers. Two clandestine notes from Larry, the first happy and short, the second more gloomy: "Worried about you. Miss you. School's boring as usual. Except for D. He scares me. He's been playing with the computer and so R's using it less. I think D wants to keep me away from it. R suggested that we both pretend we don't care for a while. We don't want to get caught with the Berry . . ."

She had taught her sons to be wary about their privacy. Still, Elena wanted to believe that her son's imagination had sparked the distrust of Derry. Did Larry merely dislike the phoniness, the way of life that Derry represented? Or, did the boy sense a more specific threat? She had to talk to the boy immediately. Elena went to the phone and dialed her sons' school. Of course, the call would be monitored by the school staff and Lord knew who else. But maybe she could pin down the nature of his fear . . . And at least Larry would know that his mother cared.

"Your Royal Highness, Lawrence is in the fields now," the school secretary explained. "It will take a few minutes."

"Fine. I'll stay on the line."

"Certainly," the woman said with polite nervousness. Ten minutes later Larry was at the other end, breathing hard from running.

"How are you, darling?" Elena said. "I got your note."

"Yes," the boy replied. Someone must be in the room with him.

"I understand. You have your scrambler?"

"It's on now . . ."

"Good, go on. Tell me what you can without using names. I wanted to know why you said you were scared."

"He told me that only one of us was going to Pepperell this weekend and not me. I wanted to play some trick and I went to his room."

"The tricks will only make him angry, Larry. You must be careful. But go on."

"I found something, but can't say over the telephone."

"Did you tell your guard?"

"No. They're all chummy with him."

"Does your brother know?"

"No. Derry's always around. We hardly get any time alone."

"Stay near and try to talk with your brother. And attend the activities at school. Don't wander off alone."

"I don't."

"Stay away from his room. Promise me."

"I do."

"And have a good tennis practice tomorrow."

"I don't have tennis then, Mum. Thursdays nights are free. We might have a concert by the river."

"Oh yes," she paused and hoped he would catch her meaning. Her younger son despised tennis. "No one will be on the courts. That gives you time for extra practice. Don't they have that big wall, the one you can bat the ball against?"

"Yes, but . . ."

She interrupted him. "I'm looking forward to playing with you the next time we get together. Get some practice in. When the evening is cool is the best time. And stay close with your brother."

"If you say." Larry was eager and she could tell from the tone that he understood. She had to see her children before that weekend trip to Pepperell. She'd drive to the school. The tennis courts were not far from the roadway. She could hike through the woods and talk to Larry alone, without staff around.

And in the meantime, she had to pretend not to care about Walter. With any luck, the guard had carried no documents or messages that hinted at their suspicions. If that had been the case, she would soon be dead, too.

CHAPTER 20

"She forgot about Walter."
"Thank God we intercepted his note."

The restaurant inside the Graycott Hotel was small, intimate, with few windows. Every table was set for two, each adorned with colorful, quaint lamps. Except for the table reserved by Michael McLarrity. Elena stood by, watching as Michael requested a table on the opposite side of the room and that the table be left bare, including no tablecloth. The princess raised her eyebrows in surprise.

"I don't want anyone trying to listen to our conversation," Michael murmured.

"You want an exclusive on my family's story?" Elena asked.

"Try Walter's story," he replied. "And I'm not worried about other reporters. Why did you send him to me?"

Elena was surprised. "So he did get in touch with you . . ."

Michael did not answer while the waiter delivered coffee and juice. "You think he was murdered, and no one believes you. In fact, some suggest that you're the most hysterical woman in the country."

Elena straightened her shoulders. "Do you believe that?" she asked and held out her arms. She was dressed professionally, in a fitted black skirt that went to her knees. The black knit top was more intricate, with tiny strips extending from her shoulders, meeting in a smooth plait that ended in a snug belt coiled around her waist.

"I wouldn't be here if I did. No, I believe you're being framed by your in-laws."

"Why do you believe me?" Elena stared into his eyes. "No one else does."

He let out a slow breath out. "I've been trying to reach you. Walter came to speak with me the afternoon that he had the heart attack. He was worried about you. He thought that someone was plotting to kill you."

"Walter didn't have a heart attack."

Michael looked unsettled.

"I was supposed to meet him in the garden. I found him, dead, and panicked. It was horrible—he was on the ground, cold. I touched blood on his chest, and it was on my hands when I came inside. But my staff at Kirkington sedated me, then insisted that I cut myself and that Walter died of a heart attack."

"Your entire security system is warped. Walter seemed like a decent man who knew what he was talking about. When I spoke with him, he was not afraid for himself. So why did he get killed?"

Elena put both elbows on the arms of her chair and shook her head. "They hate anyone or anything that reflects poorly on the system. They love the system more than themselves. Whether they hate it enough to commit murder, I simply do not know."

Michael looked down. He had not touched the drink. "I did you a favor once. Can I trust you?"

"You don't have to remind me," she said.

He dropped his voice lower. "Walter did some work for the Americans. The CIA."

"What?" Elena exclaimed. Then she leaned back in her chair and laughed. "That can't be true."

"He filed some reports with the intelligence agency and the

state department. They raised some concerns, to put it mildly. He didn't know it, but I was sent to verify his work."

"But why would Walter spy around me?" Elena folded her hands around her warm cup. "What would be the point?"

Michael leaned forward. "You are the point. You are probably the most influential woman in the world. Since your divorce, you've traveled to the world's poorest nations and met with leaders from all sorts of governments. People clamor to meet with you, and those leaders care what you think."

"But I'm not an enemy of the United States!"

"Please lower your voice—for your safety, if not mine," he politely ordered. "You're a figure of interest. On your own, without controls from the palace, you could be dangerous. Walter came to worry about your safety."

"You're not a reporter," Elena said, nervously.

"I'm a reporter. I do write articles. But that position is minor compared with my other post."

"You're a spy."

"Please don't use that word. I prefer analyst."

"But allies shouldn't waste energy on other allies! Especially a woman who has nothing to do with the government."

He shrugged. "Directors of intelligence agencies don't like sudden surprises."

"And what could change about this country?" She was skeptical.

"The monarchy. It's an odd system, mixed with democracy. Fewer people support the system of royalty . . ."

"The Americans couldn't possibly think of me as a problem," she interrupted.

He lowered his head. "Some in the government are worried—all these countries have more polarized politics than ever before."

"The royal family brings in tourists. And I'm an ordinary

woman. Of course, the divorce didn't help the monarchy. But I have no ulterior motive. My expectations did not mesh with what my husband and his family wanted. My husband had an affair. He doesn't want to spend time with his children, let alone me. He wants a certain order in his life that suits his immediate pleasure. I, on the other hand, want a normal life, for both myself and my children. And time's running out for that as my children grow older. I didn't want this divorce, but if I get half of what I want out of life, it's better than nothing."

He sipped his coffee. "I need help from you, and I suspect you're not happy about Walter's death. But you must understand something first. I'm not a spy. If you called the U.S. Embassy, they'd claim no connection with me. The same with the CIA and the National Security Agency. Still, I make my living doing research for the United States in friendly countries. I also enjoy working as a journalist and asking questions. There are plenty of people in Washington who are concerned about your divorce and where you stand on certain issues."

"I oppose war. I want to help children. It's not a very difficult job to know my positions."

"That interferes with the plans of some who see conflicts as a way of, let's say collecting resources from countries in the Middle East and Africa. No one worried when you first married. The royal family never talked politics before. Now you're getting a divorce—and are more active than before."

"They're worried that I'll speak out even more," she mused. "That I could be used by some?"

He nodded. "Your country has thrived on monarchy, and no one wants to see the system demolished overnight. Some political leaders in the United States are alarmed about the erosion of values and traditions. Others worry about any global personality. They want power tied to nations and worry about chaos."

"I'm not after any power," Elena said. "I'm a nobody. This is so farfetched."

"Is it?" he asked. "There have been rumors to the contrary. There are people who want to keep you in place, keep the system in place. They want no big changes. We're afraid that Walter's cover was broken."

Elena shook her head and used both hands to pull short strands of hair behind her ears. "Walter's dead, and I'm responsible."

Michael shook his head. "It's not your fault. You got caught up in something that's bigger than you or your family."

Elena finished her coffee. "My husband's family wants me out of the way. They despise me for not meekly blending in with whatever the family did. And my own family, what's left of them, is not much better. They're furious at me for not pretending at my marriage. I'm even less sure about everyone's feelings for the children. They're only pawns."

Michael reached for her hand. "Walter worried about them. His opinion was that they were not safe."

"I have no one left to trust," Elena said. She had appreciated Walter and Henry and the others over the years, but had never fooled herself about their priorities. The palace paid them to do a job.

Michael leaned over the table. "I think you should leave. As soon as possible. Then you can decide what to do, without all the pressure."

"But where do I go? I'd have to pack, get ready, make calls."

"That's like calling your would-be assassins and giving them your schedule," Michael advised. "Once you make the decision, you should take off. Abruptly. Give no one time to think, let alone follow you."

"Hmm." Elena held her temples and could not decide.

"Tonight," Michael pressed. "While this guard is still new."

"I can't leave my children."

"Then take them with you."

"But the family would regard that as treason."

"And what do they think about murder?" Michael shot back. "Unfortunately, bringing the children along complicates leaving the country."

"My sons could be easy targets outside the country." Not ready to walk away, she fretted.

"I don't know." Michael slowly shook his head. "The murderers are bold and trying to pin it on the IRA. Who knows, any recent IRA activity in this city may have just been a ruse."

"But why?"

"One suspect is your husband. Remarriage can't be easy when one's ex-wife is the most celebrated woman in the world."

"Neither he nor Kay cares enough about that," Elena scoffed.

"Then there's your sister-in-law, Caroline. She manages to conceal her feelings, but in truth, she envies you and your children. She would like to control the throne."

"You've done your research," Elena said.

"It could be someone with an investment in some country, some mine, some oilfield. They're worried that you may interfere with their investment. Or, it could be some members of the palace staff."

"The staff's always working for someone," Elena said thoughtfully. "The royal family thinks that they choose the staff. But that's not the way it works. Rather, staff chooses whom they'll serve."

"And that's not you," he said pointedly.

She cocked her head sideways. "Oh, there have been a few exceptions. Such as Henry and Walter. But then Walter wasn't working for me, was he? This morning, I find out that he was working for you."

"Elena," he said in his most convincing manner, "I'm being

truthful with you. I admit that I don't know everything. But does it matter who's trying to kill you? At this point, we know someone's trying. You must get away from the palace and figure this out from a distance."

"Maybe that's what everyone wants?" Elena lifted her eyebrows. "For me to run away and hide."

"It's better than being dead." He finished his coffee and sat back. Elena shook her head as the waiter approached, holding the coffeepot, and she thought about her secret meeting later with Larry. "To leave, I need to lose my new bodyguard. I mean, if I walked into the bathroom right now and didn't come out in five minutes, he'd raise an alarm all over town."

"Good. So you've been thinking seriously about walking away."

"Ever since my marriage fell apart," she admitted. "But I have to leave when I have the most time. I could go home, go to bed, and then sneak away off palace grounds. I've managed before."

"They can check your room. You need a window of at least two hours. More time is better, if possible. If you really want to get away."

"There's another plan," she offered, tapping her finger on the table. "I go to your hotel room, and pretend to spend the night."

Bending his head, he lowered his voice. "How do your guards handle that? A meeting with a lover?"

"I wouldn't know since this would be the first time it ever happened," Elena retorted. "You shouldn't believe the rumors. But this guard is new and he doesn't know my habits at all. I'd expect him to call the office and notify his superiors—who'd be thrilled, I might add. They'd probably call the newspapers themselves—we'd have hundreds of cameras out there the next morning."

Michael signaled the waiter that he wished to pay. "Let's try the hotel room, but add a twist that removes me by one step. It could buy us a little extra time." He slipped his hand into his pocket and extracted several credit cards. He examined a few, before sliding one across the table along with a single key card. "I'm going to make a call and arrange a meeting now—with a good friend, staying in an ideal room here. We have him come down and the three of us will chat over drinks. There's laughing, some flirting. After I step away, you tell your guard that you intend to stay in the hotel."

"He'll want to know the room number."

Michael nodded. "You go to the ladies room first and then to the desk. A message waiting for you will let you know the next move. Tell the guard that room number and insist you don't want to be disturbed. He'll get nervous."

"Or he'll call the press. Both the palace and snappers will have fun with the fact that I check into a hotel room. How will I leave the room without him noticing?"

"If you order him not to disturb you during this tryst, will he pay attention?"

She thought a moment, then nodded. "He's new. I think he'll try to take it in stride, as long as he can check the room beforehand and keep watch at the door. But he'll tell his superiors."

"Okay. Explain to the guard that you need privacy. Not long afterward, I'll head upstairs, create a distraction. That's when you slip out of the adjoining room and take the stairs down to the car garage below. That will be the door immediately to your left."

"You really think we can do this? My guard won't take his eyes off the door to my hotel room."

"Leave that to me. I'll be in a jealous rage. You'll hear me talking with him and I'll shout, 'Damn it all to hell!' That's your cue. The garage has valet parking, so watch out for any attendants. My car's blocked in, against the wall. The BMW." He slid a key across the table, then reached for his coffee. "You can't miss it. Get inside and hide, and oh, and excuse all the papers on the floor."

"I'm a large person," Elena warned. "Someone could spot me."

"Get in the back. I keep a blanket back there. Cover yourself and stay still. I'll argue with the guard a bit and then act annoyed that you took off."

"If he doesn't suspect you, then perhaps he won't follow you later on," Elena agreed.

"Exactly. I'll linger in the lobby a bit, check for my mail, and possibly have another cup of coffee—maybe even check how the guard reacts. When it's all clear, I'll head to the car and we take off."

"I want to go to VanCrendon Hall, my sons' school. My younger son will be hanging around the tennis courts this evening, and I arranged to meet him there tonight."

Michael frowned. "No one else knows about it?"

She shook her head.

"How far is the school?"

"Less than an hour away."

"Let's not keep the boys waiting."

Finding the car, hiding inside, that was easy. Elena's biggest problem was trying to maintain a straight face, especially after meeting Michael's acquaintance, Douglas Hill, who waited in the hotel room. The man was impeccable and well-dressed, but only in his twenties. Looking awkward and guilty, he stood and watched as Elena's guard checked the hotel suite. Meanwhile, Elena hurried into the bathroom and blasted the shower full force to muffle her giggles. Not long after the guard left and Douglas closed the door, she quickly ordered room service, as directed by Michael and left instructions that the room should not be disturbed.

Not long afterward, Michael stormed through the hallway, shouting questions and accusing the guard of whisking Elena away from the bar. Other guests complained, and hotel security joined the fray, as well as the manager on duty.

Young Douglas opened the door and scolded both his friend Michael and the guard, asking that the discussion move to some other part of the building. Michael charged toward the room and both Hill and the new guard tackled him and held him to the ground. Hill fumbled with his phone, calling hotel security, and together, three men moved Michael around the corner to the elevator. There, he shouted the phrase. Elena took off her heels, carrying them as she slipped out of the room. Without looking back, she rushed down the stairwell with its green concrete walls to the parking garage and found Michael's car parked nearby. Using his key, she climbed into the back passenger seat and quickly closed the door. Tucking the blanket to hide her skirt, pulling it over her head, she slouched and waited. For what seemed like hours, all she could do was listen to the sounds of valets shouting and engines gunned as vehicles were rearranged into narrow spaces.

Finally she heard footsteps approach her car and Elena held her breath, worrying that some valet or her guard would discover her before Michael arrived. Her knees and thighs hurt as she tried to curl up even tighter. What if Michael were lying? What if he sided with Edward and really wanted to embarrass her?

She shook her head. If she could worm away from palace security, she could escape anyone, including Michael. The car door opened, and a strange voice shouted out: "This one's finally ready to go!" Moving briskly, a valet started the car with a loud roar and turned the wheel sharply for the front drive of the hotel. The driver then hopped out, and she could hear Michael casually chatting about his disappointment with the hotel, as he leaned against the open door. Michael's voice was calm, but Elena sensed that palace eyes were on the vehicle. She tightened every muscle, wishing she could shrink into the space.

The door slammed, and Michael drove off in silence, at a reasonable speed. Seconds later, he turned the radio on to a low volume.

"How did it go?" she questioned.

"Wait," he said. "And don't move." He turned on the radio and sang with the music.

Stiff, tense, Elena waited.

About ten minutes later, he spoke. "Good work," he murmured.

"Yes," she said her voice muffled.

"Don't get up," he cautioned. "God knows who's following." He used a singsong voice. "And if someone's following, let them to think that I'm singing with the radio."

"It's so warm back here," she complained. "Can you open a window? Did my bodyguard suspect anything?"

"Don't think so . . . room service was keeping him occupied when I left. There was champagne for two at the room, all ordered by you. Douglas assured your man that you'd be busy through the night. The guard's face was red."

"Poor chap, he's probably worried that tomorrow he'll be out of a job."

"It depends if he falls for the charade. How long do you give him, before he gets curious and checks?"

"No idea, he's too new for me to know," Elena said. "But they'll immediately suspect you."

"That's why we're going to ditch this car. I called a friend and arranged for the rental of another one." Elena pulled her arms out from underneath the blanket and braced against the front seat, as Michael twisted the car, making numerous turns.

Frustrated that she could not see where he headed, Elena kicked away the blanket and moved her elbows to the back seat. She could not resist lifting her head to peek out the rear window. No cars followed, and Michael took a lonely driveway through a park. Pulling into a small parking area, he parked close to a nondescript gray Toyota. A thin woman with long red hair and a gray suit was walking away from the vehicle, and no other cars were in sight.

Michael looked about and then handed Elena a baseball cap. "I'm going to open the door and you jump into the other car quickly. Stay as low as you can."

He hurried out, transferred a suitcase from the BMW to the Corolla, then opened the rear doors to both vehicles. Elena gathered her skirt around her knees and, despite the stiffness in her long legs, climbed nimbly into the Corolla's back seat. "Pray no one has caught on," he murmured, before jumping into the driver's seat and starting the engine. "And stretch out some so no one realizes how tall you are."

As he exited the park along a side street, police cars with shrill sirens came from the opposite direction. She noticed that Michael had since removed his jacket and donned a gray sweatshirt. He tossed another sweatshirt back to her.

She slouched in the corner of the vehicle and stretched her legs out, watching as they drove away from the quiet neighborhood. Schoolchildren had already headed home. Lights and televisions were already on, and the few people on the streets were intent on getting home for dinner.

Michael took another slow tour of the neighborhood streets to ascertain that no one followed before taking off for the motorway leading to VanCrendon.

CHAPTER 21

"Should we worry?"

"She always plays this game with new guards."

The Corolla approached the outskirts of the boarding school before sunset. Michael drove slowly along the road, glancing up the hill. Only a few of the auxiliary structures could be seen beyond a tall gate, also wired for security purposes. Elena leaned forward. "Just a bit past the main gate."

"I don't know about this. The place looks like a fortress."

"The wall is not so high by the tennis courts, and the thick brush gives us cover."

"I'll break my neck!"

"Not you." Elena grimaced. "Larry has climbed that wall plenty of times. Whenever I visit the boys here, I can't sit still and neither can they. We've walked the trails around this school countless times. And Larry doesn't just go on a walk. The child runs, climbs, leaps, every step of the way."

"I haven't noticed anyone tracking us here," Michael said, driving slowly. "But it's unwise to leave the car by the side of the road."

"Drop me off and you'll find a church just ahead. Hikers park in the rear lot. You can stay there or you can walk up the road and join us here."

"I'll wait. Tell Larry to find his brother fast. I'll give you twenty minutes before I drive back around. Hopefully, all four of us will take off."

"Michael, I'm not sure what to do if I can't convince Richard."

"Don't underestimate yourself. You're his mother! He'll listen to you."

Elena shook her head and stared out the window, staring at the forest. "It's not that simple, I'm afraid. For years, he's watched palace staff treat me as inconsequential. I've had to fight time and time again to have my way with those boys—in terms of schools, activities, friendships, little freedoms that most people take for granted. That's hard for the children to ignore. The family cares for Richard. He feels an affinity with his grandmother, the queen. She's the center of that family's world, and Richard enjoys being part of the family." She was quiet a moment. "What I'm saying is, it won't be easy for him to leave."

Michael slowed the car. She still wore the black skirt from lunch, with the braided top covered by a green sweatshirt. She thought about stripping the silk stockings from her legs. But then she didn't have sneakers. She opened the car door, and Michael twisted around and reached for her. "Wait—what will you do if the boys refuse to leave?"

"I don't know," she admitted.

He frowned. "I'll swing by soon. Stay back in the woods to make sure there's no other traffic on the road when I pass by to pick you up," Michael urged. "Try to get back in twenty minutes."

Minutes later, she ducked her head to avoid the tangle of raspberry, wild rose and other prickly branches and stepped carefully over piles of rocks and old branches. The area between the road and wall was not landscaped at all and the wild bushes had twisted together into a scratchy barricade. Her stockings were ruined in minutes. In a hurry, Elena wasn't sure how long Larry would wait.

At last she reached an imposing stone wall that divided trim school grounds from the wild tangle. Weather and time compacted the pile of dull and oversized gray stones, arranged by hand hundreds of years ago. With no holes or spaces, the wall was just over six feet tall, enough that Elena could not see beyond and check the exact location of the tennis courts. No sounds of children came from the school grounds. She wanted to call out her son's name, but was afraid. She didn't want to get Larry into trouble.

She paused and whistled the distinctive two-note call of a black-capped chickadee, the first note high and the second note low: *fee-bee, fee-bee*. Chickadees performed more in the early morning than at dusk—and lived in the United States at that—but she doubted that many at VanCrendon were familiar with the bird. Larry had learned about birdcalls during a program about Henry David Thoreau, how the chickadees returned calls back and forth, and he had since practiced with his mother. She waited a full minute before calling again: *fee-bee*.

The wrong birds twittered, unseen in the darkening canopy. The sun was still up, but underneath the trees, the light had vanished, and the leaves looked more gray than green. At last, came a wavering reply: *fee-bee*. Elena instantly recognized Larry because his first note fell short. He was not far. She tried calling out his name softly, but the boy did not reply.

Elena checked her watch, studied the wall and then chose a foothold, grappling with her hands. She clutched onto the edges and finally managed to get her hand over the top of the wall. Boosting herself to the top, she prayed that the old wall would not topple as she looked about. The campus resembled a still life of lonely perfection. She was not far from the empty tennis courts. She whistled the chickadee call once more, and Larry emerged from a stand of trees and waved. No one else was in sight, but Elena put a finger to her mouth. Wearing dark clothes that blended with the setting, he ran along the wall toward her.

She held out her hand to help him climb to the top, and they sat close together, near a low tree limb that shielded the pair from curious eyes.

"Your call's better than mine," Larry complained. "I couldn't get a good one out tonight."

"We found each other, dear," she whispered. "How would you like to leave with me tonight?"

"That would be the greatest," the boy said, his eyes wide with glee.

"Wait, Larry," she cautioned. "I want you to find Richard." The boys didn't have to wear school uniforms during the evening, but his outfit was mismatched dark colors, brown and blue and an old dark hat covering the red hair. She grimaced, thinking how the dreadful outfit probably attracted notice.

"I don't know about Richard." Larry hesitated.

"What's the matter?" Elena pressed.

"I don't think he'll come. He's been awfully tight with Derry the last day or two. Ever since two security men came up from the palace last week. They spoke to us about self-defense, running away and staying away from strangers. That sort of thing. Then, before they left, they told us to contact them immediately if either you or father tried to talk us out of leaving the school."

The comment startled her. "Your father?" Elena bent over to look Larry in the eye. "Are you sure they mentioned him, too?"

The boy nodded. "They said that the procedure might be part of a security test for all of us. The usual gibberish."

"Indeed." She didn't want to frighten her son, but wondered why security had included Edward in the cautionary note. Did the palace really mistrust her husband, or did Edward have reason to remove the children? She studied her son's eyes. "I'm worried about our safety and I'd like to leave tonight. But I can't leave without Richard. Do you really think that he'd contact security right away?"

Larry nodded vigorously. "He's big on duty these days."

"You sound frightened."

The boy shrugged and looked up the hill. "I am."

"Why?" his mother asked.

"I can't stand it. Derry tries awfully hard to separate Richard and me. He doesn't want us to enjoy each other's company anymore. It was never like this when we stayed with you or father. Richard sometimes falls for his tricks."

An anger swept through Elena. But she had to remain calm.

"Anything else you want to tell me?" Elena pressed.

"I caught him messing with Richard's computer. I'm sure he doesn't know the password. Derry doesn't know what he's doing. But he forbids me to go near the computer or Richard's room! He was furious that I caught him."

"I haven't received many E-mails from Richard lately. He keeps the BlackBerry hidden, doesn't he?"

"He's watched constantly, Mom. He's stuck with Derry, and I feel bad for him."

Elena tried to remember recent messages she had sent and how Richard had responded. Most were short, light and included nothing that the palace could use against her. But the staff were odd and could create problems where none existed. And of course, she had never signed her name. Paul had promised that the BlackBerry could not be tied to her.

"Go find Richard," Elena urged. "Get him to come here."

Larry shook his head, as if scolding her. "I doubt that I can keep Derry from tagging along . . ."

"Do your best!" she cried out. "We can't just walk away without talking with him!"

Elena decided that she would have a better time convincing Richard if she could take him into her arms, hug him, and whisper into his ear. And that would best be accomplished on the ground and not from her shaky perch on the wall. She looked for handholds and poked about with her feet, looking for crevices that would hold her weight. Slowly, she lowered herself, scraping her shoes beyond repair. Only a few small pebbles tumbled. She looked about and decided to hide behind some brush near a massive oak. She leaned against the rough old bark and somehow felt that once Richard was over the wall, he would be more likely to go with her. At least ten minutes had passed, and she wondered how soon Michael's patience would run out.

Suddenly, she heard branches snap behind her. Elena imagined Larry's young legs running up the long grassy slope that led to the dormitories and the boys' rooms, and estimated that he was in the room, convincing Richard at this moment. Darkness was almost complete, and a golden glow came from most of the rooms. Reading time would start soon, with bedtime not long afterward.

Elena paused to listen, and hoped Michael was near. She edged around the oak, crouching and listening. Not the boys, she knew. Together, they'd be talking or bickering. Alone, Larry would simply clamber over the wall.

She pressed against the tree and waited, hoping the boys would be circumspect about returning to the wall. She checked her watch once again. Only a few minutes had passed. She heard another branch snap from the direction of the road. Elena closed her eyes, waiting to see who approached before calling out.

The boys could be here any minute, she thought to herself. Suddenly, a shape lunged at her from behind and grabbed the top of her arm and wrist, yanking her arm behind her back. Elena cried out in pain as she bent forward, unable to break away.

"You!" Derry pushed her to the ground. "I knew, as soon as I heard your security detail lost you in London. So, when Larry was missing from the evening games, I followed him. And look at what I find."

"I'm allowed to visit my sons!" she protested, twisting to see his face.

He pressed her arm tight, keeping her to the ground. "Why the deception? Why don't you visit the conventional way?"

"You've ruined my outfit!" she snapped. "Let go of me immediately or I'll scream."

"You have some explaining to do." But he let go and she slowly backed away. Reaching for the oak, she stood, feeling nervous, guilty, afraid all at once. She reminded herself that guilt was ridiculous because she had done nothing wrong. The man had no control over her or her children. "I have a right to see my children when and how I please. Without a lot of staff or press around."

"The press!" he scoffed. "They're the only ones left who care about you."

Elena laughed. "The difference between me and my husband's family is that I don't care what people think of me. Especially you!"

He grabbed her shoulders and shoved her against the tree hard. "You're no better than me. You're no longer part of the family, and I don't have to listen to you."

"Get your hands off of me," Elena shouted, hoping that Michael would hear and come to her rescue. "You can't possibly care about my son if you want to keep him away from me. He won't allow it!"

"You have no control," Derry said.

"I'll talk to the Prince of Wales about this. Do you hear me? You're not to go near Richard again!"

Derry lifted his hand and slapped her hard. She cried out. He curled his hand into a fist and went to strike her again. Turning to shield her face, she heard someone running and then a horrible thudding noise.

Derry slumped and fell against her, knocking her hard to the ground.

Terrified, she could not speak or move. But then two sets of arms pulled the valet off her, and awkwardly cradled her. "Mum, Mum, are you all right?" Richard's voice sounded distant to her.

"He hit her!" Larry said, in horror. "You saw it, Richard! Please talk, Mum. Are you all right?"

Elena reached to touch both of them with her hands and struggled to keep from crying. "Thank God, you're both all right. No, he didn't hurt me much. I suppose I'll have a nasty bruise."

"Sorry, Mum," Richard said sheepishly. "We came down the hill and heard the arguing, everything. We climbed the wall farther down, and decided a surprise attack was in order."

"Don't apologize, Richard," Elena said wearily. "I think you saved my life." She leaned over and checked Derry's neck. "He's still breathing, but you knocked him out good. I was frightened."

"I hope that he doesn't realize it was me," Richard said nervously.

Elena stared at her son and realized that he was terrified of a staff member who was supposed to work for him. "This isn't right, Richard," she said. "We can't be afraid of what they think of us."

"The palace won't believe us, Mum," he said. His voice was panicked.

"Tell me what went on tonight," she said, trying to keep calm.

"He ordered me to stay in my room after dinner. Some call came in and he rushed out. He said he had heard from security in London that some threats had been made against us again."

She thought a moment and tried to reassure her sons. "I

doubt it's true," she said. "Derry seems to be the biggest threat of the moment. But we have to get out of here. Too many strange things have been happening, and he'll wake up soon. Derry is part of a group that wants to get rid of me—maybe even kill me. And I'm not sure if you two are safe, or for that matter, your father."

Richard frowned and shook his head. "But we can't just leave. Where would we go?"

"I can't take the chance," Elena said. "I want you both to leave with me."

"Tonight? Now?" Richard asked.

Elena nodded. Larry stood, ready to go. Richard hesitated.

"Sweetheart, we can't plan a trip or announce we're leaving. They won't allow us to leave. The only way we can be safe is to get away and explain what happened later. We can't be sure whom to trust here."

Richard's lips were tight with anxiety and Elena hurt for her son. "Mum, they think you're crazy. I know it's not true. But if we leave . . ." He shook his head and didn't finish.

"I can't change that," Elena said. "But I'm your mother and have to do what I think is best. I can't make you go, Richard. But I want you to leave."

"I wouldn't have gone before," Richard said, gesturing toward Derry. "Grandmum always told me that the system was sacred. That we were part of a tradition that could be trusted. I always believed her. Before."

"A system can never be fair if it holds that one person is better than another, if the opinion of one person or a group of people matters more than others," Elena said softly. "You're at the top of that system, Richard. But believe me, that system hurts you more than anyone else. That system forces you to fall back and rely on it for strength. Your ideas, your character, your very essence, have no worth on their own. You're only as good as this bizarre system."

She put an arm around each of her sons. "You boys are good. I married your father when I was too young and did not understand the implications. It's only in recent years that I've come to see the challenges the system imposes on our family. The inequities. All I know is this—how important you are as individuals. Not as royalty, but as individuals. The system doesn't have to take over your lives, your choices. I should have thought about all these matters before I married your father. But I didn't. I know more now. We must leave."

"I'm out of here," Larry piped up, without looking or waiting for his brother.

On the ground, Derry stirred, startling Elena. "What about him?" Richard asked.

Elena bent and tentatively checked the man. "He's not bleeding," she whispered. "You knocked him out good, but he'll come out of it soon. There's not much we can do other than escape and reach a phone." She held out a hand to her son and waited.

"I can't," he said, with finality, avoiding his mother's eyes. "I feel like I can perhaps do something to change the system. That I'm the only one. Please don't let that stop the two of you. I love you, but I also love Father, and he needs us, too. . . ."

Elena started to talk, but Richard reached for her arm. "Look, I love the both of you, and if anyone can talk to him and explain your dilemma, it's me. Give me at least until tomorrow evening."

"I don't know," she said. "That seems so dangerous to me, especially with Larry and me on the run."

"Don't you understand?" Richard said with a smile. "That gives me a safety net. That's why you both should go, and I can stay. I'm sure Derry didn't see the two of us out here, so I'll be okay." Elena rubbed her head, resonating with pain. Maybe her son was right—about being okay with Larry and his mother away. She took him in her arms and hugged him. Richard let go first, and nodded at Larry. "Take care of each other," he said. "I'll talk to Father tomorrow, and we'll work something out. Father will believe me."

Elena stared at her older son. "You have courage," she said, hugging him. "I love you. Hurry back to the room and be safe."

Larry tugged on his mother's arm and the two headed through the dark woods, startled by the sudden appearance of the road. At least forty minutes had passed. They walked along the edge of the motorway—and hid when they saw headlights. Elena guessed that the car traveled at least half the posted speed, but waited, holding tight to Larry's arm. Security could be on the alert for missing princes.

She waited to see the driver. The car passed. Inside, Michael hunched over the wheel, worry etched on his face. She leaped into the road and waved her arms wildly. Michael braked— Elena and Larry ran up the road and opened the doors.

Michael pulled over to the shoulder. "Hurry and get in." He glanced back to the side of the road. "What took so long? And where's Richard?"

"He wants a little more time. He plans to talk to his father tomorrow."

He stared at her. "Your face . . ."

She leaned back and closed her eyes. She worried about leaving Richard behind, but knew she couldn't convince him. Still, she didn't feel right about separating the two boys.

"Richard fought with you?"

"Not at all," Elena snapped. "Floor it and let's get out of here."

Michael pulled onto the road, using the turn signal. "I don't dare go over the speed limit with you two as cargo. Besides, we need to think of someone who will be willing to hide you."

"You don't know anyone?" Elena asked in surprise. "Why not your embassy?"

He shook his head. "I told you, they're polarized. You have some enemies there. Besides, they wouldn't keep it a secret. And what proof do we have about someone trying to hurt you— despite your face." He glanced at her with a worried look. "No, think of someone else. Not family. No close friends. Who would be the last person they'd suspect?"

Elena moaned. "I could make some calls."

"Surprise is the better tactic," Michael said. "We cannot afford to use our cell phones or anything else that can be traced. You need serious help from someone you trust like nobody else. Because security will be watching your family and your closest friends."

Elena thought a moment and made an impulsive choice. "I know. Head back to the city."

"Are you sure? They'll be checking all the roads, the airport. . . ."

"They won't expect this neighborhood. Trust me."

CHAPTER 22

"She left with the youngest."
"Proof of her instability. Track her down. And the other boy?"
"He claims to know nothing of her plot."

Michael handed over a New York Yankees baseball cap to Larry, and advised Elena to tuck any strays of gold hair under her hat. Urging them both to slouch low in the seat, he took small roads back to the city. Frequent lights and stops doubled the length of the trip, making him nervous, but he wanted to avoid every major road with tolls or security cameras, police or anyone with a security radio. They neared the Brent neighborhood after midnight, and the streets were quiet.

Larry huddled against the window in the back seat and fell asleep. Elena studied a map with a small torch and called out directions. She kept her head down and gave no reason for weary motorists or impatient dog walkers to assess her with more than a passing glance.

Michael kept checking his rearview mirrors and scanning ahead for police cars, occasionally reminding her to keep her head low. With her head tilted a certain angle, she looked too damn regal. But then he was biased, coming from the United States. As a newcomer, he noticed how many British women tried to copy the hairstyles, the mannerisms, the fashions of the Princess of Wales and didn't quite measure up. With any luck, any passersby who took a quick glance would assume the woman in his car was a more talented copycat than most.

He tapped the buttons of the radio, switching from station to station, searching for news. The news reports were brief, with no mention of the missing princess and prince. Security was undoubtedly aware, but probably decided against releasing the information until the morning.

Michael checked his rearview mirror again, thankful so little traffic was on the roads. Larry stirred, sat up and looked startled and then changed his position and settled back into sleep. The boy had engaging eyes, like his mother. Michael noticed the boy's lips tilted into a slight frown that revealed an odd combination of defiance and relief. How many children went to sleep like that every night, Michael wondered. How many could really trust that their parents were trying their best? The reporter eased his foot on the accelerator and tried to shake off the strange thoughts that popped into one's head late at night. He had to concentrate and keep his driving perfect.

"I don't like how close these houses are," Michael murmured looking at the rows of brick buildings. "You'd be amazed how much neighbors notice."

"Third right after Dudden Hill," she directed.

"Keep your head down," he advised, as he took the turn. "This could be good in other ways—not at all your sort of neighborhood. So, this friend, she lives alone?"

Elena frowned and replied, "I'm not sure."

"What?" Michael said. He abruptly pulled the Corolla to the side of the road and braked hard. "What do you mean?"

"I just don't!" Elena snapped. "I've never been to her home!"

"How well do you know this woman?" he questioned.

"Well enough," Elena said, stubbornly. "And she knows me better than most. She was my nurse in the hospital, after the car bombing. She could have divulged a lot about my problems. But she didn't. So I trust her. She treated me more like a human being than most people I know in this world. I may not know her well, but I trust her more than friends or family."

"How long were you in the hospital?"

Elena hesitated. "Almost a week. But she was with me constantly."

"And you haven't seen her since," he guessed. Elena slowly nodded, and Michael shook his head. "I hope you know what you're doing."

"Keep driving and stop arguing." He wondered if her confidence was real. "Or, the police will think we're having a domestic dispute."

He groaned. "A nurse that you knew for one week."

"What are you complaining about?" Elena asked. "You told me to select a person whom I trust. A home that police would never dream of searching. And how well do I know you?"

"I'm headed there. It's your life at stake. I have to trust your judgment." He pushed his hair back from his eyes. "Tell me she's not some silly adoring fan."

"She's not," Elena said. "And believe me, I can detect the difference far better than you. Let's call her on your cell phone."

"No calls—they'd trace us."

"Then, let's stop at a callbox over there. We're not far away. I don't want to drive up and just knock on the door, standing there and having to explain, not knowing who's inside her home. You can talk with her yourself."

Michael pulled the car over and dialed quickly.

Rita answered sleepily. "You don't know me," Michael began awkwardly.

"No, I don't!" the nurse snapped. "Or, you'd know that I'm expected at the hospital before seven tomorrow morning. You better not be selling anything."

"Not at all," Michael hurried. "I'm calling for someone who needs your help."

There was a long pause. "Who?" she asked warily. "What did Danny do now?" Michael noticed that Rita did not seem alarmed or surprised. Odd, he thought.

"No, a former patient. You once mentioned that you would be willing to help her. I can't say who over the phone."

She did not sound surprised at all. "Where are you?"

"In your neighborhood. Not far."

"Come on by," Rita replied. "I'll leave my backdoor open, and we can all talk."

"We'll be there in ten minutes," Michael replied.

"Do you have a car?" Rita asked suddenly, and Michael told her yes. "There's not much parking in my neighborhood, and people complain if you take their spots. But my next-door neighbor is away on a business trip, and his garage space is empty. Pull behind the green house next door and park in the middle slot. Then come to the back. I'll only put one light on—more could attract attention."

"Sounds good."

"I'll start the tea kettle."

Minutes later, the car pulled into the driveway without lights. Michael turned off the engine and urged Elena to wait a moment. He was anxious, half expecting dozens of men, armed and angry, to swarm all over the vehicle and remove the sleeping boy. He turned to Elena who looked wan, more nervous than tired. She had made difficult choices during the last few hours, each utterly changing the direction of her life and that of her son. And there were more to make in the hours ahead. He had to get her out of the country before either of them dared go public with the tale and accusations. If they got caught, he had no doubt that the family and staff would confine her, insisting that she was mentally unbalanced.

But he didn't voice these thoughts with her. Michael reached out and held her hand. "If you, we, get caught, we'll simply lie," he whispered. "I'm a rambunctious reporter who went too far in getting an interview. That would be the easiest."

Elena looked at him, her skin pale, almost translucent in the night. Tiny lines etched around her eyes gave her dignity. Her hair was tousled and gold. He was not supposed to feel this way, but he wanted to clean and kiss her bruise.

"I can't get caught," she murmured. "If that happens, they'll toss me into an asylum and never let me out. They could do it, too."

He didn't nod, didn't want to pass on his growing anxiety to her. Instead, he squeezed her soft and ringless hand. She had left impulsively with nothing. He could try and explain in articles, but no one would believe a sole reporter. Alone, he'd be labeled as a troublesome eccentric.

"We won't get caught," he promised. "We'll get you out of the country and before another set of journalists. They'll see you and talk to you. The palace will have trouble refuting basic common sense, particularly if we're standing on soil in another country."

A smile briefly swept across Elena's lips, followed by a deep breath. "Let's begin the next part of our adventure," she said, opening the car door.

"Wait—maybe I should go in and check the house first," Michael cautioned.

"No," Elena said with soft firmness. "I must thank Rita with my trust. She's done so much for me. Would you mind staying with Larry? He'll make a fuss if he wakes up alone in the car."

"Get your hat back on," he ordered. Elena complied, and then reached back and tucked the green sweatshirt around her child's shoulders. "She said the door would be open."

Without another word, she glided out of the car and across the small yard, heading for the light of Rita's kitchen, with far too much grace for the time of night or the neighborhood. Michael kept his hands on the wheel and watched every step of the tall woman in black. By the time she reached the small porch, Elena blended with the shadows.

Elena paused at the door and knocked tentatively—there was no sound from inside and the kitchen light was low. Not wanting to stand outside for long, she slowly turned the doorknob and opened the door, stepping into a small hall before the kitchen. Rita hurried into the small kitchen with a worried face and her arms crossed. She threw her hands up and beamed as she recognized her midnight visitor. "I knew it had to be you," Rita whispered, glancing out the window.

The two women hugged quickly, as Rita took her hand and led her to the table. The tea kettle gave a shrill whistle, and it was only after Elena sat at the table for two that Rita moved it to another burner.

"With any luck, no one else will make the connection that I'm here." Elena removed the hat and shook her head. She moved her neck in a slow circle. The night was long, but she wasn't nearly ready for sleep. "I had to find a safe and private place—one that the family or police would never suspect." She paused. "You haven't told anyone?"

Rita shook her head. "No, I never spoke of you to anyone. Even about the photo, which I posted as you suggested. The sum helped my mother. But I'm not a gossip, and I kept your secret."

"I know," Elena said. "All manner of gossip could have come from that hospital stay. But it didn't, and that's why I knew I should come here."

Rita fussed with teacups and sugar and spoons. "It makes me feel good that you could trust me. I saw how unhappy you were in the hospital. I've worried about you ever since."

"Yes, but now I'm going to leave—the family, the country."

Rita paused. "But how can you run away from it all? Where can you go?"

"This is a first stop," Elena admitted. "I didn't plan ahead—an opportunity came up, and I took it."

"The man who called—he's helping you?"

Elena nodded. "He's in the car, with my son."

"The prince, too?" Rita's eyes went large.

"The younger one. Outside—with the American man who's going to help get us out of the country."

"You're leaving with one of the princes," said Rita, as if in a daze. "That will take some doing." Then she shook her head. "Let's get them inside. And if you don't mind, I'm going to put you in the cellar for sleeping. There are no windows down there, and the neighbors might wonder if I suddenly start pulling the shades upstairs. I've always been a fanatic about sunlight!"

"A cellar sounds lovely."

Rita smiled. "It's not so bad. It's finished with carpet and two sofas. And I have sleeping bags. . . ." Rita stopped and waved her hand, looking around her small kitchen with embarrassment. "But it's a cellar, and nothing in this house is as fine as what you must be used to."

Elena paused to look around the room, taking in the plants on the window sill, a tiny shelf with its array of spices, the pile of bills on the counter's edge, a plate of muffins, and the mismatched potholders. Little frames held tiny photographs, most sporting a gray tabby. The room was pale yellow and white, cheery and normal even in the middle of the night. "This is much finer than you can imagine," Elena declared. "This is a home."

"Then make yourself comfortable," Rita said. "I'll go out and collect your friend and son." She donned a black sweatshirt and slipped out the backdoor.

Moments later, Rita guided the sleepy child into the house, and Elena quickly tucked Larry, clothes and all, into a sleeping bag downstairs. The boy closed his eyes and clutched a pillow. Then Michael and Elena took turns with quick showers. Elena could not fit into Rita's petite clothes and instead donned men's jeans and an Oxford shirt that belonged to Michael, all comfortable and loose. Rita located a beat-up pair of men's trainers, which fit Elena's feet when she wore two thick pairs of socks. She then set out to apply some ointment to Elena's cheek.

Rita turned the lights low and checked a twenty-four-hour news channel, which still carried no word about Elena's tryst, the abduction of a prince, or the attack on the valet. The three adults, too excited for sleep, lingered at the kitchen table and sipped hot tea. Elena kept taking deep breaths and also poured some cream into her tea, trying to ease her nervousness. Abduction. The word was harsh, considering she was the boy's mother. All her life, every decision regarding the two princes had to be approved by the palace. The palace knew the location and activities of both boys every moment of their lives. Until this evening. She wondered if the reaction would be different if Richard had gone missing as well. Had her older son somehow found a way to explain his missing brother?

Elena was pleased about the silence from the palace—until she saw Michael's tight lips.

"They want to avoid publicity, or they don't know yet," Elena said, trying to assure him.

"They know—Derry must check in occasionally," he pointed out, then shook his head glumly. "No, they think they can catch you—before word gets out." He stared into his cup of hot tea. "Then they can control the situation." He ran his hand through his thick hair. "And I'm probably your biggest liability at this point. You're nowhere to be found, and neither am I—one of the last people to be seen with you. They'll guess that I gave you some help. I can't decide what to do. Go back out in public, act like nothing happened. Or stay with you until we leave."

"I think it's best if we leave the country quickly. They might not expect that."

"Do we hide together or separate?"

Elena was nervous. Escape was not so easy, and she could not decide. All she knew was that she didn't want to be alone, but she wasn't sure that clinging to Michael was the best plan for Larry or Rita.

"All three of you can stay here," Rita offered, with a worried look.

"If I do stay, then I must ditch the car."

"It's hard to leave Richard behind," Elena admitted. "I keep hoping that he'll change his mind and get in touch with us."

Michael frowned.

Rita interjected, "What would happen to you, Michael, if you returned to public, pretended that you knew nothing and went on with your business. Even if the waggers did suspect that Elena had driven away with you tonight? What would be the consequence?"

He shrugged. "They could detain me. I'd call my embassy. They'd need firm proof to hold me. I'm sure they have no proof."

"No one saw me enter your car," Elena said firmly. "But if you leave here, then it will make it that much harder to return."

"And the same goes for Richard," Michael cautioned. "Once they know for sure that you're leaving the country, they won't let him out of sight. Hiding is the way to go. But can we all stay here?"

Rita nodded. "Yes, of course."

"Could Rita get in much trouble for hiding us?" Elena asked.

Michael was quiet for a moment. "Not as long as the palace is keeping this a secret. Not as long as Larry is with his mother."

He looked at both women. "But let's be honest—the authorities and the press could make her life miserable."

Rita closed her eyes. "Every life can use a bit more adventure. I'm game. I have plenty of space."

"I left nothing important behind in the hotel room, and I'm paid until the end of the week. But I could move the car somewhere and try to throw them off our tracks."

"Maybe I should telephone someone at the palace," Elena mused. "Find out what they know."

"No calls!" Michael insisted. "Certainly not from here. It's too dangerous."

"Of course," Elena agreed. "But I wish I knew what they were thinking."

"We'll keep the telly on, and we'll wait for the morning paper," Rita said. "And I'll keep my ears open to any gossip. The entire royal family can't keep a secret about you and Prince Larry being missing for long. But moving the car could be dicey."

Michael tapped his finger on the table. "It could be on some tracking list by now. They probably already connected it to terrorism of some sort. I don't want it linked here."

"Me neither." Rita swallowed. "I suppose it's best if you move it sooner than later. We could even go out and borrow a set of plates from the neighbors—just until you get it moved. Maybe the police won't be as alert."

"I should leave now," Michael agreed.

"Hold on," Rita said. "First a little change with the hair." With that, she hurried to a drawer and pulled out shears and directed him to another room.

Less than fifteen minutes later, Rita and Michael emerged from the bathroom with his hair short and slightly spiky with gray streaks. He resembled hundreds of working men who rode trains every morning to mundane jobs and punched time clocks.

"I was a witch one year for Halloween," Rita explained, holding a can of spray.

"It's four in the morning," Elena noted. "We could all use some rest."

Michael looked exhausted. "But I should move the car soon."

"Dark circles under his eyes are good," Rita observed. She disappeared into her bedroom and emerged with dark eye shadow, and lightly applied some under his eyes.

"You look older." Elena was gleeful. "And perfectly dreadful!"

"I'll keep my head low, no eye contact," Michael assured the women.

"Make sure no one follows when you return here," Rita urged.

"It might be later in the day," he said. "I'll get my turn to rest tomorrow."

Rita turned to Elena. "And you, stop laughing at him." Rita was stern. "Your new look is next."

"Coming here was a good idea," Michael said, looking at Elena and then Rita. "This woman knows what she's doing."

Rita placed the eye shadow on the nearest table. "I loved dress-up as a child, and I guess that I never grew up when it comes to that."

Elena hugged him and whispered, "Thank you. And be safe." Then Michael slipped out the backdoor.

The two women stood at the kitchen window and watched the car disappear into the night. "Are you tired?" Rita inquired.

"Yes, but too wired to sleep just yet," Elena admitted.

"Then let's get to work on a new look for you," Rita said. She checked the clock. "I've got some time, and I don't want to wait until I get back from the hospital. Who knows who could come to the door?" With that, Rita ran to a hall closet, returning with a plastic bin containing several boxes of hair dye, in shades varying from chestnut to dark brown. She also had an array of makeup and a home kit for permanents.

About ninety minutes later, the two women could not help but giggle at the results. "Not bad," Rita said, standing back to assess her creation. The princess had dull brown hair, styled with an overdone perm. The baggy clothes that belonged to Michael disguised her lean frame. She could almost pass for an ordinary working woman—one who packed groceries, cleaned the hospital rooms or delivered letters.

"Though you'll always stand out because you're so tall," Rita said. "Not much we can do there."

"One of my biggest regrets," Elena said, wrinkling her nose. "When I was a girl, it kept me from dancing, put me in the back of every classroom, and frightened most of the boys away."

"Stupid boys," Rita said. Elena was checking a hand mirror, when she saw Larry edge nervously around the corner, trying to hide a yawn. His eyes darted from one woman to the next, and his eyes widened as he recognized his mother behind her new look.

"Mum?" he asked. "Your hair looks dreadful."

"Get ready," his mother warned. "We're going to change the way you look, too. Did you sleep okay?" The boy nodded slowly. "Larry, this is Rita, she's going to let us stay with her a while."

"It's an honor," Rita said, briskly nodding her head. "Let's get a start on my next client. We have time before I have to leave for work."

Elena watched as Larry stared at the woman so different than all of her friends. She hugged the little boy, rubbing his shock of red hair.

"Larry, are you sure you want to go through all this and leave?" Elena said. "No second thoughts?" The weary boy nodded slowly.

Rita and Elena set to work trimming, dyeing, and perming,

all at the kitchen sink. Larry howled at the oily smell of the permanent solution. When done, Rita pulled out a hair drier and the boy squirmed. "Oh please, I want to see the finished product before I head off to work!" she teased. "Hold still, and this will go much faster."

As Rita carefully fluffed Larry's hair, Elena automatically cleaned up bits of hair and drips left over from the operation. When she finished, Elena stared, silently reaching out and fingering the boy's shorn hair—the fiery locks gone. The shorter hair made him look older. With a set of worn clothes, he'd be an ordinary ruffian. The enormity of what she was doing suddenly hit her.

Rita sensed Elena's dismay. "I wanted to make him look different . . ."

Elena held her hand up. "Don't apologize. Of course, we do need to look different than we did yesterday. I was only thinking of how most children in the royal family would look if they were part of normal families. Most of the parents virtually ignore the children—and never have to do the actual work of bathing, feeding, choosing clothes and grooming."

"What would the world be like if all the children were treated like princes and princesses?" Rita said.

"What would it be like if all the children had parents who really cared?" Elena added to herself. "Anyhow, Larry looks splendid. I daresay that even his grandmother would pass him by on the street without a second look."

Rita bustled about the kitchen. "I'm making coffee and then I must head for the hospital. I'd call and change shifts, but I think it's best not to change my routine."

"Rita, please don't worry about us. You don't need to entertain us, and we'll behave here. In fact, if you can think of anything for us to do . . ."

"No, not at all," Rita said with embarrassment.

"Well, this is your home, your life, and we're the invaders. We owe you explanations and help. You owe us nothing."

"Please, you remind me of my older sister." Rita blushed. "She always makes me nervous."

"Oh dear!" Elena said, giggling, feeling relief about resembling someone's sister. "Do call if you can think of something for us to do." The two women hugged as they laughed out loud.

"I'm going back to bed," Larry announced loudly with a yawn. Rita directed Elena on how to make scones while she changed.

After Rita hurried to the bus stop, Elena set about to straighten the kitchen, piling dishes in the sink, cleaning counters, putting items back in the refrigerator, feeling awkward only because the setting was new. She had handled such tasks for herself as a child. As she was finishing the dishes at the sink, Larry returned to the kitchen and quickly got antsy.

"I wish we could go outside and explore," the boy complained. "I look different enough."

"But people in the neighborhood would spot you as a new child and they might ask questions." Elena shook her head. "Why don't you read a book? Rita would not mind if you borrowed one."

"But I want to finish the one that I was reading," he complained. "And I left that one in my room."

Elena was too efficient to argue. "Come here then, I have a job for you." She handed the boy a tea cloth and directed him to dry the dishes on the drainboard. Larry looked at his mother with disbelief. "Well, you complained that you were bored, and I'm giving you something to do!" she admonished.

Larry held the towel out as if it were a dead animal. "I don't know how. And I've never seen you do dishes before!"

"There's a first for everything," Elena said, plunging her hands into the bubbles. Too much soap, she thought to herself.

She turned to him as he held a saucer with thumb and finger and dabbed at it with the cloth. "Be careful with the dish. Rita has done us a tremendous favor. Do we really want her coming home and washing our dishes for us? Seeing that we don't have the slightest clue about how to take care of ourselves? We're guests and should help out any way that we can."

"But of course, she wants to help us. We're part of the royal family. I don't think she expects us to do this sort of work for her!"

Elena leaned against the sink, and turned to study her son, and indeed, he was completely serious. She turned the water off, took the dish and towel out of his hand, and sat on the floor, pulling Larry close to her. "Look here, we need to talk a moment." She kept her voice light. She did not want to scold or frighten the child, but she had to make an impression. He was young and had no idea that his life was nothing special away from the palace. "Why are you or Richard, your father or myself, so special that people should bow to us and treat us different from ordinary people walking along the street?"

"Because we're part of the royal family. We're part of British history, and British people love the royal family." Larry automatically parroted lines that had been taught to him since birth.

"But all British people don't love the royal family," Elena explained. "Should those people be forced to bow to us? Pay taxes for our castles? Follow our example? We didn't do anything important or special, Larry."

"But people want to work for us, Mum! It's not like the old days, when they received no pay. Look at Derry. He's thrilled to work with Richard."

"Is he really? Or do you think he pretends?" Elena asked. Larry was quiet and she continued. "Rita's not a servant, Larry. She doesn't have to help us. Everything she does for us comes from her heart, because of a sense of friendship. She'd be insulted if we tried to pay her to escape washing a few dishes. Trust is possible only if there's some assumption of equality."

The boy looked perplexed. "Why don't all people love our family, Mum?"

Annoyed by his question, Elena kept trying to drive home her point. "Many people believe that all people are equal and should be treated as such—that no one person is automatically better than another simply because of the circumstances surrounding their birth. Yes, some people are more intelligent, more creative, or hardworking. Some are more willing to work at learning about nursing or farming or banking. The jobs are different, and some people make more money than others do.

"But our family is regarded as special only because of our background, regardless of anything we achieve as individuals. Take you and your brother as examples. You could be the most intelligent boy. The best at diplomacy and statesmanship and analysis and everything! And still, your brother would be king."

Larry sighed. "That's not fair."

"No, it's not," Elena agreed. "I don't want you to ever feel as though you must compete against your brother. We love him. He did not design this system. All I want for both of you is to find work that you love, to enjoy living, and help others whenever you can."

"I love Richard, too, but I envy him . . ."

"It's natural," Elena cut him off, not wanting to hear a confession. Some words should not be spoken, especially by brothers and sisters who had reason to envy the other. "You can't blame Richard for a massive system out of our control."

Larry made a face. "I'm annoyed that he didn't come with us."

Elena nodded, understanding even though she was more worried than annoyed. "It's more difficult for him," Elena said. "We have to respect his decision. In many ways, your life will be easier because you won't be king. Richard's life is more limited. Larry, I'd be less than honest if I didn't tell you that I detest the monarchy. When I was younger, I had no idea that I'd feel this way. It only hit me when I held you and Richard in my arms as babies. And I saw so much potential there—and so little freedom." She let her breath out hard. "How can I expect Richard to break this dreadful system at his young age, when I couldn't?"

Larry listened as his mother continued. "Remember some of your harshest thoughts about your brother—and try, for one moment, to put yourself in the place of the staff. Think of how they must feel. All the protocol combined with working and caring for us. Thinking for us. And yet, they get little credit."

"Why does the system exist, if you hate it and the servants hate it?"

"I don't know." Elena wrapped her arms around his shoulders for a hug. "Some people prefer safety and tradition, no matter how it must be attained. But I think some change is inevitable. And that's what you and I are trying to do—hurry along some change."

Larry squirmed out of her arms. "Change! And that means that I, a prince, must dry dishes!"

Elena laughed. "Yes, indeed."

"Good thing Richard's not here. He'd be horrified!"

A sharp pain went through Elena's chest, as she stood and resumed washing dishes. She missed her older son and suddenly felt as if she had abandoned him. It was hard to think about him and laugh. But she couldn't dwell on it. She'd been losing control for years—and would have very little if any if she stayed. At least now, she had tremendous control over one son. But the compromise did not feel good.

"Wait until I talk to him next time," Larry said, holding a

flowered plate high in the air. "He won't believe it!"

Elena stopped. "Next time?" she asked. "What do you mean?"

The boy rubbed the dish dry. "Why, I sent him a note when I got up this morning."

Elena pulled away from the sink and turned to him, ignoring the water dripping all over the floor. "Lawrence!" She stared at her son. "Please tell me you didn't try and contact Richard."

Larry was startled. "Don't worry, it wasn't signed or anything."

"But how?"

"Michael has his computer downstairs. I signed on and got into your account."

Elena closed her eyes. "You know that Derry has been nosing about the computer. It could be dangerous! We could get Rita in so much trouble! Why, I wouldn't even risk using the Black-Berry."

"I was careful and wrote in a code we have at school."

"Derry makes it his business to know those sorts of codes," Elena snapped. "God knows if security can track E-mail messages." She ran to the front door and peered out the window. The scene of the ordinary neighborhood street was no different from earlier that morning. A few more cars were missing. A few trash bins had been removed from the street and returned to their hiding places. Elena felt claustrophobic, as if eyes watched from all the nearby houses. It was hard to pull away from the window.

"Show me the computer," she ordered, and followed him to the cellar. The small laptop was on the floor.

"It's different from mine," Elena moaned. "Oh dear, show me how to use it."

Larry had the Internet and E-mail up in less than a minute, by using a wireless network connection that belonged to one of Rita's neighbors, FourGayDudes. "But I erased my message,"

Larry admitted.

She forced herself to be calm. "What did you write? Did you tell him where we are?"

"No," Larry said, happy to give her the answer that he knew she wanted. "I told him you were nervous, that you believed someone was trying to kill us. I said that we missed him and would call when we reach the States. That's where I'd like to go."

"That E-mail could make getting out of the country impossible," Elena said wearily. She fought the urge to pull Larry by the hand and run.

Michael returned later that morning. At the sound of the front door, Elena waited in the kitchen. He looked exhausted, and Elena wanted to let him head to the cellar for sleep, except that she had to tell him about Larry's E-mail.

Opening the refrigerator and pouring some milk, he didn't notice her agitation. "The car is at airport parking. I made some calls and have someone arranging flights for us. That should distract your security team." He started for the cellar. "I'm ready for a nap."

"Michael, we have a problem," she spoke up. "We didn't warn Larry to be careful and he sent an E-mail to Richard."

"No . . ." Panic crossed Michael's face. He immediately hurried for the living room and, without moving the curtain, scanned the street. "They could be watching us now! How did he do it?"

"He got into your computer. I'm so sorry. Through a neighbor's wireless connection."

Larry joined them and looked sheepish. "I'm sorry, Michael."

"Did Richard reply?"

"Not yet," Larry said.

"Check again," Elena suggested.

"No," Michael said firmly. "We stay off the computer and phone—and we plan on getting out of here."

"I should have asked," Larry said.

Michael held his hand up. "What did you write? Exactly."

Larry repeated what he had told his mother. "I wrote when he's usually online, and he didn't reply. I also wrote in code."

Michael went to the computer, pulled the plug from the wall, and returned the computer to its case. "No more calls or messages from here." He was firm. "They're going to monitor any message that goes to Richard and trace anything unusual. With any luck, he gets lots of spam and they have hundreds of messages to check over. If we could only be that lucky. It's only a matter of time before they connect this neighborhood with a woman who was your nurse. We don't have much time."

"Sorry, Mum. I didn't mean to ruin everything." Larry clutched his mother's hand.

"The E-mail was sent," Elena said impatiently. "We can't go back on that. Larry didn't say where we went. Do you think it can be traced to this house?"

Michael rubbed his eyes, weary from lack of sleep and the new problems. "Did you use your school account?"

Larry shook his head. "An old Hotmail account."

"They can connect that message with that wireless account and this neighborhood. I honestly don't know how fast they can do it."

"We could ask the man who set up my computer," Elena suggested. "You could ring him from a callbox."

"We've already put Rita in danger," Michael said. "I don't want to rush and set up a trail to someone else. Before we make any calls, we should probably figure out what they know. We have to get out of here today and let Rita know somehow. It's her decision about whether she should lie outright, or say vandals broke into her home while she was out working."

Elena put her arm out. "You're afraid, aren't you?" she asked.

Michael held her shoulders and stared into her blue eyes. "We don't want to get caught by the wrong people. They'll put you into a psychiatric facility so quick, and they'll arrest me for accessory to child abduction. They'll allow me to make a plea bargain with the condition that I get the hell out of the country and shut up. And you'll be stuck. So yes, I'm terrified. For you. We have to get out of here right away. But first, we have to remove any trace that we were here."

Larry helped the two adults go from room to room, collecting hair dye boxes and food wrappers, and any other evidence that more than one person had spent time in Rita's home. In all, they collected enough for two small bags. Then they took hand towels, and wiped door knobs, tabletops, bathroom fixtures, glasses, and dishes for prints. Elena found some winter gloves and ran the vacuum, then Michael helped her remove the bag, adding that to the rubbish to be removed from the home.

Michael walked from room to room. "I think we're ready," he said, after cautioning Elena and Larry to wait in the kitchen and not touch any surface. "Unfortunately, we have no choice but to leave my suitcase here and let Rita get rid of it. In the meantime, we'll take the garbage with us and toss it in some public bin."

"Maybe we're worried for no reason—let's try and get in touch with Paul Miggins," Elena urged. "He knows about computers and Richard's account specifically."

"All right, write his number down for me," Michael said. "I'm going out and maybe I'll call."

"Don't leave us." Elena's voice was edgy.

"We can't exactly travel around in a flock," Michael warned.

"Why not?" Elena protested. "They're looking for a woman and child! We should travel together."

"Let me take Larry—a boy and dad. You can play along at that, right, Larry?" He turned to Elena and held her shoulders. "You stay here until we check on the details of our trip and find out what they're doing about Richard. Your disguise is good, Elena, but with your height, you still stand out like a sunflower among daisies."

She let out her breath. "Okay, someone should be here if Rita comes home."

Michael nodded. "I spotted a library not far from here. We'll walk there and we can get rid of these bags along the way. When we're ready for you, we'll ring twice on the phone and hang up. Don't answer, but that's when I'll call to have a cab sent to the house. Don't keep the driver waiting and keep an eye out in case you're followed. We'll do the same."

"Wait, I have no money."

Michael pulled out his wallet and handed Elena a twenty-pound note, with its illustration of her mother-in-law.

Elena accepted the money. "I don't like being separated from Larry," she insisted. "Can't we all leave together?"

"It's not a good idea. Look outside. Do you see entire families walking down the street? Even a father and son strolling along in the middle of the afternoon looks strange. But they're not looking for a father. They expect you to be with Larry."

"They may not be looking yet."

"We'll just be one jump ahead of you. In the library, we'll both find a corner and read. Don't come up to us. When we see you, you go sit by the copy machine. I'll make a copy of some magazine article and leave one page on top of the machine. It will have a message about what to do next. You retrieve the paper and pretend to take some notes."

"Be careful," Elena warned.

"You, too. Don't look around, like you're expecting someone to notice you, and no matter what, when out in public, we pretend that we don't know one another. Change your gait, keep your head down. And above all, don't look at anyone directly in the eye."

"Rita wanted us to stay out of sight until she got home," Elena fretted. "How will we let her know?"

"Plans change," Michael said. "We have to move fast. She'll understand." His light kiss on her cheek did not erase her frown. "Don't worry, we'll be back together in less than an hour."

Seconds later he was out the door, refusing to discuss the issue further and clutching Larry's arm. She watched them leave from the kitchen window, as they crossed a few back yards and walked out of sight.

Elena turned to face the kitchen, the dishes all clean and neatly put away. The house was spotless—and she really couldn't touch anything. She couldn't exactly make herself at home anymore, not after all the work they had gone through trying to remove any sign of themselves. In Rita's sitting room, Elena studied the old paperbacks lining the shelves. Tempted, she chose a mystery book, sat on the floor in the main room, and started to read.

She read three chapters, when the phone rang twice. She left the book propped on the floor, stood and checked the front window. Elena thought about leaving by the backdoor and waiting in the driveway, but it was too early for the cab yet. She went to the kitchen for a paper towel, ready to wipe the book and the door handle when it came time to leave. As she ripped the towel, she heard a rattling noise. Someone tried the backdoor. A man's voice called out: "I need the key." There was a pause, before she heard a key in the lock.

Elena panicked and backed away. Rita was not due back for at least another hour. Had security pinpointed her? Were they ready to move in and arrest her? What in the world would Michael do with Larry? Would he take the child to the United

States or hand him over to the palace? She berated herself for not making more plans with Michael in case something went terribly wrong.

Another furtive rattling sound came from the door. Elena slipped behind the door that led to the cellar and left the door cracked. At the bottom of the stairs was a makeshift closet. She ducked inside and crawled into the far back corner, then arranged a few dresses and a coat to shield her face. She curled her legs tightly underneath, pulled some shoes and boots close around her, and waited. It was the best Elena could do without turning on a light. She could be in here awhile or she could be exposed in two minutes. Either way, she might as well make herself comfortable. Forcing herself to take slow, deep breaths, Elena listened.

Two men were upstairs in the kitchen, and they complained about being hungry. The refrigerator opened and bottles clanked—followed by the sound of a ripping bag. Elena's heart beat faster. Rita had been in a hurry to dye hair, but had not mentioned any specific visitors. "We don't have time to cook anything now," one man's voice grumbled. The door to the refrigerator slammed, and a dish clattered in what had been a clean sink.

Suddenly, steps approached the cellar door and the light flashed on. Both men hurried down the stairs, just a few feet away. Elena held her breath.

She could hear one man walking about the small sitting area and the other one shoving a door open to what Rita had explained was the unfinished part of the cellar—with the furnace and storage space.

"I thought you said your sister didn't use the cellar much," one man said.

"She doesn't," called out a muffled voice. "It's my part of the house. I stay down here whenever I'm in town."

"Well, I have news for you, she's letting someone else stay here, too. Come here and check this out."

The two had to be examining Michael's suitcase. In the closet, Elena pressed her knees to her forehead, thinking. In the hospital, Rita had mentioned a brother, but this man did not sound friendly. So Elena remained still. The cellar was eerily quiet, and she worried the two men could hear every breath she took.

"Damn her, I can't believe she did this without asking."

"It's her house, and she thought you were in Dublin. These are men's clothes, good ones. She have a boyfriend?"

"The suitcase would be in her bedroom," the voice snapped.

"Let's see if our package is okay." The two men went quiet again and Elena heard boxes move about in the back room. "Hey, did you leave this here?"

"No, that's not mine. Don't tell me that bastard was in here snooping around."

"Calm down—let's pull the boxes into the other room and check." There was some shuffling around. "The tape is loose on this box. But the others look all right. Do you think your sister was in here?"

"I don't know. I'm sure it's not her hat. Let's get everything back to the way it was in this room. Close that suitcase back up."

Without talking, Elena could hear the men move about the room. Then the door slammed to the furnace room. "These are heavy, but not as bad as I expected."

"Let's get them upstairs and out to the car. Rita's shift does not end until three, but who knows about suitcase man," the brother's voice was steady. "You got a good hold?"

"I thought you said they were safe." The voice was nervous.

"We still need to be careful."

The two men took several trips up and down the stairs. The

boxes had to be heavy, because Elena could hear the one man breathing hard. About ten minutes later she heard the slamming of a trunk and a vehicle pull away from the driveway.

Elena slowly stood to stretch her legs. The men had a key. Some sort of pickup, she thought, and Rita must have forgotten to mention it.

Then she heard the kitchen door open again. Footsteps passed in the upstairs hallway and lingered in the sitting room. Elena edged back to the floor and brought her knees close to her chin, and realized she had left her book propped open in the middle of the floor.

Elena listened, but heard no sound. Without voices, she couldn't be sure if the person upstairs was one of the two men who had just left the cellar or a new visitor. Surely Rita would have called out.

She tried to reassure herself. The person carried a key and probably was Rita's brother. Elena wished she could peer out, study the person—figure out if he was connected with palace security. But that was farfetched and she wasn't about to move from her dark corner of the closet. Not without making noise and not until she was sure.

A sudden noise came from upstairs as something was flung to the ground, maybe the book she had been reading. Then came a slight cough, a man's cough. Elena cringed. She should have slipped out the front door when the two men first tried the kitchen door or when they were loading the vehicle outside. Now she was stuck.

Her biggest worry was palace security. Surely a professional, a serious investigator working for the palace, would not use a key, open a refrigerator, or lug a few items away. And surely the palace would not send a man inside alone. But maybe he wasn't alone. Maybe more men waited outside. Or, maybe he operated on his own, hoping to collect some reward. Elena shivered, and tightened her fingers about her arms. Dipping her head, she was thankful that her hair was dark and plain, blending in with the clothes and the darkness of the closet.

A nagging thought suddenly entered her head. She really knew nothing about Michael or Rita. What if they were more loyalist than they had let on? What if they had managed to separate her from Larry and then called security to come and trap her inside Rita's house? The two could have colluded to obtain favor and collect some reward. She had been relying on their word for so many matters. Indeed, security could whisk Larry away and ignore her. Elena's nerves were on edge and she felt sweaty and sick to her stomach. She realized how much she needed to escape.

A horn beeped from outside. One short blast and then a much longer one. Elena almost moaned. Her cab. The man was in the room upstairs, and she couldn't exactly emerge from the closet, stroll upstairs, and explain that she had been waiting for her taxi. The horn blared once more, before the doorbell rang.

The front door opened.

"Yes?" The voice was muffled, and Elena thought it might be the man who spoke about his sister.

"Let's hurry it up!" shouted the cabdriver, with a south Asian accent.

"What do you mean?"

"I was called to pick someone up at this address. I was told to get here fast. Please, let's get moving!"

A long pause. Elena visualized the upstairs plan, wondering if she could slip out the kitchen door. But both front and back-door were visible from the hallway stretching the length of the house. Damn, the home was too small, and Elena had no sure means of escape without catching the brother's attention.

He was calm and spoke as if he owned the place. If Elena headed upstairs and walked out the backdoor, what could he possibly do to her in front of the cabdriver?

But Elena was nervous. She couldn't take a chance by step-ping away from her hiding place, possibly revealing her identity to another set of people. Not yet. The cabdriver was already an-noyed and she couldn't count on him coming to her assistance.

"There's no one here but me." The male voice at the front door was polite, and Elena was sure it was one of the two men who had been in the cellar a few moments earlier. "I'm sorry. The call must have been a prank."

Curse words streamed from the taxi driver's mouth and faded in the distance. Elena heard the engine, her means to escape, roar away. She swallowed, and tried to breathe naturally. Footsteps moved about the rooms upstairs, opening and closing doors, until he eventually entered the kitchen.

"Where are you?" The man's words were quick, and Elena was uncertain that she had heard correctly. Surely, the question, with all its mean determination, was part of her imagination. She closed her eyes, sat still, and forced herself to breathe steadily.

When he started talking again, she jumped, but this time he was on a cell phone. Elena could only catch a few phrases as he paced back and forth.

"It's me, yeah, it's on the way . . . will connect in the car . . . Yeah, but something's up at my sister's house. Give me a half hour, if she's not home by then, then I'll take off . . . thought we could trust her, but now I don't know."

The television then went on upstairs. Indeed, the man was Rita's brother, but he sounded so angry, impatient, so different from his sister. Elena didn't dare leave her hiding place and decided to wait and hide for a bit longer. She could only hope that the man didn't search the cellar or that Michael didn't return with Larry. She couldn't afford a big fuss and didn't want to explain her plans to more people.

She shifted a bit. Maybe coming to Rita's had been a terrible mistake.

Chapter 23

"Do you think Richard knows where she headed?"
"That doesn't matter. We can entice her to return."

Richard focused on keeping his knees and feet together and still. Wearing his uncomfortable dress uniform of black swallow-tail coat and pinstripe pants, he sat straight and still in his chair. Queen Catherine deplored unnecessary movement from her grandchildren almost as much as unnecessary words. Richard knew better than to exhibit any behavior other than self-control and a subtle sense of superiority in her presence.

The two quietly regarded each other across a small table covered with white linen and fine china. A maid arranged scones alongside the tea set that had been presented to a queen of an earlier century. Women in the family had relied on the priceless, delicate set to teach lessons of etiquette to the family's children. Queen Catherine's mother had banished one of her nieces from royal functions for several years after the girl had dropped a sterling spoon and chipped a saucer.

Richard handled his silverware lightly, remembering the tale and wondering about his own grandmother's reaction. The woman strived to remain nondescript, a way to mask most emotions and personality. Her lids were heavy over her watery eyes, unhappy but alert. Pale powder gathered at the lines etched onto her face. Her mouth was straight, always determined. Her hair was short and curly, a medium sort of brown going gray.

Attractive as a young girl, she had grown plainer with age. Except for the palatial setting, she looked no different from the typical grandmother.

But her nature was anything but grandmotherly. Richard met Catherine by weekly appointment, with Larry included only occasionally. During their meetings, the queen was attentive and stern as she spoke about politics, history, economics, and classical music. She expected courtesy, common sense, and an occasional show of wit.

After the maid finished pouring, Catherine thanked the woman and noted that the two would finish the preparations. She made the same comments during every tea with Richard. And as with all the other teas, Catherine and Richard remained still until the maid left the room and closed the door. This tea would be awkward, Richard knew, because of his mother taking off with Lawrence. As always, he waited for his grandmother to begin.

"And how do you find the world this week?" she asked, stirring sugar into her tea, studying the delicate cup intently.

He gave a short smile, then moved his eyes toward the steam drifting from his teacup. The thin cups failed to keep tea hot for very long, and the steam wouldn't last long. Her initial question was the same every week, and his challenge was to please her.

But how was he supposed to answer this week? His advisors had always warned him never to be the one to introduce unpleasant topics during the so-called informal meetings over tea. But how could she possibly trust him if he didn't make some comment about his mother vanishing, taking off with his brother. Was he expected not to notice or care? For a person who received so much advice, he was at a loss as to what to say.

Catherine placed her teaspoon in the saucer without sound, but her glance was sharp at his delay. She didn't want candor. He had to play her cryptic game. Undoubtedly, he'd learn more if he pretended not to care about his mother.

"Grandmother, this week it's only the world according to VanCrendon. Small and confusing amid the global network of information. All influenced by English culture, of course."

She took a minute bite of her scone. She returned a short, thin smile. "Appropriate response about your lessons, Richard. Most fail to recognize how this country continues to influence the world. Probably better that way. Our control is subtle." He knew she snidely referred to the United States. But her criticism was always indirect, never mentioning the country by name. Catherine had made many more trips to the country than Richard had, but thanks to his mother, his trips had been normal, more relaxing. Like his mother, he liked the place, but they could never admit so much to the queen.

"Undoubtedly much easier to manage ignorance," the boy commented. Somehow the conversations about the world had a way of moving toward his opinions and personal affairs with a life of their own.

"A valid observation," she said. "Who could argue that this civil life is not an aspiration for most people in the world?"

"We're fortunate," he murmured, holding his teacup.

"You're too humble," she replied, testily. "You deny your destiny." Richard busied himself with a scone, slowly applying butter and strawberry jam. He could not argue, and he was never allowed to change the subject. His only defense was evasiveness. He looked up and pretended to be at his most attentive.

"Your mother did not understand that influence must be subtle. She did not appreciate that hundreds in this building have dedicated their lives to shaping your life, preparing you for your duty, maintaining this way of life."

"I am most appreciative, Grandmum." He managed his grandmother by pretending her comments were compliments.

He dipped his head and took a small flaky bite from his scone and the dab of warm butter. The scones were perfect. He wanted to finish it off in a huge bite and then accept a second one. But he had been long taught to exhibit self-control. The best in life surrounded him, but he had to refrain from indulging.

"Your mother," the queen spoke without emotion. "She's left with Lawrence—without permission."

"So I heard," he said, pouring more tea for each of them. He took his time, handling the old, fragile teapot with care and avoiding her eyes. Maybe the statement would be enough. He wanted to avoid her questions and forget about leaving his room the previous night, crossing the school grounds, climbing the wall. Forget the awful thud when he aimed the heavy rock at Derry's head. Forget his mother clutching his shoulder, urging him to leave, explaining that their lives could be in danger. Forget the image of his mother clutching Lawrence's hand tight and the two of them disappearing into the night. He had wanted to cry out for them to wait, that he, too, wanted to run away from the rigid and phony life. But he stood still and watched. He had to forget his anger about a decision that led to his overwhelming loneliness—was it his fault or his mother's?

Damn, he had to stop thinking. He pushed all the thoughts away. His grandmother could read his thoughts, his soul, the way that security could wire up a room. Like his mother, the older woman had little formal education, but she had made it her business to study the psyches of those who surrounded her, especially those who would carry on in her place. That had always unnerved his father, and Richard was no different. But then the three had all been trained for the same role in life.

"Your valet tried to . . . help her," Catherine pushed her cup to the side, finished with her tea. The meeting would not last much longer, Richard thought with relief. "Most commendable of him."

"Indeed . . ." Richard echoed her tone, more question than accusation. For once he followed the dictum that children were best seen and not heard. As he grew older, he found that he more often than not preferred the role of child rather than adviser.

"He would have stopped her, wanted to get the poor thing some help, but someone struck him on the head. Not Lawrence. He's not big enough, and the poor child was probably taken against his will. So your mother had help. Do you have any ideas?"

Richard made a ritual of pushing the small remaining portion of his scone to the side. Gentlemen never overindulged, in scones or in lies. He stared steadily into her eyes. "No," he said simply.

The queen smiled at him, then lifted her head high and stared out the window. "No one loves this garden more than me." The panes in this part of the castle were old, rippled with age, and Richard usually avoided staring through the glass because he detested the illusion of rain or tears. But this time he followed her gaze. A gardener walked about a rose garden, the section with massive whites. The man studied blooms, pruning prime blooms for some bouquet and trimming branches that had reached too far. He tugged a canvas bag, collecting remnants. "But I delegate its care to an expert. He has no emotion, no sentiment. It's his job. I do the same with my horses, my hounds, and everything I love. It's for the best, Richard. But your mother never learned." The queen sighed.

Richard stared at the man outside and wondered how he would ever find friends or someone who loved him as much as his mother and brother. He gritted his teeth, determined to avoid any expression. Neutrality was the best protection in these sorts of wars.

Queen Catherine continued: "The impulsivity makes your

mother a dangerous woman. That's not to say she does not love you and Lawrence. But she does not understand her limits. Someone could get hurt."

"I would hate that," Richard admitted firmly. At last, he could look into her eyes with sincerity. "You won't allow her to be hurt. If she's found, that is." He dipped his head at his poor word choice. Why didn't his mother have a right to walk away without being regarded as some criminal or lunatic? He worried about whether his grandmother sensed the comment as agreement or challenge, that he knew his mother had no plans to return. He feigned a nonchalant tone. "I'm sure she'll be back soon."

"Oh, she'll be back, my dear boy. Security has leads." Catherine laughed. "And indeed, where can she go?"

Richard shook his head, wishing he knew the answer.

"And Derry has been generous enough not to go public over his assault. He took a nasty blow to the head. No, once your mother is found, she'll get the help that she needs."

"Help?" Richard asked hopefully.

"Treatment. Not our concern, Richard. Again, we must rely on experts."

"Mmm, of course," he murmured.

"But enough about her. The entire country's looking forward to your speech today, at the . . . what is it?"

"The Technology Campaign."

"Oh, yes," she said, bored. "Technology—moving the world along too fast. Be sure to let them know that. And don't be surprised if the press is critical of your mother for not attending or standing by you. Don't let it bother you. Don't fall into their trap—letting them describe you as distraught or unfocused."

"Not at all," Richard replied. "I'll be fine." He kept his voice flat. If his mother could really escape the life that made her so unhappy, then he was relieved. Maybe her escape would have repercussions for the rest of the family. "They may not notice."

She nodded slowly. "It's disturbing when staff and bystanders go off describing our feelings to the press. Invariably, they're wrong."

Richard nodded his agreement.

"If only she'd return to the palace. All the differences could be resolved." She stared at Richard. "If your mother or Lawrence contact you, at any time, you will let security know. Immediately." She slowly folded her napkin.

"Of course." Nervous about lying to his grandmother, he followed her example with the napkin. She didn't mind lies, as long as they supported the palace. Lies that diminished the power of the family were regarded as ultimate disloyalty. But how could she possibly know about the E-mail? He had checked his computer this morning—and was surprised to see the message in his index. He wondered why they had written so soon and wondered where they had gone, whether they were already in the United States.

But then Derry had entered the room and Richard had no time to click or read the message. He clicked to erase the unread message. An unread E-mail message could hardly count as contact. Not yet, Richard rationalized to himself. Richard had turned the computer off in a hurry, and commented that the valet did not look well. Derry had rubbed his head and responded that he had not slept well, asking Richard's permission to rejoin the prince when he got ready for the technology show. Richard nodded, avoided eye contact, with only a bit of guilt. His mother and brother were not the criminals.

Richard remained quiet about the computer communication. If he mentioned the possibility of such messages, the staff would confiscate his laptop.

The queen laid the napkin gently on the table and smoothed it out several times with her hand. Then she stood. Richard quickly stood to assist. She held out her hand, and he took it, trying not to shudder as he felt the soft papery skin, the hard edges of the heavy diamond ring on her left hand. They walked to the door, and Catherine said farewell. Richard offered a deep and respectful bow, as they parted. And as he stared at the elaborate inlaid marble floor, he thought about her self-control, what she believed to be her finest quality, giving her superiority over others. But Richard wondered if the control really existed. Maybe she was merely a creature of habit, or her individuality had been polished away by the palace system when she was a child. Or perhaps ancestors and ghosts lurking behind palace walls and throughout the English countryside controlled her somehow from their graves. Would they do the same to him? Maybe they already were controlling him. Maybe that's why he didn't leave with Lawrence and his mother. It was something he couldn't explain, and Richard shuddered.

Back in Richard's palace suite, a tutor from the school offered a stern reminder that the rest of his class worked on math exercises in Dowling Hall. School staff could order the princes about; if the directions were in the boys' best interest, the queen would approve. Richard didn't like the tone but had given up arguing long ago. He nodded, but instead headed for his room and closed the door.

Switching the computer on, he typed in his password and entered the mail server, which allowed the list of messages to emerge—several new ones from friends and nothing more from Lawrence. He placed the cursor on the trash to retrieve the message from the morning and clicked on it, immediately regretting his hurry. He had not checked if the message was new or marked as read. And he should have checked. He closed his eyes and tried to remember, then returned to the index and stared. But it was too late. Whether the message was new or read vanished forever with the one unfortunate keystroke. Richard tried to shake his doubt. Of course the message had been unread. He scanned the message, disappointed that the note was from Larry and not his mother. Even more frustrating was the fact that the letter was short and silly:

"Hi! Mom's nervous, but going ahead with IT! She thinks someone's trying to kill us! We miss you and wish you were here. Will write again when we reach final destination! With luck, the West!"

Typical Larry, thought Richard. Lots of enthusiasm and little real information. He had never told anyone, but he truly believed that Lawrence was part of another generation. Even his mother would laugh. The boy actually looked forward to growing up in the United States, while the very idea terrified Richard.

He remembered one time the family had visited the country. His mother accepted an invitation for him to sit in on an afternoon of classes at one of New York City's public schools. Richard had protested, but she insisted. He had quietly observed from the back of the classroom, later refusing to admit that the visit had been impressive. The students had so much more freedom, walking around the classroom and collecting supplies and advice from one another. The teacher lectured less and the children were expected to choose topics for independent projects. They didn't simply write compositions. They wrote speeches and pretended to be broadcasters. Often, teachers expressed more pleasure at the questions students asked than the information they knew. Every project required persuasion.

Richard had been puzzled. The exchanges had been real, not rehearsed—genuinely engaged, the students had bantered with him and seemed to care about his ideas. They were not performing for media or parents or even the teacher. Richard had always been taught that individualism was selfish, and could breed materialism and violence while eroding loyalty and values. But people could love freedom for the individual more than themselves. He wondered if his mother knew how much he had learned that day.

Throughout his education, only one of Richard's courses addressed the American Revolution, a section called "A World in Revolution." The instructor took the attitude that laws, culture, history, sports, details, that took place across some distant ocean simply didn't matter.

Influence. The word that used to sound so worthy connoted intrusive and dangerous control. His grandmother would say that he was thinking too hard. She often had the same complaint about his father and his mother, constantly advising them to leave matters to the experts. Then nothing could ever be their fault. Likewise, he thought with a scowl, nothing would ever be their triumph. He struck the R to reply to Lawrence.

His little brother was young, and still resisted being shaped by an expensive and rigid education. Larry would walk about one of those colorful, noisy classrooms in the States and, in time, forget about Richard, duty and influence—his place in the palace hierarchy. Larry would compete for himself on a level playing field, make plans for himself, and forget a family that thought of him as second best. The boy would regard Richard's role in the world as a quaint and archaic custom and probably would not long for such a role in the palace. Richard was surprised. Larry was supposed to envy Richard. But indeed, the opposite was true.

Richard didn't know what to write. His younger brother did not need reassurance or advice, not nearly as much as Richard did. After a few minutes, Richard typed a reply, and then took care to delete the clandestine messages—and empty the computer's recycling bin.

Chapter 24

"Do you think she intends to ruin the family?"
"It doesn't matter, she's dangerous and must be stopped."

Despite having no sleep the previous night, Rita managed to conclude the hospital shift without any big errors. She looked forward to getting home, making a cup of tea, then perhaps taking a nap. She was confident her guests would not mind.

She unlocked the backdoor and entered her kitchen, pleased to see the room clean, except for a few dishes in the sink. Everything from the morning meal was cleared. The house was quiet.

Tossing her keys to the counter, she plopped her purse and a shopping bag with snacks and the makings of a dinner on the table. "Hellooo?" called out Rita, cheerful despite the long day at the hospital. "I managed to leave on time. Where is everyone? Hello?"

She went into the sitting room and was startled by her older brother standing in center of the room. Danny Whittaker took a few quick steps and stood in the doorway, essentially blocking her inside the room.

"Hey, Rita, who is everyone?" Danny asked.

Rita was too tired for a row with her brother. He was bossy and possessive, jealous about every minute Rita spent with friends he did not know. She tried to be pleasant.

"Why, Danny!" Rita exclaimed. "I thought you were traveling this week."

Danny walked up to her. "Back early. I had to pick up some supplies downstairs. But tell me, I saw the suitcase downstairs. Who is he, Rita?"

Nervous, she didn't want to say much. "Some friends stayed over last night. You didn't see them?"

He shook his head with annoyance. "I rent that space from you. I didn't know that you were letting other people use it as well."

"It was sudden, Danny, and not for long. Look, let's sit over a cup of tea and talk about this." She smiled and tried to walk past him into the hallway. But he stepped to the side, blocking her and grabbing her arm. He was only a few inches taller than her, and moved his face close. With his dark hair and sharp blue eyes, there was no doubt they were siblings.

"Who are they? Where are they now?"

"I just got home from work. I have no idea." She was too tired to think of a story that might calm her brother or come up with fake names.

"There is a suitcase down there with men's clothes—not the kind your dates usually wear. What's he doing here?"

"Some people from the hospital needed a place to stay. You wouldn't know them." He squeezed her arm tighter, as if he expected more information. "Ow—a friend and her new boyfriend. Her husband is a mean bastard, not much different than you and daddy." Danny glared at her, but let her pull her arm away. Still, he did not budge from the doorway, and she badgered him more. "I'm the one who should be annoyed. I asked you to call before you came for a visit."

"What are you hiding from me, Rita?"

"Nothing!" she protested. "This is my home, Danny. I let you stay, but that doesn't mean you can tell me what to do with it."

"I try to help you out with expenses and expected a little privacy down there, that's all."

"For fifty pounds per month, you get more than enough privacy—and no right to tell me who I can invite into my home." She tried to relax. She couldn't let him push her around. "What are you hiding in my cellar, Danny?"

He smiled. "Some supplies, that's all. None of your business."

"They are my business if they're in my house. What kind of supplies? You don't have a job."

Danny smiled. "It's better you don't know. I found a hat in the back room, a Yankees hat. Someone was in my stuff."

Rita put her hands to her hips. "You have no right to come into my home and make demands," she shouted. "And you shouldn't have put anything in my cellar without asking me!"

Suddenly, he looked at his sister with sadness. "Rita, what happened? You got a job in London, you bought a house, and you changed completely."

"This is my home and life, Danny. Not yours. Not our parents' house. I control my life now. I don't need your approval for friends or what I do."

"I'm just trying to keep an eye on you and help out."

Agitated at his cockiness, Rita said, "You expect me to trust you, but you don't trust me. You're a jerk—and I'm through with you."

Danny's shoulders slumped and he looked sheepish, but only for a moment. "Why don't you call the police on me?" he challenged her. "You don't dare, because then I'll tell them about you."

She scowled at him. "Only because I listened to you a few times, which was a big mistake. Get your stuff out of here now. No more renting a space in my house. Maybe when you calm down and stop bossing me around, act more like a brother than a father, then you can come around again."

"I'm not leaving this house until I find out who was here."

"Don't be so stupid, Dan," Rita murmured wearily.

The offhand comment enraged the man. He stepped forward, his face red and his hand raised. Rita flinched and he held off striking. "I have conviction. That's more important than anything else. Don't ever call me stupid, Rita. I thought you were one of us."

"I love you. But I don't want to hurt people." Rita was earnest, hoping to convince him.

"Anyone involved with this government is a legitimate target," he responded. "Anyone who supports it. Why, you were this close to one of the Wyndhams, the most important one, and you couldn't tell me." He held his hand up, touching his thumb to his forefinger. "I had to hear about her from Patty."

"I'm a nurse," she hissed. "My job is to care for patients. Not get involved in their politics."

"Don't start on your good-nurse routine. You could have told me. You weren't too good to sell a photo of the bitch. You did it, and everyone knows you did. No matter how many times you deny it."

"I didn't do anything wrong." Rita tightened her lips into a frown.

"Don't play games with me, Rita. Patty told me about how the supervisor commended you. That the princess wanted you in the room more than anyone else on staff. You let her use you!"

Rita ran her hand through her dark hair. "I did my job, that's all. The woman was a patient, and patient information is confidential. I refuse to talk about her."

"Patty said no one else had more opportunity to take that photo."

"Dozens of people came in and out of that room," Rita insisted.

"And you've avoided me ever since," he accused her.

"I refuse to hurt people. I always said that, Dan."

"Talking doesn't work. The governments ignore people like us. Bombs get attention."

"Did you ever think that your bombs and violence might compel people to cling to the system and reject anything you have to say?"

"Some of us have lost patience. The days of ignoring poverty, preening for the monarchy, wasting money on war, and other such foolishness are almost over." Her brother was smug. "And now we have help from inside the palace."

"What are you planning to do?" Rita demanded.

"Wouldn't you love to know?" Dan shot back. "So you can run to the police?"

"I'm going to find out." With that, she pushed by him and rushed for the cellar, determined to check the sealed boxes he stored down there.

As she swept past him, he grabbed his sister by the arm. "You're too late," he snarled. "We moved those boxes this afternoon." As he dragged her into the kitchen, she tried to bite him, stomp on his feet, twist away, but the struggle was futile. He had always been stronger than her and easily pulled her arms behind her back that much tighter.

"Stop it," Rita screeched. "What are you doing to me?"

He managed to open the cellar door while holding her. She pulled away one arm and gripped the doorframe, twisting to face him, hoping some eye contact would get him to come to his senses. But he was like the angry brother of old, never understanding his younger sister's happiness or independence. He couldn't control her emotionally, but he could do it physically. As her wiry brother shoved her to the floor, past the doorway, Rita lost her step and pitched forward, flailing her arms to clutch on to the railing. She scraped both shinbones, but avoided falling down the stairs.

Danny slammed the heavy old door shut and turned the key.

Rita banged on the door and screamed. "Danny, think about what you're doing." She leaned against the door to listen, but couldn't tell if he was still in her kitchen or not. "How do you know you can trust this person on the inside?" She banged again, harder. "It could be a trap. I watched those servants, Dan, while she was in the hospital. They're vipers!"

"Doesn't matter. The old man and his kids will be history after today. There's no stopping it now."

Rita heard rustling from the dark closet downstairs. The surreal sound of a woman's hysterical shriek came from downstairs, inside the closet. "No!"

Her brother laughed on the other side of the doorway. "Give up, Rita. I'm right and you're wrong. And at last I'm taking action."

Terrified, Rita hurried down the stairs, turned on the light and opened the closet door. Elena stepped out, disheveled and angry. Rita shook her head and held her finger to her lips. From upstairs, they heard Danny speaking, another telephone call. But his voice was too soft, the conversation too abrupt. A few minutes later, the backdoor slammed and a vehicle left the driveway fast.

"I'm sorry," Rita whispered.

Elena stretched her neck and then her legs before answering, and when she spoke her voice was puzzled and cool. "Why didn't you warn us about him?"

"I didn't expect him here." Rita sat on the bottom step and started to cry. "He's supposed to call."

"He talked about a bomb," Elena pressed. "How dangerous is he?"

Rita could not keep her secret anymore, the words tumbling out. She explained to Elena her brother's early involvement with the IRA, his fury at the ceasefire, and his growing involvement with more radical groups—early tentative curiosity turned into fascination, then extremism. He fervently believed society could not tolerate any system of inequality or elitism, and he no longer trusted the government to be fair. "I thought it was all talk, but he's my brother. I was never sure. I didn't want to believe Danny could be so rash, so hateful."

Elena shook her head. "What's sad is how much I might agree with him," she said. "But his methods are so wrong. Attacking Edward and the family will accomplish absolutely nothing." She paused a moment and looked up the stairs at the door. "Can we get out of here?"

"There's no key down here," Rita said. "He had the only one."

"Maybe we can find some way to break out?" Elena asked. She ran to the top of the stairs and felt around the old door, which fit snugly in its frame. Rita hurried to a set of shelves, and found a screwdriver, a hammer and some other tools, before joining Elena at the top of the stairs. "Do you have a phone down here?" Elena asked. "We could call the police for help and I could hide . . ."

"In my bag on the kitchen table, not down here."

"And Michael took the laptop." Elena was distraught.

"Here's some tools we can try," Rita offered.

Elena stared at Rita. "Let me ask, did you deliberately arrange to be my nurse at the hospital?"

"I was curious," Rita admitted. "And yes, I volunteered. I wondered if you would fulfill all my brother's expectations."

Elena looked thoughtful for a moment. "Danny was upset that you didn't tell him. Why didn't you?"

Rita gave a short laugh, and waved her arm. "I didn't want to

---

be pestered with his questions—or his advice on what I should do. I just didn't want to hear it. Do you remember your last day in the hospital? He called my cell phone, wanted to know if it was too late to try some poison or search for some evidence so he could bribe you later. You were sitting in the room—you heard me! I didn't want any part of it. But he's my brother, and every day, I keep hoping that he will change his mind."

She paused a moment. "At first, you were just another patient for me, but in a good way. I was furious about your staff and my superiors making such a fuss, urging you get special treatment. I only wanted to do my job. Eventually I realized you didn't want much more from me—except maybe some friendship."

Elena was quiet. "When I was in the hospital, I really thought you cared for me. I trusted you."

"I cared for you like I would treat any other patient, no better and no worse." Rita sighed. "Except for that last day, when we took the photo and then, we were like friends. I suppose that I should have told you about Danny. But when? Last night? I didn't plan on him coming today, and if I had said something about my brother possibly stopping by, would you have left?"

"I had nowhere else to go," Elena admitted and shook her head, looking more sad than worried or angry. She looked around the tight space. "I have no right to expect anything more from you. I was trapped yesterday and I'm trapped today. Every family has its odd ones. Sometimes that makes us try harder as individuals."

Rita nodded and turned her attention to the door. "Let's do what we can now to get out of here, so we can help your sons and husband."

"And stop your brother from ruining his own life," Elena added.

Chapter 25

"The system is more important than any individual."
"The boys' lives depend on the system."

Larry sat curled in a private study carrel and was about seventy pages into a book describing squids, when Michael approached and bent down to whisper. "Your mother should have been here by now."

"She's always late." Larry shrugged, then looked up. "But that's almost always because of reporters."

Michael looked toward the library's entryway. "I better go back to Rita's and find out what delayed her."

Larry suddenly felt shaky. He didn't know if he was more worried about his mother's lateness or abandonment in the library. "What happens if she got caught?" Larry asked.

"She didn't," Michael said, but Larry knew it was false confidence. The man was obviously fretting. "Rita probably came home early, and they started talking."

Larry raised his eyebrows. He started to stand, but Michael put his hand to the boy's shoulder.

"Stay here," Michael urged in a low whisper. "I'll run back and fetch her."

"What if she's not there?" Larry pressed. It never failed to annoy Larry that he thought far more in advance than most adults. "And what if you don't come back?"

Michael reached in his pocket and pulled out his wallet and

gave the boy some coins and a ten-pound banknote. "You should have money, just in case. But wait here. I'll come back, and we'll make a decision together about what to do next. She may be on her way. If she shows up, you can slide her a note in a book that explains. You both wait—in separate parts of the building. I'll check Rita's house quick and be back in less than thirty minutes. Let's hope she beats me here." He paused a moment.

Larry took a deep breath and decided that Rita's house was more dangerous than any library. "Leave your pack and take this." Larry handed over his backpack. "It has something I found in Rita's cellar. You might find it of use."

Michael took the pack with a puzzled look and started to look inside.

Larry stopped the man's hand and shook his head. "Not here. Wait until you're outside and alone." The boy turned his attention back to squids as Michael turned for the exit.

The moment Michael was out of sight, Larry removed the man's laptop from the pack and placed it on the table. Unlike his dorm or his room in the palace, the library had wireless. He glanced at the librarian, and she didn't seem to pay any particular attention to him. He flipped the switch, and the machine gave off its soft hum. Larry typed in passwords quickly to retrieve his mother's E-mail from a remote location.

Two conflicting messages, both from Richard:

"I carefully thought over the circumstances of the last few hours. You both betrayed me and the country by leaving. I'm not sure I can ever trust you again. I need to talk with both of you. I'll be at the Technology Campaign today. It's your only chance or I'll refuse to see you again. Your son, Richard."

Then the other message in their code: "Have fun, little brother. Wish I was there."

The boy studied the notes. Even though logged a few hours

apart, the two could not have possibly come from the same person, especially Richard. That could only mean that Derry had access to the computer and Richard didn't know it. Larry should know—he had managed to pirate his older brother's laptop plenty of times without his knowledge.

Maybe this was why his mother had not come to the library. She somehow had contacted Richard and decided to meet him at the Technology Campaign. With luck, his mother planned to attend the event and convince Richard to join them. Larry could help her. Or, if she had been apprehended by palace security, Larry could still help by pleading her case to his father. Larry returned the laptop to the backpack and waited in the line at the reference desk. All he needed was directions for the nearest bus.

CHAPTER 26

"He insists she's coming back."
"That would be ruinous."
"There's no room for her in the royal future."

Michael walked the full length of the street twice. The small brick home looked the same, no sign of unusual activity. The street was quiet, no lingering groups of gossiping or gawking neighbors, as would be expected if police had raided the place during the previous hour. Of course, Elena could have been quietly apprehended during her taxi ride, and even Rita could be totally unaware.

He went along the back path and saw Rita's car was parked in the garage. As he approached the house, he pulled the zipper open to Larry's backpack and reached inside. A chill went through him as he touched the barrel of a gun. He looked inside, and saw a Beretta 92G Elite. The manual safety was on, so the thing was probably loaded. Closing the zipper, Michael looked around. No one was watching.

Where the hell did the kid get the gun? Surely, his mother didn't know. Michael wanted to hurry back to the kid. He pulled out his cell phone, but didn't dare dial Rita's number. Elena wouldn't answer the phone anyway. He couldn't just wait outside, pacing back and forth, or a neighbor would call the police for sure. Michael would have trouble explaining the contents of the backpack. Where the hell was Elena? He had to get inside Rita's house.

Striding purposefully to the back of the house, he knocked firmly at the kitchen door. No answer. Michael peeked inside a window. The kitchen table was clear, no big changes from when he had been there earlier. He paused and knocked again, stopping when he thought he heard a noise inside. A thumping. He tried the door and swore. Locked tight.

Looking about, he checked to make sure no one was about, thankful for how the back stoop blocked the view. He removed his sweatshirt and balled it around his hand. Without hesitation, he struck the center of the window firmly. The pane cracked easily with little noise. With a few more hard taps, the glass falling to the floor inside, he made a hole large enough to reach inside and flip the lock.

Michael walked inside and listened, hoping that no one called to file a police report. It would be tough to come up with an explanation, especially if he couldn't find Rita.

But Rita's purse and keys were tossed on a nearby chair. The kitchen was neat. No note or sign from Elena. He walked softly into the hallway and into the sitting room. He saw a rumpled rug and a book propped open on the floor—but not a clue about why Elena did not show at the library.

Michael sat on the chair and listened. The house was too quiet, and he had the feeling that he was not alone, that he was being watched. Someone waited for him to make a move. He wondered if Elena could possibly have had a change of heart. All the reports from the palace indicated she was impulsive, flighty, thoughtless. But she had seemed so sincere about leaving, and he could not imagine that she would have abandoned Larry.

But then she did leave her other son, Michael reminded himself.

Maybe he had already crossed paths with Elena. Maybe she

had stood outside the library and watched, waiting for him to leave in search of her. Maybe she retrieved the boy and headed for the nearest palace. If she had, he was a terrible judge of character. Or, she wanted to escape on her own.

He shook his head and returned to the kitchen. He opened the backdoor and checked the garden. No one seemed to notice the break-in. What the hell, he thought, deciding to call out. "Rita?" he said softly. "You home?"

Pounding and shouts burst out right behind him, just behind the cellar door. "In here!" screamed Rita.

"Michael!" Elena shouted. "Let us out! We're locked in the cellar."

Startled, he went to the door and tried the doorknob. The door was heavy, with a lock that opened, not with a deadbolt, but an old-fashioned skeleton key. "How did both of you manage to get stuck down there?" Michael said with a scowl. "Where's the key?"

"Look around—on the table or near the sink," Rita advised. "I usually kept it right in the lock."

Michael checked the counters, table, the shelves.

"No luck?" Rita called out. "He must have taken it."

"He?" Michael shouted. "Who are you talking about?"

"My brother," Rita said in a forlorn voice.

No key was in sight. For the heck of it, he tried the few on Rita's key ring. None came close to fitting. He swore, and on the other side of the door, Rita groaned.

Michael opened the drawers in the kitchen. "Do you have any extra?" A sad "no" came out from the other side of the door.

"Any other ideas?" He stood and looked around the kitchen. The knob on the door twisted back and forth. "Even if you find the key, it may not work anymore," Elena said. "We've been hitting the doorknob and lock on this side with a hammer.

Not much good, I'm afraid."

"Don't do that anymore," Michael cautioned, examining the knob. "You don't want to make it more difficult to get out."

"We don't have much time, Michael," Elena spoke, edging on panic. "The man who locked us down here, Rita's brother, he has plans to kill Edward and Richard today. It has to be at the Technology Campaign—Richard's giving a speech there. We don't have much time to get out and stop him."

Michael knelt and studied the cellar door. The door was actually heavier and stronger than the frame itself. "Rita, do you have an ax or anything out in the garage, something that I could use on the hinges?"

"No," Rita called out. "But I do have a few more tools under the kitchen sink—a hammer and some screwdrivers. We're not making much progress from this side."

"Maybe you should head off to the pavilion alone," Elena said. "You could at least warn Edward."

"Or make a call on the cell phone," Rita added. "Anything to stop him."

Michael examined the hinges, old and covered in layers of paint. Using a hammer and some screwdrivers would take a while. "I doubt that I'd get near your husband at this point," Michael said. "Let me give something a try," he muttered. He reached for the backpack and extracted Larry's gun. "If this doesn't work, I'll head off by myself. But first, I'm going to try and shoot the lock. Do you mind, Rita? It will ruin the door . . ."

"Shoot away! I just want out of here."

Michael studied the door of solid wood. He did not want to jam the lock for good and decided to aim for the hinges. "Okay, can you two get off the stairs and head to the back corner of the cellar? Shield yourself because these bullets could ricochet. And this isn't my gun, so I have no idea how this thing works." All he could do was aim and hope for the best.

"Be careful," Elena cautioned.

"Tell me when you're clear and I can start."

He heard the two women scramble down the stairs, and waited for them to position themselves around the corner. "All right!" Rita called out in a muffled voice.

But from how far back? Point blank or back a few feet? He didn't want to hurt himself. He checked the gun. It was fully loaded. Michael moved some of Rita's glassware away from the nearest shelf. He moved the kitchen table a bit closer to the cellar door, so that he could take aim from behind that. Holding the weapon with two hands, he fired.

He barely had to press his finger against the trigger. The Beretta responded like it was attached to his nerve endings—at least six shots emerged from the cartridge. The shots were good, splintering wood with deafening cracks. Nice. Michael whistled and handled the gun with more respect. He went to the door and checked. The hinge was loosened. "Stay put until I call out all's clear," he hollered. "It's going to take a bit more time." Then he fired again. Four more shots, and the door was weakened. "I'm done for now. You two look for some kind of metal tool—and see if you can't help pry it open more from your side."

Putting the gun on the table, Michael found the hammer and the biggest screwdriver, and went to work on the hinges. Ten minutes later, the hinges and that side of the door frame were in shambles. "Can you push hard from your side?" Michael asked.

"Stand back," Rita called out from her side. He could hear the women hit the door hard with their shoulders, and the old door cracked open. With his hands, he shoved the battered door to the side.

Both women ran forward and hugged him with relief. "Let's get out of here," Michael urged.

"Where did you get that?" Elena pointed to the weapon left on the table. "That looks just awful."

"Your son lent it to me," Michael said. "He handed it over in the library of all places."

Elena looked horrified.

"But it came in handy," Michael admitted. "He was better prepared than we were. I didn't think the British condoned such weapons, even for princes."

Rita cast a mortified glance to Elena. "He must have found it downstairs."

Elena shook her head with obvious fury. "Michael, we have a lot more to worry about than the palace and we better hurry." She quickly explained that Rita's brother was an extremist, intent on attacking the Prince of Wales with a bomb. "He said he's working with some member of palace staff—we don't know who. But it has to be at the Technology Campaign. We must hurry there, and I don't want Dan or anyone else to catch us."

"Shouldn't you ring the palace?" Rita asked Elena. "Or the police?"

Elena shook her head, frustrated. "Honestly, they'd believe you before they would believe me. They think I'm hysterical and they wouldn't lift a finger about a bomb threat reported by me."

Michael immediately asked Rita for her cell phone. "Let me call my agency. They'll know which authorities to contact. That's the best chance of relaying a message to your husband's security detail, and maybe they can shut down the Technology Campaign."

"It's worth a try," Elena agreed. While he dialed the phone and talked, Elena stood by the back door, nervous, as Rita hurried about, filling a bag with some cheese, crackers, fruit.

Michael hung up. "They're contacting British authorities. I hope you're right, that it's the Technology Campaign."

Rita and Elena each looked a bit more relieved, and they dashed for Rita's car. As Michael drove, Rita explained Danny's past in detail, his connections with the radical remnant of the IRA and what he had said about his plan to attack the members of the royal family. Michael looked in the rearview mirror, but no one followed.

"I'm sure he's headed to the Technology Campaign," Elena said, leaning forward. "And I hope palace security listens to your people. They get dozens of calls like that before every event, and the palace often ignores them."

"I'm worried about you stepping into that pavilion," Michael spoke up. "That could destroy any chance you have of leaving this country."

"We have no choice," Elena said. "I must do whatever I can to help Edward and Richard."

Michael and Elena both accepted a small sandwich from Rita. Elena paused before taking a bite. "Where's Larry?"

"I left him at the library," Michael replied.

"By himself?" Elena exclaimed, dropping the sandwich and leaning forward in panic. "But we can't leave him alone!"

"It's been less than forty minutes," Michael said, checking his watch. "I had no idea why you didn't show up. If he had to be alone, what's safer than a library?" But then, the last time the boy had a few minutes alone, he had sent out the problem E-mail.

"We have to pick him up, and we're running out of time to get to the pavilion!" Elena turned to Rita and started pleading. "Maybe we could drop you off at the library, and you could let him know what's going on while we try and stop Danny."

"Not at all!" Rita was adamant. "You don't think I can just sit at the library, do you? Who knows, maybe I can find Dan and talk some sense into him."

"Stop arguing." Michael was resigned as he parked near the

library. "At this point, we better stick together. We have no other choice."

CHAPTER 27

"The evidence has been placed in her bedroom."
"Well done. When she returns, she'll be implicated."

"The blue and gold stars," Derry said, as if surprised about the tie. "A daring choice for a public event. Why, a brilliant choice, I declare."

Richard nodded, far from amused. It was still hard to believe the man had slapped his mother. But Richard couldn't confront him and the man was more cheery than usual. Too damn much chatter about ties and so-called choices on ridiculous matters. He wanted to shout and explain that, dear God, man, he had merely plucked a tie from the wardrobe! Nothing was clever or worthy of comment. The banality of it all was about to make him snap.

The man's job was to attend to Richard's personal needs. Such attention was supposed to be a luxury—allowing Richard more time to ponder intellectual matters. That's how his father had explained it before his birthday. But the constant, shallow conversations about colors and clothes and meals irritated Richard and made him feel less of a person. He yearned for time alone. Time and privacy were the ultimate luxuries.

Granted, Richard had a grand time with Derry during the first few weeks. After a while, the novelty wore off, and Richard tried to make a point of not relying on the valet so much. But the man was hard to shake off, and Richard was appalled to discover that he actually had to request time alone. The man refused to abandon any of his duties. Every day, Richard had to remind the man that he needed no help with dressing.

"Someday, you may change your mind." The smug valet puttered about the room and complied when asked to leave. But then he rang a few minutes later asking if further assistance was needed. Richard rubbed his forehead and realized that his life amounted to avoiding, anticipating, and handling interruptions. For the first time, Richard understood his father's need for distance, even from his own family and children.

"Your note cards are on the desk, Sir," Derry added helpfully. "Let's pop those in your jacket before I forget. Your father inserted a few revisions."

"Yes, he told me."

Derry stood to the side, eager. "Would you like to review your presentation with me, Sir?"

Richard stared down at the notes in his pocket. Shallow words of good will, all written by a member of staff. Not that he could come up with much better. He sighed. "Perhaps it's best if I sound more spontaneous?"

Derry cocked his head considering the idea and then nodded. Everything that Richard said was correct, but only because the words traveled through an endless series of filters.

"Of course. Still, keep the cards close at hand. Excuse me, Sir, for intruding, but you seem somewhat down today."

"Not at all." Richard kept his voice light. "Only preoccupied. Thinking about later today, addressing the public, standing with my father . . ." He purposely drifted off.

"You'll do fine," Derry said, patting the boy's shoulder. It was all Richard could do to keep from cringing. What exactly was he fine about? What did such accomplishments mean? Richard flashed a warm smile and felt completely fake and empty inside. The man Richard used to regard as a friend was now an annoyance. Another human filter against the real world.

Derry rearranged items on Richard's desk. "Of course, all this business with your mother and brother must have you concerned."

"I want only their safety and happiness." Richard was firm.

Derry lined some pencils to the one side and then put them into a drawer. "Admirable thoughts, especially since she's abandoned you without word. Or have you heard from her?"

Richard felt alarm course through him, to his fingers and toes. The question was a test. Of course, Derry already knew the answer. Richard sighed, acting as if his family was a minor irritation. "Not really. Larry may have sent a brief and pointless note. I'm not even sure it was from him. It wasn't signed." Richard turned and took a long time placing the cards in the front pocket of the jacket. "My grandmother knows about it."

"Do you know where they're going?"

Richard frantically tried to remember the note. Larry had mentioned "west." That could be taken as west anywhere—west in any city or country of the world. If Derry had access to Richard's E-mail, why would the man ask? Or, could he read his mind?

"No." Richard dismissed Derry abruptly, with despondence. He couldn't fool Derry into thinking that he did not care for his mother. "It wouldn't matter if I did. You know how they change their minds." He paused. "They'll settle down and get in touch. Or, they'll return, and life will go on."

Derry's head snapped up, surprised.

Richard shrugged. "Anything's possible."

CHAPTER 28

"The boy lied."

"His mother has a plan. The younger boy said something about 'IT.' "

"Unconscionable—they must all go!"

Michael grasped Elena's arm to prevent her from running through the library and making a scene. The three adults separated and checked every section of the library, including all the carrels, the stacks, the toilets. They went outside and walked around the block. They met at the front of the building and Elena slumped down on the front steps. "No sign of him at all, and your laptop's gone. What do we do?"

Michael and Rita looked at each other over her head. Michael wanted to wring the kid's neck. But he knew Elena was distraught about the missing boy.

Elena looked up. "Maybe we should ask at the desk? Maybe he left a message."

Michael scowled. The library staff were not like palace staff. He wanted to attract as little attention as possible. But Elena was getting frantic, and the kid was a menace. After seeing the gun, Michael didn't put anything past Larry.

"Is it possible that he got scared and changed his mind? Went back home?" Michael questioned.

Elena shook her head, and Michael knew she was right. The kid was hot to leave, and maybe was afraid the two adults had left without him. At any rate, they had to find him.

"I'll go," Michael volunteered. "People have already seen me with him." He directed the two women to sit on a nearby bench and handed over a newspaper. "Elena, sit with Rita and read. Hold it so it shields your face. And don't speak with anyone. Let Rita do all the talking. And please, don't you two disappear on me."

Inside the library, he approached the circulation desk and then paused. Librarians were meticulous researchers. He knew Elena was in a hurry, but he didn't want to ask a lot of questions and start an alarm about a lost child. He had to think this over.

Michael strolled toward the children's section and sat at a carrel between the children's section and the young-adult section for nonfiction. The squid book, the one Larry had been reading, was on top of the desk, closed.

Michael opened the book and scanned the pages. No note inside. But then he did not expect one. If the boy had followed him to Rita's, wanting to check on his mother's safety, then surely he would have joined the group as they left the house. Michael frowned, glanced around the room, mulling Larry's reason for leaving and the direction he might have taken. Had someone approached the boy? Scared him? Recognized him?

As Michael stared about the room, he caught the eye of the young woman sitting at the children's reference desk. Her dark hair was swept into a hefty roll behind her head. Her navy dress was far too stern, but her eyes were big, even without makeup. She stood and walked over to the carrel.

"Are you looking for your child?"

Michael nodded dumbly. He had to keep words to a minimum. Maybe he should have let Rita come inside. Librarians were quick. She might notice the accent and wonder how a father could possibly have such a different accent from his child.

"The boy sitting here earlier with the laptop?"

Michael panicked. Why was she asking questions? He had a few questions himself, but he had to fake an accent. "Thank you," he mumbled in what he hoped passed for a British accent. "I had to run a short errand." With any luck, she might think he was not from London.

The librarian frowned. "He was fine while in the library. Actually better than most children. How he's doing at the moment, I have no idea."

"He left?" Michael asked nervously.

"After tapping on his laptop—for a minute. Not a toy and not to be left with children unsupervised, I might add. The boy packed up, came to the reference desk, and asked how to catch a bus to Town Centre." Michael felt her disapproval through her stare.

"Ahhh," Michael said, nodding and pretending to understand.

"Your son, he's about eleven?" she asked.

"Ten."

"Tall for his age then," she said, with disapproval. "I must have a word with you. This is an area of grave concern for me—parents rushing childhood. I watch every day. Dropping children off in public places, expensive toys compensating for time. One can't be too careful about children these days. It doesn't hurt to protect them and allow them to be little children for a while."

Michael ran his hand through his hair. He would have loved to grab this serious woman by the shoulders and explain he knew nothing about kids. Her advice was a little late. But she'd probably turn to the telephone and call the police. He had to be agreeable. "Of course, you're right. I never thought about it before."

She smiled, as if relieved. Most parents were defensive.

"Why, you could probably write a book about it!"

The smile turned wary. Enough, Michael thought to himself.

He aimed for his best British accent. "But now I better catch up with that boy. Can you give me directions for the same bus?"

She shook her head, but jotted them down on scrap paper. He thanked her for both the directions and her advice on child-rearing and then took off for the exit.

"What took you so long?" Elena cried.

"Sounds good," he fired back. "Most unlike a princess. Come on, let's track Larry down."

"Where is he?" Elena pressed.

"He took the bus for Town Centre. Maybe we can catch up with him. The bus will make dozens of stops and perhaps we can intercept him."

"A bus! But how, without a pass or money?"

Michael shook his head. "I gave him some money—but would he use it?" He paused a moment. "I can't believe I'm asking that about a kid who handed over a loaded gun earlier today. Never mind—he's resourceful."

They ran for the car and Rita, who was accustomed to the constant stream of city traffic, drove. "Don't you realize?" Rita murmured. "Town Centre and the pavilion—that's where the Technology Campaign kicks off."

"It can't be a coincidence." Elena sat in the front seat. "And your brother has such a head start."

"Did Larry know that his father and brother were supposed to make an appearance there today?" Michael asked.

"We didn't talk about it much, we were so busy this morning," Elena said.

"Why would he take off and not say anything?" Michael asked. He reached for his pocket to check his wallet, but didn't notice any missing money. Perhaps the decision was not planned. He leaned forward, watching Rita navigate Edgware Road. No use in urging her to go faster—she was driving as fast as she dared in the heavy traffic. He turned to Elena. "You're supposed to be running away, not checking schedules."

"Somehow, Larry found out," Elena said to no one in particular. "He knows his father and brother are in danger."

"The librarian mentioned that he was using the computer just before he asked about the bus. Maybe he wrote to Richard again."

Elena shook her head. "I asked him not to. He knows how dangerous it is." She paused and Michael heard excitement creep into her voice. "But maybe Richard replied and gave him some kind of message. Maybe Richard needs our help—or he changed his mind."

"There's no use speculating," Rita said. "Let's just find the boy before someone else does."

"Thousands of people will be at the pavilion," Elena fretted. "I don't know how we'll ever find him."

"With any luck, he'll be waiting outside, disappointed because they won't let him in," Michael said. "He doesn't have that much money."

"He'll blend in with a school group," Elena retorted. "Or, he'll convince them that he's a prince." Rita pressed the accelerator harder, and they traveled the rest of the way in nervous silence.

CHAPTER 29

"The case of explosives is inside and ready."
"Her boys do not deserve to be king. They chose her over us."

The bus headed straight for the pavilion, and Larry had no problem figuring out the best entrance for sneaking inside. A tall blond man in his twenties grinned as he accepted tickets and answered questions from a threesome of attractive college-aged women. Larry extracted one of Michael's documents from the backpack and scribbled for a moment. Then without waiting, he dashed through the man's gate. The ticket taker called out, annoyed about the interruption: "Hold on, lad!"

Larry didn't pause, but shouted back: "Sorry, Sir, I must deliver this message to my dad." He waved Michael's document overhead. Then crouching low, Larry darted about the crowd. He joined the line waiting for a security check and knelt to tie his shoe. But he didn't have to worry. The man had already resumed his conversation with the women. Larry opened his backpack, displayed its contents and entered the great hall.

The boy had never been to the pavilion before and, with his head ducked, walked around a bit to figure out the massive sections. If he asked for directions, some guard might realize he wasn't supposed to be on the premises. Most of the sales reps ignored him, but a few smiled. One handed over a free pencil and another offered a visor. Larry thanked the man and immediately donned the visor, shielding both his hair and eyes.

Groups of children explored the displays, laughing with one another, followed by weary school chaperones, and Larry enjoyed mingling with the crowd in a way that was new to him. He had been to plenty of large events before. But the feeling wasn't the same when he sat on a stage, separated and alone.

His family was kept locked up. If people recognized him, they'd approach and ask for autographs. Or if his brother were near, they would shove Larry aside to reach Richard. Larry had seen how crowds could behave with his mother and brother—overwhelming, hysterical, intrusive. Less so with his father and himself. But this crowd was lovely, as long as he was on his own and no one knew who he was.

Larry found a sign—a guide to displays on the floor—and studied the map and list of exhibits. He immediately headed for the stage area. That was where his father would deliver some speech, and indeed as he approached, he saw the ring of security scurrying about. He even recognized a few of the men.

He paused by a table near the stage and studied the scene, trying to figure out from which side Richard would make his entrance. One of the few women with an exhibit was nearby. Dressed markedly better than most of the men, she wore a red suit with black trim and precision makeup to match. Her eyes were intelligent and mean. "Hey, there," she called out to Larry. "Move on. I don't need you hanging around here."

"I'm waiting for my school group," Larry exclaimed. "They're coming along in a minute."

"There's been no school group allowed in here for the past hour. No pass?" She smiled with false sweetness and pointed to the door. "Get lost."

"But . . ." Larry began.

"Young man, you need special passes to stay in this room." Larry had never seen a woman hiss with a smile. "And they're not handing them over to kids. You don't even have a name tag.

I want no commotion around my table. The Prince of Wales is here today. Now, leg it, won't you?"

Larry walked slowly along the table, scanning the artful arrangement. "Can I have one of those?" He pointed to a pen filled with water and miniature floating figures.

"No!" the woman was furious but kept her voice low. Larry guessed that she did not want to call the guard and create a disturbance. That would keep Prince Edward and his entourage away.

"My father's around here," Larry said, in his haughtiest voice. "Somewhere."

"Who gives a damn?" the woman snapped. She immediately resorted to coaxing. "The prince and his son will be in here any minute," she said. She snatched the basket of pens out of his reach, but reached in for one. "They'll stop at a few tables, with a trail of media nipping at their heels. Look, kid, I need the publicity." She held the pen up.

"Has anyone from the palace been down this aisle?" Larry asked eagerly.

She frowned. "Not yet, and they won't if you're around. Anything unusual, and I lose a lot of free publicity. So do me a favor? Take the pen and get lost! Bother the pinheads on the other side of the room."

Larry thanked the woman, held the pen like a trophy, and walked away. He could have offered the woman some advice on how to attract the courtiers. They'd appreciate her desperation, much like moths attracted to light—but then they would never send his father this way. Too much intensity or calculation would work against her. Of course, she wasn't about to listen to Larry.

Odd that the courtiers had not been by, the boy thought. They loved to interview and tease at such affairs—talk to the audience and find out who was most suitable for photo-ops with members of the royal family. Security was already clearing aisles and making final arrangements. His family would arrive soon. Larry had to find a place to wait and watch. Perhaps some distance was wise.

"Damn, I thought it would be good to have my display in the same room as the prince," said a nearby technician, slouched in a chair and playing with his keyboard. "But these damn guards are chasing all the real buyers away."

"Give them a chance—the guards might buy a few," offered his neighbor, a cheerful young Indian man. His hair was long and pulled back from a thin and thoughtful face.

"Hah!" said the complainer. "Do they really look like the types who like technology to you?"

"It's not so bad—they're letting people in with passes." Larry liked the man's eyes, large and kind and brown—the kind that instantly signaled friendliness and intelligent tolerance. But then wasn't all tolerance intelligent?

"And look at who has the passes. Old goats and media dogs— all the cheap bastards!"

Larry looked about at the crowd; the people slowly filling seats in front of the stage did not look anything like the young people sitting around the computer displays. His mother scolded him about stereotyping, but Larry understood what the man meant. For the most part, the palace guards and the computer reps at the tables were mostly men. The guards wore dark conservative suits that matched their cautious stance, while the men behind tables with the computer equipment uniformly had long hair in need of cuts and wore rumpled shirts. Maybe the mean woman in the red suit would get her chance.

Larry paused by the friendly man who stared at his screen, typing in lots of strange code. The programmer looked up and smiled.

"Can I sit and watch you for a while?" Larry asked. "I promise to be quiet."

"Here?" He looked up surprised. The boy nodded. "I want to watch someone who knows what he's doing."

The man laughed, skeptical, but pulled a chair close to his computer. "I'm Nikhil, but most people call me Nick. Who are you?" Larry told him his first name, the real one.

Nikhil returned to his work on the computer, typing furiously. "I'm working on a web page for a friend," he explained. "This is xml code. There are page programs, even word-processing programs, that revert type into code at the push of a button, but you don't get the detail, unless you do a lot of pain-in-the-ass typing. Are you sure you want to sit here and watch?"

Larry stared at the code. Rows of type surrounded by arrows and slashes. "Cool," he said.

The man laughed. "Actually, it's hot. This is the code for my background page. I'm going for a flame effect."

Larry nodded and watched a few moments before asking, "Did the courtiers from the palace come around?"

Nikhil stopped typing. "Is that all you care about?" He looked more disappointed than angry.

"No . . . and yes." Larry stuttered not wanting to lie. The man was nice, decent, so damn different from the unhappy woman with the pens. "I know the prince. He's not a stranger to me."

"Hm, I thought I recognized you," Nikhil said, with a smile. "Except for the hair. You're not going to get me into some kind of trouble, are you?"

"I promise to walk away before that," Larry said. "Sometimes I like to get away from the . . . commotion."

"That's okay," Nikhil said. "You don't have to explain. You're either Larry, the kid brother, or some kind of relative. Look, I have a stepmother and two stepbrothers. People think computers are complicated, but families are worse. Do you like computers at all?"

"Sure!" Larry said. "I like Internet and E-mail and Halo."

"But that's all canned," Nikhil said, earnestly. "Do you like to make your own programs? Invent your own games?"

"I wouldn't know how to begin," Larry admitted.

"Hey, don't feel bad," the man said. "How old are you anyway?"

"Ten," Larry said.

"Okay, I didn't start until I was twelve myself. But it was different then. Who had a computer to play with when I was a kid? And now, kids have them at school, but they teach you all the wrong things."

"Especially my school."

"So teach yourself at home. Let me show you a few tricks."

"To make my own page?"

"Sure, why not?" Nikhil said, nodding. "You could learn the basics in an afternoon." Larry reached into Michael's backpack for the laptop. Typing a moment, Nikhil downloaded a program, typed in some code, and then showed Larry how to switch back and forth from the browser revealing the result of any code. He also pointed to a manual on formatting. Both became engrossed in their tasks, and neither noticed the royal entourage enter the room. Neither stood. Nikhil kept typing away, with Larry following suit, occasionally asking questions. A uniformed representative of the palace walked by and used his fist to knock sharply on the table.

"Please, Sir, some courtesy is called for," the man whispered.

Nikhil hurried to stand and Larry, blushing, hid behind his new friend. He looked about for his father and saw the executives of the campaign welcome the royal visitors and guide them into a nearby room to prepare. Most people returned to their seats, but the volume and speed of the chatter increased.

Organizers of the Technology Campaign scurried through the pavilion repeating advice on protocol suggested by palace representatives. A young excited man, accompanied by a member of the palace staff, dispensed the patronizing advice quickly to the group in Nikhil's area. "The prince and his son want to walk around and examine a few simple demonstrations. The key word, here, is simple. Most importantly, do not approach members of the royal family. No questions to the royalty at all. If they're interested, they'll come to you. Protocol demands that the public waits to be addressed and then speaks only if spoken to."

The stuffy and overdressed palace representative concluded, "Otherwise, proceed with what you were doing and no formalities are necessary." He gave the table another irritating tap and then headed for the next section with the same advice.

"How do you make friends with someone like that hanging around?" Nikhil asked under his breath.

"It's not easy," Larry murmured, staring at the slow-moving entourage, full of smiling faces and shallow chat, not very far away. He located his brother, in the center, and watched as courtiers pointed and directed attention this way and that. Richard laughed and spoke with people, but never more than a minute. Larry crouched low and decided he had to stay undercover, that he couldn't bear to get hustled away from his new freedom. And somehow he had to convince Richard of the same. If only Richard looked his way, surely, he'd recognize Larry.

"Look at the man standing next to the poor young fellow," Nikhil observed. "He hovers over him. Looks like he's positively going to explode."

"That's Derry," Larry said. "He's never happy unless he's completely in control. And now that I look at it all from the outside, I'm amazed. They think they have control, but I'm not sure any of them has control over anything."

"So you're not kidding me," Nikhil chuckled. "You do know

these folks, but somehow you don't look the type."

"That's because I'm still a kid," Larry replied, echoing his father's sentiment. He had a webpage started, relying on photos from the official web site of the royal family. He asked Nikhil how to get the page online.

Nikhil turned back to his monitor. "I'll show you that later. If the royal club comes around to this table, I'm supposed to show them something flashy." He typed a few minutes. "What about this web page?" Larry checked the screen and laughed.

Animated caricatures of the royal family waved dumbly and moved about the screen. His parents loomed large, and Richard was on top of them. The figure for Larry was small and made to look as though he was running and pulling at his parents, trying to catch their attention.

Larry laughed, as Nikhil exited the program and searched for another file. "Richard would like it," Larry said. He glanced across the way and noticed his older brother strolling about the exhibits. "You have time to find another display before they get over here."

"They may not make it over here at all," Nikhil said, with a shrug.

"Can we send an E-mail between computers in this room?"

The man smiled. "I have a few friends here."

"Are any sitting near the prince?"

Nikhil checked that part of the hall, smiled and typed, then waved.

"What are you saying?" Nervous, Larry did not want to get caught by Derry and be forced to return to the palace. "I don't want them to know I'm here."

Nikhil typed some more before shoving the keyboard toward Larry. "I set up a chat line with a friend of mine over there," the young man explained. "Hold on—he's going to tell the prince that he has a message from an old friend. Don't worry, he'll be mum on the source."

Larry hunched his shoulders, clutched the edge of the table, and watched the other side of room. He could not shake the feeling that he might have to jump up and run from the room. A man who didn't look much different from Nikhil hovered over a computer and extracted some paper. He leaned over and tapped one of the guards, startling him, then he handed over the note. The man looked annoyed and said something sharp. Other security men surrounded the man to read the note from the computer.

"What did the note say?" Larry asked, cringing.

"Asked if he was having fun and told him a friend, Larry, is in the room," Nikhil said. "He can type a reply, if the goons hand the note over."

Larry stared as the guards carried the message to Derry, who laughed as if he had read a joke. But Richard must have overheard, stepping forward and insisting on seeing the note. The older brother read, nodding absently, and looked about the crowded hall, before turning to ask some question. The security guard pointed to the nearby exhibit, and the young man stepped aside and showed Richard how to use the chat line.

"You sure they don't know where we're sitting at?" Larry whispered.

"Don't worry," Nikhil said. "I told my friend not to point us out. And he won't relinquish his laptop for anything."

Larry watched as Richard bent his head low and typed slowly. Words appeared on Nikhil's screen: "Good to hear from you. D doesn't believe it's you."

Larry typed fast. "Tell him to stop hanging over your shoulder, reading every word. He looks like he's permanently attached." He signed off with the top-secret name, *Cordulegaster*, that security attached to him. Guards who knew the password were supposed to be trusted. Didn't matter anymore, Larry thought to himself.

Richard ordered the staff to stand back.

"Are you really in this room?" As Richard wrote, Derry spoke to the guards and waved his arms. Security men spoke into radios and began spreading out through the hall. Derry returned and hovered behind Richard. Larry forced himself not to look over in that direction.

"Is your tie blue and yellow stars?" Larry wrote back. "And look over your shoulder."

Richard turned and snapped at Derry to stand back, before typing, "They're gold, not yellow." The man bowed, just enough to be sarcastic, before scanning the crowded hall. Then he headed for an exit, speaking into his radio. The man wore a smile on his face and Larry wondered if security would soon surround the pavilion. He swallowed.

"Tell him not to bother security. He won't catch Mum. I'm alone."

"Believe me, I have no control over the man, even though he constantly reminds me that he serves only at my pleasure. That I'm free to make changes at any time. He can't believe that you're at the show. Says he wants to see you, make sure that you're all right. He almost had a fit when I told him this morning that Mum intended to come back. He probably thinks that she's planning a coup!"

"Tell him that we've never been better." Larry regretted being so cocky and erased the words. But how could Derry possibly find him. Hundreds milled about the room, with more trying to enter and get a peek at the stage. "He can try and catch me, but I'll get away."

"Derry's history. Remember you told me about Derry fooling around in your closet? I checked again and found your science set, dumped in a plain box. But don't you remember the day of my party? He insisted packing the science box in Mother's car.

I told security. Don't know why he's still here. Will talk to Father tonight."

"So, what do you think? Do you want to join us?" Larry typed fast.

"It's not as easy for me, I'm afraid. How could I possibly explain? To Father, Grandmum, and everyone else."

"Don't forget what's important for you," Larry wrote.

"Derry thinks he can keep me contained, as easily as blocking these exits."

"I see that. But I got in here. We can both get out."

"Maybe I'll give my last speech today. Larry, really—what I'm hoping is that you and Mum can get away. Once everyone gets used to that idea, the control will stop. I can visit. If that doesn't work, then I promise, I'll leave."

Larry sighed. The palace would never let Richard leave, but he gave his brother credit for trying. "That might work out. Good luck."

"Thanks, I need it. And I appreciate what you're doing. Godspeed to you, little brother."

CHAPTER 30

"Both boys are here, but not the mother."

"Without the two boys, she's nothing. She'll have to live with herself the rest of her life.

"I hope you're right."

Traffic slowed to a crawl a few blocks away from the pavilion. "What's going on?" Elena muttered. "Edward never attracts this sort of attention!"

Rita pulled the car into a lot and handed the attendant a few pounds. "We'll get to the pavilion faster if we walk!"

Running, they were less than a block away when they heard the massive explosion on the far side of the pavilion. Fear, memories of the last explosion, swept through Elena. She felt a blow to her chest. Her ears hurt. This time, alarms rang and smoke filled the sky. Not far from the building, some people hit the ground while others took off running, every direction away from the pavilion. "My God, my boys," Elena screamed, pushing against people who were trying to head in the opposite direction.

Michael held her arm, but looked helpless. "We don't know that."

"What do you mean?" Elena shouted, tears streaming down her face. "That was the pavilion—and both my sons are there."

"Ten more minutes." Michael pushed his hair back. "All we needed was ten more minutes. I should have made more calls!"

"They never would have listened!" Elena screamed in frustration.

"We should have tried," Michael retorted.

"Both of you, calm down, and wait for me!" Rita caught up with both and grabbed each by a shoulder. "Stop talking like either of you had any control over any of this. There's no use arguing. This is a huge emergency. Let's do what we can to help people now. We get inside and we might find the boys. But that's only going to happen if we stay calm!"

Michael nodded, and the three took off for the pavilion. The building still stood, but one entire side sagged, the corner ripped apart by a bomb. Some flames spurted and all the glass windows had been blown out. The ticket office for the Technology Campaign was deserted, and a sign announcing "SOLD OUT" hung haphazardly. Screams and wails came from inside. Security guards hired for crowd control looked confused as an immense crowd tried to escape the location.

With hundreds of people pushing their way out through the doors, Elena could see they would have trouble entering the pavilion.

Rita went to a police officer and flashed her hospital ID. "We're here to help with triage. Can you help me get inside?"

"Are you sure, young lady?" the officer asked, before pointing to a door around the corner. "Go in that way. But you're entering at your own risk."

"What do you mean?" Elena pressed.

"We already got a call from our supervisors," the officer replied. In his forties, he looked worried. "They suggest the structure is none too stable and we're not to go in or let anyone else in. Those are our orders. We're just trying to keep the exits clear and assist people out."

"Do you know where the Prince of Wales was last seen?" Elena asked, desperate.

Rita glared at her, and the officer shook his head with irritation. "No idea, lady."

"We have to go in—come on," Rita ordered. She nodded sternly at the police officer and then guided Elena and Michael, holding her ID out as a way to move forward.

Elena followed behind, hoping that she would not get asked for an ID card. She could never leave the site without her sons. The place was noisy, smoky, and dangerous—with people, dusty and coughing, straggling for the exits, many helping others to walk. She hoped that someone helped her sons, or that the boys were well enough and helping others.

Michael, Rita, and Elena entered the hall and stopped in amazement.

To the left, most of the great hall was intact, with glass walls and futuristic displays of intricate electronic equipment. Some computer monitors still flashed colorful scenes and messages. To the right, the pavilion was unrecognizable. The building leaned inward, gutted. Literally all that remained was a pile of concrete and metal rubble, broken glass and plastic, and thousands of hanging wires. Smoke billowed from the corner, with all the choking, harsh odor of an electrical fire. A few people walked around the perimeter of that area, dazed, staring at the piles, perhaps hoping to find survivors. But nothing in the smoldering mess resembled the human form. Piercing alarms went off, forcing everyone to shout.

A few people sat against the wall, holding their heads, as if trying to squeeze images from their memory, perhaps trying to stop blood oozing from head wounds. A few others climbed gingerly about the wreckage, tugging at pieces, with the hopes of finding anyone who might still be alive. Elena felt paralyzed with horror, not knowing where to start. Richard and Larry could be anywhere, in any condition. Along with Edward.

Surely, staff would be swarming to help Edward, Elena

thought to herself. But she didn't recognize any faces. A group of men struggled to move a heavy beam and called for Michael to help, and he hurried off.

Elena felt useless and looked around. "I don't know where to start."

"Do whatever you can to help," Rita advised. "We're the best hope there is for anyone trapped underneath. Listen up. If you hear someone, work with someone else to remove them. As much as you're tempted to rush, move the odd pieces carefully and don't tug on people. A blast like this—they could have severe internal injuries and not realize it." She dropped her voice to a low whisper. "And please don't be too obvious about asking questions about Richard or Larry."

With that, she turned away and hurried to the nearest rescue operation, where one young man helped extract a moaning man, an older one in a suit, from a heap. Elena followed and watched as the rescuer, less than thirty, worked steadily, showing more calm and control than anyone else at the scene. Once uncovered, the older man limped away. Rita introduced herself to the young man, and the respect was immediate. "I'm a nurse who specializes in traumatic injuries," Rita explained. "How many people do you estimate are still underneath?"

"At least two hundred, maybe more, I'd say." He looked relieved to see her uniform and, shouting over the noise, explained that he was a systems analyst, who had left the pavilion for a few moments. "My name is Cam and I just started in here . . ."

"You're doing fine, Cam," Rita assured him.

"The damn hall was packed! And security had just started clearing this area for the bloody royalty. If not, there'd be hundreds more buried."

"The princes, tell me did they arrive?" Elena could not control herself.

Rita closed her eyes and looked away as Cam gave Elena a cool look. "Yes, the father and the son."

"Tell me, where was the boy standing?" Elena couldn't help it. She had to know.

"In this hall. I can't tell one exhibit from another. Look, I've got to get moving here. My friends are under here and every minute counts. And it would be nice to have help, regardless of who's underneath." He kicked a hunk of plastic and walked away.

"Just start helping," Rita urged Elena. She handed over some tissue and advised the woman to stuff some small pieces in her ears. "That will make it a bit more bearable. To find your sons, it's best if we spread out. Work with anyone and start moving debris. If you find someone, call out for help. We can only hope that the boys got out—or someone is helping them. It won't help if anyone guesses that you're their mother." Rita broke away and started guiding rescuers to move the most seriously injured near the doorway.

Elena still didn't know where to start and stared at the wreckage strewn about on the one side of the room. A few people crawled over the piles like ants. She looked down and tugged at a large piece of metal in her path. It didn't budge.

"Here, you can use this," a young man with long hair called out, waving a broom. "Poke around and go through systematically. Be careful moving any wires—some could still be live. There's enough people on the injury list. And once you find someone, hand the broom over to someone else."

"Better hurry, the police will be chasing us out any minute," advised another man, clearing metal away from one area, despite burns down the side of his face. "They'll want evidence to catch the bastards." Elena wasn't sure how anyone could possibly get their bearings in the confusion. A team of firefighters, donned in helmets and heavy suits, stormed the hall and spread out, spraying a stream of chemicals that immediately doused the flames along the one side of the hall.

The firefighters shouted orders and waved their arms, but the tissue in Elena's ears muted that noise. Most rescuers ignored the commands. Not far away, Rita shouted for people to bring water, towels, makeshift splints, bandages, as she took over triaging patients, directing people to lay the unconscious and most seriously wounded near the doorway, so that ambulances could whisk them away.

Every surface, everyone in the room, was covered in a powdery dust. The color of people's clothes, their hair, or skin no longer mattered. Everyone looked the same.

Elena approached the man who had handed over the broom. "I just want to find someone alive," she pleaded. "Where do you think I should look?"

"Stay away from the smoke—waste of time going too far back." He pointed along the edges of the wreckage. "All along the edges here and especially under any tables."

She started working, poking with the broom and using her hand to move away blackened computer monitors, ripped poster board, chunks of plastic, wood, keyboards, and pieces from the wall. She worked methodically, distraught to think of people trapped nearby and she didn't know where to look.

Michael came to her side, and quietly started working. Together, they clawed away at what she thought as their pile of once expensive, shattered, unidentifiable equipment. All around them, small groups negotiated plans for moving material about. Otherwise recklessly tossing material about could smother another victim of the blast. Ordinary people lined the perimeter, doing what they could to help, and Elena was inspired to work harder.

Poking about with the broom, she found a long flat surface—a table! She grabbed Michael's arm and shouted, tossing her broom to a group working not far away. Michael fell to his knees, desperately clearing some space. "A moan—I hear someone," he shouted. Part of the pile moved—a leg covered in dust and blood. A leg in ruined nylons. Elena could not help but swallow some disappointment, even as she forced herself to keep on working as fast as she could, carefully removing plastic and metal away. She could not walk away from someone so badly hurt, in search of her own child. She no longer felt that pull inside, and only wanted to help this woman.

"Here's one!" Michael shouted to people carrying wounded to the doorway. They asked him to help move another person and promised to return and help. As Elena kept picking away at the pieces covering the other leg and the table, another frantic young man approached, tearing away at the rubble. "Don't pull at her," Elena advised, as she gently pulled jagged pieces away from the woman. For the first time since walking away from the palace, she was dressed appropriately for an occasion, she thought, with Michael's baggy jeans and sweatshirt making it easy for her to move throughout the mess. "We have to clear more of this junk away from her somehow. And then we can lift her out."

Elena managed to grip the edge of a broken table and pulled. No use. So she patiently kept clearing more tangled wires and debris away, but still had trouble dislodging the table. Elena worked with steady intensity, focusing on saving this one person. Somehow, Elena thought, if she saved this one woman, then somewhere else in the hall, some other person might do the same for her children. Underneath the table, the woman groaned and cried out.

"Let me give the table a try again," the young man said. "I'll be careful." As he struggled to lift the table, Elena used her hands to shield the trapped woman's face from bits of glass that slid away. The man hefted the table over to its side, and Elena brushed away dust from the woman's eyes and nose. The woman gasped and struggled and cried, and Elena whispered, urging her to remain calm and to wait just another few moments until they could free her. The woman's hair was dusty and matted with blood. But she was conscious and fought to breathe despite a raspy cough. At least Elena helped one person. For an instant, Elena wondered to herself why she didn't continue searching frantically for her own children. But somehow, it didn't matter anymore. First, she had to work on getting this one woman to safety.

"Come," Elena said gently, using both arms to help the petite woman to stand. Elena couldn't determine much about the woman, even her age, because she was so dusty. Her trim suit—it had to be at least a size two—was torn, grubby, and gray. Coughing, the woman swayed, then leaned against Elena's tall frame. Gasping, she tried to catch her breath and talk. "There's some water over here," Elena said, leading the woman to Rita's makeshift triage area.

The woman nodded through a rough series of dry coughs, clinging to Elena's arm. She tried to talk, but only coughs came. Supplies were scarce—only a few large bottles of water—and one man in a security uniform retorted that water was for medical personnel only. Elena ignored him and reached for a used paper cup that had been tossed near a large container. She filled it with water and knelt beside the woman, touching the cup to her lips. The woman spat dust out of her mouth, and Elena held the edge of her shirt up, wiping mucus from the woman's nose. Then Elena offered another sip of water. The woman grasped the princess's arm and retched.

The needs in the hall were immense, but for Elena to try and hurry away would be cruel.

"Take it easy," Elena whispered. The woman coughed more and tried to speak. Elena poured some water once again onto the end of her own oversized shirt, using it to wipe the woman's face. "You're out in the open now and safe. Ambulance crews will be here soon, and you're going to be fine." The soft words calmed the woman and her coughs subsided enough that she could hold the cup herself and take a few swallows. "Relax," Elena whispered.

Another woman stumbled nearby—and ambulance workers passed by with stretchers.

"We'll be back for you next," called out one of the paramedics.

"I probably should go back and help others," Elena said. After uncovering this one woman, she couldn't bear the thought of anyone waiting beneath the huge dusty piles, slowly suffocating.

The woman nodded. "Yes, go back and help the others." Then she pointed to an area of the room that was farther away from the main area of the blast. "Children here . . ." The woman gasped for air, and took another sip with a shaking hand. "A little boy, he's around somewhere. I chased him away . . . but he went to another table, not far away. Oh, God, my head. I feel so awful."

Elena looked at the woman's eyes. "Red hair? No! I mean, did he have dark hair?"

"Yes, dark, about ten or so. Go on and hurry. It's hell being buried alive in this mess. Please go and help the others. I'll be out of here soon." She squeezed Elena's hand. "It's strange— you look and sound so familiar to me. Like you're my guardian angel. I can't ever thank you enough."

"Thank you," Elena murmured automatically and pulled her arm away to stand. She didn't know what else to say, so she turned and hurried back toward Michael, already clawing at another pile.

"Thank God, the first one we found was alive," Michael said. "I'm not sure I could go on otherwise."

Elena nodded. "That woman told me that a small boy had been hanging around not far from here," she said, breathing hard, more from excitement than exertion. "She described him. It had to be Larry."

"Look, Elena, you can't count on anything." Michael did not stop moving pieces away from the pile. "But at least there's a lot of people working around here."

"I could use help—someone's under here!" shouted Cam, working not far away.

"Go ahead," Michael urged her. Elena rushed to Cam's side and helped him lift the larger chunks of wallboard and pieces of chair. As they worked, a muffled voice called for help. Once again they reached a long solid flat surface.

"It's another table blocking them!" Elena shouted.

"These tables probably saved some lives," said Cam, pausing a moment to wipe sweat from his brow and leaving smudges.

"Let's hurry." She moved pieces of plastic and cardboard, computers and walls, all mixed together, trying to locate the edges of the table. "With this dust, they can't breathe under here. And we're running out of time!"

A commander from the fire brigade stood in the main entrance with a megaphone and called for attention. "This is the fire department. The structure's not safe and could come down any minute," he announced, his voice breaking. "We urge everyone who can to assist one other person and leave the premises immediately. All fire personnel are ordered to leave immediately." The men, donned in helmets, heavy canvas and leather gear, reluctantly started heading towards the exits. The firefighter moved to the wall, where patients waited for stretchers, and waved his arms, as if pleading with them to do whatever they could to get away. He roughly pulled one woman to standing. Then he hefted another woman over his shoulders and stormed for the door.

Then suddenly, a cracking sound interrupted all rescue work in the hall, as everyone paused and looked upward. A huge steel beam had broken loose and dangled, pulling at the framework that supported the glass ceiling.

"We don't have much time," someone called out from behind them.

"They aren't forcing us to leave yet." Elena stubbornly tossed scraps aside, ignoring her sore and bleeding hands.

Cam looked up at the ceiling and then at Michael and Elena. "Sorry, but I don't like the way that beam looks. Two more minutes for this person and then we're out of here." As he tugged at the table, someone pounded from the other side, then gave a muffled cry.

Elena climbed closer to get a better grip on the mess covering the flat surface. Shaking, she tried not to imagine the fear felt by the trapped people who might have heard the announcement or the panicked conversations all around. Throughout the hall, more rescue workers abandoned their efforts, rushing for the doors, ready to escape the horrible smoky hall with its unstable rooftop. With fewer people, the room seemed larger, with more debris. Suddenly, Elena realized that the room was quiet, that the piercing alarms had stopped.

"We're coming," Elena promised the people who waited below, her voice croaking. "We're going as fast as we can."

"Elena!" Michael cautioned.

"No—I can't leave, not yet," Elena insisted, pulling away pieces, no longer caring. She had to reach this one person—just one more person to save. "Come on, it's time to get out of here," shouted one man, stumbling over an office chair in his race for the door.

"Michael, I understand if you want to leave." Panting, Elena did not stop moving pieces.

He just shook his head and joined her and Cam, systematically clearing the plastic, wallboard, even a shoe covering the table top. As they worked, they could feel someone pushing from underneath. Still, only part of the table was exposed. "If I could just get a grip on one edge," Michael said. "It's a big table."

Elena started to call out for Rita, but the nurse was supporting a man who dragged one leg, obviously broken, to the exit. The commander from the fire brigade approached, and Elena put all effort into uncovering more of the table.

"Didn't you hear me?" he barked. "This block must be cleared. Now!"

Elena scolded him. "Anyone who's trapped and conscious can hear you! And I'm not walking away while I know there's someone alive underneath here. Please think about what you're saying."

The man, taller than anyone in the group, looked nervous and lowered his voice as he spoke with urgency. "Yes, that is all well and good. But the engineers want to come in and prop up some of the beams. They might make it safe, and we'll be right back in here. But they won't start work until everyone's out of here." He tugged at her arm. "Please, Ma'am, we must leave. Immediately."

"Let me go!" she shouted.

"That could take all day!" Cam exclaimed. "We're finding people alive—they don't have much time."

The commander roughly pulled Elena from the pile. "I want you to leave now."

"God damn it!" Michael bellowed. "Give us a hand and two lousy minutes, and then we'll step outside."

The man stood tall. "We have security rules here."

"Look, we're almost through with this one," Michael argued. "We think it might be a kid. Can't we at least finish here?"

"A child! My God, and the prince is missing." Uncertainty

crossed the man's eyes. He was one of the last officials left in the hall, and Elena could read the man's mind. He could become a national hero by saving the young heir. The man kicked a computer monitor out of the way and went to work, even more eagerly than Michael, Cam, or Elena.

"All right, we'll try this one," the firefighter agreed. "But quickly."

Michael nodded. "If we can just expose an edge, we can move the table and maybe pull him out."

The firefighter was lucky to be wearing tough gloves. "Look at how the table slants slightly downward. It's best to work from this side—everyone do what they can to uncover this side first. It will be easier to lift that way." With his hands protected, he could remove glass and other sharp rubble at twice the speed of Elena and Michael.

"What the hell are you doing over there, Paul?" shouted another firefighter from the main doorway.

"One more minute!" the commander yelled, intent on getting the table moved. "I'll be out in one more moment." He lowered his voice and addressed the small group working around him. "Got it! Here's an edge! Help me lift now. We don't have much time—and they're going to arrest the lot of us and drag us out if we don't hurry!"

Elena backed away as Michael, Cam, and the firefighter uncovered a corner, gripped their hands underneath the heavy metal table, and tried to lift with all their might. But the large slab didn't budge. The sound of a weak cough came from underneath. A muffled adult voice called out, and pushed, followed by more high-pitch coughing. There was more than one person underneath the table.

"Have water ready, Elena," Michael ordered. She hesitated, wanting to see who waited under that table. "Now!" he shouted. She took off running. A policeman held Rita by the arm and was tugging her toward the door, shaking his head. "Wait!" Elena called out. "We need her over here. Only one more minute. We promise! That firefighter needs us!" She pointed.

"Damn fools," the officer said with a shrug, let go of Rita, and took off for the exit himself. Rita collected two bottles of water long abandoned by the rescue workers and caught up with Elena. Michael was swearing. They had cleared a few inches of space along the table's one edge. But not enough to peer underneath.

"Just enough to get a grip," Michael said, frustrated. "So much damn dust around—who would think it weighed so much?"

"What if all of us try?" Elena offered.

Another screeching sound came from the sagging roof. The fire commander glanced at his watch. "I'm sorry, but one more minute! If there's a kid under here, he's better off under the table than standing here with us underneath that." Sweating, he pointed to a dangling beam and cracked roof. "That's ready to go."

Michael fiercely kicked at the pile blocking the table. "Okay," he said. "Spread out and I'll count."

"Our last try," the firefighter warned, under his breath. "So give it all you got."

"On the count of three," Michael said, and counted. They all worked on lifting the table. Rita fell. Elena's feet slipped in crumbly glass and plastic fragments all over the floor, but she hung on and put all her weight into lifting the table away from the wreckage.

"We're getting there," Cam shouted.

Elena held her breath, closed her eyes, and used all her force. When she opened her eyes again, she could see that they had made headway. And they also had help. Two dusty arms pushed the table from underneath.

"Hurry," Michael said, gasping. "But watch, there's a lot of glass around here."

"Damn the glass," the firefighter scolded. "Just hurry."

Elena couldn't speak, didn't dare look. It took everything she had to hold the heavy table and push. Broken computer parts, cardboard, unrecognizable pieces from the technology displays fell away. More dust filled the air and everyone in the group let go of ragged coughs.

The men held the table up and a small body stretched out his arms. Rita took hold underneath the armpits and dragged the figure out. The group struggled to lift the table even higher, and another figure, an adult, crawled out from their protected space, groaning as he scraped against broken glass and metal. The two figures were gray, covered in dust, and couldn't stop coughing. "Anyone else in there with you?" Michael asked, peering into the pile. The biggest one, the man, dirty and bleeding, collapsed on the pile and could only shake his head.

"Okay, stand back and let it go," Michael ordered. The long table fell with a crash, raising another small cloud of dust. Exhausted, Elena crawled toward the smaller of the two people pulled from the wreckage. Oblivious to sharp bits all around, Elena sat near him, ready to cradle the filthy person in her arms, because it no longer mattered who the child was.

"God damn it all," the commander swore, obviously disappointed. "This one's too young to be the prince."

The others stared as the man walked away. Elena wanted to scream at him, tell him how wrong it was to feel that one human being was so much better than another. Instead, her arms automatically tightened, hugging the filthy boy, and only then she sensed that it was her Larry.

Rita held a cup of water to the man's lips and then asked whether he was ready to stand. But he couldn't even reply. Elena worked on clearing dust away from her son's mouth and eyes, but her hands were bleeding and made him look even worse. Larry closed his eyes and sucked in air.

"Time to get out of here," Michael cautioned. Elena clutched Larry tightly, and he opened his eyes and smiled. But Michael frowned and pointed upward.

Elena glanced up and knew it was not her imagination. The beam dangled at a lower, more precarious angle, as if it hung from a few delicate threads.

"The place is going to cave in," Cam called out and he turned to help Rita, who pointed out the twisted ankle of the man. "We'll stand on either side of you and lean on our shoulders," Cam ordered.

"My name is Nikhil," the man said, coughing furiously. "And thank you." He held on to them and they started hobbling away.

"We're right behind you!" Michael shouted, as he removed Larry from Elena's arms and helped him to his feet. The boy was unsteady and almost fell, but Michael caught him. The hall was strangely empty, the only noises were crackling noises of breaking or burning plastic, sirens beyond the walls, and a low straining noise from the ceiling.

"Make a quick decision, Elena," Michael said. "Do you still want to walk away from the palace?"

She nodded.

"How would you feel about not being bothered by paparazzi, at least for a few years?"

She couldn't imagine it. "It would be heaven," she said. "But how?"

"Do you have anything that you can leave behind here?" he pressed. "And hurry, there isn't much time."

She had left with so little, and it was hard to think of parting with anything. But her hand automatically reached toward her neck—and she extracted a gold chain from underneath her shirt. Hanging from the chain was an old cross with jewels that had been a gift from her grandmother. Also on the chain was her wedding band. She unclasped the chain and removed only the ring—and looked at Michael. He took the ring and flung it far into the ruins.

Then, he turned, took a quick step toward her and reached for her head. "Excuse me, for being thorough." He grimaced, and she felt a sharp pain on her scalp.

"Ouch!" she screeched.

"Sorry about that." He looked about and found the woman's shoe. Tucking the strands of hair deep inside, he threw it, aiming for the same spot where the ring now lay hidden. "They'll check every article of clothing closely. It gives them some DNA and will allow the family to declare you legally dead. And you can walk away with closure." He lifted Larry in his arms and started for the door, noticing the threesome struggling ahead. "You help Cam with the other guy," Michael called to her.

The hall was deserted by now and the small group had to make its way by climbing over the rubble. Elena caught up with Cam, and urged Nikhil to lean on her, as Rita moved ahead, trying to guide them, shoving aside obstacles that blocked their way to the door. A wheezing noise came from the ceiling, and some glass panels sagged and cracked with the pressure. A few large squares fell, landing with shattering bursts.

Rita pointed to the exit used by the firefighter and everyone moved in that direction.

With another loud cracking noise, the beam overhead jerked out of place and dipped lower. Even carrying Larry, Michael moved fast and the others struggled to keep up with his pace. Moments later, another glass panel fell not far away, showering the group with a spray of glass. Michael bent his head and used his arms to shield Larry, before turning back to the group, blood streaming from his face. "Keep moving, no matter what!" Michael ordered. "Don't stop for anything." He hurried even faster, increasing his lead, moving ahead of Rita.

Without talking, the group steadily moved for the exit. As Elena, Cam, and Nikhil passed through the door, the beam fell with a deafening crash behind them. Elena turned to see a section of the building folding downward, almost in slow motion, smashing the table that had covered Larry only moments earlier. A billow of dust and glass emerged, almost as if chasing them.

Even with the help, Nikhil was in severe pain and had trouble walking. Ahead, Michael looked back and paused to give the stragglers time to catch up. But Elena screamed at him. "Don't wait for us! Keep running."

Rita heard the shout and paused, too. "There's no point in all of us getting buried alive," Elena shouted. "Keep going. If you get outside, you can always tell someone where we were last seen."

But Rita hurried back. "No, it's faster if the three of us carry him." She directed Cam to take the shoulders and then she and Elena each grabbed a calf. Seconds later, they lugged the young man into a small connecting hallway that was only one story high. Thankfully, the crowds had long since vanished, and only a few rescue workers hurried by, so it was easy to move away from the pavilion. Behind them, Elena could hear the larger structure cracking and shuddering.

Pain ripped through her legs, her hands, and throat, and tears streamed down Elena's face. Not slowing her pace, she could not help but glance back. "I hate to take off without knowing about Richard and Edward and the others."

"For all you know, Edward and Richard made it outside a long time ago," Rita shouted, panting and struggling to keep up. The thought kept Elena moving.

Ahead, Michael must have deliberately slowed his pace, and Elena noticed that Larry lifted his head up and tugged on the man's arm, speaking earnestly. Michael shook his head somberly, as the boy broke out in another coughing fit. Elena couldn't hear her son's words, and could only watch as Michael shook his head and quieted the boy. "Don't talk, little man," Michael said. "Let's just get out of here."

He turned around and urged the group to hurry, shouting, "We need to get far away from this block." Elena felt relieved as he moved faster. "Don't stop now. Anything can happen when something that big falls."

At the end of the hallway, they reached another large structure—and an exit, but to an open courtyard surrounded by a maze of other structures. "Couldn't we be safe here?" Elena called to Michael. "In the center?" Her shoulders ached from carrying the full-grown man, and Rita, who was smaller, couldn't even speak.

"Safer, but this place could come down, too. A domino effect."

And so they hurried the length of the hallway—following signs that pointed to the open streets. Elena, Cam, and Rita managed to catch up with Michael, but that was only because he didn't hurry ahead. "Mom, thanks for coming for me," Larry spoke. "Getting me out of there."

"Almost," Michael promised. "Give us a few minutes and we'll be out for sure."

Elena couldn't wait to ask what bothered her most. "Did you see your brother or father in there?" she asked.

The boy's eyes had tears. "Mom, they're gone," he said, closing his eyes. But Elena wasn't sure what he meant. Maybe her other son escaped. Just then they heard a giant crashing noise, the deafening sound of the ceiling of the Great Hall falling away.

A large door was all that remained separating them from open space. Michael reached the door first and slammed into with his shoulder, holding it open so that the others could pass through. Another shrill alarm shrieked behind them. Outside, the air felt so clean. Some police bustled about and looked horrified to see more people emerge from the tangle.

"Get away from this block immediately," shouted one.

"No kidding," Cam replied.

"Keep going," Michael urged. "Let's just keep going." He turned to Elena. "Keep your head down and just keep moving. We don't want to answer any questions, we don't want to stop. We want to get as far away from here as we possibly can."

Elena nodded, but didn't worry. Covered in gray dust, no one in the group stood out. "We'll just finish helping Cam here." Once outside, the group headed for the nearest ambulance, which was empty and waiting. The driver opened his doors, eager to assist, as Nikhil thanked the group and apologized for slowing them down. Even as tears streamed from his eyes, mixing with the glass and dust, he spoke with calm amazement. "I owe my life to you. Any of you could have walked away, but you didn't."

"We'll get him to the hospital quickly," the ambulance worker promised. He pointed to their shredded hands and eyes. "You could use some help, too. All three of you get in, too!"

Cam urged Rita or Elena to climb inside. But they shook their heads and explained that they had promised to meet and leave with Michael. "I don't want to leave here without a full load," the driver admitted, turning to hunt for others in need of care.

Cam took Elena by the shoulder and bent down to whisper in her ear. "I recognize you, and I'm sorry about how annoyed I was when we first met in there. I thought you cared only about the prince. I didn't realize you were looking for your son."

"But you were right," she agreed with a smile, touching his arm. "And that's why I don't want to have any part of this system anymore. Please don't tell anyone that you saw us in there. If anyone ever suspects anything, do whatever you can to convince them otherwise."

"Are you sure?" he asked with a frown.

"Please, you saw how it was in there—what people care about. It's best for us if they think that we're all dead."

Cam nodded and, dusty, weary, the two hugged. Then he turned and hugged Rita. The ambulance driver returned with another small group carrying an unconscious woman, and Cam broke away to help him load the woman next to Nikhil. "You ride in front with me," the driver ordered Cam, before slamming the rear door. Jumping into the ambulance beside the driver, Cam gave a brief wave and a nod. Pulling away, the driver did not put on the siren or lights—the emergency was just too big.

Turning away, Elena had to keep moving and help Larry. She still carried a shred of hope that palace staff had somehow whisked Richard and Edward away to safety. The two women hurried back to Michael, who waited, still holding Larry. But the boy's eyes were open and alert.

"Do you think he needs a hospital?" Elena asked.

Rita asked the boy some questions about where he had been hit and then checked his eyes. "He's going to be fine," Rita assured her. She had a small bottle of cold water and was patting the boy's red skin gently. "We need to clean him up and let him rest. The burns on his arms are mild. Nothing we can't take care of ourselves . . ."

"So, let's go." Michael set off, and as the group walked toward Rita's car, the pavilion collapsed, almost in slow motion. Larry buried his face into Michael's arm, and the man walked quickly, intent on shielding the child from the gruesome sight. Clouds of smoke and gritty dust spewed from the building.

"We got out just in time," Michael said, passing lines of firefighters and police who surrounded the block. A few ambulances pulled way with other ones taking their place. Photographers clashed with the police to move in closer. Crowds gathered, curious and horrified, crying and pointing. Anyone inside the building now could not possibly have a chance.

Rita's car was parked beyond those crowds. As they approached it, Michael slowed his stride and the other three caught up. Michael was frustrated. "All that, running down here to stop this, and we still don't know who attacked your family. Whether they're still after you—or Larry. You may never know."

"It doesn't matter anymore." The feeling was genuine, Elena knew, and not just because she was exhausted. "We're going to be okay." Elena no longer felt compelled to hide or worry, at least for the next few hours. No one glanced twice at the bedraggled group, with hundreds of others walking away from the scene who were just as dazed and dirty. The entire country focused on the tragedy and not just a few missing members of one family. Everyone's mind was on the disaster at the Technology Campaign. Anything else was unimportant. And that was how it should be.

The women waited as Michael unlocked the door, and Larry was quiet as Michael loaded him into the backseat. Elena sighed and paused, looking back at the empty space where the Great Hall had once gracefully reigned over the Centre. "I don't feel right about just driving away," Elena murmured. She didn't feel right about running away from her other son, even if he was no longer alive.

"No," Michael insisted, as he took her by the shoulders and guided her into the back seat next to Larry. "There's nothing we can do for them. You saw it back there. We did our best."

He slammed the door, and then jumped inside himself, taking the wheel and starting Rita's car. He eased the car away from the scene, taking care to use signals and maintain speed limit while driving away from the ugly scene. Elena realized, with every action, he was intent on helping her escape.

Elena let out a soft moan. "We never should have left Richard. I should have insisted that he come with us. God, was it only last night?"

Larry sat up and tried to talk, but the only result was some dry coughs. Rita passed water to the back seat, and Elena held the small cup to his lips. He took a sip, then pushed it away, his eyes filled with tears. "Mum, I'm sorry, but they're dead. I'm sure no one on that side of the room made it."

Elena squeezed his hand, suddenly worried about Larry feeling guilty or perhaps even changing his mind about walking away from the family. Everything had changed for him, and she had to be strong for this son. "Did you get a chance to talk with your brother?" she asked.

"He wanted to join us, Mum," Larry said. "I sent him an instant message and he wrote back, saying he was going to wait until we got settled. If Grandmum and the palace didn't let him visit us, he was going to walk away from it all, too."

Elena wrapped her arms around Larry. "Our Richard . . . I can't believe he's gone."

"After seeing what Derry did to you, he didn't trust Derry anymore." The boy's voice was hoarse. "He reported Derry to security." The boy took a deep breath. "Richard told me that he found the experiments and equipment from my science kit, dumped into a plastic bag." Puzzled, Elena asked what he meant.

"Don't you see? Derry ordered that the box get packed into the trunk of your car the day of Richard's party. He wanted it removed from the castle and taken back to your house. I was fine with that—they never let me do anything at Wyndham that could possibly involve a mess. But I think he must have used the box for whatever caused the car to blow up." Larry leaned his head against his mother's chest.

Elena felt a chill slice through her chest. "Dear God. So it was Derry."

"It could involve others besides Derry," Michael interjected. "And who knows where the conspiracy starts or ends—or the reasons why."

Elena nodded. "Knowing about Derry only makes it that much easier to leave the country. But can we just walk away and let him go unpunished?"

"If Richard is dead, then Derry is, too," Larry said. "He was standing close to Richard in the hall."

"I have contacts with the police—I'll tell them about the science materials," Michael said. "Maybe they can investigate. Maybe the truth will come out."

"But there's proof," Lawrence said hoarsely. "In Mum's bedroom. Richard said in his E-mail that he teased Derry. Pretended like you might come back. Later, Richard overheard that they hid something in your room to implicate you."

"I hope it wasn't a mistake leaving the rings behind," Elena murmured.

"It wasn't." Michael sighed, but kept his eyes on the road. "As long as they think that you're dead."

"It gives you time to decide what to do next," Rita added. Her voice broke. "I'm so sorry, about what my brother did to your son and husband." Puzzlement crossed Larry's face, and Elena realized he did not know that Rita's brother had helped with the blast. "If only I had known," Rita said through the sobs.

As the woman cried, Elena thought it didn't matter why the woman wept, whether for the victims of the blast or the crimes committed by her brother or the loss of his soul. Rita hurt inside, whether Danny was alive or dead.

Elena reached for Rita's shoulder, leaning forward to comfort the woman in the front seat. "But it wasn't you," she said. "You can't blame yourself. We all did what we could."

"I only hope they don't try to shift blame," Michael said, with a scowl. He turned to Rita, offering her advice on immediately reporting her brother's involvement and cooperating with the investigation. Then he glanced in the rearview mirror. "We don't know if Danny is dead or alive. And if they blame you, Elena, we'll have to respond. Perhaps police will get access to Richard's E-mail account. Or maybe others will step forward."

"With any luck, they'll think I'm dead and just leave well enough alone." Elena looked out the window with a sigh. Who knew how many were involved besides Derry? Giller and others from security; senior staff like Barringer, Barnes or her own Fanley; perhaps even members of the family, like her Uncle Gregory or Caroline.

She shuddered, but then shame swept through her. Elena's family was as complicit as Rita's brother. Rita had helped her through so much, and all Elena had done was get angry after finding out about Danny's plans.

"Rita, we owe you so much." Elena leaned forward to thank the nurse. "Who knows what would have happened if you had not taken us in?" Wiping her eyes, Rita flashed Elena a grateful smile.

She turned to Larry. "And do you realize that you're the heir? Are you sure that *you* still want to leave?"

The boy looked surprised, then shook his head with stubbornness. "I don't want it," he insisted. "I refuse and I want to leave. Tonight."

Elena rubbed her head and felt relief. "Do you mean it?"

"How can I forget—they never liked me," Larry insisted. "I would never trust them, and I'm sure that they wanted to kill us all." Elena squeezed his hand.

"Then I have your trip arranged," Michael explained. "We'll drive north to a place where we can stay tonight and can clean up. A fishing boat waits for us in Fraserburgh, along the eastern coast in Scotland. It will take you and Larry to Norway. I'll meet you there, and we'll head to the States."

As he headed for the M1 motorway, the group fell silent. Elena could feel Larry's hand relax as he fell asleep.

"I can't wait until we're done running," Elena murmured, leaning back and closing her eyes.

Michael glanced at her with a small frown. "But there's no clear end point. You can never stop being careful."

"I hope it's enough to convince them that I'm dead and they give up," she replied.

"In the meantime, we cover our tracks," Michael said.

Tears glistened in her eyes, and she stared back toward the city, where a small plume of smoke rose over the skyline, all that was left of the Technology Campaign. Her heart ached for Richard. She could have done more so long ago. "It means we'll be hiding and running from them for the rest of our lives."

The car broke away from the motorway and the traffic, and turned off for a small road that aimed for the coast.

EPILOGUE

"The funeral arrangements are complete?"
"All protocol is in order."

Elena watched as a battered black Jeep pulled up to the small cottage that leaned against an unnamed peak not far from Castle City in Montana. Night was falling, and a few windows glowed with light, though the curtains had long been drawn. Autumn arrived early to the mountain areas. Irregular bursts of wind swept down the slopes and whipped the tall grass and sage. Elena watched Michael pause outside, scanning the lonely and peaceful scene. She was confident no one had noticed or cared that the little cottage was in use. Yet, silence and peace could be deceptive.

That was why he had driven more than a hundred miles away to the nearest university and made copies of recent newspapers from Europe. They didn't dare purchase copies during the past two weeks and show any special interest in a subject that dominated the news. Michael prohibited Elena and Larry from searching the Internet for news during their travels. The cabin had no phone line. Michael had wanted to leave no sign along the trail they had taken from Europe to Montana.

Elena welcomed him as he entered the cabin and noticed the relief cross his face, probably because the comfortable scene had not changed since he had last left. Dry logs had been added to the fire and it snapped pleasantly. Elena wore jeans and flannel. Larry read a book and asked about going outside. Elena smiled, nodded, and put on the tea kettle.

"Well?" she said.

He hugged her. "They claim to have found four bodies—the Prince of Wales, his ex-wife and the two boys," he whispered. "Blood tests were performed. The funerals were held last week."

She shook her head. "But if we're not dead, then maybe it's possible Richard and Edward are alive?"

"I don't know," he offered. She held him tight but did not cry. She had tried to convince her older son to leave. She had done what she could to stop Rita's brother from attacking the pavilion. Michael had called top security officials in the United States. If the palace staff had ignored those calls, then no one would have listened to other warnings—even if Michael and Elena had reached the site an hour or two earlier. She couldn't argue with him. Officials would never have evacuated the hall based on her word alone. She sat at the table and pulled some of the copies close.

"Rita's brother died in the blast, and Scotland Yard has named him as a suspect. The reports don't mention anything about palace staff. Of course, they might be holding back, investigating a conspiracy."

"Does the report mention Danny or Rita?"

"Only that his family is cooperating with investigators." She nodded. "And more than one person swears to sighting you and Larry immediately after the Technology Campaign," he added. "There are reports of sightings of you and the boys all over Europe."

"I thought my disguise was so clever." Elena patted her dark hair.

"The accounts are hardly reliable," Michael scoffed. "Except for one. A report by Commander Paul Blakely, who insisted that an odd group lingered behind, long after the blast and after occupants had been ordered to evacuate the premises . . ."

Elena's eyes widened. "The firefighter who helped us pull Larry out . . ."

Michael nodded, held his hand up and kept reading: "Blakely insists that he helped pull a young boy out from underneath rubble and a large metal table with the help of the Princess of Wales and other bystanders. Blakely noted that the princess expressed concern for victims of the blast before leaving the premises. He claimed to have no idea of her whereabouts, but suggested that he had urged her strongly to leave the premises. He said he could not be certain whether she perished in the collapse.

"Police insisted that Commander Blakely take a lie detector test, which produced inconclusive results. The royal family insists that the four bodies of the Wyndham family have been found and identified.

"Parliament will hold hearings, but it's presumed that Prince Edward's sister, Princess Caroline, will be named heir to the throne in the upcoming weeks. The deaths mark a shift in power for the family—putting Princess Caroline and her two daughters under a new spotlight of attention."

Elena turned to a page describing the funeral. A photo showed four caskets carried by horse-drawn carriages in the pouring London rain. She gently touched her fingers over the grainy part of the photo and the third casket, the one that carried her older son. Another photo showed the remaining members of the royal family. The copy was poor, the queen's mouth was set, her blotched eyes cast downward.

"She looks so lonely," Elena said. She had no real proof, only an inner certainty that the woman had nothing to do with destroying her son and his family. Elena wondered if she could have read the woman's face so well standing next to her in person. If Elena and Larry had meekly returned to the palace, would life have changed? Would the staff prod Elena and Larry on how to behave and what to say? But Elena wondered only for a moment—the funeral probably was no different than Richard's birthday party and hundreds of other events, with staff directing every move and word, where everyone should stand, what to wear, and when to cry. The tragedy probably made staff more cautious, more controlling, than ever before. Elena closed her eyes and felt pity for her mother-in-law. "It's over," she murmured.

"You won't have Larry officially abdicate? End it for once and for all?"

"If only that were true." She shook her head. "But I have read far too much about others who have abdicated. People were fascinated with them only because of the path not taken. Larry would never have a chance to do anything worthwhile. The tabloids are worse now than ever before, they would dog Larry constantly. I can't put my son through such an ordeal.

"No, he can wait until he's an adult and has a chance to explore his goals. Until then, Caroline will resume the foolishness with relish, and the groups that killed Richard and Edward will go on. But if Larry remains heir, and lives out of their control, they lose all power. No, Larry will neither accept nor abdicate. He's a child—and he can always blame the escape on me!"

"You'll never have a moment's peace," Michael warned. "If anyone guesses, they'll try and track you down. They would do everything they can to ruin you, possibly even accuse you of murder."

"Ending that way of life is worth it for me! They don't dare do much—as long as I stay hidden. They really won't know what to expect!"

"That means living a normal life," he said, looking at her with worry in his eyes. "It's not just your son's future—it's yours, too. Do you really think you can do it?"

"It will be heaven," she exclaimed.

"I hope so," he said. "My friend who works at the Witness Protection Program is developing a profile—based on your answers to his questions. He should be ready with a new life in about two weeks."

"So I can go to nursing school?" she asked.

"He said it fits. You must be careful about your accent."

"I've been working on it," she said, with only the faintest twinge of a British public-school accent.

"Not bad. And you must be careful about strangers."

She nodded.

"Now that your husband's dead, you might want to think about marriage—but you'll have to be patient with every new person that you meet. And for the time being, avoid old habits and leaving fingerprints on cans, tables, or surfaces in public places."

"I remember—I think I can do it, Michael. I want to try."

He nodded sadly. "To make it work, I should probably never see you again. The two of us together would be just too dangerous." He reached for her hand and stared into her eyes. "It's too late to say this now—but I love you."

"I can't just separate from you," she admitted. "I'm not sure about love—but I have no one else. That system wasted years of my life. It destroyed my husband, my marriage, and my son. I don't want to deal with them. But I'm not sure that I'm ready for love again. I'm not sure how to go about normal life just yet."

"I understand," he said.

"I hope we can still be friends. We can be careful. We're here, aren't we?"

He nodded. "We'll see. We must think about Larry. He's probably in far more danger than you or me. He stands between the throne and those who didn't trust your family."

"So much depends on what happens here—with school and friends."

Michael looked out the window toward a field where Larry ran with a dog. "He says that he's ready for change, but he doesn't know how hard it will be. No one ever knows how hard losing a routine is until it's gone. He might be okay for a week or two, a year—and then one day he might just long for the palace. He may resent you for walking away from so much power."

"Larry's stronger than the system, and we can find other paths to power," Elena said, with more confidence than she felt. She stood and shoved the copies of the newspapers into a drawer. "For now, we both simply want to be free."

ABOUT THE AUTHOR

Susan Froetschel is assistant editor of YaleGlobal Online.